RISE
OF
SERPENTS

B. A. VONSIK
AWARD-WINNING AUTHOR

D1570874

CELESTIAL FURY
PUBLISHING

Primeval Origins®

By B. A. Vonsik

Paths of Anguish
Light of Honor
Rise of Serpents

Visit www.primevalorigins.com to gain access to the Primeval Origins Encyclopedia and Lexicon.

Awards and Praise for Primeval Origins®

AWARD WINNING, Fantasy Book of the Year, 2018 New York City Big Book Award, Winner

AWARD WINNING, Epic Fantasy Book of the Year, 2018 New York City Big Book Award, Winner

Praise

"With the Primeval Origins Epic Saga, B.A. Vonsik has skillfully created an exciting and fantastic tale of mankind's origins which pushes the edge of imagination and thrills with cliffhangers galore. Vividly detailed and engaging, Mr. Vonsik's remarkable storytelling shines in this multiple award-winning series that is sure to entertain any reader. A brilliantly imagined and beautifully crafted narrative full of suspense and adventure." -- Mitch Reinhardt, author of the award-winning, Amazon best seller Darkwolf Saga

"Primeval Origins: Paths of Anguish" is an epic journey to the origin of mankind in our struggle against evil. It is a page turner sure to thrill young and older readers for sure! I definitely recommend it is an awesome read!" -- Arianna Violante for Reader Views

"Between the artful handling of suspense and the skill in descriptive narrative, Primeval Origins: Paths of Anguish is loaded with action and is very hard to put down. This is the first in the series, and I can't wait for the next volume!"-- Maria C. Cuadro, Bookideas.com, 5-STARS

"From the opening scene to the very last pages it was impossible to put it down... The action scenes were simply incredible and made me turn pages faster... Just like with the best fantasy/epic novels, the reader gets completely immersed into a new universe, where the young heroes fight for their freedom." -- Ellie Midwood, author of The Girl from Berlin; The Indigo Rebels; and The Darkest Hour

"Are you looking for something to test the boundaries of your imagination, with the feel of a wonderful tapestry depicting a magical tale? Primeval Origins: Paths of Anguish will do that and more!" Tomb Tender Book Blog "Primeval Origins will get into your blood, and you will not want to put it down before reaching the final page ... [It] is, in a word, outstanding." -- 5 STARS, Readers' Favorite

"Vonsik's series opener offers an engaging plot to keep the fantasy fan reading." -- KIRKUS Reviews

"Author B. A. Vonsik has done an absolutely amazing job in creating characters that readers will connect with and relate to... Vonsik's skill in world creation is simply second to none." -- 5 STARS, Tracy Slowiak for Readers' Favorite

"Wow, this book should definitely be made into a movie!" -- Ellie Midwood, author of A Motherland's Daughter, A Fatherland's Son; Emilia: The darkest days in history of Nazi Germany through a woman's eyes; and The Austrian: A War Criminal's Story

"An absorbing read throughout, "Primeval Origins: Light of Honor" is an original science fiction story that is highly recommended for high school and community library YA Fiction collections." -- Midwest Book Review

"All readers, regardless of them having read the first volume or not, will feel like they have been deposited onto a whirling tornado or the crest of a tsunami, and the best thing to do is ride it out to the very end. I find it to be a very exhilarating ride!" -- Maria C. Cuadro

"An epic fantasy that will take you to the edge of time and keep you on the edge of your seat." -- 5 STARS, Rabia Tanveer for Readers' Favorite

"This series is destined to be recognized as a classic." -- Paige Lovitt for Reader Views (Fantasy Book of the Year Award Review)

"Story that's always alive with possibilities, and it keeps readers guessing... an ambitious, often engaging adventure through time." -- KIRKUS Reviews

First Age

Humanity ... Material form of Creation's intention, conceived the vessels conducting *Lights'* essence; a reflection in fashioning of Creation's splendor, a merger, a fusion of perceivable and consciousness; meant in experience the physical realm, free will determining the path of *Lights* found; material maturing *Lights'* progressions, quality and convictions of life's temperaments; Creation's desire for *Lights'* preparations, sees kindred essence joined through measureless ages.

Serpents ... Humble in their ancient genesis, gods and renown men of lost witness; called upon in prominent service, guarding ... guiding mankind in Creation's benevolence; corruption's temptations irresistible, worship of man found most desirable; mortals learn of scornful regard, when awe and deceptions are seen through the shroud; tyrant governance by unkind hands, bring challenge and defiance in young man; Creation sadden in children's choosings, makes clean the template of all living; desiring humanity another life, champions made out of turmoil and strife; essence physical sowed in the stars, meant as rebirth in the long afar.

Of Godlings and Man

Rebirth ... Time, times, and times again pre-man evolves as ages befall, his material form molded in guidance by Creation's will; coiling serpents within man's Tree, ever shaping the mortal being; serpents reincarnate set forth man's shape anew, their hands guided by Creation true; bound in service by their godly makers, mankind learns to struggle from their repressive overseers; mankind gains worldly knowledge, from Serpents now fallen ... Creation's lost servants ... Watchers; humanity rewarded kingship lowered, make anew a civilization tainted; serpents whispering in humanity's darkness, lead weak-willed man astray as tyrants; humanity's masses rejecting oppressor's advances, see authority's hands speaking and appearing in illusionary manners; the unworthy ... undesirables muted in mass, suffer an entangled world embracing *chamas*; humanity fallen his culture in madness, led by the children of the Fallen desiring *Kedushah*.

Serpents Reincarnate ... Once sentinels serving in Creation's favor, guarding ... guiding mankind in humbled reverence; hubris embraced for the worship of humanity, believing divinity their manifest destiny; usurping and tainting the Tree of Life in man, corrupting many *Lights* while spreading wickedness throughout the lands; now fallen from grace and defiant of stooped knee, self-proclaimed adversaries of Creation with sinful needs; humanity as servants ... slaves to their masters, Creation all-seeing sends forth the savior in counter; Watchers above humanity fearing salvation, imperil the world with opposition and annihilation; the Christ the redeemer ... the Way to *Yeshua*, brings forth his horsemen to wage war and conquer.

The Harbinger of Judgments

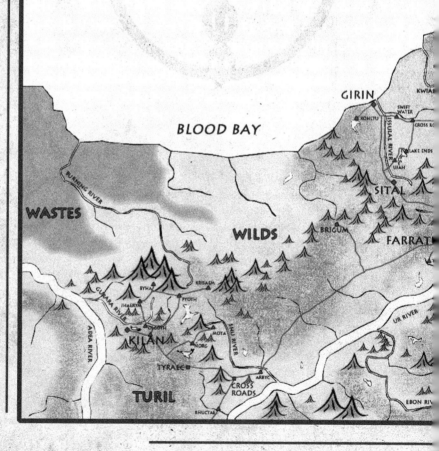

SHURUPPAK +
NORTH TURIL

BLOOD BAY

GIRIN

KWIA

SWIFT
WATER

KOHLTU

ISSUAL RIVER

CROSS RO

LAKE ENDS

UAH

SITAL

BURNING RIVER

WASTES

WILDS

BRICUM

FARRAT

GUMARA RIVER

BYHA

KRISAEM

PYOTH

IHAERYN

ADEA RIVER

DYGOTH

MOTA

SHU RIVER

UR RIVER

KILAN

NORG

TYRAEC

ARBYC

CROSS
ROADS

TURIL

EBON RIV

BRUCTAE

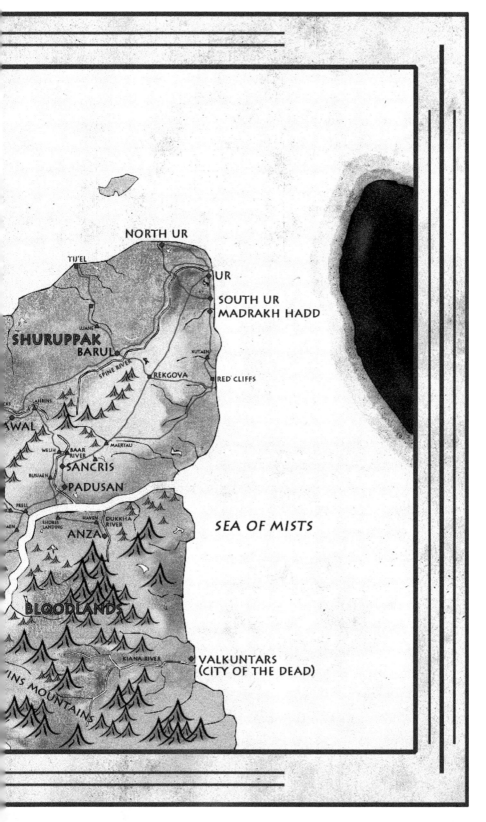

NORTH UR

TIJ'EL

UR

SOUTH UR
MADRAKH HADD

SHURUPPAK
BARUL

LUANE

KUTAEN

SPINE RIVER

REKGOVA

RED CLIFFS

LAHRINS

WAL

WEUH   BAAR   MAERTAU
         RIVER

RUSIAEN

SANCRIS

PADUSAN

PRELL

HAVEN   DUKKHA
          RIVER

SHORES
LANDING

AEN

ANZA

SEA OF MISTS

BLOODLAND

KIANA RIVER

VALKUNTARS
(CITY OF THE DEAD)

INS MOUNTAINS

Prologue

Privileges and Affluence

Fading pastels illuminated Nassau's horizon to the southwest as the vanishing sky gave way to the deepening blue of the coming cool night. A light wind fluttered the flags of the docked ships and wind sock of the vertical lift pad. The beauty of the dusk sky over the Atlantic Ocean gave Nikki a sense of comfort as she stood dockside of their yacht, a seventy-five-foot vessel, the *Sukkal*, watching the rest of the crew go in advance of them through the transparent carbon walls of the passenger module in the quadlifter heli-drone programmed to transport them to the Risen Cove Hotel located somewhere on the northwest side of the New Risen Atlantis Resort. The whirl of electromagnetic rotors grew louder as the quadlifter ascended as Nikki watched the green and red navigation lights either side of the white beacons rise into the air amidst the blast of air washing over Nikki and those who remained with her. As the quadlifter whirled off, Nikki felt the calming light wind return to the yellow, white, and green lit vertical lift and landing pad.

"I feel ridiculous in this outfit," Nikki complained again while giving her attire another look-over. The green fantasy elf costume dress, sandals, head circlet, and sheer gown revealed too much of her.

"You look stunning," Dr. Shawn Steven Anders commented in an admiring tone as he struggled trying not to stare at her too long. Nikki thought Anders looked too much in character dressed as an old movie archeologist with a brown, wide-brimmed hat and whip at his side that went about the old world trying to keep powerful ancient relics and artifacts from evildoers' hands.

Nikki felt her cheeks uncomfortably warm at his remark. Wanting to get a safe opinion, she turned to Aren and asked in Antaalin, "*Zu malga?*"

The tall Evendiir, dressed in his ancient outfit of blues, gray, and black pants, boots, tunic, and cape, ran his radiant green eyes over her body and costume as if examining a curious object before commenting. "My consideration. Your appearance is made to attract those with sweetness desires upon you."

Nikki felt her jaw drop at Aren's reply. She wanted his honest opinion that the outfit was revealing yet flattering but didn't think he would choose words confirming what she worryingly felt. What she sensed of Aren confirmed his disinterest in her.

. . in that way. Nikki shot a look at Dr. Dunkle, who was dressed in his own costume of blue pants and tunic, high leather boots, a red cape, and gold amulet with a green gem at its center hung about his neck. Now, seeing them together, Dunkle and Aren looked much too similar. Dunkle waved his hands, not wanting to comment. She then looked to Mr. Miller, the young, short-haired blond *Wind Runner* officer now dressed in black leather boots, pants, and jacket over a heavy black jersey bearing an angry white skull. *He's so not his proper mannered self*, Nikki thought. Miller tried looking everywhere except at Nikki and her partially revealing costume. Finally, Nikki turned to Rogaan, also dressed in his ancient outfit of blue, red, and black meshed metal looking the part of a very successful uniquely clad gladiator or praetorian. She stood hoping he would say something to make her feel more comfortable about the way she dressed.

"I would do you," Rogaan stated using contemporary words while wearing a roguish smile as his radiant blue eyes kindly cast upon her.

Nikki felt her face and body explode in heat. Never did she expect him to say that. Her sense of him confirmed he was attracted to her, which sent her heat higher, if that were possible. Nikki started to feel light-headed. She breathlessly spoke to herself, "Oh, I'm going to die."

"Roga!" Aren chastised. "Of the House An. Is that a manner to talk to a lady?"

"You know I am not wanting of that title," Rogaan shot Aren a friendly glare.

"I am to know," Aren replied of his demonstration that words evoke emotions and that Rogaan's words did so in Nikki.

"She . . . to ask for honest, sweet words . . ." Rogaan sounded like a teenager trying to explain to friends why he did something everyone thought inappropriate.

Staring at the unclear and swaying ground, Nikki felt kind hands on her arm. She looked up; her vision started to clear. She found concerned brown eyes that carried both a hint of jealousy and inferiority. Anders continued staring at her as Nikki regained her breath and balance.

"I'm okay. Thanks." Embarrassed at being swept up as she did, Nikki tried to sound as if nothing significant happened. Anders stood back allowing Nikki to regain her composure which she felt relieved for him giving her space. Nikki found Anders attractive and not such a bad guy to be with, but . . .

"Everyone . . ." Dr. Dunkle broke into the moment. "We truly must be going. We have a time to keep."

"A 'time' requiring these . . . interesting costumes?" Anders asked.

"To blend in, Mr. Anders," Dr. Dunkle replied. "We're going to . . . or better said, *through* one of the largest cosplay events attended by the wealthy and politically powerful where every one of us will look to fit in. Even our new friends will blend in with their functional outfits from the past."

"Oh . . ." Nikki realized. The costumes made sense to her, now, but she still would have rather had the field clothes she had on the dig and playing her own part as movie archeologist.

"To what end are we joining this . . . cosplay gathering, Doctor?" Aren asked.

"To pull off a slight-of-hand exchange." Dr. Dunkle sounded all proud of himself.

The doctor then waved them all to follow him to a nearby robotic skiff where they would be ferried across the harbor. Walking remained uncomfortable for Nikki as she felt her legs still not completely recovered from their horrible twisting and brokenness in the battle weeks ago on the *Wind Runner*. Their healing was a wonder of Aren and Rogaan using the powers of Agni and Dr. Dunkle's modern technology. Her pain now was discomforting, though she chose to persevere without complaining. *At least they gave me elven boots and not the high-heeled kind.* Nikki admitted she hated heels as they were uncomfortable and designed to make her look more sexual.

As the skiff departed the dock, being back on the water rocking and bobbing, Nikki suffered unwelcomed images flashing in her mind of the events of the past few weeks of the *Wind Runner* doing battle with that United Nations frigate, and of suffering wounds she barely survived. Grimacing as she relived her pains, she worked her leg that was all but lost before Aren's healing, bending it at the knee to relieve the pain Dr. Dunkle told her was only in her head, now. He said it was part of her post-traumatic stress disorder, her PTSD. A condition common in those exposed to traumatic, life-threatening situations who then struggle to make sense of it all, to feel safe again. Nikki wanted to feel safe again, but something gnawed at her, telling her it wouldn't be. Grimacing more as gunfire filled her mind remembering that day as rattling bursts and visions struck her of that sinister . . . malicious Tyr super soldier with his dark, gauntleted hand around her throat. And its synthesized voice pounding in her head, "How dare you defy the Tyr. Your punishment, death." All sense of comforts about the world Nikki felt disappear in that moment. Sweat now dripped from her forehead as she tried to slow her breathing . . . just as Dr. Dunkle instructed her to do when she felt the panic welling up. *What else did Dunkle tell me . . . think on something. Focus on my surroundings . . . be in the now.*

Looking around the harbor in a conscious effort, Nikki saw boats small and large and of all types, though the yachts, the size of the *Sukkal* and larger, stood out.

Nikki whispered to herself not intending for anyone else to hear, "What are their names?"

She read them one by one: *Beltway Bandit, Progressive Living, Neocon Way, The Fed, Never Waste a Crisis, The Christless, Divide and Conquer, Divide and Plunder, D. C. Gravy, It's Not Your Money, UN Hammer, Collective Justice,* and the *Sukkal.* This last name carried with it the Sumerian meaning of "courier." The *Sukkal* was their ship after getting rescued from the *Wind Runner* weeks ago. The rest of those ships seemed to be natured in politics as names of the *Privileged* in contemporary organizations in and around Washington, D.C. and New York and political statements that found their way as common slogans in the pop culture and the media. Many she heard through her teen years. Others, she heard more recently from political candidates and office holders prior to leaving the states on their South American dig.

"A who's who of politicos and celebrities," Anders commented as he stepped next to Nikki. Anders's strong voice intruded on Nikki's moment of distress and her struggle to conquer it. She blinked several times before seeing him clearly. With his dark goatee and wearing his adventurer field attire . . . including his brown hat he kept taking off and putting on, trying to get the right fit. He looked the part of that old movie archeologist, but with now tamed black curly hair instead of the dishevelment he allowed in the field.

"You know I'm not interested in politics," Nikki reminded him.

"I'm only interested enough to find ways to work around the *politicos,*" Anders clarified, ". . . and the corrupt trappings of their *system.* It's frustrating and dangerous to anyone daring to get something done."

Nikki really wanted to avoid the politics, even more so at Anders's reminder of why she just wanted to tune it all out. She found politics viciously intimidating and demoralizing and wanted nothing to do with it.

"You should know after everything you had to do to get permission for our dig in Bolivia." Nikki recalled Anders's long fight with both the U.S. and Bolivian governments to gain permission for the dig. In the end, Anders told her he had to have the university pay unlisted "fees" to get the proper permissions. A feat he refused to reveal how he had achieved it.

"You look like *our friend* standing there with that expression," Anders commented, nodding at Aren.

"That's scary," Nikki flatly replied, though she felt surprised at the comparison. "How?"

"He gets that distant look in his eyes . . . sometimes," Anders answered while watching Aren with his contemplative expression as the Evendiir examined the resort hotel and convention center structures to their north. "As if he's someplace else or seeing things we can't. It's a little unnerving."

"He *is* and *can*," Nikki confirmed Anders's observations. Looking westward at the small harbor dock the robotic skiff drove them toward, Nikki felt in the back of her mind something she couldn't quite identify. Then, she realized what he was looking at. "Sometimes, when I'm calm with a 'blank mind' . . . wandering with my thoughts and . . . always when in his presence, I can almost see what he sees. Shadows, ghostly shapes, and vague symbols and . . . lines and waves . . . mostly."

A sharp glance from Mr. Miller silently told her not to speak in the open details of anything concerning them. Nikki fell quiet. She, Anders, Aren, and Rogaan all received the same guidance from Dunkle and Miller. They explained how surveillances using multispectral, vibrational, and audio sensors would be everywhere and to act as if everything they did and spoke of was being watched and recorded. Nikki felt her cheeks warming as she realized what she had done. Feeling their amusement, she glanced at Rogaan and Aren. She found the dark-haired Rogaan openly smiling behind his short beard dressed in his blue, red, and black steel armor over a mix of tanniyn . . . dinosaur hide and cloth clothes with his blue metal blow, quiver of arrows, and sheathed short sword riding high on his back. His forearm bands . . . his *mahbi'barzil*, the Tellen name for blue steel, *Ra'Sakti* with five embedded dark Agni stones each, shaped and flowed over his muscles as if his very own skin. Feeling both comforted and unease where the *Ra'Sakti* was concerned, Nikki didn't know quite why, though she felt Rogaan constantly exerting his will over an unseen presence.

The platinum-haired Aren's appearance was different in many ways. Instead of armor, the Evendiir stood tall clothed in his dark pants of worked dinosaur leather, a dark blue, short sleeved tunic of cloth under a sleeveless, above-the-knee robe of dark cloth and dinosaur hide. A wrapping of brown and lighter colored dinosaur hide belt bands tied off to a dark metal circular buckle kept his robe closed and well fitting. His boots were high to his calf with his pants drawn over the tops and leather crisscrossing bands of dinosaur leather wrapped about his upper boots and lower legs. Aren wore dinosaur hide and cloth forearm wrappings also with leather band wrappings. Nikki knew he wore the wrappings to cover what was underneath, a set of black, steel, arm bracelets half the length of Rogaan's *Ra'Sakti*. Being very guarding of them, Nikki only viewed the bracelets briefing in Dr. Dunkle's lab before Aren reclaimed them. A pair of Agni-encrusted *barzil* rings on each of Aren's hands and a necklace pendant with yet another blue Agni stone completed his look. Rogaan and Aren carried the full look of any cosplay characters she ever saw, yet she knew they were real . . . and despite their lightheartedness, they confidently carried themselves in a way that gave a sense of dangerous power to any giving them more than a glance.

Nikki struggled a little hopping off the robotic skiff to the dock. Anders and Rogaan both gave her concerned gazes. She felt her cheeks warming at their attentions. Aren playfully slapped Rogaan on the back of his armor.

"End with the eyes," he teased his friend. "That one is to show enough *pal* as Suhd and pleasing eyes as *pili* as Dajil."

"Nikki . . . looks nothing like them." Rogaan sounded defensive.

"Truth . . ." Aren continued to tease as he walked off following Dunkle and Miller. Aren then spoke in Antaalin instead of English. "*Maa bi unsa til za pad kana gerebu sha.*"

Nikki felt her warm cheeks turn into a raging fire. *How does Aren see me as charming . . . in that way . . . and trouble?* She looked down at her split green dress to ensure she wasn't showing more than she thought; then she yelled after Aren, "I am *not* showing any crotch!"

Anders looked at her, his eyes filled with confusion and jealously. She forced herself to speak calmly as if nothing just happened, hoping to deflect Aren's teasing of his friend as just that. "We should be keeping up, Shawn."

The six of them moved quickly along wide concrete pathways between a parking lot half-filled with parked robotic passenger vehicles to their right and a heavy trafficked road on their left emerging from a tunnel running under the water harbor entrance to the resort marina. Off several hundred yards to their right, the massive Royal Heaven Towers and casino stood.

"Welcome to the New Risen Atlantis," Miller announced to the group in his Southern drawl. "The rebuilt resort after the original was destroyed decades ago in the tidal wave caused by a large fragment from the Apophis asteroid strike in the Atlantic Ocean."

"We've all learned about it in school," Anders commented. "Apophis passed close to Earth in . . . 2029, missing the keyhole that would have brought it to Earth on its next orbiting return in 2036. On its second pass, it was much closer than should have been, just at the edge of another keyhole. The scientists couldn't explain its trajectory. The world held its collective breath while nations in their U.N. eventually decided not to try to destroy it because they couldn't be certain of success. Instead, they decided to track it and launch spacecraft to push it away on its next return."

"If not for the Chinese secretly sending two nukes to the asteroid . . ." Miller chimed in speaking with disdain. "Two thirty-megaton nukes to blow it to hell."

"Well . . . They didn't get it all," Anders commented.

"No," Miller answered. "What remained of the asteroid was a large fragment field about a third of the original mass among a cloud of smaller debris. On the next return of Apophis to Earth, many of the smaller fragments from the broken asteroid struck parts of the Pacific, the U.S., Central, and South America. The large fragment struck the Atlantic causing the massive tidal wave wiping out many of the islands of the Bahamas, including this one."

"As I recall from the history archives, much of the East Coast in the U.S. suffered a lot of damage from the tidal wave, as well," Nikki added.

"Almost all of the East Coast suffered great damage," Dunkle confirmed and clarified.

"Damn Chinese," Miller let out a disdainful rebuke. "They never admitted their wrongdoing until about a decade ago after an old Chinese scientist confessed on his deathbed in the U.S. as being part of the nuking."

"After this island was wiped out, *he* had the opportunity during the restoration to install in *secret* an ancient artifact that we're headed to, now," Dunkle informed in a hushed voice. "One of *his* companies was contracted to rebuild parts of this resort."

"Looking at what was once a family place before Apophis . . ." Miller's words continued to be filled with disdain. "Now, it's become a place of debauchery for the well-to-do and government types. They used the disaster to get control of the U.S. government and surrounding territories such as this and have never let go their grip despite our elections."

Nikki looked up at the massive hotel on their right. It stood lit up with multicolored lights everywhere and a giant holographic marque projecting above the facility's main entrance welcoming this year's cosplay festival and TM²A Tournament.

"What is T-M-Two-A?" Nikki asked.

"The reason we're taking this path to the Risen Cove." Miller pointed with his thumb at the crowded front entrance to the Royal Heaven Towers on the far side of the parking lot. Nikki took one look and agreed with Miller. The entrance was packed with vehicles and people and many in black uniforms she took as security.

"The Transhuman Mixed Martial Arts Tournament is centered in the Towers in that hotel, where the cosplay crowds are all over the resort," Dunkle explained, but not such that Nikki understood.

"It is dense with . . . *technology*." Aren tried to explain in English when he seemed to feel Nikki's confusion. The Evendiir swept and swirled his arm at the hotel casino's entrance area. "Difficult to see the people beyond the utterances of their tools."

"That much tech and security presents a problem for our decoy PDA and ID devices keeping us masked," Dunkle further explained in a hushed voice. His ability to understand Aren's and Rogaan's translations of their lexicon into English impressed Nikki. "The transhuman, especially in a tournament like this, will have all the latest surveillance tech that we've not yet programmed countermeasures for. And, the security is likely to have upped their tech in the hopes the transhumans won't penetrate and compromise the resort's cloud and core as they did last year. It was a big issue and a threat to Global Eye and I9. Our Mother-Brother Government was all in a buzzing irritation over the incident. I'm surprised you didn't hear of it."

"We don't follow the transhumans," Anders broke into the conversation. "We don't agree with their pursuits to becoming superhuman or immortal."

Nikki felt unsettled at thinking of the transhuman rave and what they do to their own bodies—replacing healthy tissue and organs with synthetic and computer-enhanced parts. "There is something . . . just not right doing that to themselves. It's . . ."

"Not natural," Miller finished her thought.

"Nor ethical in much of what they do," the doctor commented, then continued to provide guidance. "Some of the transhumans are little more than walking cybernetic drones controlled by unseen others either on these grounds or linked in from elsewhere. Try to keep your distance from them."

"What do you think it does to their . . . souls?" Nikki asked Anders hoping he had an answer that would satisfy her.

"Transhumans don't seem to think of a life after," Anders spoke as the scholarly one, though his bias against transhumanism carried clearly in his tone. "They are fascinated by the possibilities of the technology like people were back when they built personal computers and telecommunications devices in their homes. They want to create and be acknowledged for it, to have built the better 'rig.' Others want superhuman abilities. And others still wish to hang on to this world, forever . . . becoming immortal through technology, downloading their minds into it."

"But their . . ." Nikki felt conflicted at the freedoms allowing people to become transhuman and even encouraged by their governments, implants infused into flesh without understanding what they were being transformed into.

"Souls . . ." Dr. Dunkle spoke of what Nikki didn't say. "Ms. Ricks . . . are not believed to be something special by many of the transhumans. They think cybernetics only changes them for the better. In the early days of prosthetics, the war-wounded, accident survivors, and those unfortunate to suffer disabilities found freedom and restored purpose in life by getting artificial limbs. Technology restoring function to the body and the person was good. But then, we went further, seeking to tie the machine . . . and more carelessly, the computer, to all parts of the human body, to the complete nervous system and deeply into the brain . . . becoming cybernetic beings. We disregarded the cautioning voices, the voices of human ethics and those understanding the nature of humanity as few, including our Founding Fathers, did. A truth that not all people are kind and benevolent or unselfish . . . Not all people are good. Immoral people with enhanced abilities. And worse, these cybernetic systems and connections go both ways . . . allowing access, monitoring, and control of many transhumans by mega-corporations, governments, and those skilled in the tech and with ill intensions. Humanity's arrogance and ability to dismiss away the unpleasantly obvious . . . 'it won't happen to me' type of wishful and arrogant thinking almost always ends in bad things happening."

Rogaan and Aren looked at each other as Nikki felt a knowing feeling passing between them. She glanced at them. "What? What is it?"

"Your people are little . . . different from what we . . ." Rogaan started to speak, then stopped. Nikki felt a deep sense of regret and pain in Rogaan and even emotional pain in Aren. The latter surprised her.

"What?" Nikki pressed Rogaan knowing Aren wasn't the type to talk about his feelings.

"It takes a strong *Light* to fight the . . . longings of the body." Rogaan continued with measured words translating his lexicon into concepts Nikki and the others could understand. "And to fight the . . . call . . . calling of the Agni . . . and to your machines. A fight to *not* consent . . . to its ruling or to its sway."

"The Agni holds within the voices of those possessing it past." Aren further clarified as he attempted to inform. "Not their *Lights*, except rare to . . . take place. The voices are of the learned head without their *Lights*. Or what powerful and skilled *Kabir* and *Kabiri* leave behind . . . with a faithful task provided to the empty Agni."

"A program?" Dunkle asked to confirm. Aren thought for a while as they walked the concrete path crossing a busy intersection congested with driverless vehicles stopping for them and then starting, again, driving around a large water park on their right. More robotic vehicles traveled back and forth on the road at their left with passengers dressed in all sorts of costumes. Almost everyone they saw was enthralled with their holographic PDA displays. Some had even worked them into and parts of their costumes.

An occasional breeze carried the aromas of delicious foods to Nikki's nose, making her stomach grumble. Upbeat music and splashing waters came from inside the waterpark to their right, coming from beyond several sizable two-story buildings, both with large and tall outside cages attached to them. Between and beyond the buildings, Nikki and the group spied a lighted lagoon with entertainers jovially speaking on loudspeakers and jumping water animals of some type flying in the air before splashing back into the waters, making an unseen crowd yell excitedly.

"Yes. A program, Doctor," Aren finally answered. Nikki felt a sense of satisfaction fill the Evendiir for working the translation. "It . . . holds the empty Agni from performing more . . . than it is 'programmed,' but the stones are unsafe. They at times take a *Light* without . . . care of their . . . 'programming.' It is then they become dangerous if a troubled *Light* is taken."

"Would you stop speaking in terms of 'voices' and 'Lights'?" Anders complained. "It all sounds like magic and mysticism to me."

"Yes . . ." Nikki answered with a sense of knowing. "It would. The 'voices' they speak of are the data of the mind; the memories, experiences, and information we collect over our lives."

"And the 'Light'?" Anders asked.

"The . . . *soul*," Rogaan answered with a prideful grin for figuring out the translation so quickly.

"The *voice* means little without the *Light*." Aren tied it all together, or so he thought before seeing the confused looks from the group . . . all except Rogaan. "The *Light* . . . the *soul* is that which makes you, *YOU*."

"Data on storage, your 'voice' known as experiences," Dunkle summarized to ensure he understood. "Your soul the program with algorithms within it using the data to choose what to do with it."

"Interesting theory, or dare I say, a philosophical belief," Anders the skeptic stated almost as a challenge.

"Doctor, you are soon to touch a dense utterance," Aren warned.

"What?" Dunkle looked at Aren, then all about himself. "I don't see . . . an utterance."

"Fields . . . electro . . . magnetic fields surround this place." Aren gave a subdued wave of his hand at the busy vehicle welcome plaza of a well illuminated high-rise building across the road to their left. The Risen Cove Hotel name displayed boldly in glowing blue holographic letters above the plaza. Higher above light-colored quadlifter transports sounding as hives of bees with flashing lights, flew repeating paths as they went to and from the roof ferrying people.

"Everyone . . . speak only of trivial matters as we pass the hotel," Dunkle cautioned the group.

x

No one spoke as Dunkle and Miller led them on a walkway paralleling the road and roundabout plaza. At their right, blue villas separated them from the crowded lagoon beyond. Ahead, increasingly thick crowds, mixed with natural and non-natural skin and hair colors and dressed in their favorite character costumes, some holographically projected, of heroes and superheroes, hindered their way as they approached holographic welcome and marketing ads in front of sliding glass doors giving access to a covered walkway attached to the exterior of the hotel. Nikki felt increasingly uncomfortable being surrounded by so many people who appeared to be GENANCING . . . genetically changing and enhancing themselves. Her uncertainty of the GENANCING was confirmed accurate after being brushed up against several times by orange- and green-colored skin cosplayers, and not getting paint rubbed off on her.

Dunkle didn't hesitate to pass through the sliding glass doors causing a synthetic beep to sound off and a natural-sounding voice to speak. "Security Scan complete. Welcome, Isaac Edison. Your luggage has arrived by quadlifter and will be ushered to your room."

Nikki followed Dunkle with Anders and Miller following her closely. As each of them passed through the doors, more beeps were heard as their wrist-worn PDAs projected holographic images displaying their biographical data. A genderless synthetic voice sounding much as a human spoke from somewhere near the security station.

"Security Scan complete. Welcome, Elizabeth Bathor, Thomas Veigh, and Jeffery Domanner. Your luggage has arrived by quadlifter and will be ushered to your rooms. Please find your directions, Risen Cove special events, and discounts accessible on your personal data assistants. To ensure your joyful experience, staff servants will attend to any of your needs. Please request services through your personal data assistants, at one of our android servants, at our service desk located in the main lobby, or at kiosks throughout the grounds. Welcome to the Risen Cove Hotel at the New Risen Atlantis Resort."

Nikki looked over her holographic displayed biography to reaffirm in her mind her alias, given to her on the *Wind Runner* before they ferried to the *Sukkal*. Nikki still wasn't certain why they needed fake identities, but she went along at Dunkle's and Miller's insistence. Nikki looked up from her PDA-displayed information, feeling a bit insecure. Rogaan and Aren were not with them. A wave of panic rippled through Nikki as people with blue, green, and purple skin dressed in expected skimpy attire for the warm island and those in traditional material and holographic cosplay costumes passed by her and Anders.

"What?" Anders asked her.

"Where are Rog . . . they?" Nikki replied, remembering Dunkle's instructions to them about using true names. Quickly scanning the crowd, she found dark-haired Rogaan in his blue, red, and black armor, and platinum-haired Aren looking his part as a mystic monk in his dark-blue tunic and dinosaur hide clothing. They stood outside the sliding doors discussing something as they looked about purposefully. When they seemed to agree on whatever they talked of, Nikki felt a chill sweep through her as Aren started manifesting something she was unfamiliar of. Aren closed his eyes. Nikki felt him concentrating on . . . unclear images flashing in her mind. Concentrating on the images brought some of them into focus in her mind. She saw into Aren's thoughts, him speeding through dynamic electromagnetic fields and along electrical pathways seeking . . . circuits filled with ones and zeros . . . binary code. The code changed so quickly, making it impossible for her to read the code even if she knew how, but she recognized it for what it was. Aren stopped at a piece of code, changing it as it continued executing. Then, he did it again in another section of code. Suddenly, the lights and holographic displays all around them started flickering, and the sliding doors stopped opening. Everyone around Nikki slowed or stopped at the flicking lights. Aren put on a pleased demeanor, then walked through the open doors with Rogaan in trail. The security system with its scanners failed to examine them or react in any way, nor did it trigger their PDAs into displaying their aliases. The pair casually joined up with Nikki.

"Want to walk through the garden of eyes and . . . ears?" Aren asked with a deep sense of knowing and satisfaction as he waved his hand to the hallway leading away from the inner hotel lobby and toward another set of open glass doors. "To the place of . . . joy we walk."

Nikki exchanged looks with Rogaan to confirm he had confidence in his friend. Rogaan simply nodded with a knowing smile. Anders, Dunkle, and Miller had confusion written all over their faces.

"Did you . . . just do all of this?" Dunkle asked of Aren tilting his head left, right, and up.

"Oh course, Doctor," Aren replied. "I don't . . . care for eyes . . . watching me everywhere I go . . . or those . . . utterances by objects . . . examining me."

"How?" Dunkle asked incredulous of what Aren just insinuated.

"Difficult to explain," Aren informed him. With a half-smile, Aren held out an open hand as he made a slight bow. "Lead on, Mr. Isaac Edison."

White and blue can-shaped robots rolled from concealed wall bays immediately surrounding the malfunctioning outer door and security station. They appeared to be scanning and probing the station for what Nikki didn't know. Dunkle wasted no time guiding the group through the open malfunctioning glass door leading to the inner resort grounds, working their way through a small crowd of guests, all wearing rather revealing costumes. Nikki blushed for them. The guys simply stared. Their group followed a covered paved pathway lined with humming stone pedestals, each with a fist-sized floating rock a foot or so above.

"There has to be a trick to these floating rocks." Nikki found herself fascinated by them.

"No trick," Dunkle replied. "Technology of our ancient gods. Sound focused on the rocks levitates them. Only recently did we learn how to levitate objects heavier than a ping-pong ball."

"No way," Nikki challenged, still not believing sound held the shaped rocks in the air.

"We were levitating objects up to several hundred pounds a few feet high back at the university when you were on your leave," Anders confirmed Dunkle's accounting. "It's real fascinating tech."

Nikki wondered at the floating rocks as they continued their short walk to an intersection. The path right led to the lagoon. The path straight ahead to the Royal Heaven Towers Hotel and Casino and through crowds of costumed people. Dunkle led them left following a wide paved walkway deeper into the resort and park as the last of the day's light faded engulfing them in darkness and walkway artificial lighting.

"Attention, resort guests," a male synthetic voice announced in English. The voice sounded as if it came from everywhere. "Guests under the age of eighteen are now restricted to indoor spaces. All young adults and children, please follow the instructions provided on your personal data assistants. Please comply with security personnel and artificial life-forms while exiting the outdoor grounds."

The park's voice repeated its message in multiple languages as Nikki observed everyone she presumed underage having their PDA's holographically projecting instructions to them. As she and the group walked along the wide, winding, paved path now illuminated in soft white light as dusk passed away, robotic white and blue mini-drones buzzed all about the resort finding younglings. *Why did I think younglings?* Nikki asked herself. Many of the young complied with the instructions, though just as many protested both their now red, flashing holographic instructions and their parents. Those in protest quickly found white and blue human-form android ALFs or less prolifically similarly liveried personnel directing them more forcibly indoors. With all the walking, Nikki's leg started becoming painful enough to cause her a visible limp, slowing her. She fell to the back of their group while trying to keep up.

"Are you okay?" Anders fell in beside her after Rogaan and Aren gave her sympathetic glances when she fell behind.

"My leg is getting sore," Nikki answered as they covered another game field length of strides along the winding path with the Risen Cove Hotel on their left. A slowly flowing almost lazy water ride to their right with voices obscured by well-placed tropical trees and bushes told Nikki they were not the only adults still outside. Here too were more humming pedestals with floating rocks occasionally lining the path on both sides. Watching the last of the children and teens being ushered indoors by parents, uniformed resort attendants, and ALFs, Nikki grew more curious about the resort's night happenings. "What's all this about?"

"After-dark adult cosplay . . . as Miller told me about on the *Sukkal*," Anders answered with purposely made wide eyes. His eyes swept over Nikki in her green, almost revealing elf attire.

"Stop that!" Nikki blushed feeling uncomfortable at being objectified, though liking the attention.

"Sorry," Anders replied as he stole another glance at Nikki's legs.

The path curved to the right, away from the Risen Cove, setting them on a stroll toward a large group of something other than cosplay people crowding an intersection ahead. As they neared, Nikki realized many of these people were tall and exceptionally well fit. Others, visibly shorter and with all different colors of skin . . . natural and not, were mingling with those tall. None wore costumes. Instead, the taller men and women had on sports clothing of purples, blues, and reds, while most of those shorter had on skimpy outfits. Nikki felt her body flush warm at how skimpy some of the outfits were . . . if they could be called outfits. The crowd appeared to be celebrating under holographic banners of pink, white, and silver with the bold letters and words "TM^{2}A Champions." As they closed the distance to the crowd, Miller slowed slightly, offering Nikki a little welcomed relief for her leg. Though, another urgency grew.

"Miller . . . Mr. Dom . . ." Nikki attempted to get the attention of the *Wind Runner's* officer with a hushed, then louder voice as she hoped the facilities she needed were near.

"My name is Domanner, Jeffery Domanner," Miller chided while stopping short of the crowd and whirling around on his heels. He gave Nikki a scolding look with furrowed brows.

"I need to go," Nikki stated sheepishly.

"Where?" Miller looked confused.

"You know . . . the bathroom," she answered, a bit surprised at Miller not understanding the meaning of her words.

"You're kiddin' me." Miller sounded flabbergasted in his Southern drawl. "Now? Didn't you go before we left?"

"Yes," she answered defiantly.

Miller rolled his eyes before putting on a face of frustration and pointing to a building beyond the TM²A crowd. Nikki found the blue glowing symbols of a woman in a dress, a man, a man with half a dress, and a wheelchair set into a stone obelisk next to the building she assumed had the restroom. She groaned at the signage. She didn't like all-genders restrooms. Too many less-than-desirable experiences in them. She looked around the celebrating crowd of tall athletes hoping to find another restroom symbol . . . for woman only. *Nothing!* Nikki's anxiety built.

"What?" Miller asked impatiently.

"I . . . would rather . . ." Nikki started to protest her lack of choice in accommodations.

"It'll be all right," Anders sounded playful. "I'll go with you. You know . . . to watch your . . ."

"You'll watch nothing of me!" Nikki retorted.

"All right." Anders defensively raised his hands. "I didn't mean anything by my offer."

"Time is critical, Ms. Bathor," Miller urged Nikki with an outstretched arm in the direction of the restroom.

"Men!" Nikki snorted as she trudged off toward the glowing blue symbols, preparing herself to navigate the crowd of TM²Aers. "When you're not acting like dogs, you're acting like—"

"You're welcome," Anders interrupted with a smile.

Banners fluttered, and holo-signage flashed all around the boastful crowd of powerfully built athletes as Nikki weaved through them. The signage and the conversations she overheard told her they were celebrating winning the title in the International Transhuman Mixed Martial Arts League. The strong smell of alcohol and a haze of intoxicating smoke wafting heavy in the air as a stout electronic tune, someone thought was music, pulsed, making her feel the score as much as hear it. All of it quickly caused her to feel a "buzz" and headache. *This is not my kind of crowd.*

She started to wonder what "transhuman" meant in terms of the martial arts when she brushed past two preoccupied martial artists, a dark-skinned woman slightly taller and more muscled than Nikki and a white man more than a chest and head taller and much bigger than the dark-skinned woman. The feel of cool carbon fibers and metal alloy brushed against her arms making her look down from the blue glowing symbols she was navigating toward. The two athletes each possessed prosthetic arms and hands shaped closely to their biological replacement forms, the hands having artificial flesh covering them that to Nikki didn't feel exactly like human flesh. The woman's hands were colored in her natural skin tones while the man's hands were colored in a purple, blue, and red pattern. Nikki suddenly felt uncomfortable as she realized all the martial artists and some of the team staff had prosthetics and implants. Many the prosthetics had built-in holographic PDAs in which a noticeable part of the crowd used, but not to interact with each other. They seemed to prefer the physical for interacting with their fellow athletes, coaches, and trainers. *Interesting.* Some also appeared to possess cybernetic enhancements in their necks or heads. One even had a cybernetic eye that looked like it came from a killer robot out of an old movie classic about the end of the world. To Nikki's relief, they paid her little attention as she "pardon me" and "excuse me" while getting through them.

Breaking free of the flesh, carbon, and metal throng, Nikki found herself standing before several wiry-built, above-average height men, one brown-skinned and one white with a hint of oriental heritage. Both wore loose-fitting purple athletic shorts and shirts with a woven-in display signage that was shifting in blues, then reds, then blues again, "Transhuman Mixed Martial Artist." Both sported purple, blue, and red patterns on their prosthetic legs and arms. *All of their limbs . . . quadriplegics. Cybernetic-controlled limbs!* She felt even more uncomfortable than moments before. *Not natural . . . not what He meant for us.* Nikki heard her Bubba Jules's words in her head about the mingling of technology with the human body. Clinging on the arms of the martial artists were what appeared to Nikki as four young women. She gave them double and triple takes but remained uncertain of their gender before realizing she stood staring at the red bikini "enthusiasts" with jaws agape. The young "*women*" adorned their bodies in colors and patterns of orange and black tiger stripes and yellow and black leopard spots. Not painted . . . No, the coloration and patterns on their bodies were skin pigment deep. Two even had cat whiskers sprouting out around their noses. All four displayed long manes of yellow hair with black highlights and a red stripe. Each had their own variation on hairstyles. *Awkward*, came to Nikki's mind. One of the "*women*" growled at her like an agitated cat. Awkwardness turned to anxiety and alarm. With all four "cat women" staring at her as if a threat, Nikki quickly resumed her navigation around the six, continuing to make her way to the restroom.

Walking with a slight limp and a headache, the buzzing of something larger than an insect drew Nikki's eyes upward. A small swarm of multicolored mini-drones, each able to fit in the palm of her hand, hovered just outside of the restroom. News and paparazzi drones. Nikki had second thought about her needs as she felt certain each carried a powerful camera, maybe one of the new ten terapixel micros or something close, able to see the finest flaws in a girl's complexion . . . *and me revealing so much*.

"Just not right," Nikki spoke aloud with unmasked disdain as an uncomfortable shiver rippled through her. She stepped under the mini-drones and onto the tiles of the restroom entranceway as her inner physical discomfort grew.

Inside the restroom, Nikki's breath was taken away. She again considered finding another place to do her *business* but knew she would never make a new destination. Instead, she pushed forward into the heavy drug-scented haze obscuring much of the upper half of the restroom. Worse, noises filled the restroom of people "enjoying" themselves and others from the stalls. Another shiver rippled up and down Nikki's back. She had to almost dance through the throng of multihued people interacting with one another through their holographically projected PDAs or talking and pawing at each other . . . and worse. *How can they do that in public?* Nikki felt both amazed and repulsed at their displays that went *far* beyond public affections. Many of the occupants she brushed past looked to be women . . . in varying states of nudity, making it a bit easier for Nikki to know what she was looking at. Almost all were surgically enhanced, but she couldn't say if they were originally male or female, or something in between.

A hand groping her backside startled Nikki, causing her to jump while looking for the offending person. The crowd swallowed both hand and owner. Now with an urgent need to relieve herself, Nikki started forcing her way to a stall she thought unoccupied. Relieved she was right and in a state of cleanliness she could stomach, Nikki closed the stall door bringing on a sense of security and welcomed isolation from the depravity going on beyond the door. A quick maneuver of her clothing found Nikki sitting with a deep sense of relief.

A heavy thud against the stall door sent adrenalin shooting throughout her body. Through the din, she heard the unmistakable sounds of heavy, raspy breathing and moaning outside her stall and more down the line of stalls along with words that just should not be spoken in public, like "Oh . . . just like that . . ." and "Such a good girl, Senator . . ." and "I want more of that!" Nikki felt herself both blushing and alarmed.

The sight of feet shuffling under and just beyond her stall door concerned

Nikki. Heat bloomed in her face . . . some from embarrassment, more from anger. *A girl can't even get some peace and privacy in a bathroom stall*, Nikki thought as she finished with her business, stood, and redressed.

"Hi, gorgeous." The wide-eyed face of a platinum-blond woman appeared above the stall door. The woman's eyes were unnaturally red beyond her drugged, bloodshot appearance. Her facial features told Nikki she was of European descent, but her skin was colored light blue. At a glance, Nikki thought her hair a wig and skin painted for cosplay.

"Yum," the woman continued, then looked to someone outside the stall, but near. "You've got to see her. She just must *play* with us."

"Leave me alone!" Nikki snarled at the woman.

"That's not nice," the woman chastised with a wounded pout, then dropped from the door and backed away from the stall.

Nikki stared at the door not knowing what to do. Her hair felt as if it stood on end as she held her breath listening for the woman. The din in the restroom pitched up and down with voices both female and male. Soft and deeper moans accompanied by rhythmic thuds, heavy breathing, and some grunting came from the line of stalls Nikki now stood in. She felt dirty just standing there. She wanted badly to leave. *Is it safe to leave the stall? Is she . . . Are they waiting for me . . . or gone?* Nikki worried at the unknown. She just couldn't be certain. With a deep breath, she unlatched the door, then opened it slowly—no platinum-blond woman. A sense of relief washed over her. Several clusters of women and what Nikki thought were estrogen-treated men dressed in skimpy, feminine clothing took up most of the walking area of the restroom. That haze of smoke hung heavy in the air with the scent of drugs. A throng of women beyond them were at the wash counter touching up their makeup and hair. All of them had pigment-color alterations to their skin, as all had interesting styling to their equally colorful hair. Some had eyes of unnatural colors with one pink- and blue-skinned woman showing off her glowing, yellow eyes to those surrounding her. A short-haired blond man with cybernetic prosthetic legs, dressed in those loose-fitting purple, blue, and red athletic clothes left one of the stalls for the wash counter. Several of the women made room for him to wash his hands. He appeared unfazed by the surroundings . . . as if all were normal.

Nikki stepped from the stall and around one cluster of colorful women before going to the only open wash basin at the counter. She turned on the water and started washing her hands when she heard that woman's voice behind her.

"There you are," that blue-skinned, platinum-blond woman sounded triumphant. Nikki froze with her stomach feeling as if she dropped from a tall building. She felt hands on her shoulders . . . Strong, lean hands that quickly made their way to her neck where they lightly wrapped partially around her throat. "You're just too yummy not to be enjoyed."

"Please, let me go." Nikki tried to keep her voice steady but knew it quivered more than she wanted.

"Not before *we* get a taste of you." that woman stated with a certainty that made Nikki's hopes sink and skin crawl. She felt a hand slide over the curve of her backside, then slip between her legs as the hands around her neck applied just a little more pressure.

Nikki felt violated. Panic welled up in her so quickly that she lost her ability to think soundly. *What can I say to get out of this . . . get away from them?* Rationality started slipping from her. *What's happening to me?* Confusion gripped her as she was spun around by both pairs of hands and held against the counter. That blue-skinned, red-eyed woman stood close and eye-level to Nikki. She wore only a red bikini revealing a body as slender as her face and athletic. The other person, unseen till this moment, kept a left hand wrapped around Nikki's neck. Taller than Nikki by a little, she had blue eyes, lavender-pigmented skin, long, blond hair, and a well-endowed chest. She squeezed Nikki's neck hard to the point of giving pain when Nikki tried to pull away. *Too strong.* Nikki looked down at her lean body wrapped in a revealing black, wet-look dress showing off lean legs to the thighs. Nikki didn't find the telltale sign of a man or a transgender as she suspected.

"She has one . . . be sure of that," the blue-skinned face came close to Nikki's. Her breath reeking of alcohol caused Nikki to crinkle her nose. The platinum blonde's hands roamed over and gripped Nikki's breasts. Nikki's skin started crawling worse than before, and her mind went numb. She felt powerlessness, and that took away her strength to fight back. "Kitten show her. Give her a touch."

The lavender-skinned blonde grabbed Nikki's right wrist while wearing a sadistic expression. She . . . He then pulled her hand down to the hem of the black dress. Nikki realized what was happening and where her hand was being forcefully guided. In a burst of panic and anger, she pulled her hand back to her hip trying to find some part of her clothing to grasp with her thumb. Again, the lavender-skinned blonde pulled at her wrist, this time forcing Nikki's hand under the hem of the black dress. Nikki's eyes went wide in panic as she felt her body electrify with what she could only describe as crawling insects all over her. *No!* Her attempt to scream cut off into gurgles by the blonde's strong left hand on her throat. Nikki then tried to pull both of her arms in tight to her body, but her right hand just wouldn't move. Panic, her violation, anger—all mixed into a single tempest of emotion. Nikki swung wide and high with her left hand, slapping the platinum blonde hard on her right blue cheek staggering her back a step.

"You . . . bitch!" The platinum blonde's red eyes turned bloodred with rage as she rubbed her face. She raised her hands, so Nikki had a clear view of them. With a flick of her wrists, small silver claws extended from under her red-colored fingernails. "Now, we're gonna make you *sorry* before we have a taste of you."

The hand around Nikki's throat squeezed hard, slowing the blood flow to her head as she choked. Nikki grabbed at the hand on her throat with her free hand, trying to pull free from the blonde's grip, but the blonde was too strong. Nikki started to see tiny flashes of light in front of her eyes.

"Let her go!" a woman's voice demanded from deeper in the haze-filled restroom.

"Stay out of this, Tigress." The platinum blonde made her own demand.

"I said, let her go, or I'll bring in your martialist!" Several octaves lower, the unseen woman repeated her demand for Nikki's release. Footfalls to Nikki's right drew her eyes to the newcomer, a head taller than the platinum blonde, dressed in a differently styled wet-look outfit, and having naturally tanned white skin with black and orange tiger stripes coded into her dermal layer. The dark-haired woman . . . no, another transgender, stared down the blue-skinned, red-eyed, platinum blonde as if this were all a normal evening for them.

The platinum blonde held her ground for long moments before Nikki saw her "retract" her claws. "You spoil all our fun."

The lavender-skinned blonde kept a powerful hold on Nikki's throat and wrist throughout the whole exchange, controlling Nikki from any useful movement or calling for help. More tiny lights flashed in Nikki's vision. She felt light-headed, almost euphoric, almost . . . a tingling sensation Nikki felt in her head . . . somewhere deep. A strange sensation unfamiliar to her. It grew larger . . . more intense as it spread throughout her body. The tingling transformed into a mild burning sensation, almost like an electrical shock, only not painful in the sense Nikki felt any potential harm. The tingling burn grew again and intensified, alarming Nikki now, but before she could act, the tingling burn radiated out to Nikki's arms and hands, then burst in arcs in all directions.

The lavender-skinned blonde reeled back in pain as arcing electrical discharges bridged the gap between Nikki's hands and their bodies. The blonde started cussing in a swirl of anger and pain, her voice now deeper by an octave or three. Looking up at Nikki, she half-demanded, half-asked, "What in the hell did you do to me?"

"I . . . I don't know," Nikki choked out in-between sucking in breaths of air. She felt them . . . him in her head. Nikki didn't understand it, but she felt him clearly . . . a linkage between her and Aren. Her body felt charged up, alert, alive with the residual of whatever was that shocking charge. Everyone in the restroom who saw the sparks stared at her with surprise and some with fear or awe. Now with a clearing head, Nikki realized she no longer was restrained. Taking advantage of the awkward standoff, she scurried left out of the restroom, not knowing what to think.

Concentrating on walking steady, Nikki feared her nervous system damaged. *That shock thing seemed to have injured me, making me a bit wobbly.* Stumbling out of the restroom, Nikki looked to the spot where she remembered the group, but the crowd of martialists and colorfully skinned companions obscured them. She thought the music loud before she entered the den of debauchery. Now, it felt deafening and painful. Whatever Aren did to her, she found it both a blessing and something she didn't want to experience again.

Walking toward the crowd, Nikki searched for her friends. A ruckus of voices behind her found the three "cat women" from the restroom hotly arguing as they hurriedly approached the dark-skinned female and large male cybernetic martialists. The pair of martialists seemed confused and annoyed at the trio's ranting explanations and accusations. That is . . . until the two blue- and lavender-skinned cats pointed at Nikki as they made more accusations at her. Nikki couldn't hear what they said, but when the body language of the martialists changed to something of sympathy as they stroked their cat companions to being calm, Nikki thought it best to get out of there.

Nikki plunged into the crowd, hoping she was making her way toward Anders and the others. Martial artists, martialists, companions, and others celebrating gave annoyed and dirty looks at Nikki as she brushed past them. She dared not look back for fear of seeing a bunch of them hot on her heels. After what felt like much longer than it took, Nikki emerged from the crowd close to where she aimed. Anders and Miller were standing off to her left looking into the crowd, likely for her. Miller looked almost as anxious as Anders.

"I'm here." Nikki called out to them while waving her arms. Both looked her direction, then annoyed as they approached her.

"How long does it take to relieve oneself?" Miller asked callously in his Southern drawl. "Come on, Ms. Rick . . . Bathor. We have to get goin'. Timing is of utmost importance."

Miller ushered Nikki and Anders down the paved path away from the Risen

Cove, trying to catch up to the trailblazing Dunkle, Rogaan, and Aren. As emotional relief started to fill her, Nikki's right leg started becoming painful again, though she didn't complain for fear of them stopping. Nikki wanted distance from the TM²A Champions and their companions. Anders kept looking at her with questioning eyes, as if he knew or sensed something wrong.

While on their brisk walk, they passed scantily dressed patrons enjoying each other a bit too much in the open sky of adult hours of the resort. Numerous blue and silver service bots going about their business carrying food and drinks and things Nikki couldn't identify were all around them. Some got in their path before moving out of the way at the last moment. It was a short walk at the edge of another large pool off to their left before arriving at a large, paved courtyard peppered with occupied round tables topped with open, circular, shade umbrellas. Now with the nerve to look behind, Nikki found more scantily dressed patrons pawing at each other as they walked with Rogaan and Aren strolling behind them. Rogaan seemingly enjoying the view. Discussed and feeling wounded, Nikki turned her gaze back to the courtyard. Her heart almost stopped at what lay ahead and with her two ancient friends still strolling some distance behind.

In front of the tables stood the dark-skinned cybernetic martialist. She appeared to be waiting with eyes fixed on them. Surprised and confused, Nikki admitted aloud she was fleeing this one. "How in the hell did she get in front of us?"

"I have a bone to pick with you," she spoke in an aggressive American accent as she pointed at Nikki with her right prosthetic hand. The cybernetic arm and hand moved as naturally as one of flesh, maybe faster. "You slapped one of my kittens and tasered the other."

Ahead of Nikki, Miller had tried to maneuver around the woman, but she easily cut him off at every angle. When the woman made her accusations, he stopped and looked back at Nikki along with Anders. Miller asked in his pronounced Southern drawl, "What happened in the restroom?"

"This redefines . . . 'I need to go'?" Anders looked at Nikki with raised eyes. He clearly was hoping for an explanation.

"They assaulted me," Nikki answered the dark-skinned, cybernetic woman dressed in purple, blue, and red shorts and a matching athletic top. "And I didn't TAZER them. I don't know what happened."

"Not what my kittens told me," the dark-skinned woman countered in disdain. She aggressively approached the three. Miller instinctively stepped between the woman and Nikki, as Anders closed to Nikki's side. Nikki didn't know if she should feel safe or not, but she appreciated their intent.

"That's far enough." Miller held out his hand like a law officer might in one of those old movies. The woman came to a halt in front of him.

"Get out of my way," she spoke with determination and anger.

"I cannot," Miller replied in a calm, almost matter-of-fact, manner. "We are short on time and need—"

The barely audible whirl of micro-gearing and an intense hum of electrical systems delivering energy to powerful mechanisms mixed with the gurgling sound of Miller's choking gasps. The woman's right arm moved in a blur, clamping its hand and fingers around Miller's throat, lifting him slightly to his toes as he grasped the artificial arm trying to pull himself off the carbon fiber and metal mechanism. Nikki stood in shock, both at the speed of the attack but also for the action lacking any sense of social civility or respect for lawful behavior. *I see where her kittens learned their ways.*

"Let him go!" Anders left Nikki's side to help Miller without a thought or hesitation. He surprised Nikki in his brave act . . . more so for him defending Miller. Anders ended up on the bad end of a powerful sidekick, sending him flying backward beyond Nikki, losing his hat while in midair, then landing with a thud on his back on the paving. He groaned in pain as he rolled into a ball hugging his chest. Nikki stood paralyzed, not knowing what to do. *She has cybernetic legs too. I thought they were human legs.* Miller had other plans. He started kicking at the woman's midriff. The first strike caught the enhanced martialist by surprise, staggering her and forcing her to lean over with a winch of pain. Miller pressed on with his feet now solidly pushing off from the ground. He kicked her again with little additional affect. His next strike she blocked with her free arm, stopping the kick as if he hit a steel rod. Miller cried out in pain.

"You . . ." the woman martialist growled while grabbing Miller's leg with her left hand, then let out a *kiai* as she drove him downward with her right arm, slamming Miller into the paving stones. Miller lay motionless. Nikki let out a gasp fearing the worst for him.

"Stop!" Nikki heard the shout directed at the martialist who now hovered over Miller's still form. She then realized the shout came from her own mouth. Nikki swallowed hard when the woman cybernetic martialist looked up at her with intense, angry, bloodshot eyes. *I have to make this end . . . How?* She decided to plead. "I'm sorry. I'm sorry for anything I did to offend you or your friends."

"You can apologize to my kittens . . ." the growling martialist countered as she forgot about Miller and stepped in front of Nikki, staring her down. The scent of alcohol and synthetic drugs wafting heavily from her as she spoke . . . giving reason to Nikki for her bloodshot eyes and unfriendly mood. In a lightning move, the martialist grabbed Nikki by her top hairs with that prosthetic right arm, pulling Nikki upward, so she had to raise herself up on her toes to lessen the pain in her scalp. "After you're taught manners. You people . . . think you're so much better than us. You're not. You're pathetic compared to us . . . to me . . . and my kittens."

Nikki grabbed the martialist's hand and arm trying to give herself leverage to lessen the pain inflicted on her. The synthetic flesh felt unnatural and slightly cool to the touch. The flesh had a tiny bit of give over harder things beneath.

"What . . .? No. I'm not better than you." Nikki attempted honest reasoning with the impaired cybernetic woman.

"No more am I hearing that wounded confidence in my kittens caused by the likes of you and others," the woman martialist avowed with growling words.

"I didn't . . ." Nikki tried more reasoning. *She's protecting her . . . kittens,* Nikki realized. *She can be reasoned with if she knows the truth.* The woman martialist yanked up on her hair "Ouch!"

"No!" The martialist pulled Nikki close. The wafting of intoxicants on her breath made Nikki's stomach sour, nauseating her. "No more useless excuses."

Nikki felt herself being pulled and half-dragged back the way they came. She tried to keep up with short, choppy steps but continued stumbling. Realizing ration and reason weren't going to work with this woman, Nikki tried struggling to get out of her grasp. *Nothing.* Another harsh tug at her hair delivered more sharp pain, making Nikki angry. She tried pulling at the martialist's fingers but found them unmoving mechanical digits under their simulated flesh. *This isn't natural . . . not right.* Nikki gave in to the fact she just wasn't a physical match against this cybernetic woman. But then, she didn't need to be her match. A smile came to Nikki's grimacing face.

That familiar feeling of presence began growing in her head. Not the tingle and burning of earlier. The presence in her mind. The lights suddenly started flickering all about the resort grounds as if power somehow was being interrupted, and that booming electronic music from the TM^{2}A Champions celebration fell silent along with the pleasant melody playing over the park's outdoor speakers. The flickering lights finally settled to a steady on state, though dimmed, providing shadowy illumination across the grounds. Nikki then felt . . . him.

"Release the youngling," the deep voice calmly demanded from somewhere behind them.

The martialist stopped and looked back while still holding Nikki high and tight by the hair. Nikki painfully spun a little on her toes to confirm with her eyes what she already knew. At the edge of the courtyard stood the six-foot-tall, broad-chested, blue, red, and black armored figure she expected.

"You're not my mother." The martialist dismissed the armored character as if she expected her confidence to intimidate and see immediate obedience. "Leave me alone, if you know what is good for you."

"Do I appear to have . . . lost my manliness?" Rogaan directed his comment beyond the martialist and Nikki.

"Not something I . . . care to confirm, old friend." Aren's sardonic tone brought a low growl from the cybernetic woman. Looking back towards the courtyard, Aren stood in his dark blue monk-like clothing. Putting his stare directly on the martialist, he spoke at her. "What is good for you is to let our friend go."

"Go back to playing your childish cosplay and get out of my way," demanded the cybernetic woman martialist, her focus on Aren.

"Release our friend," Rogaan demanded again as he calmly walked toward Nikki and her captor. As he drew near, Nikki could make out more finely his well-groomed hair pulled into a tail, revealing his brown skin, short beard, and radiant blue eyes that held in them a life of skills, experience . . . and confidence.

Nikki felt Rogaan's raw emotions . . . He feared nothing here. She waited for the *tell* he almost always gave when readying for conflict. She waited a few moments but didn't see it. Really wanting her hair free of these artificial fingers, Nikki complained with pain-filled words, "Are you here to talk or get me out of mecha-woman's paws?"

"Shut your mouth," the martialist angrily demanded of Nikki as she gave her a shake. Nikki yelped. The woman martialist then put on a knowing smile that seemed out of place now as she dragged Nikki to the side of the path, allowing the martialist to watch both Rogaan and Aren with minimal head movement. She spoke again at Aren and Rogaan. "I said, get out of my way."

"Old friend, more like her to approach behind you," Rogaan warned Aren while he continued closing to sword's length of Nikki's abductor.

Aren smiled knowingly as he too moved to the side of the path opposite the woman martialist and Nikki while casually speaking to Rogaan. "Do you need my help with this troop, old friend?"

"Your aid is always of value but let us to keep the Powers in store and to not notice," Rogaan conferred with Aren.

The path beyond Aren started filling with the cybernetic woman's fellow martialists. The biggest, a male martialist, with prosthetic arms, dressed in his purple, blue, and red athletic attire, made strange-sounding pounding gestures fist to palm. He stood taller than everyone and carried himself dangerously. With new confidence filling her words, the woman martialist chastised Aren and Rogaan once again. "Stop with this cosplay crap and leave before you're made to regret us."

Nikki felt the change in the half Tellen's demeanor just before he set his jaw and shifted his weight on his feet . . . readying himself for physical combat. It was ever so slight a change, but Nikki knew what to look for. Rogaan spoke with more heat. "Once more, release the youngling."

"There's the *tell*," Nikki defiantly announced with a pain-filled groan as she hung at the end of the cybernetic arm. She hung impatiently waiting for what was to follow. Rogaan cocked his head sideways slightly looking at Nikki as if asking an unspoken question.

"What *tell*?" the woman martialist sneered.

"The *tell* that says my friend is going to put a hurt on you," Nikki confidently answered. "Better listen to him. I've seen that look . . . It sank a ship a couple of weeks ago."

The transhuman martialist dismissed Nikki's provocations by jerking her about. Nikki yelped in pain again, seeing the martialist sneer with satisfaction. A strong brown hand grabbed the wrist of the prosthetic arm gripping Nikki's hair. The pain Nikki endured from being jerked back and forth subsided. The cybernetic martialist tried pulling her artificial arm from Rogaan's grip but found it held in a vise. She growled at Rogaan's impassive, unflappable gaze as dim light glinted off the half Tellen's dark blue metallic forearm guard.

"You're transhuman too?" The cybernetic woman martialist sounded shocked with her realization and accusation.

"Release my friend," Rogaan spoke calmly in a lower tone. Nikki knew him better. She felt his anger heating his actions, despite his outward stolid presentation. A surprised expression swept across the martialist's face as her prosthetic forearm, designed for abusive TM^{2}A combat, started crushing under Rogaan's grip.

"What the hell are you?" the martialist asked as she tried frantically to pull free of Rogaan's hold.

In the struggle, Nikki fell free of the synthetic grasp. She stumbled away from the struggle before she got her feet under her. Concern and anger simultaneously swept through her as she ran adrenaline-trembling fingers through her hair, worried some was taken by the prosthetic hand or that she bled. When satisfied neither was the case, Nikki looked back to Rogaan to thank him. Instead, Nikki saw the martialist strike Rogaan with a left hook to his face. The martialist's eyes went wide with surprise and a growing fear when Rogaan simply glared back at her.

"Competition safeties remove," the woman martialist commanded, speaking to nobody that Nikki could see.

The martialist then struck at Rogaan again with her synthetic left fist and legs. The sounds emitted from her arm and legs now more aggressive, power-filled . . . maybe overpowered. Nikki felt the impact along with Rogaan. *That's new.* Nikki rubbed her jaw. *That hurt.* The strike angered the half Tellen though he still maintained his composure and an impassive expression. Nikki felt Rogaan's reluctance to hit her. The woman martialist then burst into a flurry of strikes—hand and knees—on Rogaan until he released her right wrist and took a step back, forcefully blocking with ease her trailing strikes. The woman martialist stopped her assault, instead, stood looking at her deformed hand and hanging arm, bent slightly at the wrist with fingers limited in movement. She looked at her damaged right appendage with shock that then saw her transforming loss into a growing visible anger.

Rogaan simply rubbed his jaw and side where she made particularly hard strikes. Nikki felt them too. Still, Rogaan held his anger in check. In fact, he was calming himself, to Nikki's amazement. *Such self-control and no desire to inflict undue injury on a woman.* The intoxicated and drug-high woman with her deadly transhuman tools now without strength limiters readied herself to attack Rogaan. She went at Rogaan with everything unbridled: arms, legs, hands . . . damaged as well as undamaged, feet, knees, and elbows. She attacked straight on, with spinning moves and kicks, and with jumping strikes. The speed and anger in which she attacked Rogaan was a blur and more intense than anything Nikki ever saw live or in video flicks. The cybernetic woman martialist wanted to hurt Rogaan, maybe kill him as her strikes told. She growled, grunted, and did that power yell with her attacks. Rogaan deflected them all, every strike, without counterattacking. Nikki felt Rogaan purposely seeking an inner calm.

Suddenly, Nikki felt hands tugging on her, pulling her back from the two combatants. Looking over her shoulder, the dark-haired and tanned face of Dr. Dunkle met her eyes with a wide-eyed *"You should know better than to be in the mix of this"* look. He quickly positioned her a short distance away behind a waist-high, stone-faced, holo-signage emitter that now sat cold and dark. Dunkle then left her, making his way to Anders, who still lay on the ground clutching his chest. Watching the one-sided fight between the cybernetic woman martialist and Rogaan frustrated Nikki. *Hit her, Rogaan. Hit her hard . . . as hard as she deserves for hurting Shawn and Miller.* Nikki hoped Rogaan heard her and felt her anger at the transhuman martialist as much as she felt his emotions.

Nikki felt the other one near and found him kneeling over Miller. She almost missed him in the dim light and shadows as they blended with his dark monk attire. He placed his hands on both sides of the unmoving head of Miller. Nikki knew what was to come . . . the searing pain and euphoric joy of that which is broken is healed. *How does he do that?* Nikki wondered at it for the countless time. Miller's body jerked and convulsed, then lay unmoving. Nikki felt a tingling . . . a touch of the energies flowing through Aren the *Ra'Pa*. It always manifests as a chill felt throughout her body when he was near and using the Powers of Agni. The unresponsive Miller drew a look on Aren's face matching the surprise Nikki felt in him. He attempted another healing with Miller's body convulsing again as Nikki felt another chill sweep through her. Aren then placed his hand on Miller's chest. To Nikki's relief, she felt satisfaction in Aren, and that meant Miller drew breath.

Looking to Dunkle and Anders brought Nikki more frustration. The woman martialist kept stepping in front of what Nikki wanted to see. When she finally stopped bouncing about, the transhuman martialist appeared winded as she stared at Rogaan with frustration and what looked like fear-filled eyes. Rogaan appeared calm, casual . . . almost unconcerned by her relentless attacks, though Nikki felt his desire not to injure the woman starting to wane.

"I need some help with this one," the woman martialist reluctantly admitted to her fellow teammates. She raised her right hand high for all to see the twisted fingers and bent wrist of her battered synthetic arm. "He bent my graphene, bad."

"Stop this . . . foolishness." Rogaan attempted an offer of reason to the woman, wanting to stop events before he would need to act decisively.

Nikki knew better. Reason was not at play. The woman martialist wanted this because of a sense of being wronged through her *kittens*, despite their troubled moral values and behaviors. She carried a sense of entitlement, allowing her and her friends to behave in any manner they saw fit and that everyone else must accept, even encourage, their ways, or be forced to do so. *Sad . . . The ones once seeking acceptance decades ago now demand all others conform to their desires in living. The bullied are now the bully.* Nikki shook her head in disgust at the realization.

When Nikki looked up, she found Rogaan surrounded by six transhuman martialists, two she took for women and the other four men. Fighting hand-to-hand, Rogaan easily dodged and deflected their strikes except for a few. Those, despite the sharp ringing tones caused by cybernetic appendages powerfully striking Rogaan, his armor seemed to absorb it all without him noticing. Rogaan moved with a blur. Despite the odds against him, Nikki still felt Rogaan unworried . . . even calculating, as if events were unfolding as planned. Dunkle now had Anders up on his knees but found themselves surrounded by three more hostile team-colored transhumans. A troubled expression on Dunkle's face said what he thought of their situation as another chill swept through Nikki, drawing her attention back to Aren. He stood off to the left of the rest in his dark blue monk-like clothes. *It's a good look for him*, Nikki decided.

With his left hand raised, Aren held at bay three more aggressive transhuman martialists with some form of unseen barrier he created between him and them. His right hand extended horizontally, Miller levitated, his body gliding silently toward Nikki. The transhuman martialists looked in awe. *You think that would be enough to get them to back off*, Nikki thought. Instead, their drunk and high states of mind would not suffer such obvious reason.

A loud whistle sounded. Fearing it was security forces, Nikki looked for its source before realizing it came from Rogaan. He now pointed at the three martialists surrounding Dunkle and Anders. "Are you three . . . so cowards as to not fight me?"

Nikki thought she heard Rogaan's words wrong. *Did he just challenge another three of the transhumans to join the fight against him? What's he thinking he's doing? Maybe he translated his Antaalin incorrectly to English?* Then, it became clear to her as Miller's unconscious body settled on the inactive holo-signage display surface in front of her. Rogaan and Aren were working as a team to get them out of danger. Aren turned his focus to Dunkle and Anders, pushing his unseen barrier past them and into three more martialists. He now pushed back six transhuman martialists, keeping them from getting into the fight. No longer surrounded, Dunkle helped Anders to his feet, then got him moving toward Nikki. *Rogaan bought Aren time to protect Shawn and Dr. Dunkle.* Nikki now saw and realized how they fought as a team.

As Dunkle and Anders stumbled to Nikki, she felt Rogaan transform his thoughts into a mind-set of resolve. Looking between the six transhuman martialists doing all they could to harm him, he calmly growled, "Let us finish this—now."

The big martialist growled, then started swinging angrily at Rogaan. The remaining martialists hesitated a moment before joining their big teammate, all six attacking as a coordinated team. An air of calm surrounded Rogaan as he blocked the brute's and others' mechanical arms and legs, sounding as if he was damaging them as he did. Then Rogaan called out in Antaalin, "*Aren, idaalam!*"

Nikki understood the Antaalin words "Aren, now!" and their meaning as she felt a chilling tingle sweep through her when Aren stretched out his hands and fingers. Blue-white arcs of energy danced across his hands, then lanced out to the nearest transhuman, then another, and another; then to all the other transhumans and several metal poles aside the patio as the sound of electrical burning buzzed all about. Amidst the screams and groans of surprise and pain, the entire crowd of transhuman martialists fell to the ground, many with their cybernetics now smoking, having been disrupted or destroyed.

Rogaan stood tall surrounded by the withering bodies of transhumans, all now unable to stand or attack as their cybernetics were rendered useless. Camera flashes from various places around them, most at some distance, a few just to the water-side of the patio where a small group of towel-wrapped resort patrons stood among arched pillars leading to a giant, irregular-shaped, illuminated pool told Nikki they and their fight had been noticed . . . and on video. Pleads of mercy and shouts of anger came from the fallen championship team. Some of the transhuman martialists feared they were about to be slaughtered in their defensiveness. Others kept up their air of arrogance and superiority, continuing with threats of revenge.

"He's going to have my hide," Dunkle groaned as he noticed the growing interest and video recordings being taken by the resort patrons.

"Too much?" Aren asked Rogaan in Antaalin.

"Too . . . little," Rogaan replied in English, as he noticed Aren looking about the area for something. "They still . . . wiggle."

"And . . . make too much noise." Aren discharged another handful of arcing blue-white energy, looking much like lightning, striking and dancing all about the complaining transhumans. More camera flashes Nikki caught out of the corner of her eyes told her Aren's acts were being captured on still images and video. When the electrical burning buzzing and the screams of pain it brought out ceased, Aren stopped his assault. He looked at Rogaan. "Superior?"

"Superior." Rogaan nodded in agreement.

The two were a fighting pair, Nikki realized, balancing and complementing each other in almost every way. Rogaan took on the martialist mob to draw them to him so Aren could take them down in one act without killing. *Creative. Merciful.*

"What . . . do you to seek?" Rogaan asked Aren, who looked about the area searching for something or someone.

"I recognized the Powers in . . . usage," Aren revealed. "Not from me . . . or from you. That . . . deduces others are near."

Rogaan started looking around the perimeter of the patio filled with its custom-placed bushes, trees, ferns, flowers, and rocks. More camera flashes visibly irritated him. Nikki felt his irritation before he forced a calmness on himself. Appearing to realize the uselessness of his physical vision, Rogaan then stood perfectly still with his eyes cast down as if he were looking at something other than his immediate surroundings. Nikki felt something more of Rogaan. He was . . . His mind was adrift. Not adrift . . . connecting with intelligence . . . a presence. That familiar presence. The Wind.

"We need to get Miller . . . Komann . . . whatever in the hell name I gave him, to a medical facility," Dunkle told Nikki and the pain-suffering Anders as he held his MediScanner on Miller's forehead. "He's in poor health. His waves are all off norms. He has a severe concussion, and I think he is bleeding on the brain."

Aren placed his hands on Miller's chest. The chill of his manifestation made Nikki aware that he attempted another healing. Looking at the motionless young blond officer, Aren grunted. *Not a good sign*, Nikki knew. Aren spoke to Rogaan without taking his eyes from Miller. "He needs you, old friend."

"They approach from everywhere," Rogaan informed the group as he joined Aren. "They arrive with fly . . . ing eyes and *Tusaa'Ner* in front."

"And the sexless beings?" Aren asked calmly as if expecting these events to unfold as they did. "Are they changed from servants to . . . enforcers?"

"Consider them not friends," Rogaan replied as he looked for where to place his raised hand on the unconscious Miller.

"Sandu," was all Aren said as Nikki sensed him begin another manifestation.

Rogaan placed his right hand on Miller's forehead, allowing his blue steel arm guard to change as if liquid-forming tentacles that penetrated the young officer's skull. Nikki winched at the pain she thought Miller felt. She felt Rogaan as clearly as she did Aren. He willed his *Ra'Sakti* to link with the Wind above. Fragments from a vast knowledge repository flashed in her mind. Nikki assumed she saw only a tiny bit of the information Rogaan did. With it, he searched for the injuries, allowing his blue steel tentacle to fix them. She stood motionless trying to see as much as she could of both Miller's brain and the knowledge vault.

Aren's completed manifestation drew Nikki's attention away from Rogaan, some. She was torn between seeing the wonders of what Rogaan was doing, and those of Aren. This manifestation of his felt different . . . aggressive, evasive, probing, even a bit malevolent, with fragments of numbers spinning in Nikki's head, not unlike those Aren suffered in his long-ago civilization, in another time. The whine and beehive buzz of flying security drones started drowning out all other sounds. Looking up, Nikki found the shadows of dark, flying security drones surrounding them while approaching from the ground the resort's blue android ALFs came walking into view from multiple paths leading to the courtyard and patio. Their synthetic eyes now glowed with a red tint. More camera flashes than before gave Nikki a concern more people were assembling to witness them.

"This doesn't look good . . ." commented Dunkle.

"Miller?" Anders asked.

"No, the new company we're keeping," Dunkle clarified. He then spoke to Rogaan. "Any chance you can be done with Miller? Of course, after you save his life."

Rogaan appeared to be concentrating and not paying the doctor any attention. Dunkle placed his MediScanner back near Miller's forehead to take new readings. A hopeful expression grew on his face.

Something new entered Nikki's conscious mind. The feeling familiar, but vague. She turned to look behind, but before she did, the stinging pain of two weighted pricks struck her in the back. *What?* Nikki's muscles suddenly tightened and seized up painfully as she felt electricity flow, jab, and lash through her body. She staggered backward, and the pain went away as quickly as it struck her. Nikki sucked in a breath of air filling her lungs. Again, her muscle bound up as she suffered painful stinging, convulsing this time as she let out a scream that sounded more like a long grunt. As she fell backward, she saw Dunkle, Anders, and Aren look back at her. Nikki knew she hit the patio hard, but the shocking electrical current kept her muscles taunt and head from snapping back into the concrete. The racking pain left her once more. She tried to take in a breath, only to find every movement of her ribs painful. A shadow above her drew Nikki's eyes up. Fright gripped her. The stoic face of the gray-suited U.N. blond agent stared down at her, a void of compassion with that practiced smile of a sadist.

"A bit underdressed for the occasion." The blond agent spoke coldly with a cruel smirk. "I have more questions for you."

Nikki retained vague memories of the blonde's questioning in Bolivia. What she did remember sent chills down her spine. *A cruel woman . . . a sadist.* Nikki never heard her name spoken. Her fellow agent only called her "Agent 19." Meeting Agent 19's eyes confirmed to Nikki that the agent was devoid of compassion, sending another chill down her spine.

"I demand your surrender," Agent 19 snarled at Rogaan and Aren.

Looking past Agent 19, Nikki saw a flash of a spark in the air open into a swirling man-sized circular rainbow revealing a black void inside. Tyr super soldiers . . . *No, these are bigger and darker*, jumped from the darkness of the resort's bushes at the edge of the patio taking positions next to the void as they revealed themselves by turning off their stealth camouflage. They stolidly stood guarding three to each side of the swirling circular colors. Two more super soldiers jumped from the void before taking up positions on either side of the swirling rainbow. Sensing Aren manifesting an attack of lightning against the agent and others brought hope and a sense of satisfaction to Nikki. Another manifestation, not Aren's, though familiar to her . . ., formed just as quickly. Aren's lightning lashed out for the blond smirk and super soldiers lighting up the entire area as it struck an unseen barrier protecting the insanely dangerous rabble. A blinding brilliance caused Nikki to shield her eyes for long seconds. Wanting to be out of the line of this fire, she tried to get up, but instead, was painfully slammed back onto the patio concrete by a black-armored boot solidly planted on her chest. Looking up, she found Tyr super soldiers armed with rifles of some kind flanking the blond agent, one with his armored boot on her. A figure emerged from the void. This one in a dark cloak casting deep shadows over his face and covering much of his red, glinting armor. Nikki didn't need to see his face. She felt his presence as much as she did Aren's and Rogaan's. Dread firmly gripped her.

"Subdue the whore," snarled the cloaked figure, his voice familiar to Nikki, his eyes gleaming mauve from under his shadowy hood as he walked up behind Agent 19. The Agent still facing Nikki, wore a mix of fear and anger in her eyes. The Tyr raised their weapons in anger, only to settle them back into ready positions at the wave of the newcomer's hand. Nikki felt him do something to their minds . . . a manifestation. The cloaked figure glanced at the two super soldiers accompanying him through the step-gate. Nikki thought she felt the cloaked one experienced an intense moment of disappointment. He then set his gaze on Aren and Rogaan as Nikki felt the first twinges of pain from another electrical surge of the taser starting to flow through her. The shadowy figure spoke, "Let us finish . . . this."

In Nikki's screams of agony, darkness overtook her.

Chapter 1

Enduring

Blurry appeared the dirt beneath Rogaan's sandaled feet. His head swooned as his body felt sluggish as he willed himself to move, yet somehow, he still felt light as a feather to his mind. Tremors in the ground, he felt through his sandals, were familiar and comforting in their almost constant presences. A noise off to his left, a shuffling of feet over the crunchy ground. Rogaan swung his body around to face whatever it was but staggered off to his right, almost falling before regaining his footing. A featherwing's screech echoed above him. A light breeze was at his back carrying on it the scent of cooked fish. Rogaan shook his head forcing it all to clear, the haziness slowly receding. He both welcomed it and felt a loss for the euphoria. He took a deep breath. His thoughts returned to him, and his vision cleared. Looking up, in the light of the late day standing before Rogaan was a Tellen of light-brown skin. The Tellen was not as tall as he and filthy in appearance, dressed in a torn, dark green tunic, light green, loose-fitting breeches, and high-ankle sandals. The Tellen's dark hair hung over his broad face falling to his shoulders in a tangled mess that matched his hand-length beard. Those dark gray, oval eyes set apart slightly more than the average Baraan fixated on him with a burning intensity few could match.

"This one will kill you," Sugnis scolded Rogaan with deep and grumbling words. "He is more capable than the handful before him. How you avoided the point of this *Saggis's* diseased blade is a mystery of the Ancients."

"Staying downwind of me limits your fight options," Rogaan hinted of Sugnis's tactics to close on him as he sought to avoid the unpleasant discussion of his seriousness and commitment to the fight. The expression returned on Sugnis's face told him the Tellen got his meaning.

"Most go down with the hook punch you took," Sugnis critiqued, the flash of a compliment in his eyes and face now gone, replaced with that intense burning stare that gave Rogaan shivers. "You recover fast . . . faster than all but him. Still, you need to learn to avoid injury and pain, not endure it."

"I deserve it," Rogaan spoke more to himself than to the Tellen, filling the need to pay for all the terrible things he had caused happen to his family and friends . . . and their family. "And more."

"What did you speak?" Sugnis asked, though Rogaan felt certain the Tellen heard his words.

"Will you ever take a bath?" Rogaan continued to insult Sugnis of his terrible body odor to throw him off the coming lecture about feeling sorry for himself. "Seriously, I can smell you even with you being downwind."

Sugnis simply stared at Rogaan, his oval eyes narrowed, and his jaws clinched. Rogaan felt the intensity of that stare as a familiar shiver crawled up his back.

"Guilt clouds your thoughts again," Sugnis reprimanded. "It will kill you to lose focus against such a dangerous foe as you just lost focus allowing me to strike you."

"No," Rogaan argued with Sugnis. "You are that good at fighting. I did not see your punch."

"Your eyes tell the moment to strike at your sides," Sugnis simply stated. "They wander when your thoughts wander over that guilt you carry."

"I made a mess of things!" Rogaan growled at himself more than at Sugnis.

"Yes." Sugnis stated matter-of-factly. "A terrible time fighting against enemies far beyond you. So, few lost their *Lights* or were put in bondage or servitude. You did well for not being prepared."

"Tell that to Pax and Suhd." Rogaan felt sick to his stomach.

"Nothing you do to satisfy guilt will make well their situation," Sugnis advised. "They too were swept up in the same winds being friends with you."

"Being my friends is what lost them their parents." Rogaan felt tears well up in his eyes and his throat tighten as he fought down a wave for welling despair and rage. "Now, Suhd is being forced to do who knows what, and Pax is with us on this unkind rock of a prison surrounded by every watery set of jaws wanting to eat us."

"You have your wellness," Sugnis spoke cheerfully in his deep voice with obvious intent at redirecting this discussion more positively. Then, his deep voice dropped even deeper, more serious. "At least until the morning when you face this latest *Saggis*."

Rogaan was about to argue with Sugnis again, proclaiming his failings to Pax and Suhd and Mother and Father before getting interrupted by a group of newcomers. The group consisted of strongly built, light brown-skinned male Baraan island prisoners dressed shirtless and with breeches or loin covers. The group walked the edge of the two-stride high elevated rock rim of the fighting pit.

"Practice all you want, *stoner*," one of the Baraans yelled out as they walked. "Tomorrow, you die, and I win my *Hili'giin*. He looks to be a pretty one."

The other Baraans laughed at the statement as they strolled off to the hovel Rogaan shared with them. Rogaan felt disgusted and dirty at the thought of the

"*Hili'giin* service" as the island prisoners called it. Youngling prisoners, female and male, forced to be concubine slaves to the older prisoners. The female younglings rarely survived it. The few that did killed themselves on the rocks or threw themselves into the waters to avoid carnal and other abuses as a "*Nigilim'gardu*," spoiled concubines, for whatever time they had remaining of their jailing. Rogaan quickly learned only strong and ruthless survive this prison island.

When Pax and Rogaan arrived as the ship docked in the inlet, they were thrown into a crowd of unruly prisoners. They were immediately whisked off to a fighting pit located close to the dock where they, along with a handful of other young prisoners, one a female Rogaan has not seen since, were commanded to strip naked by the crowd. When Pax and Rogaan refused, the self-proclaimed leader of the island, Urgallis, ordered those Baraans loyal to him to teach the uncooperative a lesson. The fight was brutal and short with five of Urgallis's thug brawlers sprawled out in the pit. Pax suffered many bruises, and a crude knife wound on his ribs but refused Rogaan's offer of aid, instead, keeping to himself, even caring for his own wounds. For Rogaan, he stood tall with bruises, but otherwise well off. Before Urgallis could send real fighters at them, Urgallis's rival in this rocky prison, Kirral, showed up with his battle-ready *Ursan,* quickly declaring Rogaan and Pax to be too old to be *Hili'giin*, just to spit in the face of his adversary. Since then, Rogaan and Pax kept to the hovels controlled by Kirral to avoid fighting with Urgallis's bands of loyalists, though, even the Kirral loyalists, mostly Baraans considering themselves higher in standing than the few Tellens, Evendiir, and Skurst in their midst, treated him with contempt. *At least they talk to Sugnis and me*, Rogaan reflected, seeking something positive from the horrid experience.

"Don't give them a thought," Sugnis coolly told Rogaan. "Those needing to dominate others to feel better of themselves are best avoided. And when you can't avoid them . . . kill them. Come, you need food to keep up your strength for tomorrow. I have fish drying on the rocks."

Rogaan's first thought was to politely refuse Sugnis's offer of a meal; one whiff of the pungent Tellen churned his stomach. *Sugnis really needs a bath*. Thinking on his need for allies and Sugnis's kindness, Rogaan reconsidered. Besides, he would likely have to fight for scraps back at the hovel. "I accept on one condition."

"I'll guess," Sugnis's deep voice sounded playful. "You want to eat upwind?"

"Yes," Rogaan replied with a guarded smile and a bit relieved.

Sugnis led Rogaan to his camp. Near the fight pit and away from the hovels, the camp sat in a high crop of rocks and boulders where structures were not easily built or navigated due to the treacherous way the rocks rested upon each other from successive floods and for the tangle foot, strong vines that covered much of the island. It had a high vantage point where much of the island, the Ur River, and the surrounding area of the far shorelines were visible. Rogaan had come to this spot several times in his first days on the island, seeking solitude so to stew on his self-made predicament and blame himself for his arrogance and stupidity . . . a dangerous combination. Rogaan fell into his melancholy once more. *If I had only listened to Father and gone to the Ebon Circle temple, I would be a prisoner of them and not here on this forsaken pile of rocks, Pax's and Suhd's parents would not be dead, and Pax would not be shunning me.* Then Rogaan's thoughts turned to his family . . . prisoners, Mother at her Isin family's estate and Father in the Farratum jails. Regrets swept heavily over Rogaan, causing him to misstep and trip. Fortunately, he got his feet back under him before falling to the ground and embarrassing himself. A disapproving look from Sugnis was the worst that happened.

Approaching Sugnis's camp, the wind shifted several times almost in tune with the trembling in the land beneath him as they climbed, making Rogaan regret accepting the Tellen's meal offer. *He really needs to bathe.* Along the way, Sugnis disarmed trip-cords, made from the island's tangle foot vines, barely visible to Rogaan that he would have easily missed if he did not see where Sugnis reached. The Tellen carefully reset each trip-cord upon their passing. Several times as they went, they stirred up white- and gray-colored twin-tailed featherwings that flew off back to the colony on the western shore of their rock of an island. Soon arriving at their destination, the camp itself was a four-by-five-stride recess in the rocks, cleared of the vines, with a rocky overhang on the south side forming a small cave-like structure facing north. *The sun on an east to west arcing path through the northern sky heats the rocks by day, and the rocks keep him warm by night.* Rogaan appreciated the Tellen's knowledge and pragmatism. The camp had some unexpected features; rocks for sitting around a central fire pit with a pile of driftwood neatly stacked in the rocks, a bed of partly dried ferns elevated slightly off the ground in the cave recess, makeshift wood plates, dining ware, and a metal pot hanging over a pile of red and gray embers in the fire pit. Accommodations Rogaan thought inconsistent with Sugnis's minimalist vision of living.

"Not my usual 'hole in the ground,'" Sugnis proudly stated as he stirred the embers in the fire pit with a stick before adding several pieces of driftwood on top. "It's a bit too done up compared to my covered 'holes' needed in the wilds on the mainland. Keeps me from being a bite to eat in the night. But here, only Baraans are a danger, and I took care of that when I arrived."

Rogaan heard of Sugnis's arrival on the island, killing several of Urgallis's fighting followers, then holding a bone dagger to Urgallis's throat before the first day fell to night. Ever since then, Rogaan observed Urgallis always gave foul looks in Sugnis's direction but took no action against the Tellen. When Sugnis took Rogaan as an apprentice in fighting, Urgallis begrudgingly extended his foul looks and the immunity from physical abuse to him as well. This hatred, and more importantly, the *fear*, were welcomed by Rogaan, free of the need to look over his shoulders at all times. No longer needing to worry about Urgallis's band, Rogaan focused on the many *Saggis* who almost always appeared on the island a few days after the resupply ships arrived. Soon after the dockings, a new killer emerged from the shadows trying to extinguish his *Light*. Rogaan had become expectant of it and even felt annoyed by the *Saggis*. In truth, Pax had saved him from the shadow blades several times and scolded Rogaan to be more serious in his respect and regard of the killers.

Rogaan reflected on that first attempt on his life. It was a long fight breaking much of the shack he lived in. After that, the *Saggis* was subdued by a bunch of Baraans who took him away to ready him for the pit, the means of keeping order on this rock. Rogaan found himself in the pit the following morning facing the killer again. He had no intention to take the *Saggis's Light*, only to survive the one-on-one combat, but the *Saggis* had other plans and would not relent, leaving Rogaan no choice. He had to kill him, with a large rock to the head, of all things.

In this morning's attempt to take his *Light*, the *Saggis* caught Rogaan unaware. He was enjoying the morning sunrise—too much—and feeling the small ground tremors frequent on this island. Rogaan had let his guard down. His inattention allowed the *Saggis* to approach undetected. If it had not been for Pax rendering the *Saggis* unconscious with a thrown rock, Rogaan was certain he would not be taking breath now. Then, before Rogaan could thank Pax, he disappeared back into the shadows of the hovel and stayed elusively at the edge of Rogaan's vision all day. Since the *Saggis* was taken away by Kirral's followers, Rogaan prepared for the fight in the pit with Sugnis critically coaching him.

Now, the two sat quietly in the fading light of the day around a low fire eating Sugnis's dried fish he retrieved from a sun-exposed boulder covered over by a makeshift thin metal mess to keep animals, featherwings, shell-walkers, or biters from the meat. *Where did he get such a well-made mesh of metal?* Rogaan pondered a bit on that after he got over being surprised by Sugnis having it. Rogaan took notice how strange it was that the annoying flying biters did not bother them or even buzzed about. *What is Sugnis's secret at keeping them away?*

Sugnis was a mystery to Rogaan . . . and everyone else on the isle, it seemed.

Appearing on the island less than a month after Pax and himself were delivered to this rock and just days after that first *Saggis* assassination attempt on him. A few days later, Sugnis took favor of Rogaan and started training him in the arts of fighting, presumably after hearing of Rogaan's battle with the *Saggis*. Strange happenings, unasked for, but welcomed by Rogaan. That was almost nine months and six *Saggis* ago. And Rogaan no longer believed in coincidences.

"You never answered how you came to be a prisoner here," Rogaan half-asked, half-accused Sugnis of secrets.

"No need; that's past," Sugnis answered without missing a bite of his fish meal.

"So then, why take me on as a fighting apprentice?" Rogaan finally asked Sugnis directly, wanting to know if someone sent him or if this was all by chance.

"You need training," Sugnis spoke matter-of-factly. "So far, you survived by luck and brawn, and that thing you do, sometimes moving faster than the eye . . . Still, I haven't figured that out. But fighting skills for the pits and other places . . . dung."

"Thanks . . . I think." Rogaan did not know how to take Sugnis's bluntness.

"Most of the *Saggis* carry the mark of the Keepers of the Way," Sugnis continued explaining the unasked questions in a manner as if talking about fish drying. "The others, one of the Black Hand and one with no marks at all."

"So, what of the marks?" Rogaan asked.

"It tells me more than one interest wants your *Light* to pass to the beyond." Sugnis held Rogaan's eyes with his words.

"I thought they all came from the same place, the Keepers." Rogaan felt confused as the hairs on his neck stiffened with a growing realization that his situation was more complex than he thought.

"Some are set on you taking your last breath." Sugnis hesitated as if considering what he would next say. "Others wish you to live. The Keepers of the Way want your last breath. Know why?"

"No," Rogaan said as he searched his memories of the teachings of his father. He talked to himself as he recalled his knowledge as if reading from a scroll or book. "The Keepers are against the Agni using temples . . . such as the Ebon Circle. They have influence in Shuruppak, mostly in the east regions with their center of power in Ur."

Sugnis openly wore a look of confusion listening to Rogaan. "Where did that knowledge come from?"

"My father taught me." Rogaan paused as he answered. A revelation that came to him now that he was ready to understand. He continued talking, but more to himself than answering Sugnis. ". . . many things. Maybe it is time I listened and embraced his teachings."

The two sat silently eating the dried fish for a time until the stars shone brightly above the glowing embers of the fire pit. The numerous island tremors felt gentler against his feet and backside now that the night was full upon them. Images and words flashed before Rogaan's mind's eye as he fell into deep thought, reviewing his father's teachings and the events of this past year. His teachings were full of sound knowledge and advice on a great many subjects: nature, stones and stonework, metallurgy, smithing, history of their ancestors and of the Ancients, history of the Tellens and of Shuruppak and Turil, conflicts, negotiating and influencing, and much more. The review left Rogaan impressed with how much knowledge he had been exposed to. Now . . . if he could just remember it all. Then the events and his acts in recent times he reflected on. He felt embarrassed for many of the acts he took since even before his father was taken by the authorities of Farratum and the Shuruppak nation. Painful regrets filled him too; getting his *War Sworn* uncle killed in Brigum while being protected by him, trusting Kardul and his band of *Sharur* and being betrayed by them, then becoming prisoners of Farratum, Suhd being attacked by Farratum *Sakes* and taken from him along with Suhd's and Pax's parents. Pride filled him for some of his acts such as saving Pax from the redfin in the Valley of the Claw, besting the Mornor-Skurst and Nephiliim in the Farratum prison so they no long beat on his father and that Evendiir Aren, and saving his father in the Farratum arena. Though that last came at a high price, inflicting a terrible pain in Rogaan for having not being able to save Pax and Suhd's parents from the ravers. *That pain of my failure hurts . . . terribly, but I must remind myself my pain is nothing compared to my friends'. Can . . . Will they ever forgive me?*

"It'll do you no good in tomorrow's fight," Sugnis offered in the dimming light of the glowing embers. His features took on a dangerous and more mysterious air in the glow.

"What?" Rogaan asked in a manner trying to play dumb about his thoughts that his mood reflected visibly on his face and by the way he held himself. An observation of his mother she let be known to Rogaan every time he gave away his mood to the rest of the world.

"That loathing and guilt you carry," Sugnis answered flatly.

"It is deserved," Rogaan replied just as flat.

"He'll kill you when you lose focus like you did today," Sugnis explained. "Your focus has to be completely on the *Saggis,* to kill him or he surely will kill you in the pit. You fill yourself with loathing and guilt often enough out of the clear sky, but when your angry friend is in eyesight, you lose focus every time and get moody. You can't let that happen tomorrow. You should ask your friend to stay away from the fight."

"I do not talk to Pax much these days," Rogaan reflected with a sulk. "He blames me for his life in ruins, and he is right to do so and will not let me get more than a few words out before he off and disappears into the shadows."

"Then, let him be angry," Sugnis counseled. "You have more important things ahead of you."

Rogaan looked to Sugnis with a surprised and questioning face. *How callus! What does he mean by that?* Rogaan exchanged stares with Sugnis for long moments before he averted his eyes to the dirt at his high-ankle sandals. He understood Sugnis's counsel and found himself agreeing with it but found it hard to do with his heavy heart.

"Then off with you," Sugnis ordered with a quick wave of his hand. "Get rest and be ready at sunrise to fight the most dangerous *Saggis* yet."

Rogaan continued sitting on the rock he had been using as a stool looking at Sugnis with a dumb expression wondering at his fighting mentor's dismissal. Sugnis nodded to Rogaan, then crawled into his cave, his hole in the ground, but not from Rogaan's night eyes. He watched Sugnis fiddle with his bed of ferns before lying down, then scratching himself in his nether region and finally settling off to sleep with his hands on a long dagger and another weapon he did not know what.

Rogaan stood up to start his journey back to his hovel before realizing he had to negotiate Sugnis's trip-cords to get out of camp. *This must be another test . . . to see if I watched with care his disarming and resetting of the cords.* Rogaan considered just staying safe within the cords for the night, but then thought better of that with Sugnis dismissing him. So, off he went focused on the trip-cords and how to get out of camp without embarrassing himself. At least, he had something else to think about instead of brooding in his guilt or on the hovel with its unsavory group of prisoners he shared space with . . . and Pax.

Chapter 2

Friends and Foes

"The hovel . . . home," Rogaan spoke to himself in a deeply depressed tone as he stood in the main street of his hovel trying to swat away the buzzing biters he could not ignore. He felt it too. He did not want to be here, but to be outside a hovel all night long was spitting in the face of death. An unsecured shelter here was extremely dangerous, causing all the more wonder at Sugnis and his almost comfortable camp. Reluctantly, he admitted to himself he and Pax did not have the skills to endure the isle alone and that frustrated Rogaan. Well past a half year he and Pax called this place home and the unfriendly, ragged condemned within. More as a clan among other competing clans, with smaller clans within the clan. Living and getting along in the hovel was complex and something Rogaan found surprisingly difficult. Most of the condemned deserved it, in his mind. They were selfish and ruthless as a bunch, though there were exceptions. Unfortunately, the exceptions rarely lived long. Rogaan sighed heavily.

A strong mix of odors of discarded fish and shell-walkers remains, sweat-stained clothes, unwashed bodies, and buckets of waste dumped just outside the living spaces, all turned Rogaan's innards. He felt his stomach rise into his throat. *Bad taste.* He swallowed hard. A bite from a buzzing biter frustrated him as he slapped himself, killing the offender. *What I would do for some blue flower paste*, Rogaan said to himself. He did not want to be here. Unintelligible low voices carried on the light breeze, mostly due to the unwanted buzzing about his head. A half-moon dominated the almost cloudless sky over the small, ragged structures of salvaged timbers, wood, and rocks. Everyone did the best they could, given the circumstances. Small fires, a handful of them, in their usual places in front of some of the "dwellings" told Rogaan tonight was going to be quiet. The largest of fires burning within a circle of stones to the northwest on his left as he entered the hovel's main street, if it could be called that, gave Rogaan some solace. The flames were dying down with few folks standing around its illuminations and warmth, telling Rogaan those using the fire were no longer tending it and most likely had retreated to their dwellings just beyond the flames for the night. That area had the largest dwellings and is where Kirral ruled his parts of the island from.

Rogaan's eyes now had adapted for his moonlit surrounds. Months in the dark made his eyes sharper at night and able to see farther than he could have ever believed. Still, the dark remained uncomfortable to him, and he could not get himself not to jump at unexpected sounds. *Too many things jumping out at a person*, Rogaan whispered his thoughts to himself to make the dark not so empty. Shadowy figures slunk back into the deeper blackness as Rogaan made his way down the dirt and rock street lined with makeshift shacks, most without a proper roof to keep the rains out. Buzzing came and went from his ears as flying biters kept at him, taking his blood occasionally with a painful sting. At the only cross-roads of streets in the hovel, with the main street continuing ahead to the cliffs and Ur River, the shacks got smaller as you walked closer to the water, but this part of the main street held the most fires in front of the shacks and with the most folks visible in the firelight. As to the street off to his right, it ended in the worst of the shacks, all a wonder at how they continued to stand looking like a tangle of timbers. A single, moderate-sized fire burned in front of the shacks at the very end of this street with a small throng of folks surrounding it.

Almost undetectable tremors vibrated under him. If not at least half Tellen, he doubted he would have noticed them. As Rogaan turned to enter the smaller street, more shadow-engulfed figures moved briskly between buildings as others he could make out either sat or stood at the entrance doors of their shacks, stolidly watching him.

Rogaan found himself standing in front of the shack he and Pax shared. It was a destroyed pile of broken timbers when they first arrived. He immediately put this father's teachings to use in building up the place. He and Pax and a third fellow made it sturdy and a shack besting all the others in the hovel. They became friendly, the three of them, as they achieved in making this place a little easier to bear. That was a lesson learned, as the others in the hovel burned it down in a fit of envy and jealousy and with his and Pax's third in it. Pax's mood swung again to deep brooding and blamed Rogaan for almost everything as they set to bury the poor fellow, then rebuilding the shack. By intent, the rebuilt shack took on an outward appearance more run-down than the rest on the street. Rogaan, now, stood hesitating before entering the poor-looking structure. He worried that a newcomer was within, freshly off the ship, or one placed there by Urgallis or Kirral. It was common for Urgallis to purposely send newcomers to dwell in his and Pax's shack, some of whom were sent there to kill. Another lesson learned. Strangely, Kirral seemed to tolerate this behavior, managing in some manner to use it in barter with Urgallis.

Rogaan stepped inside the dark standing structure with great trepidation. Not for who might be there . . . those were mere lessons, but that Pax might be inside and that his friendship with Pax still stood in shambles. Upon passing through the door from the street, light from a cooking fire escaping through tiny spaces between stacked rocks. The light illuminated the small entranceway. *Pax must be in inside.* The shack took on an improved appearance inside, with timbers, wood planks, tree branches, fist-round tree trunks, and rocks stoutly building upon one another making the structure strong and visibly appealing. The small entranceway opened to a room almost four strides wide by five long. The cook pit near the center of the room gave off welcomed light and warmth. All the almost amateurish furniture around the room, three stools, several desks, two cabinets, one for him and one for Pax, were all made by Rogaan's hands. *One can only do so much with flint rocks and a metal bar,* Rogaan justified his less-than-high-quality work. Occupying the desktops and cabinets were baskets, also woven by Rogaan, and some by Pax, from the ground vines plentiful on the island. They were filled with scraps of everything edible that he and Pax could find. In truth, most of the scrounging was Pax's doing. Over the cook fire hung their only metal pot with a stew bubbling of what smelled like fish or shell-walkers and herbs. It was about the only meal they could leave unattended without attracting attention from the others around the hovel. *No sign of Pax.* Rogaan felt both relieved and yet disappointed.

He cautiously moved through the doorway on the left side of the room entering a small sleeping area that, to Rogaan's relief, looked undisturbed. A stone wash bowl at the side of his bed, also of Rogaan's hand, sat filled with water. He removed his filthy tunic, tossing it into a large basket hanging from the wall before washing the dirt and stink from the pit and the grease from the meal eaten with Sugnis. Returning to the main room, Rogaan spied a shadow of a figure perched high on the entrance wall crouching. Rogaan realized he had passed underneath him without noticing.

"You are getting better at hiding," Rogaan spoke to the shadow as he inspected the stew pot. He spoke with confidence, but inside, Rogaan was nervous, not knowing how things would transpire in talking with him. "I did not see you this time."

A slight thud, more a vibration he sensed through the floor than heard, told Rogaan the shadow had returned to the ground. The stew looked almost appetizing.

"Urgallis be after ya head again." Pax offered news with little emotion, not hinting away where he stood concerning it.

"When is he not?" Rogaan asked with a mixed hint of honesty and cynicism.

"Dis *Saggis,* Urgallis be spotting big odds ta him," Pax added.

B. A. VONSIK

Rogaan took in this new information adding it to his stack of why Urgallis did anything. *Heavy odds against me. Urgallis either must know something, or his hatred of me has blinded him. Still, better to be cautious.* Rogaan stirred the stew with a wood spoon he had made months ago. "What do you think?"

"What matter of me opinion?" Pax spoke snarky.

"I trust your thoughts, ol' friend," Rogaan spoke honestly, but almost held his breath in anticipation of Pax's response to "friend." He continued to stir the stew slowly to occupy his attention away from Pax. Silence filled the room for a time before Pax took a step toward the front door, then stopped to speak something, but did not, then moved toward the door again.

"I would be dead without your stone, yesterday," Rogaan spoke loud enough to make sure Pax heard him. Pax's footfalls stopped. If not for his old friend Pax throwing a stone striking the assassin's head and knocking him out, Rogaan would have suffered the *Saggis's* bone blade yesterday morning while sitting atop a rock pile on the eastern side of the island, preoccupied in thought waiting for the dawn to replace the dark early-morning sky.

"*Friendship* died with me parents," Pax said in a harsh way that had some practice to it as he stood in the doorway looking at the floor under his dark soft-hide boots. Rogaan's heart felt that stabbing pain sink into him once more. Losing the friendship he and Pax had would have been difficult under normal living conditions, a crippling anguish for Rogaan to endure. On this island, the loss could mean both of their *Lights*. "Da stone ta da *Saggis's* head be just practice. I no like killin' in da back, unless it be me doin' it. He be gettin' da chance ta look ya in da eye before killin'."

Pax silently stepped to the door dressed in gray and black-veined pants and tunic, stopping before opening it. "I be watchin' dis *Saggis* prepare for ya. He be good at da figthin' moves. He be good at killin'. Best one, so far."

In a blink and before Rogaan could say a word, Pax was gone, leaving Rogaan with the stew prepared for him. *Why does he cook like this?* Where Pax went at night, Rogaan could only guess. He almost as often stayed out for the night as he stayed in his bed. The few times he tried following Pax, it ended with Rogaan alone in the dark after only a short time. Pax easily made himself invisible in the dark, even to Rogaan's improving eyes. *Pax is getting good at disappearing,* Rogaan noted before agreeing with himself skills of any sort were beneficial for a fellow to have out here.

Shivers of guilt washed over Rogaan as he looked at the stew his angry friend made for him and the unwanted life he made for Pax. A guilty conscience driving him, Rogaan ate some of the stew before planning to wash, again, then go to bed.

With a small grimace, he swallowed the fish and shell-walker meats, along with an unfamiliar, bitter-tasting herb. "Pax still cannot cook."

A knock at the front door drew Rogaan's attention from Pax's poor-tasting stew. He just sat in place listening, unsure he heard it. *Nobody knocks around here.* Rogaan tried to dismiss what he thought he heard. Another knock, louder and more forceful this time. Rogaan cautiously stood and approached the door. He opened the wood plank door, also of his making, more cautiously than he approached it. Standing at the door, looking about to hit it with all his might, was an *Ursan* he knew by sight from the pits but not by name. Dressed in a padded tunic of worked snapjaw hides and high-strapped sandals and with a dagger tucked in his cloth belt, the *Ursan* stood confidently. His height slightly taller than Rogaan, though slenderer in build, made for an active brawling and blade style of fighting which Rogaan watched many times over the months. This *Ursan* Rogaan considered far better than himself in all manners of pit battling.

"Words, Tellen." The Baraan's gruff voice trailed off as he turned and walked back to the street, his long brown braids swinging with each stride. Rogaan stood stunned at the open door as the *Ursan* walked away with confidence expecting Rogaan would comply, though Rogaan did not know what to make of the situation until the *Ursan* took his place among an unlikely bunch of *Kaal'Ursa* and *Ursans*. The *Kaal'Ursa* being the brawling fighters of the pits, good battling one-on-one with hands and weapons, though mainly concerned with winning their next fight and the *Honor of The Pit*. The *Ursan* were different. They the warriors of conventional battle and warfare, though more often hired blades and spears of caravans, wealthy merchants, unaligned estates owners, the Houses, and even some temples. Trained in weapons and fighting styles of many kinds, *Ursans* made good coin as mercenaries across the lands and were renowned for their formidable negotiation skills, especially for contracts in which they gave service.

The seven never to lose in the pits stood in the middle of the packed dirt and stone street with a hooded figure standing next to the biggest of them, a *Kaal'Ursa*. Rogaan watched the big pit fighter's last victory by pulling another Baraan's head from his neck. A bit gory for Rogaan, but most of the prisoners cheered the kill. The *Kaal'Ursa's* name escaped Rogaan, but he knew that that one liked to kill. Rogaan's attention shifted to the hooded figure. Vein-patterned black and gray pants emerged from the bottom of a dark hooded cape. *Pax*, Rogaan breathed. Whatever this is, it was planned, or they would never have been able to capture Pax.

"Follow," the gruff-voiced *Ursan* demanded. "He has words for you to hear."

The seven started off walking back to the main street with Pax, still hooded, being guided and pushed along. A flash of anger passed through Rogaan as he accepted neither he nor Pax was in control.

"I hate being handled," Rogaan mumbled to himself as he followed. The seven in front of him, some who worked for Kirral, the rest he was uncertain of, moved on at a purposeful pace. *Who has words for me?* Rogaan grunted in wonder as they went. "Another matter Pax will be blaming me for."

Chapter 3

Deal

The cool night air lightly carried the scent of fish upon it as the big Baraan pushed Pax, still with a dark hood over his head, across the hovel's main street before disappearing into deep darkness between a large wood building on the left and a fair-sized shack on the right. The path between was narrow with the other six "escorts", several ahead of Pax with the rest between him and Rogaan, bumping and scraping at the wood planks of both structures despite being single file. The narrow way stank of urine and other things he chose not to dwell upon. Rogaan's night eyes adjusted quickly to the darkness, giving him a gray picture of what lay before him and to his sides, irregular wood planks with bumps and several cross beams protruding into the narrow space. Darkness forced on Rogaan an unease he still did not master. He thought his fear of it would have worn thin after all these months on the island and in the Farratum prison before. His disappointment kept the hairs pricking stiff on his skin. He stepped carefully, bringing up the rear of the line looking behind as much as to the *Ursan* in hide armor in front of him.

They exited the narrows into a small foot-worn field that appeared to be a training circle for those preparing to fight in the pits. Gentle, almost soothing, tremors under his feet betrayed the sense of foreboding Rogaan felt. Beyond, a cluster of small wood shacks surrounding a large building, the largest Rogaan had put eyes on since his imprisonment on this island. It appeared to be where they were prodding Pax toward. The "escorts" weaved their line between the shacks and around cook fires surrounded by clusters of poorly clothed Baraans, both young and old. All fell silent at their approach with few resuming talks until Rogaan was well beyond them. The "escorts" paid no heed to those they passed by as if they did not exist.

As they approached the north side of the large central building, Rogaan found the foundation and steps to be of granite stone blocks . . . rare on this island patch. *And well-made and fitted together*, Rogaan noted. Fires wafted more than a stride high from braziers to each side of the wide stone top step. Their line *Ursan* and *Kaal'Ursa* kept an even pace walking past the four spearmen flanking the steps, two at the first and two more at the fifth. Atop the steps, Rogaan saw the stone platform provided open space four strides wide running the length of the timbers of the single-story building structure which stood some twenty-five strides in both directions from him. *A well-hidden place amongst the wood shacks . . . an illusion to the eye until you are upon it.* Rogaan wondered at the builders. *No Baraan or Evendiir built this place.*

The first two of their line swung wide large, wood, double doors taking up positions holding them open until Rogaan passed. Both wore hide armor with long daggers in their belts that they carried comfortably. They fell in line on the backside of Rogaan's sandals, making him nervous at their intentions. Lit by six braziers spaced equally around the room, the entrance hall was both grand and stunning in the flickering light of the flames. Nine strides tall at its crest, the pitched roof made of timber beams spaced every two strides held up the roof planks and the gray tiles atop them, which Rogaan caught a glimpse of when climbing the stone steps outside. *No Baraan made this place*, he was certain of it. The scent of pine was heavy in the air. It soothed Rogaan's senses as he drank it in with each breath.

"I see you approve of my choice in aromas," the voice came from Rogaan's right. A tall Baraan dressed in maroon robes stepped into the edge of the shadows, his features dark in contrast from the light of the flames. Broad at the chest though only slightly taller than Rogaan, he stood confidently with dark. His stringy hair touched by gray hanging to his shoulders matching the length of his short, graying beard, braided in the Tellen custom. Kirral.

"Why do you have us here?" Rogaan asked Kirral with an even stare.

Kirral returned Rogaan's stare, just as even and maybe a little more threatening. "Direct. To the heart of matters. I see there is Tellen in you."

"What do you mean?" Rogaan did not know how to take Kirral's implication.

"You behave more Baraan than Tellen most of the time," Kirral answered with a directness Rogaan found unsettling. As Kirral talked, Rogaan became increasingly uncomfortable. "Self-absorbed. Self-important. Then, you build brilliantly and with the pride of a Tellen, that shack. Too bad the misfortune of its burning. It did raise the value of land for this hovel."

"Ya hopper-lickin' spawn of Kur!" Pax growled from under his hood as he stomped on the foot of the *Kaal'Ursa* holding him. That succeeded in getting a groan from the big Baraan and a loosening of his grip. Pax pulled away as he struggled with his rope bindings behind his back. It appeared to Rogaan that Pax then was out of his ropes. "Ya burned us and killed a friend!"

A fist from the *Ursan* closest to Pax hammered him in the face just as he lifted the hood from his head. Pax half-stumbled, half-flew backward, landing hard on the red and green round rug covering the stone floor. There he lay unmoving for a time. It alarmed Rogaan that Pax could be seriously hurt. Four hands suddenly grabbed Rogaan's shoulders and arms just above his elbows and held him firmly in place. Rogaan braced his feet set to shake off the unwanted hands when Pax ungracefully sat up to an elbow wiping blood from his nose.

"That's the last of my grace you'll get, youngling." Kirral spoke directly to Pax. Pax looked up at Kirral returning contempt-filled gaze. "Next time, you start losing parts.

"Now, where was I?" Kirral held his right index finger up to his lips in a pondering manner while flaunting a sadistic glean in his eyes. Then he turned his attention back to Rogaan, that even stare hinting of threat settled back on him. "Yes. Artful and stoutly built your shack. It had a great amount of appeal. No, I didn't have it burnt. The locals resented both your skills and more, your will, to make what you could of this place. It told them of their sorry plights. This is home till they take their last breaths."

A pang of guilt and regret rolled through Rogaan. It made him sick in the stomach, beyond anything Pax could cook up in that pot of theirs. *My fault. Another Light lost to the Darkness because of me.*

"See, there's that self-absorbed *Baraan* in you." Kirral chided Rogaan while boring into him with his eyes intense and message. "Everyone dies. Well, except the Ancients. Everyone dies, all around you, even your friend's parents—"

"Ya howlin', dung-eatin' spawn of da daimons," Pax burst out in insult as he struggled to his feet.

"Hit him!" an annoyed Kirral commanded his men. Several made a step toward Pax when the *Kaal'Ursa* closest slammed his fist into Pax's jaw, dropping him unmoving on the rug. "Where does he think up these insults? I need to remember a few of them."

Rogaan stood staring at Kirral with a mix of unsettled regrets, contempt, and anger. He felt a surge building within him and thought to encourage it, use it, though something with Kirral seemed *off* to him. Kirral gave Rogaan a long look as if the Baraan was reading the finer markings of his *Light*. Not wanting Kirral to sense his fear of him, Rogaan decided to speak. "Insults come easily to Pax. He has had a terrible time of—"

"No more your whining about your or his loss," Kirral cut Rogaan off, then mentored him in a most unkind way. Rogaan felt insulted and more so, confused. Kirral pointed at the unmoving Pax. "And rebind that one. Do better this time."

"Time to leave all that youngling thinking and *Baraan* ways behind you," Kirral returned his attention to Rogaan. While staring at Rogaan he spoke to everyone in the hall. "Stories have it up and down the Ur, this one defying those who desire him *lightless*. Beating dagger and spear and tooth and claw from Brigum to Farratum. And his guardian, the Dark Ax, himself, in the Farratum's arena. That must have been a show for the ages, him killing the ravers."

"I killed one of the raver*s*," Rogaan injected and corrected with an indignant flair.

"That's better," Kirral smiled as he seemed to enjoy Rogaan's hot temper and defiance. "There *is* more Tellen in you. Yes, and what a tale they speak of. You besting a number of *Tusaa'Ner* below in the prison to climb tall ropes to save your father in the arena above and toppling a raver with nothing more than strength and brashness."

"How do you know all of this?" Rogaan asked in awe of Kirral's knowledge of him.

"I keep eyes and ears on those who most shape lives . . . especially my own," Kirral answered soberly. "Your *guardian* put me here half my life ago. Him and that dark-robed master of his. I'm the first prisoner of the new Shuruppak to enjoy this rock."

Danger and warning thoughts filled Rogaan's head causing him to drip sweat. Panic welled up inside as he looked about the room trying to think of a way to get away, escape with Pax. Rogaan struggled to find a way out of the situation while Kirral watched Rogaan react to his words. A smile graced the Baraan's bearded face.

"I can help you win the island from Urgallis." It was all Rogaan could come up with in his thinking.

"Urgallis . . ." Kirral smiled big at Rogaan. "That half-witted, self-bloated . . . . 'howling, dung-eating spawn of daimons' . . . The words do work. Urgallis is a useful piece to play in the game. He's the brute everyone, except his chosen few, hates and fears. Takes the attention from me. I get to be the good one stopping that idiot from hurting the rest of the prisoners. It brings me good graces with the prisoners, *Sakes*, and others above them who think they control this island."

"What is it you want of me?" Rogaan asked with a defeated yet defiant tone. *I am facing the real power of this island prison.* Rogaan's hopes of a good turn in outcomes here sank to the bottom of the deep Ur River.

"Almost a Tellen," Kirral struck Rogaan another insult for his too Baraan of an attitude. "First, I want to know who is sending these *Saggis's* at you. Why do they want your *Light* darkened and cut from your heart so badly?"

"The Keepers . . . I think." Rogaan answered honestly before he thought to use the information as a bargaining stone.

"Keepers of the Way . . ." Kirral lifted a hand to his beard pinching it as he drifted off in thought. He paced a short distance, then returned to Rogaan still deep in his thoughts and his beard between his fingers. With eyes focused on something unseen in the distance, "Prophecy. Of the Return and the defiling of the Divine Laws. Causing the Ancients to punish us all. That is what the Keepers are about trying to prevent."

"I have not heard of such a prophecy, this Return." Rogaan spoke as if he were the authority on all things historical, myth and legend, or prophetic. After all, his father taught him much in all subjects.

"No," Kirral spoke in a mocking tone. "The Keepers believe in the Return. It drives them to seek out anyone wielding the glowing stones, to keep them from using that of the Ancients. To keep all from drinking or taking a bite of the *Food of the Ancients*. To see the Divine Laws are followed by humanity."

"Too much attention—" One of Kirral's strong-arms started to speak, the *Ursan* dressed in hide armor, who knocked on Rogaan's door.

"Yes!" Kirral cut him off both with words and a glare. The *Ursan* fell silent at his leader's prolonged stare. The others in his ranks all heard the same message. *Be seen, not heard*.

"Too much attention?" Rogaan asked of Kirral in repeating the *Ursan's* words.

Kirral stood looking perplexed, undecided as to what he would say or do. He paced some more and pinched his beard, then paced some more. Rogaan kept his tongue quiet as he watched the Baraan wear out his rug. As the moments passed with each rug-wearing step, Rogaan increasingly knew Kirral was going to kill him or have someone do it for him. He looked about, again, for a path to escape. There were a number, but none that included Pax. *I cannot leave Pax to this one.*

"I planned for you to willingly have your heart silenced," Kirral confessed to Rogaan as he continued pacing. Rogaan felt shocked at the Baraan's admission and fear at the seriousness of his words. Kirral continued, "I planned to use your mouthy friend here as a hostage to see just how far you would go . . . to see if you'd allow the *Saggis* to steal your *Light* with his hands or blade."

"Then why tell me to be more Tellen if my fate is not among the living?" Rogaan asked honestly and confused.

"I detest self-loathers!" Kirral stopped pacing and met Rogaan's gaze with a level stare. "It's just not Tellen. At least, part of you is Tellen; yet, you act as a suffering youngling Baraan wanting sympathies to justify your mistakes and misdeeds. I see it enough from the prisoners sent here. Own your mistakes, accept them, learn from them, show your regret, and ask the harmed for forgiveness; then never repeat the misdeeds. Then stand with head high on your shoulders, not with chin in chest to take on the rest of the world and your death."

"And if forgiveness is not given?" Rogaan asked sincerely as his eyes shifted to Pax who was showing signs of recovery from the fist across his jaw.

"The one to give forgiveness hasn't yet stopped wanting you to share his pain," Kirral answered as he curiously looked at Pax. "He may never, as long as you give him that control. If he's a friend, he wouldn't want you to suffer as he. If he has become something else, he's no longer your friend. Now, enough about the abstract; let's talk details that I'm going to use against you."

Rogaan stood utterly confused before Kirral. He started wondering if Kirral's mind to be sick or injured. The Baraan's band of strong-arms all wore smiles as they worked to hide their snickering at Kirral's complex behavior, his multiplicity. *No, this is normal for Kirral.*

"You are bringing too much attention to this rock with all the Keepers and the Black Hand going after your head and heart," Kirral answered Rogaan's questioning scowl. "I can't take your *Light* directly. Not with your *guardian*. He'll finish the job he started long ago and destroy everything I've built here. So, the second thing I need from you is for you to accept your end willingly. And to make sure you do, I'll end your friend if you choose differently. Deal?"

"What be dis deal puff and blow be tellin' ya?" Pax slurred his words as he stirred. He was awake and aware enough to hear of the deal Kirral offered Rogaan. At Pax's interruption, Kirral's eyes rolled high.

"Hit him!" Annoyed again, Kirral ordered his strong-arms. Pax went down with another smashing fist to the jaw.

Rogaan swallowed hard as he gritted his teeth painfully, expecting them to break.

Chapter 4

Pit of Decisions

Squawks and songs from colonies of waking featherwings and leatherwings increasingly filled the cool, predawn air of the island. Their vocalizations were overtaking the grunts and hissing of the water-dragons and snapjaws patrolling the flowing waters below the cliff and all in between the main island Rogaan sat on and its rocky smaller brother across the narrow channel. The cliffs were thick with flying creatures of all sizes and colorations, the latter hard to see in the gloom. The scent of decaying fish and perfumed blossoms from the island vines carried on the breeze. He would wrinkle his nose at the smell of it all if he thought he would not sneeze. Rogaan's eyes adjusted to the half-moonlit night long hours ago. His unease of the dark and its unknowns diminished a little over the long months living on this island without the amenities of a civilized world and with it the numerous candles, lamps, and lanterns lighting both the insides of huts and the streets of the hovels. Several ground tremors, large enough for even Baraans to notice, shook the island not long ago. They're occurrences common ever since he stepped on this rock. Everything around his vantage point from atop a rise of rocks he could see: The Ur River flowing around and in between the rocky islands; a misty patch marches away obscuring the far shorelines of the mainland; the swirls of surface water giving away where the currents were their most dangerous; dark-colored water-dragons breaking the liquid surface to breathe air before returning to the dark depths of the water; the vine- and moss-covered rocky landscape of the island; lights from more cook fires coming from the hovels within eyesight . . . and the clay surface of the fighting pit below.

The "deal" kept Rogaan awake all through the night. He tried sleeping in his shack, but missing Pax, who remained in the hands of that bizarre tyrant, Kirral, made rest difficult and sleep impossible. *Pax or me*, Rogaan had to choose. *How do I know the small poisoned blade Kirral gave me will do as he claims?* Rogaan wanted to trust Kirral but could not find it in himself to give that much to a person who openly admitted he wanted to silence Rogaan's heart. The plan simple, though filled with unknown dangers . . . Trusting Kirral was key to its success and that the *Saggis* Rogaan is to fight would not end him with a blade. Trusting Kirral was a problem for him. Believing he held something coated in a *Light*-taking liquid was also difficult, though Rogaan decided not to test the blade before he faced his opponent in the pit.

While eating the last of his dried fish, Rogaan watched snaking lines of burning torches make their way from the hovels toward the fighting pit closest to him. They periodically kicked up single and small flocks of featherwings as they went. Most in the lines would be watchers of the fight to come, and many would wager coin or goods or services for and against him. Rogaan, in truth, did not know how well he would fare against this *Saggis*, an assassin by profession and training, not some *Lugasum* cutthroat with only street experience developed skills. Rogaan felt nervous. Reluctant to enter the pit, he found rising off the rocks difficult despite his inner voice nagging at him to do so. Then, the fear of forfeiting the fight, and the lashings that would be demanded, if he did not stand on the clay at the moment the sun's rays touched the ground. The thoughts of lashings combined with that nagging inner voice motivated him to stand. An old and almost forgotten sensation . . . a tingle at the top of his neck where his spine met with skull . . . A feeling in his head gave Rogaan pause. *What? Where is this coming from?* He surveyed the island and waters looking for something he did not know what or if he would recognize it when he found it. He saw nothing out of the expected. With one last scan of the island and waters about him, he dismissed the feeling as his nervousness playing tricks on him. Ending his procrastinating, he set off on the descent into the pit.

As his footfalls navigated the treacherous rocky slope shadowed in the morning gloom, Rogaan caught sight to the north three tall galley ships speeding eastward with sails fluttering and oars rowing. Even with his better-than-average night eyes, Rogaan was unable to determine the colors of the flags flying from their masts. Stopped, he watched the ships for a short time until they disappeared into the mists northeast of the island. That tingling feeling in his head, teasing him, diminished as he returned to descending the hill. Without more excuses to keep him from the pit, Rogaan made his descent to the round, clay-surfaced grounds. The Pit was rimmed and shaped by a stub of a stone wall further surrounded by rising terrain, all around except at its north end where a small strip of dirt gave way to a rocky cliff overlooking the west end of the watery channel between this rock of an island and its brother just north of it.

Halfway to the clay ground, Sugnis, with a dirt-stained face and his disapproving scowl framed by his dark tangle of shoulder-length hair and hand-length beard, stood in his now-resewn green tunic and green breeches waiting for his apprentice. Rogaan walked by Sugnis without speaking a word but did exchange somber glances that told his fighting mentor he understood the seriousness of the morning and approaching sunrise. Sugnis silently followed Rogaan to the stacked-rock rim wall of the sunken clay in the fighting pit, where for only a short time they would be alone.

"What of the offer?" Sugnis asked in a serious tone. "Will you go through on it?"

"How do you know of the *deal?*" Rogaan asked in surprise having been caught off guard with Sugnis's seemingly omnipotent powers.

"It's what I do." Sugnis sounded more of his usual overconfident self. "You're avoiding answering?"

"I cannot leave Pax to that tyrant," Rogaan answered soberly. "He will kill my friend. And, no, I do not trust Kirral. The blade he gave me is still in its clamshell, though I do not see another way for both Pax and me to live through this . . . complexity."

"Difficult decision." Sugnis sounded both proud and pragmatic. "Tellens are known to shrug off poisons. Not certain that he gave you is strong enough for taking your *Light.* I have your back guarded. Now, let's speak on your opponent one more time to ensure he doesn't end your *Light*, first, and change the *deal.*"

As the cloudy sky brightened with the predawn glow, they exchanged knowledge as experienced master and well-learned apprentice, talking through how the *Saggis* would fight Rogaan, and how Rogaan was to fight back, as well as defend himself from the venom dagger they expected the killer of men to use against Rogaan. Small crowds started arriving around the Pit taking up spots at the rim informally assigned through past brawls and rituals of intimidation. The strong ruled this island. The weak served or perished, usually both. Soon, they stood surrounded by a rabble of prisoners. Two prominent spots elevated above the crowds, one to the south where Kirral and his followers would perch, and the other to the east was reserved for Urgallis and his band of thugs. Both were occupied with standards waving atop poles in the slight breeze, the red banners of Urgallis and the yellow of Kirral. The sun neared breaking above the far hills to the northeast across the expansive swirling waters of the Ur River. Rogaan and Sugnis watched as the *Saggis*, accompanied by several of Urgallis's *Ursan*, stepped onto the clay.

The lean, muscular, brown-skinned Baraan *Saggis* stolidly stood in the Pit. Slightly taller than Rogaan, he stood confident and imposing with his clean-shaven face and sandy-colored hair pulled back into a tail. The expertly trained *Taker of Lights* wore a black and bloodred hide kilt, vest, wrist guards, and soft-soled boots. Rogaan tried finding a blade on his opponent. *Nothing*, as he touched the small clamshell holding his own coated blade secured in his pants just below the waist. With a nod from Sugnis, Rogaan hopped from the stacked stones to the clay ground. A roar from the rabble erupted more loudly than previous fights Rogaan had survived in this place . . . in fights deciding who served whom or who died and who lived. This morning, the fight would see one of their *Lights* depart unbreathing flesh. Rogaan swallowed hard. The seriousness of the morning started weighing heavier on him as moments passed. The *Saggis*, a Baraan sent to kill him by the Keepers of the Way, stood five strides in front of him wearing an unshakable confidence in his stance, face, and eyes. *Ancient gods of old, give me the strength and skill to send my opponent's Light to your heavenly abode*, Rogaan prayed. Not often did he do so, but now seemed a fitting moment for it. To Rogaan's left, the sun was almost clear of the far hills. A drum, deep and booming, sounded a handful of times from the east. The noisy rabble fell silent.

"We gather here upon these clay grounds to honor the Ancients with a blood sacrifice of combat," Urgallis announced with his deep voice while standing tall atop his rocky rise with a bone dagger raised high and dressed in hide armor adorned with colorful feathers. "The Tellen, Rogaan, and the Baraan, who has no name, are to fight with hands bare till the *Light* is forever gone from one of their skins. Let the rays of the sun strike the clay to see blood to run freely."

Rogaan stared at the *Saggis* while swallowing hard. The *Saggis* stood returning his stare unmoving like a stone statue without a hint of emotion. Upon Urgallis finishing his introduction, the crowd began the customary *Kaal'Ursa* chant, preceding the bloodletting.

Fight!
Fight!
Fight for honor.
Battle for redemption.
Slay for reckoning.
Let the Ancients judge, condemn the guilty.
Lights of the wicked suffer in Kur.
Lights of the pure victorious honor.
Fight!
Fight!
Fight!
Let them fear your rage!

Rogaan soaked in the spirit of the chant as the sun warmed his left cheek. Sunrise upon the clay was moments away. His left shoulder and arm warmed. Bright rays struck the top of the stacked-stone wall forward and off to his right; then it started walking downward. Rogaan's breath quickened as his heart beat even faster. He felt sweat begin dripping from his forehead as his body tingled with anticipation of battle . . . or was it fear, he did not know which. As clay to his right brightened with the rays of the sun, an explosion of cheers and shouts from the rabble deafened Rogaan, momentarily startling him and drawing his attention beyond the stacked stones.

Soft-soled boots solidly impacted Rogaan's chest and midsection, launching him backward through the air. His breath knocked from his lungs as he hung suspended above the clay in what seemed both a moment in time and an eternity in realizing his mistake. Rogaan landed hard on his upper back, shoulders, and neck, jolting his jaws and skull before rolling feet over head. Fearing the *Saggis* would be upon him, Rogaan painfully snapped his head and eyes up in his opponent's direction as he rolled into an upright squat. He found it impossible to suck in a breath despite his gapping mouth and painfully working midsection. He wanted to inhale the morning air but found it difficult. Charging at him, the brown-skinned Baraan launched himself forward, colliding with Rogaan and driving him back into solid stone. Pain racked Rogaan's back and neck despite the stacked stones giving a little as they were pressed back into the dirt behind them. Flashing specks of light started filling Rogaan's vision as the edges of his sight grayed. His head felt light, and his body floating, almost unresponsive to the commands he screamed out from his mind to fight back.

"Ya can never be allowed ta fulfill da prophecies," the deep voice of the *Saggis* spoke into Rogaan's left ear. "Time ta end ya *Light*."

Alarmed at the promise of death, a surge of strength exploded through Rogaan. With the stones cutting into his back, he pushed the brown-skinned Baraan up and away with arms and legs. Sending him airborne into the low rock wall of the arena. Free of the *Saggis's* weight on him, Rogaan rolled to his hands and knees as he tried to suck in a breath. More sparkling flashes of light as the gray edges of his sight expanded. Rogaan tried to scream, but nothing came out of his burning lungs. Agonizing desperation filled him as he both worked at drawing a breath and somehow scream at the same time. The feel of the trembling clay beneath his hands and knees disappeared, replaced by a sensation of floating in the warmth of the sun as he started feeling light-headed.

Suddenly, a breath of air painfully rushed into his lungs as his midsection released its straining muscles. Disappearing from his vision were the gray tint of the world and the flashing of lights. Looking up as he sucked in another breath, anger and determination filled his being, pouring over and silencing the fear, doubt, indecisiveness, and embarrassment he felt moments before. With his sight almost clear, Rogaan found the *Taker of Lights* unsteadily regaining his feet from a sitting position against the stacked stones across the clay arena.

Rogaan staggered to his feet before taking determined, confident steps toward the *Saggis*, intending to beat him into the clay. On the other side of the arena, the *Saggis* stood shaking his head and arms before also closing on Rogaan with the same determined strides, but with eyes wild and burning in a fanatical rage. They met almost at the center of the clay with the *Saggis* striking a punch to Rogaan's cheek first. The punch felt light to Rogaan, underpowered, as he threw his own right sweeping punch striking the *Saggis* on the jaw, staggering him. Quickly recovering, the *Saggis* swung back, only to find his punch blocked by the half Tellen. Rogaan and the *Saggis* quickly descended into their own personal world, punching, blocking, and counterpunching each other in a fury of action. Nothing else existed, each consumed with their intent to drop the other. Rogaan landed a left uppercut sending the *Saggis* staggering back with a bloody mouth and nose. A surprised look engulfed the *Taker of Lights* face, immediately replaced with the return of that fanatical searing gaze and determined jaws. A small bone blade appeared in his right hand as he charged Rogaan. Focused on the blade and the deadly poison that had to be on it, Rogaan grabbed the right wrist of the Baraan with both of his hands as he rotated away from the blade strike, exposing his back to his opponent. The *Saggis* impacted Rogaan midback, sending him off balance, then driving him forward toward the north end of the clay. The two spilled over the stacked-stone wall, rolling onto the dirt vacated by the yelling crowd standing there a moment earlier.

Rogaan kept an iron grip on the Baraan's blade hand as the *Saggis* repeatedly punched and struck him in the right-side ribs and face. Rogaan rolled to escape the unanswered pummeling by trapping the *Saggis's* right arm underneath him. Unexpectedly, he felt as if floating, then falling a distance embraced in battle with his adversary. A jolt of pain seared through Rogaan's left side, forcing some of the air from his lungs as he realized they landed hard on a surface before rebounding into the air, then falling again. Moments later, they impacted a giving surface of moist sand, sinking into the ground before coming to a motionless position with Rogaan under the *Saggis*. Still, Rogaan held the blade-wielding hand of the wild-eyed Baraan, but only with his own left hand. The *Saggis* pushed himself up while remaining on top of Rogaan, then pulled his blade hand free of Rogaan's grip. Blood covered the *Saggis's* face and soaked his hair as more dripped onto Rogaan with every move. The Baraan's eyes smoldered a wildness with unshakable intent that the victory he sought was only a moment away.

Bone blade raised high, the *Saggis* drove his right hand down with all his might at Rogaan's chest. Rogaan crossed his arms defensively at the wrist, blocking the blade's descent in the wedge formed by his arms. He awkwardly gripped the blade hand with both of his hands and reversed about the *Saggis's* wrist. The *Saggis* tried to pull his blade hand away but found Rogaan's grip too strong. Then, with a flick of his wrist and hand, the *Taker of Lights* tossed the dripping bone blade into the air before catching the poison blade with his left hand. The blade now raised high above the *Saggis*, Rogaan knew he was defenseless to the killing strike he was to receive.

The morning sun went dark, blocked by a large mass of teeth towering over them, curved fangs gleaming. The beast struck with a crunching bite on the *Saggis's* left arm and shoulder. The Baraan screamed out in pain and frustration, his eyes still fiery hot with intent to take Rogaan's *Light* as the massive beast twitched its body, ripping the *Saggis* from atop him while showering Rogaan with water, blood, and sand.

Near-panic propelled Rogaan off the sand and into a crouch facing the cliff, looking up a shear wall of wet rocks and slick moss. Spinning around to face the beach, he found a scene of horror. The beach, only four to five strides wide, ended abruptly thirty strides to his left and a hundred of strides to his right where it ended just before a wood pier where ships docked to offload cargo and prisoners. The thin, sandy beach, at low tide, as it was now, brought air-breathing water-beasts to use it as a resting place away from the dangers of the deep Ur River. Filling the thin stretch of sands in both directions lay snapjaws and water-dragons of all sizes and in great abundance. The water-dragon near him, a twelve-stride long, black-and-white-colored beast with a head as long as an Evendiir is tall, looked more fish than land dweller, with flipper-like forearms and hind legs and with a tail made to propel its massive body through water. It bit down on the *Saggis* while lying half-buoyed in the shallows in front of Rogaan. The beast was readying itself to gulp down its screaming and punching prize before other water-dragons or snapjaws could steal its meal away. As it fed, the dark-hued water-dragon drew attention away of the surf-dwelling animals from Rogaan except for another ten-stride water-dragon close on Rogaan's left and an eleven-stride snapjaw nine strides to his right. A green-gray beast with thick armored hide. Its four short legs kept the animal low to the sand and surf dragging its long, armored tail topped with twin rows of vertically pointing plates, and a robust bony, triangular head filled with conical spikes for teeth. Both momentarily eyed him as if not real before closing on him, the snapjaw quicker on its short legs than the water-dragon on its flipper like legs.

Without pondering his fate, Rogaan broke into a run to his left, hoping the water-dragon would be too awkward out of the water to catch him in its jaws. He took several steps directly at the air-breathing water monster before breaking hard to his left, jumping up on rising rocks as the water-dragon lunged, snapping closed, with a loud whop, its curved, spike-toothed jaws just under Rogaan's drawn up feet. At the peak of Rogaan's jump, his sandals touched down on wet rocks, but the surface was too slick for his flat-bottomed sandals. His feet slipping out from underneath him, upending and landing him hard and painful on his back across several boulders. Fearful of the tooth-filled dangers near, Rogaan opened his eyes with head upside down, expecting to see the water-dragon's black-and-white maw close on his head. Instead, the massive water-dragon and the snapjaw hissed and threatened each other in displays of aggression. Neither gave Rogaan another thought. *A blessing from the Ancients and my ancestors*, Rogaan recited to himself, giving thanks, before trying to sit up and remove himself from the giants' battlefield. Pain racked him head to feet as nausea gripped him. He lay flat on his back for a moment to recover before trying again. Slowly, he managed to roll to his knees, then crawl to the rocky cliff where he began his dangerous eighteen-stride high climb.

His nausea grew worse with each passing moment. Halfway into his ascent, it threatened to overpower him, leaving him hanging from the rocks fighting to keep conscious and unable to climb farther. Making matters worse, pain rippled through Rogaan's muscles which made it difficult for him to keep hold of the tremor-filled rocks and exposed roots as his breaths turned more painful. He was almost certain his ribs were broken. Rogaan was stuck, unable to climb higher. Fearing he would fall, again, he decided to descend and try to find an easier path up. As he looked for a foothold below, a rope fell past him, then dangled an arm's length away.

"Grab the rope," a voice called out to him from above.

Concentrating hard, he fought through blurring vision grabbing the rope with his left hand, wrapping it around his wrist before grabbing the rope with his other hand. He then hung on the rope with all his might as he felt himself ascending in surges. Time started to not matter to Rogaan. All he knew was that he needed to grip the rope with everything he had. He felt hands tugging at him, then the cool sensation of the clay pressing on the back of his head, back, arms, and legs. He realized he was lying down. Looking up, he saw Sugnis hovering over him, with his dark, untamed locks and beard framing a concern-filled face. Rogaan felt hands on him inspecting his head, chest, arms, and midsection. Pain seared through him when hands touched the ribs on his left side.

"Forgive my slow timing of aid." Sugnis sounded genuinely repentant for something Rogaan did not know what. Looking up, Rogaan's blurry eyes found his fighting mentor inspecting him with intense focus.

"You used the blade on yourself after all that." Sugnis sounded sadly impressed.

"No," Rogaan corrected his mentor with a mumble. He clumsily patted his waist where the blade given to him by Kirral was, still unused. "That blade is in its shell. See?"

"No," Sugnis said with concern reverberating in his voice.

"What bothers you?" Rogaan asked with slurring words, his vision now almost dark, and his muscles unresponsive to his wishes.

With blurred and waning sight, he saw Sugnis holding a broken partial blade of bone in his fingers. "I pulled this from your side. It seems the *Saggis* stuck you with his venom-coated blade, after all."

Chapter 5
Mortals and More

V oices disjointed and distant spoke with words unintelligible. Some sounded concerned while others seemed gleeful, even rejoicing. Nausea and pain endured in the pit left him as he felt himself being picked up and carried, where, he did not know or now even care. All was replaced with calm, a peacefulness. He felt serenity with the warmth of the sun and the cool touch of the wind all around him. The scent of blooms from island vines and decay of that taken from the waters guarding the shoreline of this rocky hold all filled his senses. He could not make out where hands held him or if he was upright, upside down, or something else. Orientation had no meaning. Rogaan vaguely heard voices and no longer sensed motion, nor knew if he still moved. His chest tightened, giving him a moment of pain, then nothing. All sensations gone.

Rogaan opened his eyes. He looked about confused and disoriented. Slightly below him, five strong Baraans and a Tellen carried a pole stretcher, three to each side. Others flanked the six trying to spy a look at what they protectively transported between them. Looking down at the limp body lying on the stretcher, Rogaan gasped in disbelief. *Me? No!* Rogaan denied what his eyes saw . . . a strongly built, brown-skinned half Tellen wearing hide sandals, a dirty gray cloth kilt and torn tunic with disheveled, shoulder-length, dark brown hair and a short brown beard. *This is wrong! No. This cannot be.* He called out to the six. No response. They kept at their even pace walking. No matter how loudly he yelled, they ignored him. Rogaan called out to the Tellen, Sugnis. *If anyone will answer me, he will.* Again, no response to his calls and screams. Reaching out to the nearest Baraan, Rogaan found his fingers sinking into his shoulder. *No! How?* A plummeting sensation of desperation gripped him as he looked around hoping for answers . . . from anyone. Not a person near or far seemed to see him. Rogaan returned his attention to Sugnis, his mentor's back to him, with hopes another scream would get his attention. Rogaan then realized he was moving, keeping pace with the group. *But I am not walking.* Looking to his still body being carried, Rogaan saw a silvery-white glowing cord from his body lying on the stretcher with . . . his glowing naked body floating just behind the six . . . and himself. *How?* A thought came to Rogaan that he immediately dismissed. *Cannot be*. He looked at the slivery-white glowing cord again. He recalled the stories of those losing their *Lights*. He always thought their descriptions as a figure of speech for what could not be understood. *I am Lightless . . . dead?*

Numb from the realization of his situation, Rogaan looked about again. The rabble of a crowd thinned some as the six made their way toward Rogaan's . . . Kirral's, hovel. Urgallis was engaged in celebrative discussion with one of his *Ursans* to the right of the six as they kept pace with the stretcher. Both Baraans seemed genuinely joyful. *Urgallis must have scored large at my death.* The five Baraans carrying him were all Kirral's followers. Most he could not read, though several joked as they walked. Sugnis kept looking back at Rogaan's body with sorrow and anguish flowing from his eyes and his dirty face bearing evidence of tears. A loud call from a hunting featherwing above drew Rogaan's attention upward. A single, midsized featherwing followed the crowd in repeated circles, the sky around it clear of all other featherwings and leatherwings. As the animal turned, Rogaan caught sight of what he thought was a dark-tinted glow. *Father. Mother.* Rogaan started remembering who he was, how he arrived at the island, and why his body lay lifeless on the stretcher. *Keepers. Saggis. Poison.*

"Nooooooo!" screamed Rogaan defiantly at the heavens, at the Ancients. His eyes fell to his lifeless body, the cord tethering him to it glowing more brightly than before. A question formed in Rogaan's mind that gave him hope and purpose. He grabbed the cord with both hands and pulled, desperate and hopeful. He remained frustratingly anchored at a fixed distance, unable to move. He tried again and again, growing more frustrated and angrier with every effort. The cord glowed brighter. A whisper spoke. Rogaan thought it everywhere then knew it was in his mind. Its words broken with only some understandable, "...not...time." Renewed determination filled Rogaan. Again, he pulled hard on the glowing cord. He budged, just a little. Hope. He pulled hard, determined to touch his body, the distance to his goal shortening. More hope. Rogaan kept at it, relentlessly, pulling, desperation changing to determination. A sickly sensation and taste came to him as he closed to just beyond arm's length from his paling body. The silvery-white cord now glowed brightly in his hands, as if it would burn him; yet, he felt no pain.

Everything exploded, engulfed in bright blue-white light. Quickly, Rogaan's eyes adjusted, revealing arcs of lightning dancing all around the six. The rabble, to a Baraan, fell to the rocky, vine-covered ground, withering in pain from burns and more. Many vines covering the rocks sizzled, popped, then lay withered with rising wisps of vapor from the intense heat of the arcing lightning as it withdrew. The six stood motionless, carefully looking around trying to figure out what just happened. Rogaan caught sight of him, first, a lone Baraan, tall in stature . . . a head taller than himself, on the trail to the hovel. Dressed in calf-high, bloodred, tanniyn hide boots, a dark hide kilt with red metal-plated thigh-guards, a wide, red, tanniyn hide belt over a dark gray, cloth-weaved shirt, bloodred layered metallic shoulder guards, metallic silver and gold wrist guards and armbands, and a head under a dark gray, cloth-weaved hood. The stranger was armed with a heavy, curved, long knife the size of a sword resting in its sheath at his right side. Memories of his father's teachings brought images of the Ancients to Rogaan's mind's eye. The stranger wasted no time approaching them with determined steps. A *Kaal'Ursa* opposite Sugnis holding the stretcher panicked and ran off leaving the rest of Rogaan's bearers to keep his stretcher upright with grunting efforts. Without breaking stride, the stranger raised his right hand, then struck the fleeing Baraan with intense bolts of lightning. The *Kaal'Ursa* dropped to the rocks without a scream, unmoving, his body burnt black and smoking.

"Ground young Rogaan's body," Sugnis ordered the Baraans. They hesitated at first, not certain they should follow and be found without the stretcher in hand. When Sugnis crouched to set the stretcher on the ground, they all followed, then stood and stepped back as the stranger made his final steps to them.

The eyes of the stranger caught Rogaan by surprise; tilted and radiant green. Now close and with the morning sun peeking under the hood, the stranger appeared very tall, a head and some taller than the Baraans, with a slender nose and chiseled features under a short, trimmed, yellow-white beard and what appeared to be hair of the same color. The stranger was strongly built and wearing well-fitted armor and clothing. He paid Sugnis and the Baraans no attention as he inspected *lightless* Rogaan's body. After a few moments of looking at Rogaan's skin and eyes, the stranger placed his large hands on Rogaan's body and concentrated. A glow under his white cloth shirt immolated red for a long moment before fading. Suddenly, Rogaan felt sickly.

"How long?" the stranger asked nobody specifically, yet everybody.

"Since sunrise," Sugnis answered, his hand on his belted knife.

"How long without his breath," the stranger asked intensely, urgently.

"Not long ago," Sugnis clarified.

The stranger's head swiveled as he looked for something, but not finding it, he placed his hand on Rogaan's chest before concentrating again. That red glow immolated the stranger's shirt, again. Rogaan felt a presence through the silvery-white glowing cord. The stranger again swiveled his head about until his eyes fixed on Rogaan, not his lifeless body, but Rogaan himself where they locked stares with each other. Confusion gripped Rogaan. The red glow disappeared as the stranger placed another hand on Rogaan's lifeless head. With head bowed and hands on Rogaan's head and chest, the stranger mumbled something unintelligible as he concentrated. The red glow appeared once more, steady and strong. The stranger kept at his concentration and mumbling. The intensity of the red glow grew as Rogaan felt a tug, then a pull, a pull as if falling into a great depth ever increasing his speed, a vortex, darkness, pain everywhere, a sickly taste in his mouth, and an urge to suck in a breath. Rogaan breathed, sucking a lungful of air. Gasps and alarmed words surrounded him as he opened his eyes.

"What happened to me?" Rogaan coughed.

"He drew your *Light* back into your body," Sugnis answered his apprentice with a hint of awe.

"You are not whole, yet, Roga of Blood An," the stranger told Rogaan. "The poison in you is strong, stronger than any I expect your kind to endure. Some time and added healings are needed to make you whole."

"Why?" Rogaan asked the stranger with a croak; his throat felt painfully dry and sore.

The stranger regarded him for a long moment before answering, "I need your blood. Without poison."

"You protected me twice before?" Struggling though feelings of being separated from the world . . . detached from everything around him, Rogaan sought confirmation he lived. He searched his memories of the stranger, ". . . In the ravine in the Valley of the Claw with that cutthroat *Lugasum*, Akaal, and then in the streets of Brigum, cutting down the town guard allowing Pax and me to escape."

"Do not forget the clearing in the forest against ravers and that Dark Ax," the stranger added as if ensuring the record was correctly scribed. "I thought him your enemy. He proved more formidable than expected, requiring my time to recover. Your kind has made a number of surprises for me."

"Who are you?" Rogaan asked still with a croaking voice and hazy head.

"Who follows me?" The stranger looked to Sugnis and the four Baraans. An *Ursan* and *Kaal'Ursa* waved their hands in front of them as they started backing away. The stranger raised his hands, blasting both with streams of lightning. Their burnt bodies fell to the ground twitching uncontrollably after their screams were cut short. He turned his attention again to Sugnis and the other two looking too frightened to run.

"I follow," the two remaining *Ursan* answered almost together as they kneeled. The stranger turned his full attention on Sugnis.

"I go with him," Sugnis said confidently without flinching while pointing at Rogaan.

The stranger regarded Sugnis for a time. As the moments passed, Rogaan grew increasingly nervous another stroke of lightning would appear. Sugnis held his position and his tongue. *Courage of his convictions and loyalties*, Rogaan regarded, impressed with Sugnis. Rogaan really hoped the stranger would not strike him *Lightless* with lightning.

"He mentors me in hand and blade," Rogaan broke in while fighting through his light-headedness, fearing something terrible was about to happen.

"Then he is not very good at it," the stranger commented with a stern glance at Rogaan.

"I fought an opponent beyond my skills," Rogaan offered an explanation as he tried to rise from the ground. He realized he felt exhausted and without the strength to stand. "That I am alive . . . my gratitude to you, and that the *Saggis* no longer lives, I think, speaks of Sugnis's mentoring skills."

"Very well-spoken, young Roga of Blood An." The stranger stared at Sugnis considering him before nodding to Rogaan. Then, while looking at Sugnis and the two Baraan *Ursan,* the red-clad stranger spoke pointing at Rogaan as if he were accustomed to commanding and for others to follow. "You all follow. Gather him. He will be weak for a day or more. We sail immediately."

"What of Pax?" Rogaan asked with the intent to have the stranger help free his friend. "I cannot leave him a prisoner of Kirral or on this island."

"Your defiant and ill-mannered companion from Brigum?" the stranger sought confirmation.

Rogaan nodded, "Yes."

The tall stranger regarded Rogaan as Sugnis and one of the *Ursan* lifted him to his feet, then carried him with Rogaan's arms over their shoulders. Rogaan found amazing the knife wound on his left side was closed and no longer painful, though he considered it might be an illusion of his mind.

"Where is this Pax?" The stranger sounded resigned to do something. Relief poured over Rogaan as the free-handed *Ursan* volunteered to lead them to where Kirral held Rogaan's friend.

After a walk that seemed timeless to Rogaan, they stood in front of Kirral's timber house, though at a distance. Rogaan now able to stand on his own with shaking legs, stood next to Sugnis with the *Ursan's* continued help. They watched the other *Ursan* escort the tall stranger into Kirral's home building through its main entry.

"Who is this one, Rogaan?" Sugnis asked quietly.

"I do not know," Rogaan answered honestly. "He has been watching over me since Brigum, though I do not remember him so tall. He has been at task to keep me safe . . . I think. He killed a cutthroat *Lugasum* by tossing him off a cliff in the Valley of the Claw and cut down a bunch of guardsmen in Brigum who captured Pax and me. That is how we escaped."

"And Im'Kas . . . his Dark Ax reference?" Sugnis asked almost too eagerly, if not protective.

"He and the Dark Axe battled each other in the middle of the wilds allowing us to escape." Rogaan recounted the event, his head and thoughts a little clearer as a chill rippled through him. "Then, I did not think either of them wished to keep me with my *Light*. They tossed about strange powers and sorceries."

"He scares me ta Kur," the Baraan *Ursan* commented.

"As he does all of us," Sugnis spoke with an uncertain reservation.

"Was I truly *Lightless?*" Rogaan asked Sugnis.

"Seemed so," Sugnis nodded to Rogaan, then in the direction of the house. "And he returned you from the *Darkness* returning your *Light* from where it was off to. I thought it could not be done with someone who has not bonded to the Agni. We need to be ready to escape him—"

The doors to the timber building swung open. Emerging from the doorway, a bloodied Pax staggered out while looking over his shoulder. Following him out with confident strides, the tall, red-clad stranger picked up Pax throwing him over his shoulder as if Pax weighed a few feathers before striding as without a care to rejoin Rogaan and companions. The stranger walked past the trio without speaking a word, continuing his way with confident steps. Sugnis and the *Ursan* carrying Rogaan tried to keep up. A short distance farther, the stranger dropped Pax to the ground, then turned to face the house.

"Stay low and behind something," the stranger warned. The bloodred sheen of his metallic armor plates took on a living quality, moving, vibrating, blurring. After a moment's hesitation, the four realized something big was about to happen that needed them to move somewhere safer. They took cover behind a nearby mound of dirt and rocks, peeking over and around the tremor-filled rocks to get a look-see of what was to come next.

The tall stranger stood facing the timber building fifty-four strides distant as a figure emerged from the house staggering, momentarily standing in the doorway. Rogaan saw it to be Kirral. He looked injured. The stranger started concentrating, then mumbling as he held his hands out in front of him, as if he were to hold a large pot, and as the shirt under his chest immolated in a reddish glow making his bloodred metallic armor plates appear malevolent. A spark ignited in between his hands, then rapidly grew into what appeared to be a ball of blistering hot red, yellow, and blue fluid crackling lightning across its surface. With a gesture of his hands toward the timber house, the ball of crackling power sped off. It passed through the doorway, burning Kirral in flames as it passed. The Baraan never even screamed as he twitched and fell. A brilliant flash of reddish light inside the building followed by a deafening roar and dreadful explosion splintered the timbers of the structure. It threw the remnants of the building up and in all directions. The stranger stood tall making arm gestures as if throwing and swiping things from his path with his hands. Burning timber fragments arcing high and toward him inexplicably changed directions, impacting left and right of him and the rocks Rogaan and the others hid behind. After the falling debris ceased, Rogaan and the others surveyed the area. The stones making the slab underneath the timbered building now stood split apart, burning and smoldering as parts of the building lay in all directions as some of the lighter pieces continued to fall from the sky for a time. The tall stranger dusted off his hands, then turned north toward the docks in the channel between the islands. He strode past them with confident strides without giving them the slightest of glances.

"Very well, now," the stranger commented as if checking off tasks needing doing. "No eyes who have seen me or mouths to speak of my passing."

Pax, Sugnis, and the Baraan *Ursan* stood up with Rogaan raised up in between them, all looking at the stranger, dressed richly in clothing and armor unlike anything they had seen and with extraordinary abilities, walking off with the expectation they would follow.

"Who be dis one?" Pax asked with his thumb pointed at the stranger, blood still freely running from cuts in his arms and his head.

"A long tale," Rogaan answered without explaining. "He keeps his name from us. Though that matters little. He is our way off this rock."

"I have pressing matters to attend to, young ones," the tall stranger spoke loudly for them to hear, prodding them to get moving. "It is time for grand adventures and a story of the ages."

Chapter 6

Bindings

Symbols, bright and boldly colored, spun in his head. No longer did they dance in random, confusing ways. Instead, they moved and spun in patterns he now could follow. He felt confident, given time and few interruptions, that he could figure them out, all of them, and stop them from tormenting him. Head throbs accompanying the symbols were painful, but he found a way, a mind trick, to endure them, allowing him to concentrate on the puzzles instead of just wishing them gone. The method was crude, inflicting physical pain upon himself with small sharp sticks, but effective. Still, he rather the whirling symbols not be about in his mind and wanted relief from them, like when that Tellen was around. *I wonder what became of him*, Aren thought. A knock on the door startled him, causing the small stick he pressed into his left side to slip from his hand as sparks of popping lights flashed all about him, some stinging. Growling at himself, Aren's frustration flared for not having better control of himself. He forced himself to stare forward and focus on nothing so to concentrate on stopping the stinging flashes without having to contend with the symbol puzzles with closed eyes. The stinging lights diminished, then disappeared. After a few moments of blinking and arranging himself, he felt composed enough to think. *Nobody knows of this . . . hiding place.*

"I know you to be in there, Evendiir." That irritating, high-pitched voice of the young woman *Tusaa'Ner* commander, the *sakal*, was unmistakable. She spoke with tones that grated on him, though in her words now he detected a hint of disgust. "Come out. You are summoned to *Za* Irzal's chambers."

"Oh, the indignities I must deal with," he grumbled to himself before launching into an internal tirade. *That dim-witted sow of perversion wants me back in her chambers. And to do what . . . wash her floors, help her dress that cushioned bottom of hers, empty her pots, play with her?* That last thought gave him the shivers that he allowed an overexaggerated flailing of his shoulders, head, and arms.

"What is happening in there?" The *sakal* asked with a hint of concern in her voice.

"Nothing . . ." Aren answered, trying to stall for time to compose himself before Irzal's half-witted youngling had her city guard troupe knock down the door. When Aren felt calmed enough and composed, he stood tall and dignified as he opened the door.

"As the *Za* wishes," he recited in a practiced tone as the bile rose in his throat. *Endure. My time will come.*

In the open doorway, the *sakal* glowered at him with her fists on hips. A hand shorter than himself and with her red-yellow hair pulled into a tail, she stood there with an impatient glare wearing tailored tanned hides of half armor on her booted shins, hips, upper chest, and shoulders over a white weaved tunic belted at her waist. The hide forearm guards she wore looked of low-quality workmanship, though well used. A sheathed long knife completed her tough *Ursan* look that Aren assumed she was trying to achieve. That glare from her tan face held a mix of disappointment and disgust. "Does not the *Za* do enough for you that you must find a place to pleasure yourself?"

"Whoa, pleasuring—" Aren protested as a flash of pain accompanying spinning puzzles appeared in his mind's eye. "Not what – "

"Follow me, *servant* Aren," the *sakal* ordered as she sharply turned away, expecting him to follow without the usual discourse and discussion. "I have instructions to escort you back to her."

Aren begrudgingly followed the *Tusaa'Ner sakal* through the halls of the building where the city's hands administrating the urban and surrounding areas slept and worked. Aren too worked but did so through his emotions at the distaste of being a servant instead of working on the paper and clay documents that lay about the tables and shelves he walked past. *"Servant" is too unspecific a naming, more properly a "bonded slave,"* Aren corrected the commander in his own head, knowing better than to speak his mind openly. Bonded to *Za* Irzal, at her request . . . demand, by the *Gals'* pronouncement of his sentence. It was a surprise to Aren. He stood before the *Gals*, certain he would be put in prison in the place they sent the Tellen and his Baraan friend or to remain in the city jail under the arena. It wasn't until sometime after being handed over to Irzal that he learned that it was her aide Ganzer who made issues before the court and *Gals* until they relented. Since then, he served her needs and whims. *It would be less demeaning if she had half a brain*, Aren complained to himself. The woman was beautiful despite her being in her middle years for a Baraan, but her influence over him was strong. He fought at it but unsuccessfully. *I hate her for it*. Her daughter, when she visited, offered a little relief from the *Za's* relentless demand for attention.

That daughter, the *sakal*, now kept an even pace as she led him from the stone and wood building into the gloom of the rising morning sun and onto a dirt-covered gathering area where many serving Farratum's *Sakes, Tusaa'Ner, Zas, Gals*, and everyone of position mingled after receiving morning bread and drink. The *sakal* did not slow as her boots landed on the packed dirt, swiftly transiting the gathering area as sandal-footed people dressed in neat and clean tunics moved from her path, leaving a cleared avenue for Aren to follow. Exiting the gathering area as quickly as they entered, the *sakal* led Aren onto a worn dirt path leading eastward through a thin stretch of woodlands, yellow and red blooms, and an occasional showing of blue flowers lining the way. Sweet fragrances filled Aren's nose as he chased after the *sakal*. She seemed to be in a hurry. They moved quickly in the direction of the old temple pyramid where Farratum *Zas* conduct their doings and where Irzal usually could be found working. Aren felt a sneeze building up as he tripped over an unseen root.

Symbols suddenly reappeared in his head, vividly colorful and tumbling and moving almost erratically. They made Aren miserably dizzy, and with an impending sneeze . . . *Not now, cursed things!* Aren demanded of the symbols, then involuntarily sneezed loudly as he stood in the dirt path. In the middle of his sneeze, pounding throbs hammered his head as a vengeance of new colorful cyphers whipped around spinning and tumbling. Aren dropped to a knee as he feared falling over, not knowing which way was up. The moment his knee touched the ground, he felt righted. Concerned at his display of weakness, he immediately rose and tried to walk but stumbled several times, walking into trees and a prickly bush. "Ouch! Miserable brambles."

"What ills you?" That irritating, high-pitched voice of the *sakal* rang like a bell in Aren's ears. Her tone was frustrated as her words were without compassion. She continued with more than a hint of contempt in her tone, "I thought you Evendiir were part of the wild places?"

"You Evendiir . . ." Aren started a harsh retort before thinking of the repercussions. Spinning symbols distracted him from forming an intelligent response . . . *Those two puzzles fit together.* Aren found himself concentrating on them. A compulsion took hold of him to bring them close to each other, fit them, make them . . . one. Nothing else mattered. He stopped their spinning. *Yes, these belong to each other.* Aren rotated the symbols so the lines of each matched at the edges. He then concentrated on them touching. They moved closer. Pain everywhere! Each thumb of him screamed out in stinging torment. Aren felt himself falling and hitting something. Pain . . . everywhere! *Stop! Make it stop!* Music, almost imperceptible, flirted at the edge of his consciousness.

"Servant!" the music announced. The stinging pain diminished.

"Aren!" the music called out his name as the stinging pain fell away.

His thoughts clearing, Aren searched for the two symbols to make them one. *Gone!* A sadness filled him for a long moment before anger took over him. *I was so close to ending this torment.* Unable to see anything beyond a now-empty void, Aren felt the pressing of hands on his chest and head. That music turned to a voice, sweet and concern-filled, but unintelligible. *Pay for your insolence.* Reaching for a knowledge he knew not from where it came, Aren's skin prickled as a tingling throughout his body intensified. *Release!*

"Aaaaaaaaahhhh!" that sweet voice screamed out in agony, then fell silent.

Confusion gripped Aren. *What just happened? What did I do?* His vision no longer a dark void; instead, a cloudy blur that kept improving. All the pain gone, replaced by a sense of euphoria. It filled him. *I like this.* Aren repeatedly blinked, wanting to see what transpired on the dirt path, wanting to satisfy his curiosity. At the same time, a fearful panic welled up within him that he had done something Irzal would find for him a "proper" punishment.

He sat quietly, allowing his vision to clear well enough to stand and walk without getting stuck again by another prickly bush. A low moan came to his ears, not far away, where a blurry lump lay, unmoving. Another moan. Aren grew concerned as he looked for any movement. None. In short moments, his vision cleared well enough for him to move. He then rose and approached the fallen *sakal*. Her low groans told him she still lived, but he feared she might not be well. He felt her *Light* wane when he released whatever he held. It was a strange sensation, unlike anything he ever felt, and her *Light* was almost not when she fell away from him. Now, looking into the *sakal's* eyes, he saw confusion, though with an attempt at searching, gaining focus as the moments passed. *Good. Her mind is still with her.* Aren felt relieved he would not have to explain her death. Now, to get her not to place him in an isolated cell.

"*Sakal*," Aren spoke to her in a calm way, hoping she would remember him as caring. "Do you hear my voice? Are you able to sit up?"

The *sakal* started clumsily waving her arms, almost flailing. Aren remembered his father's teaching of nature and lightning and how it affected those struck by it. The *sakal* behaved in a like manner as his father described. *What did I do to her?* The *sakal's* eyes showed focus as she attempted to speak, but all that came from her was gibberish. Then her arms flailed again as her legs trembled. Aren's sense of relief started to wane. The *sakal's* body trembled more before settling down to more normal movements.

"*Sakal* . . ." Aren asked calmly again, "do you hear my voice?"

Her eyes focused on him as more gibberish, this time almost understandable, came from her lips. Her right hand moved unsteadily to the side of his head, then grabbed Aren's ear, twisting it, causing him terrible pain.

"Aaarrrrgggggg," he cried out. "Let go of me!"

Dajil kept a firm grip on Aren's ear, and there they remained until the *sakal* could speak understandable words, no longer in a high pitch, but in a voice both pleasant and soft. "What you did to me . . . What did you do to me?"

"I don't know what hurt me . . . or you," he lied, hoping it would take hold.

"Can't feel my arms or legs much," the *sakal* informed him.

Aren didn't know how to respond. She had his ear, literally, in her hand. Each attempt he made to pull away or remove her hand was met with a painful twisting. So, there they lay and sat until Dajil managed to move well enough to sit up. She looked at him with uncertain eyes before letting go of his ear.

"I don't know if you speak truth," Dajil stated with a soft voice. "You looked confused and lost . . . in pain. Then, your eyes glowed when I touched you, and I felt . . . terrible pain and couldn't move. I couldn't breathe."

"I say, *sakal*, I don't know what happened," Aren reasserted his previous words. There was much truth in them. He truly didn't know what happened, but he knew deep down what did come from him. And Aren wasn't about to admit that. "Let me help you stand."

Dajil did let him help her up where she then stood with unsteady legs. She insisted they get to her mother before she sent the entire *Tusaa'Ner* after them. With Aren helping her keep steady, they walked out of the woodland tract and onto a busy stone plaza coming to life under the morning shadow of the looming temple.

Aren looked up at the tall, stepped pyramid with its western-facing sides and the plaza gracing its western flanks in dark gray shadows as the brilliance of the rising sun illuminated the sky beyond above the northern slope of the structure. He felt a twinge of dizziness as his eyes were drawn up to the heights of the pyramid. Aren tried shaking off the sensation but found it still with him. Tumbling symbols momentarily appeared as did the ache in his head before he managed to partition his mind and the symbols with them into a safe corner. The pyramid, once a temple to the Ancient Gula, was now taken over by those governing the city Farratum and greater Shuruppak. In there, *Za* Irzal and the other *Zas* kept offices where they conducted official affairs. A foreboding swept through Aren as he thought about entering the place. He felt it every time he laid eyes upon the ancient temple, now misused. *Disrespectful younglings. Insolent ways.* Aren was surprised at the thoughts in his head. *Where did that come from?* he asked himself. Shaking off the strange thoughts, Aren continued to help the unsteady *sakal* as they made their way to the front of the old temple through and sometimes around Baraans, mostly, going to and fro about their morning affairs, with only some paying them any attention.

"Everyone's in a rush?" Aren commented to himself but aloud before he realized he spoke the words.

"They're all in preparations," the *sakal* answered partly. Aren felt light-headed as Dajil's words felt sweet and appealing. She continued guiding Aren toward the south side of the massive granite stone construction, built by the Ancients, legends said. Aren felt the *sakal* . . . Dajil, was warming to him. *She seems taken by me . . . good*, he congratulated himself. She guided him onward, toward the main entrance sitting between the southwestern and southeastern steps, both rising from the plaza to the top of the pyramid where a temple house stood. In days of old, sacrifices to the Ancients were both plentiful and regular here, using all four staircases to ascend with offerings. Now, sacrifices were made to the officials seeking tributes and taxes and obedience by the peoples.

That uneasy feeling kept at Aren as he looked upon the pyramid entrance. Four *Tusaa'Ner* stood flanking the large timber double doors. The guardsmen were dressed in full uniforms; dark blue tunics under dark hide and metal shoulder and chest armor, bright red sashes, helms, hip guards, leg and shin guards, shields and short spears. The plumeless helms identified them as low rank. The timber doors to the temple stood open, allowing a throng of servants to scurry in with empty baskets and sacks and more servants to emerge from the structure with filled baskets and sacks.

The *Tusaa'Ner* guardsmen suddenly appeared surprised and guilty, all at the same time, when they realized one of their *sakals* stood before them and the pyramid doors. Two of the *Tusaa'Ner* quickly approached with their helm-covered concerned faces.

"*Sakal*," the larger of the two guardsmen spoke, "forgive our inattention. It will not happen again."

"See that it doesn't," the *sakal* replied in her high-pitched voice that Aren didn't seem to mind, so much.

"Are you needing assistance?" asked the guardsman standing tall and respectfully.

"Yes," she answered while her hands firmly squeezed Aren's arm. "Bind this one. He's a danger to the *Zas* and everyone else."

Chapter 7

Temple of Sully

Aren stood in a fume, his hands and arms behind him painfully in bindings. *How could she do it to me?* he asked himself while standing between the two cold-as-stone-faced *Tusaa'Ner* guardsmen that accompanied the *sakal* from the main entrance. They waited in *Za* Irzal's outer chamber, a reception room some four strides square, with walls of granite blocks covered in tapestries, several two-person benches, and more chairs lining the walls. The coverings bore images of those in arenas and fighting pits . . . Things Aren wasn't interested in and trying to forget of his own experience. Two heavy wood doors stood opposite each other, one leading to the main hallway, and the other leading to Irzal's inner office chambers. *An enchantress! Yes, an enchantress*, Aren ranted in his head. *That's how she tricked me to the temple entrance . . . and her guardsmen.* Symbols glowed brightly as they spun past his sight. *No more trusting Baraan women. They all have their sways to enthrall minds.*

Voices behind the closed door to the inner chambers were muffled, even for Aren's keen ears, but the tone and pace of the words hinted at an argument. Another glowing symbol, this one blue, spun as it sped across his vision. The guardsmen flanking Aren appeared impatient, if not bored, as if this were all normal. Aren knew better the truth of the *Za* and her daughter. He bore witness to their lively exchanges on more than a few occasions over the months. The *sakal* didn't like Aren, and the *Za* didn't like his mistreatment—unless she was the one performing it. *She has gone too far this time!* Aren told himself about the *sakal*; yet, another glowing symbol, this one red, spun and sped across his vision. *That one's familiar . . .* Aren became distracted from his anger. The door to the inner chamber abruptly opened. The red-yellow, long-tailed-haired *sakal* stood glaring at Aren with her fists planted on her hips.

"Remove his bindings," the *sakal* ordered the two *Tusaa'Ner* guardsmen. The *Za's* daughter looked very angry. The guardsmen both looked questioning at each other before complying.

Relief from the pain was all Aren thought about for moments after his bindings were removed. A green glowing symbol spun and sped across his vision. Aren worked his shoulders to relieve the stiffness before stepping toward the inner chamber. The *sakal's* hand pressed on his chest stopping him.

"Harm her and I will cut you down." Dajil's voice was both low and serious. Her eyes told him the *Za's* daughter meant it.

"I told you she wouldn't believe," Aren returned the *sakal's* gaze. Aren sniffed the air searching for her "scent of sway" that he fell to earlier. The room was absent of it. "I will not fall prey to your sway, again, enchantress."

A fist struck Aren's mouth, sending him staggering backward. Stinging pain pulsed through Aren's lips and chin for a moment before symbols of all colors and patterns spun wildly about him. He stood gazing at a constellation of glowing cyphers while rubbing his jaw. Those in the room no longer held any meaning to him. He knew they were there but were of no importance. Shapes formed out of the spinning symbols. Shapes like and unlike any before. Aren recognized a few of the patterns and managed to stop several of the symbols from spinning before fitting them together. The shapes formed by the collective of moving symbols changed again, becoming more organized, more predictable. *Yes!* Aren congratulated himself.

"You are so strange," Dajil described Aren with exasperation as she pushed past him. "Remember my words, Evendiir."

"How can I forget?" Aren sardonically replied to Dajil as he rubbed his jaw once more. This wasn't the first time the Za's daughter struck him. "You keep reminding me."

"Guards," the *sakal's* irritating, high-pitched tone returned as she walked out of the room into the hallway with her hand gripping tightly the sheathed long knife at her side. Aren listened to her distancing footsteps while she uttered more orders for the guardsmen, he presumed. "Remain in the outer chamber. Let nothing happen to the *Za*."

"*Evendiir!*" the familiar voice called out for Aren. She wanted his attention, and he cringed at what was to follow after he entered the room.

Aren put on his best mask of indifference before meekly walking into *Za* Irzal's office chambers. To his surprise, the room and Irzal were nothing as he expected. The room was in chaos with law parchments spread all over her desk and chairs with more in snapjaw hide pouch-carriers sitting about on the floor. Instructions issued by the *Za* to her aides were fast and many. Her aides were struggling to keep up with the *Za*, a young Baraan woman with dark hair who recently joined the staff and a Baraan male, neither, of whom, Aren was very familiar. They were placing parchments the *Za* read and chose into the organized hide carriers. Aren's skin prickled at the sight of Ganzer, Irzal's male Baraan male aide. Ganzer was one of two to be wary of in Aren's conclusion. Months of living and serving close to

Ganzer and his aide, Lucufaar, a true mystery with what he observed of him, allowed Aren to understand Ganzer better than even Ganzer knew himself. The short and pudgy Baraan that sported a double chin, controlling and feeding information to the *Za* and pulling Irzal's cords about which way to vote and decree. It wasn't incompetence on the part of Irzal; to the contrary, Aren considered her strong and ambitious and vicious at times. It was that Ganzer knew and used various means that she was vulnerable to, and it seemed Ganzer's "scent of sway" was particularly effective on her.

Aren took notice of Irzal's clothing. Strange attire for her, leaving Aren confused and curious about what was going on. Usually, she dressed in sheer, see-through dresses and gowns, and then moved in ways that flirted with those that had eyes on her. Aren came to understand it was all part of the tools she used to influence those near, that and her own powerful "scent of sway" that her daughter seems to have inherited. *I must be careful and keep distance from both of them and their practiced sways*, Aren warned himself.

"There you are . . ." Irzal finally recognized Aren. Today, she wore a brown, split hide dress with tanned hide walking boots, as if she planned to travel. Sweeping her left arm around the room, she said, "All of you collect these pouch-carriers and follow Ganzer."

Aren nodded in compliance despite his prickling skin. It was his "duty" as a servant to do as told, forced upon him by those he was given over to by the *gal* as an alternative sentence instead of being placed in a jailing cell . . . or worse. *That is . . . until my sentence is complete, or I find a way to escape these idiots*, Aren declared to himself. *Then . . . It'll be my turn*, he promised himself.

Aren did as instructed, grabbing up two hand-fulls of carriers, all filled with parchments. He slung them over his head and shoulders, leaving him appearing as some strange, fat Evendiir with all the pouch-carriers hanging from him layered on top of each other.

"Follow," Ganzer ordered Aren before saying something to the young, dark-haired woman. Aren didn't hear what he spoke to the woman because of shouting from the hallway. Ganzer looked to the *Za*. "There is not much time."

Not much time . . . Aren took notice of the words. *What's happening with all this running about?*

Ganzer tossed a foul glare at Aren, then motioned with his kept wavy, black-haired head and contempt-filled eyes, telling Aren to fall in line behind him. A silver-harnessed ruby gemstone dangled with a sparkle from Ganzer's right ear. Aren couldn't recall ever seeing the Baraan without it.

Out the chambers they went, past the two *Tusaa'Ner* and into the hallway. Ganzer almost ran, more of a scurry to Aren's long strides as he led the way down the granite block hallways of the old temple. Feelings of loathing and anger again rose within Aren as he looked upon the tapestries, furniture, and all that made this temple a place of worship to these foolish mortals and their governings, instead of who they should truly be worshipping. *What are these feelings?* Aren asked himself. Symbols, glowing and spinning, returned, dominating his vision. *Not now!* The symbols were more organized than he remembered. And the usual pain that accompanied them now felt intensified, significantly. Distracted away from the hallway and Ganzer, Aren tripped and would have hit the floor if not for a wood table he caught himself on. Cursing himself as he suffered Ganzer's disdainful gaze, Aren regained his feet, then continued following the aide. Wanting not to look the fool, Aren did his best to peer past the symbols, instead, focusing on the dark blue hide jacket and kilt Ganzer wore as he fell in step behind him.

Ganzer led Aren out the southeastern doors of the temple where a troupe of blue-uniformed *Tusaa'Ner* guardsmen stood in formation before several wagons with spears high. Each of the wagons had a single, midsized kyda harnessed at their fronts and a driver directing what was being loaded and where.

"What did I miss?" Aren asked rhetorically, though spoke aloud without realizing he did.

"Nothing, *servant*," Ganzer answered with more contempt thick on his words. "Your eyes see too much as it is. It is best for you to remain unaware."

All the symbols halted their motions as anger filled Aren, from sandaled toes to his top hairs. *What did I miss?* Aren asked himself again. *Was I so occupied with these cursed symbols that I missed all this under my nose?* It was now clear Ganzer and the rest were preparing for travel, but to where? Aren searched his memories, around the symbols that continued to distract him, finding bits and pieces of what he sought. *What is out of the ordinary?* The *Anubda'Ner* arriving in Farratum, or at least a small contingent of the Mighty Guardians. They belonged to the Nation of Shuruppak and took their orders from *Zas* far removed from Farratum. But they spent time with Irzal and her aides, behind closed doors that Aren wasn't permitted beyond. Their stay was only for a short time before departing east . . . to Padusan, Aren recalled overhearing. *What else?*

A gathering of supplies stored in wood crates had stood all about the temple. Looking around, Aren realized the crates were now gone, both inside and outside the misused granite monument to the Ancients. Irzal, Ganzer, and Lucufaar also seemed to be holding more "planning" meetings than usual. And then he and many of the other servants assigned to *Za* Irzal, just yesterday, were ordered to hand in all but one set of their clothes for washing. Not of normal activities as usually one or more of the servants would be assigned washing duties . . . and the timing of the washing was off by days.

"Hand me the carriers," Ganzer ordered with an outstretched hand as he sat where the driver of the lead wagon would usually be. He let out a grunt as Aren's eyes slowly focused on him. "*Now*, Evendiir."

Aren stood next to the lead wagon with symbols again swirling about his vision. Without questioning or his usual attitude on display for the aide, Aren stripped the carriers from his shoulders one by one, handing each to Ganzer, who then placed them in a crate just behind the driver's seat.

"Get in," ordered Ganzer.

"Where are we off to?" Aren asked, still a bit disoriented.

"To become of those who rule this world," answered Ganzer with a disdainful irritation.

Aren didn't find Ganzer's answer much of a help as those glowing symbols started spinning and moving wildly, but his words spoke of enormous and dangerous ambitions.

Chapter 8
Journey's Beginning

The kyda's muscles rippled as it worked hard under the whipping stick of the driver willing on the wagon through the semi-crowded streets of Farratum. Aren sat in the middle of the cargo wagon's bench with an intense and irritated Ganzer to his left and an unpleasant smelling Baraan driver to his right. Symbols continued their wild spinning and arcing paths in his vision as the morning crowds parted for the mounted *Tusaa'Ner* escorts leading on their sarigs in front of their wagon. Aren noted many in the crowds unhappy at the intrusion of the caravan passing through the midst of their morning activities on this main street circling the arena. The Circle of Justice. Aren grunted at the mockery in the street's naming. *Justice was not given to me in that place*, he angrily reflected. Symbols slowed. The four *Tusaa'Ner*, leading on their sarigs, kept a brisk pace passing business after merchant stands and crowds after throngs filling the outer left side of the cobblestone street. They followed the road in a sweeping arc to the right around to the southeast side of the looming arena before turning south onto Dock Street. The cobblestone street here was less crowded in these morning hours with two-story, brick-built taverns lining the eastern side of the street and timbered log row-type dwellings on the right side. Ahead, a portcullis, large enough for two wagons to pass through together, sat open in the large block stone wall surrounding the city. A large contingent of blue-armored *Tusaa'Ner* in and surrounding the gate appeared to be checking everyone and everything passing through to the wharf beyond. To Aren's curiosity, their wagon caravan showed no intent at slowing as the mounted *Tusaa'Ner* ahead of the wagon closed on the gate. A horn sounded, causing the crowd at the gate to part just before their caravan passed through the portcullis.

The wagons veered left as soon as their wheels rolled onto the flagstones used to surface the wharf. The stink of fish and decay filled Aren's nose, causing him to wrinkle it, hoping to block the smell. Aren, never seeing the wharf before now, looked about with wide eyes. The width of the wharf's flagstones varied, though averaged some forty strides wide running from a wedge-shaped tower to the northeast, that the sun was now trying to peek over, all the way around the south side of the city to its southwest ending. Having seen maps of Farratum on *Za* Irzal's tables, Aren knew the stone-surfaced wharf continued to the west, then turned north surrounding all Farratum's waterfront. Timber-constructed dock walkways projected out from the flagstones offering ships both small and grand places to moor and harbor from the currents of the Ner River. Aren was genuinely surprised at the hustle and bustle of the wharf. Peoples were actively moving cargo, crates, and wares everywhere. Ships less than ten strides' length moored behind him to the west on the numerous timber docks provided to ensure Farratum was well capable of being a place of significant commerce along the Ner and Ur rivers.

The driver next to Aren pulled up on the reigns, halting their kyda and wagon at the first of two docks on the wharf's eastern extreme. Extending into the Ner were wide timber docks of significant lengths able to accommodate three large moored, triple-mast ships with well-kept wooden hulls, if Aren saw them correctly. Small carts pulled by Baraan bearers quickly crowded around their wagons. Workers immediately started transferring cargo and crates from the wagons to their carts before making off to the dock of the three-mast, tall-hulled ship moored there, the *Khaaron*. Aren also made note of the names, the *Erebuus* and the *Nyx*, the other two large ships moored beyond at the second dock now with Baraans crawling about them like biters on carcasses, dismembering them; instead, they were filling them with supplies. All three ships were almost identical and large, some fifty-plus strides in length and more than fifteen in width with sails resembling folded fans a lady might use in public or at a ceremonial gathering.

For a few moments, Aren stood in awe of their size and of the craftsmanship required to envision and build such things. Then, his cheeks heated as he realized he stood with his jaws agape and looking like a fool. Immediately, he put back on his impassive, unimpressed demeanor for all to see and know that he is an Evendiir of the world. With another wrinkle of his nose, Aren still found the place smelling of decay and dead fish.

"Grab that crate of parchments and follow me," Ganzer ordered. Aren looked around for others he must have been giving the commands to as he estimated the crate too heavy for him to lift or drag alone. When he found nobody around listening to the aide, Aren looked up at the now-standing Ganzer with an unbelieving gaze. A cluster of entwined symbols flew across Aren's vision, distracting him as he winced at the pain that came with them. Ganzer wrinkled his nose in a contempt-filled snarl. "Get a bearer to help you."

Aren immediately found a strong, dark-haired Baraan atop the wagon handing crates and sacks to other scurrying bearers tending to carts. "You! Assist me with this crate."

The worker displayed an exasperated attitude while looking about and finding Ganzer before grunting and making to help Aren. The Baraan pulled the crate to the edge of the wagon gate before waiting for Aren to assist him placing it into a small cart. In truth, Aren was of little help to the Baraan but made a show of it. *I'm not built for such toils*, Aren complained to himself as the Baraan grabbed one of the two carry-poles at the front of the cart. Aren reluctantly picked up the other pole, with an effort, then panted hard to keep up with the Baraan as they pulled the cart onto the wide dock following Ganzer. Aren noted the aide now carried a small backpack over his right shoulder and a carry pouch in his left hand.

Ganzer led them to the end of the dock where they climbed a ramp pulling the cart behind them. Aren struggled mightily, pulling the cart up to the second elevated timber platform where they were level with the quarter deck of the *Khaaron*. That unpleasant feeling of sweat pouring from him made Aren unsettled as he pulled his clinging light gray tunic, now darkened from being wet from him in places. Suddenly and surprisingly, Aren realized the symbols no longer tormented him. They were gone. None of his mental efforts were needed to keep the cursed things away.

"What just changed?" Aren asked of no one while standing, panting. A hopeful spark lit within him as the Baraan worker gave him a mixed look of confusion and annoyance. Aren worked at calming his breathing enough to allow himself to enter the meditative state needed to confirm the symbols were not hiding as they sometimes did. A few moments later he entered into his mediation while standing next to the cart. He felt a smile growing on his face with only the empty void found when he closed his eyes. *They're not here . . . and my head-pains have left me*, Aren told himself, making it official. *Why?*

"Evendiir," Ganzer's voice punched through Aren's moment of joy and serenity, "get those parchments on the ship. We have little time to waste."

Aren bit back an ill-mannered remark at Ganzer's disrespectful ways, thinking better of it. *I'll get my retribution on Ganzer . . . and them all*, he promised himself as he got moving. The wood walkway across to the ship, being too narrow for the cart, found Aren struggling to carry his end of the crate as the Baraan helping him easily held up his side. Once across, Ganzer directed them to the rear of the ship with a pointed finger toward a raised section with steps to either side a central set of doors going up to a railed platform where a large lever center of the ship stood. The double doors below the steering lever lay open, allowing them entrance. Aren shuffled his feet into the opening with the heavy load of the crate, causing him to pour more sweat. *I'll get my day*, he grumbled to himself. The double door entry led to a short, low-ceilinged hallway where three cabin doors all were open, one to either side and another set of double doors at the end. The smell of wood in the cramped hallway overtook the odor of decay and fish and was a welcoming reprieve to Aren's nose.

"To the right," Ganzer called out from somewhere outside.

Aren rolled his eyes in annoyance and silent protest as he backed into the cabin on the right. The widening eyes of the Baraan on the other side of the crate they carried sent a chill rippling up through Aren.

"What have we here?" That familiar voice with its even, calm cadence sent unpleasant chills down, then back up, Aren's spine. "Gifts, son of Larcan?"

Aren froze for a long moment, not knowing what to do. *He's at my back. How stupid of me!* Aren chastised himself while wishing he'd been more careful than to back into a room with Ganzer's aide, Lucufaar, within. The Baraan just seemed to know too many things he shouldn't and always seemed steps ahead of Aren. Lucufaar unnerved him, though Aren found it difficult to admit that to himself. *Act normal . . . Ganzer ordered the parchments taken here.*

"Ganzer wanted these parchments placed in here," Aren spoke with more nervousness than he wanted.

"Put them in the aft part of the cabin," Lucufaar directed with that calm cadence in his voice.

Aft? Aren didn't know the meaning. He stood there in the cabin doorway trying to decide which way to step, left or right, knowing if he went the wrong way, he would never be allowed to forget it. *I can't just stand here looking like an idiot*, he warned himself, though his pride kept him from asking for help. *Left, I'll go left*, he finally decided. Just then, Aren noticed the Baraan bearer on the other side of the crate of parchments nodding his head in the other direction. Aren was uncertain if the Baraan intended to make a fool of him. After considering the odds in that, he stepped backward into the cabin, then to his right around a small table Lucufaar was using. They found a spot to set the crate down in the small cabin, placing it snuggly into a corner between two-fold down bunk heads. The Baraan worker disappeared before Aren turned from pushing the crate into the corner, leaving him alone in the cabin with Ganzer's aide. A wave of panic rippled through Aren as he looked upon the standing Lucufaar, a light brown-haired Baraan of slender build and middle years, checking and arranging objects in a medium-sized wood chest atop a small table. Without looking at Aren, Lucufaar lifted a hide-wrapped object from the chest with his left hand, then pulled back its red and black folds revealing the ax-and-flame Agni gemstone that brought Aren all his recent troubles.

"What do you sense . . . feel?" Lucufaar asked quietly, just loud enough for Aren to hear.

When Aren simply stared back at him with a questioning look indicating he felt nothing, Lucufaar raised his right hand to the gemstone. Aren caught sight of what he thought were tiny arcs of lightning dancing in between Ganzer's aide's fingers and the master crafted gemstone. Then, they were gone. Alarmed, Aren stared at the gemstone. *Did I really see lightning in Lucufaar's hand? What is he?* Suddenly, Aren's heart felt as if it stopped, and his chest became like stone, unable to move or take breath. Symbols, bright and complex, painfully whirled madly about in his mind, causing him to become unsettled and dizzy. Aren felt light-headed and about to topple over before finding the wall of the cabin to support him.

"Interesting . . ." Lucufaar mused. "It sleeps unlike any I have known, and yet still, has hold of you."

"What's happening to me?" Just barely able to breathe, Aren asked in a rough cough. He hoped, for once, Ganzer's aide would help him instead of seeming to enjoy his suffering.

"You, young Evendiir, are bonded to this Agni in some manner." Lucufaar offered the explanation freely. *Unusual.* He kept his unsympathetic eyes on Aren watching his every twitch. Aren understood from his experiences with this Baraan and from the aide's reputation around the workers that he stood apart from the others in *Za's* staff as strange, if not highly so. Aren's chest loosened, allowing him to breathe a little.

"What does this mean for me . . . bonded?" Aren asked Lucufaar since he seemed to be in a talkative mood.

"For you?" Lucufaar asked as he kept that uncomfortable stare on Aren. All Aren wanted was an honest answer, what had him in this "bond," and if he would survive it.

"Yes," Aren answered with a ragged breath.

"It tells of opportunity . . ." Lucufaar returned to his cryptic self as he placed the gemstone back into the chest just before Aren heard footfalls in the hallway beyond the cabin door.

Frustration filled Aren, both from his struggles to breathe and from Lucufaar's elusiveness. *What in all of Kur does he mean?* Before Aren could make at protesting Lucufaar's non-answer, Ganzer, in his blue jacket, kilt, and sandaled feet, stepped into the doorway with a clicking of his sandals on the wood decking.

"I do not know why I indulge you so," Ganzer spoke as if bored with his aide's requests. Ganzer half-yawned as he scrubbed a hand through his dark, wavy hair before realizing that he did so. He then quickly produced a bone comb and made his tuft of hair more presentable, all the while Lucufaar stood with an impatient look. "The prisoners are on the dock. Tell me again why we need them?"

"They have needed knowledge," Lucufaar answered as if it were explanation enough.

"Where do you learn of these things?" Ganzer rhetorically questioned his aide with a shake of his head and a frustrated disbelief in his voice. "Or do you make stories to irritate me?"

Aren watched Lucufaar struggle to keep control of his emotions and facial expressions. It looked to him that Lucufaar almost lost the battle before the aide put on a smile and answered his superior with a practiced voice, "I have useful eyes and ears in the right spaces."

"It is a good thing for you Irzal likes what you bring her with those *eyes and ears*," Ganzer made it a point to Lucufaar his value to the *Za* had limits and that he remained of value only if he continued to produce. ". . . or I would have none of this. Traveling the Blood Lands has been forbidden since the *Time of the Ancients*, for good reasons."

Blood Lands! Aren felt his regained breath leave him. *They have lost all reason!* Aren learned of the Blood Lands and other such places of their myths and legends from his father and the books he kept. A dangerous place protected by the mythical *Sentii*, a bloodthirsty race protecting the places of the long-departed Ancients. *I must now leave before they want me to serve them on their journey to death.* Aren coughed mildly to clear his throat, then spoke in his attempt at an excuse to get as far from this ship as he could. "I take my leave of you, Masters Ganzer and Lucufaar. I must return to my duties."

Ganzer seemed startled at Aren's presence and pronouncement and now silently held him with angry regard and hateful eyes. Lucufaar seemed amused at Ganzer's obvious display of incompetence, not being aware of another pair of ears in the room able to overhear their banter. Ganzer looked to be working hard at thinking behind his angry and hateful eyes. "You will perform your duties as the law decrees . . . here on this ship, in service to *Za* Irzal."

"I have nothing of clothing and need to retrieve my—" Aren attempted to get himself excused from the ship with the intent of never returning.

"You will find your rags below deck where you will sleep," Ganzer half-scolded, half-informed him. "I had other servants bring your belongings here. Now, finish getting my and Irzal's possessions from the wagon and bring them here to this cabin and the one directly across the hall. Do not think to run, Evendiir. The *Tusaa'Ner* on the docks are with orders to cut down any runaways."

Aren made to protest again but was cut off by dangerous stares from both Ganzer and Lucufaar. Forced to hold his tongue, he swallowed hard as he gritted his teeth. *They will pay for this when I have my turn*, Aren promised himself as he squeezed past Ganzer on his way back to the wagon on the dock. He made his way to the quarter deck while grumbling to himself at his misfortunes. *I'm trapped on a journey to my death! I must escape these idiots and their quest before it's too late for me.*

He stopped at the front rail of the quarter deck where there was a good view below to the main deck and forward elevated deck and the forecastle. People, many in servant rags, were running here, there, and all about. Watching the furious activities for a few moments allowed Aren to breathe, to catch his breath, and start thinking again. *How am I to escape this?* He looked over the dock to his right. His eyes found too many *Tusaa'Ner* and more, *Sakes*, standing at strategic locations and choke points. Aren watched those watching with predator-like intensity, all dressed in belt-held light gray tunics and low sandals. *They're watching all who are dressed in servant clothing . . . as I am. I'll never make ten strides before getting caught.* He then turned his attention to the waters to his left between this ship and the next dock where two ships, smaller than his, were moored, offloading cargo. The waters swirled between the wharf and ships with more than a dozen pairs of snouts and eyes just breaking the surface of the Ner. Aren bit his bottom lip. *Is it possible?*

"I would think thrice before making that swim," a strong, confident voice stated from somewhere behind and above Aren.

Startled and fearing it was Lucufaar . . . or Ezerus, Aren whirled around so fast he tripped and almost fell were it not for the rail he had a hard grip on. Confidently descending from the deck above the side steps to Aren's right, he watched a tall *Tusaa'Ner* dressed in Farratum sky-blue guard armor, a red cape, and with a red feather-plumed helm step to the quarter deck near where he stood. A commander in the *Tusaa'Ner*, a *sakal*, and carried himself as a dangerous one not to be trifled with. Aren swallowed hard. The gray-touched goateed guard gave Aren a silent look-over with a steely, confident gaze while casually standing just strides away. Aren held his tongue not knowing if he was to be reprimanded, maybe with an often-used hide strap or reported to Ganzer, who would then have him strapped for putzing.

"The decision is yours to make," the blue-clad *sakal* strangely offered Aren a . . . . choice, before starting his stroll across the quarter deck toward the dock. "Better ways in other times to gain freedom will come, young Evendiir."

The *sakal* crossed over thick plank boards spanning from ship deck to timber dock before strolling toward the wharf with many salutes from blue-uniformed

Tusaa'Ner, uncomfortable glances from eye-avoiding dark uniformed *Sakes*, and the many bearers and servants scurrying out of his path.

"Who in Kur is he?" Aren asked himself. *And what was that all about?*

"Aren!" Ganzer yelled from the hallway, startling him and causing him to jump. "Get moving. Time is short."

Chapter 9

Questions . . . Answers . . . Questions

The constant buzzing of biters in Aren's ears was as annoying as painful, with them drawing blood from him all night long. At some point in the night, he gave up at swatting them away and accepted the stinging from their needlelike mouths. The lower deck of the ship where he lay, dimly lit by sparsely placed lanterns, was crowded with others, all servants and bearers. The air here just didn't move like the wind to keep the flying biters away, nor did the candles made with scented purple or blue flowers. *They're making me suffer by purpose; I know it*, Aren grumbled to himself. *I will have them pay for this* . . . Tired from doing Ganzer's bidding into the late night, making him and his aide and the *Za* comfortable, opening their boxes and bags and placing their things about. "*There . . . No, put it there. No, over here . . . Oh, put that back where I first put it.*" Aren wanted to scream. Then, there were the *Za's* unwanted advances on him in her cabin that he escaped only by Ganzer's or the ship commander's unannounced but welcomed interruptions, for Aren's part. Only after all their comforts were taken care of did they send him away to these condemned conditions on the lower deck, the bottom deck with cargo and scurrying creatures he didn't know what to name. Snoring from many of the others surrounding him and the "tinkling" and smell of chamber pots completed Aren's misery throughout the night. *One would think at least the smell of everyone's urine and . . . yuck would keep the biters away.* Aren sarcastically made a joke of the horrible odors filling the air around him. At least the ship moved smoothly with little rocking in its passage on the Ner River. *I would welcome the tormenting symbols back to take my mind away from all of this*, Aren admitted to himself. Strangely, those spinning symbols that had been making him mad of mind for many months had not bothered him since he stepped foot on this ship.

Thumping footfalls followed by those scurrying from the deck above told Aren either something was happening needing more of the crew awake or the morning was about to rise. The door atop steep steps to the deck above opened. A wide-eyed, dark-haired, young Baraan woman, dressed in a clean gray tunic secured at her waist by a belt, instead of the likes of Aren's thick rope, descended halfway down the steps before stopping to cover her mouth and nose as she started gagging.

After a few moments of her in undecided confusion wanting to retreat up the steps, she held her place with a determined look to complete the task she was charged with. Looking around the cargo hold, the Baraan woman's eyes passed over Aren once, then a second time before fixing her gaze on him. She pointed at Aren with her slender arm that matched her slim body, then motioned for him to follow.

Aren felt both welcomed at getting to leave this miserable deck and cargos but groaned at what was to become soon a sparring match of questions filled with his half-answers. He made no rush at getting up and following, despite his mind screaming at him to run up the steps as fast as possible. He followed the attractive, young Baraan as casually as he could muster with stiff legs and back from the cramped conditions. Aren cursed his captors at keeping him bare of foot. Never finding the feel of stone or wood, or worse, dirt or mud, on his uncovered feet and in between his toes appealing, Aren grimaced at his steps of pure misery on the rough boards of the cargo hold and at the ladder steps. *They'll pay for this too.* The dark-haired woman quickly, though quietly, closed the door to the lower hold with a relieved expression as soon as Aren stepped onto the middeck. She silently motioned for him to follow her as she turned and nimbly climbed another set of steep steps to the deck above, her bare feet barely leaving a sound. Aren looked around the lantern-lit deck he stood on, seeking the ones making the thumping and scurrying footfalls. Many *Tusaa'Ner* guardsmen either still lay in their full blue-colored gear or dressed down to their white tunics and pants were sleeping all about more cargo containers, crates, boxes, and bags. Some of the ship's tunic-and-pants-dressed crew made sleeping places out of hammocks. About a handful of blankets were empty with signs of hastily being left behind. Aren noted everything as something might be useful in the day ahead. He then followed the youngling up the steps onto the main deck where she stood waiting impatiently.

The near moonless, predawn sky held a breeze that felt wonderful to Aren as he rose from below deck. He closed his eyes to enjoy the sensations—without the stink of the decks below—feeling the moment with the wind blowing through his matted hair as the scent of forest oaks, ferns, and river lilies with the hint of decay on the breeze filled his nose.

"Come . . . quickly," demanded the young Baraan, her voice ringing with a vague familiarity in Aren's ears. Suhd was her name, Aren recalled. She turned and scampered to the forecastle on the forward deck where Aren saw Lucufaar's prisoners led in the afternoon of yesterday while the ship was being loaded.

Aren took in the dark sky and the lights of heaven, in between the half-raised triangular sails, noting a hint of dawn in the high clouds. The morning ruckus of featherwings and the other wild's creatures waking hadn't yet started. Aren noted their ship was still on the Ner River, having set off from Farratum at midnight in light sail and with steering oars used mostly to keep the ship centered on the river waterway. On the deck lay bedding for most of the crew, now awake with long poles or oars in hand at the sides of the ship. Also, on deck, the lower-ranking, blue-uniformed *Tusaa'Ner* and some black-clothed *Sakes*, all either sleeping or trying to sleep. High on the steering and poop deck was the ship's commander accompanied by a group of sailors actively navigating the river with the use of yellow-and-blue-colored flags giving commands to the oarsmen and polemen at the side rails of the ship.

"This way!" Suhd demanded with urgency as she again motioned Aren to follow.

"May as well get this done," Aren spoke under his breath at the annoying yet dangerous game of words he was about to play.

Following the lithe Suhd, Aren cautiously approached the forecastle where two *Sake* jailers, in their black uniforms adorned with blue ribbons about their upper arms and at their belts, stood to either side of the now-open door. They behaved as the *Sakes* did when guarding a prison cell. Aren, now, was all too familiar with them. *Scum. Where is she leading me?* Aren asked himself.

He entered the forecastle filled with uncertainty and unease as the *Sakes* looked him over with a hint of disgust. The room was about six strides wide and squared with the stout forward most mast extending from the center of the almost two and a half stride tall planked ceiling and through the wood planked floor below. Stacked fold-up bunks mounted on the walls both left and right, as the room was designed to sleep almost twenty, but now looked a place for less than a handful. A folding desk and several unoccupied stools sat open next to the stride-wide mast. A small door on the far wall at the left-side corner of the room was closed and appeared locked with bar and padlock. Also, on the far wall of the room were Lucufaar's prisoners, three individuals that couldn't have been more different. The young, dark-haired Tellen's father. Dressed in the gray, knee-length tunic of a lawbreaker, the older Tellen sat awake leaning against the far wall taking in everything. Aren remembered him and his graying braided beard from the Farratum jails under the arena. Mithraam. He appeared in better health than when Aren last saw him a handful of full moons ago recovering from those almost-fatal wounds from the arena's raver. He also recalled how this Tellen missed very little, and that he had plans. Maybe plans within plans, but not with goals of escape. *A strange one, indeed.*

Asleep upright against the wall next to the Tellen sat a light brown-haired male Baraan that Aren knew not. Curled up on the floor aside the Baraan lay a sleeping white-haired female Evendiir. Aren took in her slender figure revealed by her gray knee-length tunic now at midthigh and then her face. *Not of my family line.* Aren felt relief for the she-Evendiir not being related and forcing upon him an obligation to help her situation. All were chained to each other and the wall. Aren purposely left the door behind him open so as not to be completely alone with the *Subar*.

A creaking of the door behind Aren sounded just before it slammed shut. Aren jumped at the sharp sounding of the door's metal locks. He struggled with himself to not whirl about to see *him*. Instead, Aren slowly turned his shoulders while slightly craning his head and neck to see behind him, see the *Subar*. Standing where he could not be seen with the door open, the Baraan now stood with his hands clasped in front of him, silently looking Aren over. Aren still felt unease at the *Subar's* manners. As usual, the Baraan stood patiently waiting for Aren to break the silence. Aren took several steps back toward the center of the room as he turned to face the *Subar*. There, the two stood silently looking at each other for a time.

"You're getting more confident, young Aren." The *Subar* spoke first. As Aren anticipated, the Baraan was dressed in his clean, dark gray pants and a sleeveless shirt that had wide shoulders. His dark, shoulder-length hair pulled back, as usual, ended in a short tail today. He only wore his belt sash of black and red to show his allegiance . . . but to whom, Aren still didn't know. Aren then realized he didn't even know the *Subar's* name even after a number of moon-cycles to the next *Roden'ar*. The *Subar* then, with his sharp, angular, facial features darky shadowed in the light of the room, threatened. "I'm not certain that is good for one's wellness."

"We've been at this for months . . ." Aren answered with the obvious as he fought down his fear of the Baraan. Aren continued, seeing if he could get the *Subar* to reveal his intentions with this session of questioning. "We greet in silence. I talk. You ask questions that are of importance to you. I answer. You dismiss me."

The *Subar* slowly strode to one of the stools aside the small desk, then sat. He then motioned to the other stool for Aren to join him before looking to the corner of the room where the youngling female had positioned herself. He gave a command in a firm, but not unkind manner. "Suhd, fetch us cups and drink."

Aren silently watched as Suhd scampered from the room, closing the door behind her. Without looking at the Baraan, Aren asked, "What's to be kept from her ears?"

"Bolder and more perceptive," the *Subar* put on a wry smile that Aren saw in his mind. "Who was that *Tusaa'Ner* talking to you yesterday on the tall deck?"

"I've not seen him before yesterday," Aren answered honestly. "What do you know of him?"

"*I* ask the questions, young Aren." The *Subar* corrected Aren with a hint of warning in his voice. "What words did he share with you?"

"Few," Aren answered in truth. He considered conveying his discussion with the *Subar,* almost as it happened with the *Tusaa'Ner*, but something cautioned him of doing so. "He told me not to think about leaping from the ship in search of my freedom. And that if I did somehow survive the snapjaws or worse, he'd stick me with arrows and spears, himself."

"Anything more?" the *Subar* asked with skeptical eyes as if he knew something Aren wasn't sharing.

"No, nothing," Aren flatly answered.

Silence fell on the room as the *Subar* appeared to contemplate Aren's words or his next question. "What of Ganzer's two new prisoners chained behind us? What are they that Ganzer and his aide think them valuable enough to bring along?"

Aren kept an unchanged face at the discovery of the *Subar's* true purpose for this questioning session. *He wants to know what Ganzer is about. And doesn't understand that Lucufaar is up to something unknown to his superior.* Aren decided to give up some half-truths. "Ganzer thinks they hold knowledge of use on this doomed journey."

"Doomed?" The word slipped from the *Subar's* lips. A rare event that Aren noticed by the flash of frustration on the Baraan's face. "What do you know of where this rabble is going?"

"To the Blood Lands," Aren answered without hesitation. His own fatalism added to the learned knowledge from his father of the place where they journeyed. It made Aren skeptical that anyone would survive the expedition. "And we're all going to have our *lights* sent into the *Darkness* there."

The *Subar* simply stared at Aren with a blank expression as silence fell over the room. A long moment passed. Nothing moved or breathed, except the mild creaks and moans of the ship. Even the prisoners were looking at the two while holding their breaths. Except for the Tellen with the gray-touched beard . . . who was smiling to himself.

"You didn't know of the destination we're set for?" Aren asked of the *Subar.*

"Yes," the *Subar* replied calmly with a face that matched his tone. "Though I did not know you held so much knowledge of the lands. Do tell."

Aren now felt uncomfortable at having to recall much of what his father taught him on the subject and that he would need to take care of his words and not give too much away. "The Blood Lands are the place of our legends. They speak of the mountainous lands being the home of the Ancients, our gods in the living flesh . . . where no others are permitted to dwell until their return again to rule over us—"

"Common knowledge to even younglings," the *Subar* interrupted with an impatience he seldom displayed. "If no others are allowed to dwell, then what is to take our *Lights*? Do not the Ancients dwell within the temples scattered across our lands here in Shuruppak and elsewhere?"

Aren felt embarrassed at never having thought of these questions. *Good questions*, he only admitted to himself while he sought answers in his head. He fell silent as he searched.

"Speak of something uncommon, even rare, that gives you confidence in our doom," the *Subar* calmly demanded as he broke in, interrupting Aren's thoughts.

"The Blood Lands, named so by King Darak in 2036, five hundred and more years ago, after those of Shuruppak ventured into the Twins Mountains seeking adventure and riches and power." Aren recited as well as his memory could recall, and his memory was near perfect. "They found blood and death both for the adventures and for Shuruppak in the days that followed as punishments for defying the Ancient decrees. The Twins Mountains, called the 'Bond Heaven-Earth,' the *Dur'Anki* by some and by others the *Roden'ar* for the ceremony surrounding it, by those long ago, are forbidden to mortals . . . so decreed by the Ancients before leaving humanity to this world. Their reasons unknown. The Ancients' decrees engraved in stone at the gates of Vaikuntaars, over two thousand years ago, lay the foundation of all laws. Dangerous mountains, north and west, protect that within the *Dur'Anki* from those seeking that of the Ancients. Guarding at the south, Patalas, the Forbidden Forest, stands, impenetrable, unpassable to all but the dead. The Sea of Mists, protector of all within, destroying by rock and tooth and whispers, those seeking the lands from the dangerous waters to the east. Only Anza, on the river Dukkha that feeds the river Ur, allows passage into the forbidden. In the lands looms *Tsae'Phon*, the 'Prison of No Return,' where ancient gods seeking the destruction of the earth and us remain chained within the Bottomless Pit. And Vaikuntaars, the 'City of the Dead' . . . The 'Throne of the Ancients,' where guarded lays hidden powers made unto humanity for the End of Days, when gods and mortals alike will be called upon to defend this world together. And the Watchers of the lands, 'Sentinels of the *Dur'Anki*,' Keepers of the Returning Light, in lands north and south, stand the *Sentii*, created by the gods, for the gods, to guard all that is of the Ancients."

"Uncommon," the *Subar* almost sounded complimentary. "I should have expected such from you. Your words speak from the ancient clay tablets, not the parchments read these days with lost meanings and dangerous softening of the decrees."

Aren hadn't expected the *Subar* to be so well read given their previous meetings and interchanges. Aren had considered him only a foe with a usefulness to him in gaining his freedom, a foe with unrelenting curiosity seeking the weaknesses of others and an almost brutal way of conducting manipulations.

"I see where your confidence in our doom is of source," the *Subar* concluded.

The door to the room creaked open, revealing the young female, Suhd, standing in the doorway with a large red bottle held against her lithe body in one hand and two unfilled cups by their handles in her other hand. Aren suddenly found himself thirsty as the *Subar* motioned for her to enter. Suhd quickly complied, handing a cup to the *Subar*, then filling it. Aren noticed the *Subar* now wore a red jeweled signet ring on his right hand. *That's new.* Aren noted too, Suhd seeming completely subservient to the Baraan sitting across from him. In truth, she appeared almost pleased to comply with his commands. Aren eagerly accepted the other cup from her, then allowed her to fill it before drinking almost half of it. Red berry ale that Aren found pleasant to both his nose and tongue. When Suhd didn't immediately retreat from them, the *Subar* gave her a quizzical glance that should have sent her to the corner she previously stood waiting to be called upon.

"The one named . . . Ganzeer, I think his name . . ." Suhd spoke nervously, as if overstepping her boundaries while choosing words carefully trying to omit some words spoken to her without changing the meaning of the message she was to present, "instructed me to ask you to allow him the . . . use of his *eresikim* when you are done . . . questioning him."

Facial expressions flashing from one to the next by the *Subar* told Aren that this wasn't a new conflict between this Baraan and the advisor to the *Za*. A dark mood settled on the *Subar* after a few moments of what Aren thought was him considering words to send back to the advisor.

Suddenly, the ship shuddered once, twice, then listed right a little, then righted itself as it moved up and down several times. Yells broke out from the crew all along the main deck as the ship moved strangely. As soon as the movements eased, the *Subar* rose to his feet with the help of the stout mast, then stiffly walked to the door looking out upon the deck. Aren also rose, unsteady with the deck under him again listing now to the left as the ship seemed to also rotate in the opposite direction. Aren regretted the drink as his stomach protested the unusual movements. *I need to see more than this room.* He bolted past the *Subar* and onto the main deck. Chaos! The crew ran this way and that grabbing ropes to long arms and sails while others fought the ship's motion with oars and long poles. A pale sky of the predawn allowed Aren to see beyond the ship's rails. They were no longer on the Ner River. It was retreating behind them, the mouth of which feeding into a massive waterway causing the merging waters to be unsettled. *By Kur . . . more than unsettled!* Aren corrected himself as the ship heaved upward at the bow, then plunged downward, leaving him suspended in the air until the deck rose again, slamming him painfully flat to the wood. "Oomph."

There, Aren lay on the deck until the ship settled to a more normal and kinder motion. When he rose, the *Subar* was gone from the doorway. He, like many of the guardsmen and many the crew, was at the rails looking at the extensive expanse of water in what appeared to be a massive river, unlike any river Aren ever saw. Joining the others at the rail, Aren gazed with awe at waters that almost stretched farther than the eye could see, to a far shore marches away.

"The Ur River," one of the crew spoke its name with reverence as several guardsmen beyond him gave tribute to the waters from their sickened stomachs. "Dangerous waters filled with *mu'luzuh* and *mu'usumgal*."

"Water-thieves and water-dragons . . ." Aren translated the ancient words and wished he hadn't. "We're doomed. Even before we get to the Blood Lands."

"We will not have our *Lights* taken from us on these waters," the *Subar* stated with a confidence Aren thought unfounded. He then pointed to a pair of small islands in the middle of the Ur. "It could be graver for you, young Aren. You should be sharing pain with your Tellen friend there, surviving the *eKur'Idagu,* and it's truly terrible snapjaws and water-dragons . . . the *mu'usumgals*."

Aren looked on at the small, rocky islands . . . the *Prison of the Water Land* or *River Land* or *Island,* depending on the translation of the old tongue. The closest of the two small islands had several stone towers flying the colors of Padusan, green on black, and Farratum, red on deep blue, acting as sentinels in the dawning light as the expedition's ships passed on swift currents and building winds from upriver. *From the west the wind blows, I think.* Aren drew on his book knowledge of maps trying to place himself on the Ur River, in his mind. Looking out over the watery expanse, Aren viewed a multitude of slippery black backs and fins both moderately sized and huge, breaching the surface of the waves, sometimes exposing their white underbellies as the water-dragons blew the wet from their nostrils before submerging back into the dark depths. *Dangerous currents in more than one manner,* he concluded.

He felt little for that Tellen, Rogaan, and his friend, Pax. They brought him near disaster months ago in the jails below the arena and in that cursed pit of death with ravers trying to kill him and everything else. *Dangerous times the recent past,* he reflected. Surprised he survived the arena, his thoughts turned to what was ahead, the unknown of the waters of the Ur and the Blood Lands. Aren felt certain the dangers ahead were greater and that they would all be *lightless* before this adventure's end. It was then, Aren wished for the Tellen to accompany them . . . or that Dark Ax, who saved them all in the arena. *Only to end up as prisoners and servants for the undeserving,* Aren added in his thoughts accompanying a suppressed flare of anger and indignation. *I'll have my revenge.*

"Curse you, you insufferable Evendiir!" The loud and unhappy voice of Ganzer startled Aren, causing him to bolt upright from his position, elbows having been leaning on the rails. The dark-haired advisor to the *Za* was looking out over the rail from the ship's rear elevated deck near the *Za's* cabins. "That's right. You. Come, immediately. Time is short."

Chapter 10

Loathed Reflections

Small, choppy waves formed on the waters of the Ur making unsettling the movements of the ship *Makara* as its crew feverishly worked triangular sails to capture the smallest winds, adding to their rowing oars speeding them eastward on the river for reasons still a mystery to Rogaan. Water-beast frequently breached the water's surface left and right of the ship taking in a breath before again submerging, their shadows under the waves Rogaan could make out faintly before disappearing into the unknown depths of the Ur's waters. Most of the creatures were of size dangerous to anyone unfortunate to be in the waters, and some frightfully massive, almost matching in length the ship itself. All were eerily dark in color and difficult to see in these waters as they passed by and under the ship, *mu'usumgals*, the water-dragons.

The *Makara* steered almost the center of the huge river, if the waters could be called that instead of a sea, with several marches distant to the shores on both sides of the vessel. Sleeker than the three ships Rogaan saw early at dawn, the *Makara* looked to be a built for swift transport of cargos and thieving from others given the ballista mounts about the decks and the hooking ropes coiled at even intervals along both sides of the vessel. Her five sails appeared to Rogaan like large, collapsible hand-fans, were now full open catching the wind with varying success. The main deck had in the middle of it an elevated platform that served as the roof of enclosed rooms. A single, stout mast rose, with sails full, from its center to a height of twelve strides. Aft, the decks rising two times were filled with crew dressed in all sorts of clothing and garb meant for easy movements. Two mast poles with lightly filled sails projected up from the stern decks, both to heights less than the main deck mast. On the highest stern deck stood the blue-hued-dressed commander of the *Makara*, Saalar, if Rogaan remembered his name correctly during the quick introductions when he came aboard. On each side of Saalar stood an Evendiir female who seemed to be giving the commander guidance on sail configurations and more concerning the operations of the *Makara*. Forward on the main deck, upwardly projected another mast pole with its sail deployed. It too was shorter than the center mast. Beyond that rose a single deck with yet another raised sail mast standing shorter still. At the forward most bow, standing on a platform half-surrounded by railing was the red-clad armored mystery . . . the tall stranger with a long spear in hand thrusting down into the waters at water-dragons swimming too close to the *Makara*. Two *Ursan*, in a style of eur armor unfamiliar to Rogaan, were armed with spears, swords, and bows guarding the red-clad spearman. The three were alone as the crew of the ship seemed to take paths avoiding them.

Rogaan's thoughts turned inward, troubled as he recalled that moment on the island, suffering terribly from the poison . . . when his body lost its battle, his *Light* separating from flesh and rising to the Beyond as if on a gentle wind . . . it . . . He was drawn upward. *Serenity* is how best Rogaan recalled the fleeting memory . . . that feeling, as the calling of the *Lights* invited his *Light* to join them. The material world mattering to him less and less with each passing moment. Then, that calm voice from nowhere . . . everywhere, saying something about . . . time, just before the silver cord went taunt. The intangible cord tethering him, his *Light*, to the below, holding him separated from both body and ascendance . . . the Beyond, adrift somewhere between worlds. Hands of the tall manifester then laid upon his body, first cleansing much of the poison-tainted blood, then taking hold the silver cord and drawing him, his *Light*, back into his repaired body. Rogaan held the dreamlike memory of the experience with confusion, profoundly confusing feelings. *What lays beyond?*

"Serious thoughts?" a familiar, deep, grumbling voice asked.

Surprised at not smelling his fellow Tellen approaching from the rear cabins, Rogaan sought a reason for it. *The wind must be in his favor.* Satisfied with the wind, Rogaan again returned to his thoughts focused on earlier happenings. He did not know what to make of it all on the island . . . mostly of this morning but was not about to share it. *They will think me mad.* His thoughts wondered all over, asking the same question . . . *Was I . . . lightless . . . truly dead?* His Tellen mentor would think him not right in the head if he confided in him. So, Rogaan chose to take their talking in other directions.

"What does this unnamed giant of a stranger have us entangled in?" Rogaan asked his question concerning their here and now as he turned to see Sugnis properly as Tellens do, eyes to eyes. The turn made too fast caused his head to swirl and his stomach to tell him not to do that again. Surprised, Rogaan took a double look at his island mentor. The Tellen no longer dressed in the rags of prison life. He comfortably donned a worn and stained suit of eur armor with equipment fitting of a *Kiuri'Ner* . . . crossbow, sword, and long knife. "What . . . What are you?"

The Tellen shrugged as he approached the deck rail giving a cautious look beyond to the waters. He then took a few steps back as he crossed his arms on his wide chest, all the while swallowing hard. "Let's just say . . . here to help. Too many ears about without knowing loyalties to speak freely."

Bewildered at almost everything about Sugnis, Rogaan stared at him with an open mouth before making to ask his mentor another question about the Tellen's background and his loyalties. A stern scowl from the Tellen left Rogaan with his mouth open and no questions asked.

"As to our unnamed '*friend*,'" Sugnis shifted to the question he would entertain. "Walk carefully. He is mightily dangerous and has his own motivations about you . . . plainly."

"You do not trust him?" Rogaan asked honestly.

"I trust him to use you as he needs." Sugnis tugged at his beard to straighten it to his liking. "His talk about needing your blood untainted of poison was a strange answer. One that foretells . . . possibly a not-so-happy future."

"Me . . . What does he want of me . . . or my blood?" Rogaan asked, frustrated with so many unknowns and so many questions.

"You, young Tellen, are going to have to ask that of him." Sugnis smiled in that manner Rogaan found irritating. Sugnis's unspoken words told him that he, Rogaan or Roga of the Blood An, would have to find the answers himself. "I appear to be little more than a stone in his boot and will not provoke him by speaking on your behalf. Though I will be keeping my eyes on you, along with the others."

Rogaan was unsatisfied with Sugnis's standoffish manner concerning their '*friend*.' Then, confusion hit him of Sugnis's choice of words. "What do you mean by 'eyes on me along with the others'?"

"You should put on the wears our '*friend*' provided you in our cabin . . . before asking anything of him." Sugnis blatantly avoided Rogaan's question, frustrating Rogaan even more. Sugnis took note of Rogaan's demeanor, then looked as if questioning himself while trying to make a decision. The Tellen then looked up to the skies and spoke. "You're not alone, Rogaan, son of Mithraam. Now, be off and put on your wears that are more fitting you than slave rags."

More confused than ever, Rogaan looked up into the morning sky. Clouds sparsely dotted the blue. He noted the sky strangely absent of leatherwings. *They are always above over waters.* No featherwings were aloft except for two creatures that he felt a familiarity with, having seen them periodically on the island, though never together. The two featherwings now flew high, confidently, as if unconcerned at being meals by things bigger. Both were a fair size for featherwings, predators

Rogaan thought, one brown and white in color, the other darkly black. Confusion taunted him, at how featherwings and eyes had anything to do with him not being alone. Rogaan made to ask more questions, but Sugnis's gaze warned him off. They just stared at each other for a very long moment before Rogaan broke eye contact. His body still feeling weak from the *returning* and the poison, Rogaan decided not to argue with Sugnis and disappointedly made way to the rear cabins. He did so almost without trudging his steps.

The door from the outside deck led to a narrow hallway only a bit wider than his shoulders. The hallway had a low ceiling . . . just a couple of hands above Rogaan's head, giving him a sense of being closed in upon. Sugnis, Pax, and Rogaan shared a single cabin, the first door on the left. The cabin door was even narrower than the hallway, forcing Rogaan to turn sideways to enter while cursing to himself at his uncomfortable feelings at such closed in quarters. A musty odor struck him upon entering the barely three-by-four strides-sized space. Two sets of bunk beds dominated the space, one set on each wall left and right, and built-in chests of drawers as tall as himself at the end of each bunk set. A single square window with a metal-hinged bezel around glass opposite the door was open, allowing some air in improving the smell of the cabin. Sugnis assigned him the bottom right bunk and Pax the upper. As to the *Ursan* who boarded the ship with them, Rogaan had not seen him since, leaving the bunk above Sugnis's "hole" empty. His mentor claimed the bottom left bunk as his own but it clearly did not appear comfortable with the *openness* of the cabin as a blanket already hung from the top bunk covering the bottom making a cave like hole. Rogaan smiled at Sugnis's consistency. *My assigned mentor . . . evidently. But, assigned by whom and why?*

A pile of a mess was Pax's bunk. Rogaan recognized his friend's bunched-up island tunic and other clothes. They did look like rags, he admitted. A neat bundle of clothes and equipment lay on his own bunk. He recognized most of it . . . his clothes from home, huntsman armor, his backpack, and the flint-edged long knife from the Brigum Hunt. Rogaan smiled at the familiar items and for a moment forgot his situation. *How did he find all of this?* Next to his clothes and backpack, a stout bow of composited woods and two quivers of flint-tipped arrows lay. *Not my shunir'ra, but a good-feeling bow.*

As Rogaan changed into his old clothes and equipment, he thought of the one piece that was missing . . . his *shunir'ra*, his masterwork bow. The one item showing all he was no longer a simple apprentice youngling, but an adult to clan and family . . . in Tellen society, that is. *Lost, for all I know.* Regret and embarrassment filled Rogaan at that thought and anger at himself for putting himself into the situation needing to give his blue metal bow to the Tellen *Sharur*. *Where is it now . . . in the Tellen's hands, or worse, in the hands of Farratum or Kardul?* His anger turned to remorse as it reminded him of his *Zagdu-i-Kuzu*, his Tellen coming of age ceremony and celebration. The celebration was to be held after he returned from the hunt. A celebration that never was. *The return to Brigum, only to be hunted by the Farratum Tusaa'Ner and the Band . . . and more locals.* Rogaan relived the mess of a situation in his mind a few moments before pushing the painful memories away. Pax's and his escape from Brigum came at a great cost . . . Rogaan's *War Sworn* uncle, brother to his mother, killed protecting him. Recalling that memory, Rogaan fell into despair. *How am I ever to explain this to Mother?* He did not even know her whereabouts since his fleeing Brigum but suspected . . . hoped . . . she was safe on the estate of House Isin. *I hope with protections her family name can give.* More despair filled him with thoughts of his father and friends. Rogaan feared little could stop the *Zas* of Farratum from their nefarious goals. Their reach seemed unlimited. And then there were others; Akaal the mysterious cutthroat in the Valley of the Claw, Kardul and his traitorous followers, the Dark Ax, dark robes, the *Zas* and their factions, the cutthroats . . . *Saggis'* of the Keeper of the Ways, these newly revealed "eyes" mentioned by Sugnis, and now this powerful and deadly *"friend."* Rogaan felt small and lost in it all, being carried on winds blown by others with their schemes and doings driving those winds. Feeling overwhelmed, he realized how much he missed his best friend.

Usually in such times, Pax would do strange or silly things to improve his mood in saying something stupid or utterly nonsensical before they would go off getting into more trouble. Rogaan smiled at those memories, then fell into another saddened frown. Denied his best friend because of the tragedies in their travels, Rogaan felt more regrets and fears he did not know how to fix. Both of Pax's parents now *lightless* in the maws of the ravers . . . and Pax's sister, Suhd . . . Her face brought a smile to Rogaan, a captive . . . a slave proclaimed by Farratum law. Rogaan's chest and heart tightened with that image in his mind of Suhd being *handled* by others in her servitude. The pain of that unwanted image angered him. *How do I get this out of my head?* But, even those images at times seemed kind compared to the memory of the look in his best friend's face each time he and Pax meet eyes. *Pax blames me for the loss of his family, both the death of his parents and enslavement of Suhd by the Zas.* Rogaan felt the pain of it all and agreed with Pax. *It is my fault.*

Rogaan stood in his cabin, sick in body with the last of the poison he still suffered and in his despairing heart. He felt helpless to fix, if even possible, everything he had made a mess of. His frustration rose to a boil as he did not even know where to start. *The world appears against me and filled with those having designs on me as well as others. Tyrants, small and big, seem to have run of the lands and control my family, my friends.* Rogaan's despair gripped him. Then, the words of his father came to him from when they sat together in Farratum's jail. "Tyrants reign when no challenge stands in check to the gathering of their power and authority over people." *Father told me I am seen as a danger to those in power and authority, the ones who see the people of these lands needing their rule . . . who covet authority and work influences over the masses in soft steps to keep rebellion from rising, as the Zas and their devotees enslave the people through new laws and new rules enforcing those laws . . . small step by small step.* A chill rippled up Rogaan's spine. *I do not see how I can make a difference against this beast when those like the Dark Ax have not won the day. How can I be a threat?*

Rogaan then wondered at his father's refusal to be freed from the Farratum jails. Im'Kas offered to take them away, almost pleaded with his father, several times. Yet, Father was as solid as a stone . . . and as unmovable, in seeing through their plan. *Their plan? Who's plan?* He realized, maybe for the first time, that they all . . . especially Pax's family, could have been broken free and none of the dark things would have happened . . . at least to them. *Why? Why? Why?* Rogaan asked himself. *Was it Father's attempt to educate me or his sense of duty to the allegiance they hinted about or something more?* Rogaan had not seriously contemplated these things for some moons as his time and attentions were occupied surviving the Farratum jail and prison isle.

Memories flashed in his mind of the Farratum underworld, its jails filled with those not having broken laws concerning the interactions between citizens, but because they opposed, in some way, the *Zas* and their secretive maneuverings gathered absolute power over their citizens. Their power solidified solidly in the complicit actions of those administrating for them, those in the *Tusaa'Ner* . . . the *Sakes* following their orders blindly, and those serving the *Gals* with quibbling truths. Visions of the crowds, the masses, in the streets and seated in the arena, seeming to give more and more authority to the *Zas* for stipends of food and rights they already have and for the promise of refuge from both threats beyond the walls and the worries of living. All this, Rogaan saw and experienced in the short time he was held in Farratum. *They . . . The people have become enslaved and do not even realize it with the distractions the makers and keepers of the laws provide.* Worse, Rogaan disbelievingly watched the people increasing demand as their *right* the daily stipends and the removal from the streets . . . the public square, those who disagree with them, those who called out the twisting of common meanings to justify the stipends. The most belligerent to the challengers of this community decay, removed . . . incarcerated, finding themselves with Rogaan in the jail cells and in the arena or banished to *eKur'Idagu*, the prison isle . . . that vile rock of a place. With a heavy outbreath, Rogaan recognized the world was little as he thought it was.

Rogaan recalled more of his father's words. They made better sense to him now, after his experiences. *Is this what Father was trying to teach me? No. It is more than that. He and their plans are working to change what has become. Fight the growing tyranny.* Then, the foreboding words of Im'Kas rang like a gong in his head. "Your immediate days will likely be unpleasant, but longer days to come will try you harsher." *He spoke as if he saw my future.* That frightened him . . . "harsher days to come." Rogaan stood filled with uncertainty and fearful pains of not knowing what he could or even should do with conflicting thoughts of retreating to a safe place, *if one can be found*, or to stand against the wrongs. *Am I to watch the world and my family and friends suffer while I do nothing? Why am I a threat to those . . . How?*

A new anger rose within Rogaan burning on a stoked and growing fire of self-loathing. *Am I to wallow in self-pity or fear in some imagined safe place?* He found vile what he saw of himself in his thoughts . . . a truth filled reflection that left him immobilized between doing safe and doing what he could to protect those that could not fight the tyrants. *Maybe I cannot make a difference, but then, maybe I can. I do not know if I can do anything for the masses, but I must embrace the unpleasantness of the hasher days to come, if Father and Suhd are to be freed.*

Chapter 11

Vassal

Stepping out onto the ship's deck near his cabin, Rogaan did so with a growing sense of purpose . . . live up to his father's and his own longings and beliefs to see his father and Suhd free. *In short, do what he could to make things right.* Rogaan reminded himself of his youngling hero desires to become a *Kiuri'Ner*, a Protector of Paths. It would have been a life filled with dangers and strife, maybe as is his present. The words of Im'Kas, most famed of the *Kiuri'Ner*, reverberated in his head, ". . . sometimes requiring all of that we have . . . to whom much is given, much will be required." *I understand better the meaning of what he spoke, though, I am hoping his words for me are not completely prophetic. What will be required of me to see my family and friends free?*

Looking forward out across the main deck and its multiple masts and raised folding triangular sails, Rogaan spotted *him* . . . the one who he believed could help him best. The *Makara* pitched roughly for a few moments, then settled. The movement unsettled Rogaan's innards, but he fought back the nausea successfully. *Is it the motion or still the poison?* A groan to Rogaan's right found Sugnis leaning over the ship's rail in an undignified manner. His skin coloring terribly off . . . ashen.

"He be doin' dat since ya go ta da cabin," the familiar voice came from above.

Looking about, Rogaan found his once-best friend sitting four strides up lounging in the rope rigging of the nearest mast, as if in an upright hammock. Pax wore a smile on his face until their eyes met. Then, that familiar scowl of the jails and island returned. It hurt Rogaan's heart, but he was determined not to let it keep him from making things right. He decided to keep their talk to matters present.

"It is the Tellen in him," Rogaan explained as he fought back unsettling feelings. "We feel the movement of the earthen ground, rocks, and all other things, and the ship's motion . . . Its creaking is too much for Tellen perceptions, this motion making his innards unsettled."

"Why be it different for ya?" Pax asked honestly.

"I do feel the movements and creaking and footsteps of others as Sugnis does,"

Rogaan answered. "I guess it is the Baraan in me that keeps me from illness and sicking-up."

A loud upheaval at the deck rail where Sugnis suffered made him question himself. He felt sorry for his mentor, though he had to admit the image of Sugnis leaning over the rail brought on a chuckle. The Tellen seemed as solid as the stones he slept on, but now this, sickened by waters. Suppressing a smile, Rogaan started off with the composite bow in hand for the front of the ship. He did so without looking back at Pax and his scowl. Down ladderlike steps to the main deck Rogaan went, dodging baggy-pant, bare-footed sailors adjusting ropes and riggings of the raised sails, hoping to get the most of the wind. Working his way forward on the left side of the main deck to avoid a busy crew working ropes and other things, he spied over the rails moderately sized and large black-backed water-dragons swimming just below the surface of the waves. He remained surprised at how they were so difficult to see in these dark waters. One of the beasts passing from bow to stern trailed what looked to be blood from its head or neck.

"Pardi me," a well-dressed, dark-haired sailor wearing the blues of one of those in command made to get Rogaan's attention as he partially blocked the way up ladder-steps to the forward most deck and the railed platform Rogaan sought. Surprised, Rogaan stopped just short of knocking him over before giving the scruffy Baraan sailor a simple questioning look with raised eyebrows. Without pause, the sailor continued addressing him. "I have me a question for ya, if ya entertain it."

"Yes?" Rogaan acknowledged the sailor with a guarded tone.

"Dat young one in da rigs," the Baraan, slightly shorter than Rogaan, pointed toward Pax relaxing in the riggings. "Are ya knowin' him?"

"Yes," Rogaan answered cautiously.

"He lookin' familiar ta me." The sailor continued with his questions. "What be his name?"

"Pax." Rogaan did not know where this was leading and gave the sailor a suspicious look. Ignoring Rogaan, the sailor stared at Pax for a short time before returning Rogaan's gaze.

"His fader . . ." the sailor asked, looking at Pax while he did, "was he about as tall as me with dark hair? Did he talk like me . . . as da River Folk?"

Rogaan still was not certain where the questions were taking them, but the sailor described Pax's father and very possibly knew him. "Yes."

"Daugu?" the Baraan sailor asked with hopeful eyes.

"Why the questions?" Rogaan decided it best to seek the sailor's intent in case he meant harm to Pax.

B. A. VONSIK

"I be in Daugu's debt," the sailor answered with an honest and pride-filled, clean-shaven face. "Daugu be me pally . . . and be a good one at dat. He be well known among da River Folk before he disappear."

Rogaan simply stared at the sailor while allowing this revelation to sink in. *That explains much.* As the stare between them lengthened, Rogaan felt increasingly uncomfortable and answered. "Yes, Daugu was the name of Pax's father. You described him well enough."

"Den ya have ya hands filled bein' dis one's pally," the sailor smiled while keeping his gaze fixed on Pax lounging in the ropes. "Moody as a snapper.

Rogaan nodded in agreement, not certain what a *"snapper"* was, but he guessed it something like a river shellback that would take a finger or tuck up inside its shell . . . though you never knew which before you bothered it. Or it could be a snapjaw. They often seemed moody too. Regardless, Pax took after his father in that way . . . moody and at times to a fault. *Finally, someone who understands.* Certain this sailor knew Pax's father, and well, Rogaan relaxed his guard a bit. *Pax's father a sailor . . . River Folk. Who could have known?* Rogaan felt as if a large puzzle piece fell into place concerning why Pax was . . . Pax.

"Can ya tell me of Daugu?" the sailor asked of Rogaan. Immediately, Rogaan felt alarmed and fearful of answering. The scruffy Baraan put on a questioning face when noticing Rogaan's change in demeanor. "Where be his dock?"

Rogaan did not understand the meaning of *"his dock"* at first. Then came a thought that the sailor's *"dock"* meant *"home"* or *"place"* for someone living on the land. Feeling accomplished for figuring out the translation made Rogaan a bit proud of himself, though the added pride did not counterbalance his sense of dread telling him of the circumstances of his friend's . . . "pally's" *Light* being darkened. Sadness welled up within Rogaan, causing his chest to tighten. *I cannot do anything about the past*, he scolded himself.

"*Light* was taken from his father and mother by ravers." With a sorrow-filled voice, Rogaan informed the sailor of his pally's death. Rogaan's thoughts went to the many and growing questions he now had of his experience on the prison island and with the Great Beyond. *Are they living in the Beyond?* Rogaan hoped and felt the answer was yes. "Pax and his sister, Suhd, now walk without them."

"Lightless . . . both of 'em?" The sailor stared at Rogaan with a pain-filled face of disbelief. "Daugu left da river for her. Ta keep da feud from her and younglin's day hoped ta have. Ravers? How?"

Rogaan feared revealing too much of the deadly games played by Farratum to this sailor who he just met, telling him of his *lightless* pally at the hands of the

Farratum *Zas*. Memory of the arena . . . of them, Pax's parents, in their last breaths suffering in the jaws of the ravers, made a tightness deep in Rogaan's chest. *I cannot imagine the pain Pax . . . and Suhd must feel. So much worse for Pax, for them.* Rogaan's heart sank low with sorrow. *How do I answer?*

"Son of Mithraam!" A call from somewhere above surprised Rogaan and also the sailor. The voice was familiar, but not one Rogaan considered a comfort. Anxious over more talk with this sailor, Rogaan found an escape by quickly answering his new "*friend*."

"I am here."

"Come forward and join me." He called to Rogaan with a confident and commanding manner.

"I must go." Rogaan offered the excuse to the sailor, relieved at not having to answer more of his questions. Rogaan mounted the ladder to the forward deck and climbed.

"Our talk of Daugu . . . I wish ta have," the sailor called after Rogaan, now halfway up the ladder. "Keep ya head and care of tongue, son of Mithraam."

Rogaan climbed the stepladder with a swirling mix of relief, confusion, and unease. *Keep my head and watch my tongue?* Cautiously popping his head over the top rung revealed to him the forward elevated deck much as he saw it afar with three folks occupying it. Two tan-skinned warriors he knew not of with the third, the red-clad armored *friend* stood a head taller than the others, all carrying spears and swords. The *friend* had his attention on the waters off the forward sides of the *Makara*, poking at unseen things with a long spear while the other two stood near watching every move Rogaan made. What Rogaan thought them at far glance—Baraan *Ursans*—the two warriors watching him were anything but *Ursan* mercenaries or of the Baraan race. The pair of steely-eyed warriors wore stout green-gray eur armor of worked tanniyn hide with overlapping layers on shoulders, thighs, back, and chest. The breast and back guards at the sides were laced together in a crisscrossing pattern of stout hide cords, beautifully done and unlike any Rogaan had seen. Each wore similarly subdued hued high-laced feathered sandals with layered shin and foot guards as well as matching forearm guards. Their heads and long yellow-white hair were uncovered except for the brown-black hide headbands each wore with colorful feathers attached hanging down to the nap of their necks. At their sides, each had attached to their belts sheathed metal long knives and worked hide green-gray caps with protective cheek flaps. In their hands, each wielded a spear and a drawn sword that looked more like an ax of some kind. Their heads were a little long of skull with faces clean-shaven, thin, penetrating, radiant blue eyes making Rogaan confused at how much Baraan they were and how much of something else.

Climbing onto the forward deck, Rogaan felt uncertain what to do. The *friend* had called for him, but the two staring at him seemed to have other ideas.

"Greetings . . ." Rogaan tried to get a response out of the two. *Nothing.* They did not blink as they kept their unsettling stares on him. Assuming . . . Hoping the two warriors would not confront him, Rogaan guardedly stepped from the ladder and in the direction of the *friend*. Both the warriors moved with blinding speed to either side of him yet positioned to block his way forward while crossing their ax-swords with a ringing in front of his chest. Surprised at their aggression and quickness, Rogaan stepped back raising his bow into a guarding position. Neither of their expressions gave away any hints of malice, fear, or anything useful to Rogaan.

"Test him," commanded the *friend* without taking his eyes from the waters.

Both warriors shifted their weight forward before moving again with blinding speed. Rogaan first felt the flat of the ax-sword from the warrior to his left strike him on his left thigh, then saw the warrior to his right jabbing to his face with the pommel of his ax-sword. Moving too quickly for him to dodge, the jab hit him solidly in the mouth, knocking Rogaan on his backside, his bow clattering to the deck off to his left. Both strikes hurt painfully, the jab drawing blood from his lips. Anger swelled within Rogaan . . . anger fed by embarrassment. The pair of warriors stepped back, then settled into casual on-guard stances. *Test me?* Rogaan wanted to ask what this was all about but then thought better of it. *Test me.*

"All right . . ." Rogaan spoke loud enough for the three of them to hear as he rose to his feet. Assessing his opponents as Sugnis taught him, Rogaan concluded the warrior on his left was dominant by the way the other warrior kept his position relative to his companion. Rogaan decided to act against the left warrior, first, then against the one on his right. He wanted to make this quick, disabling them, so he could talk to this *friend* to find out why he was here and what need there was for his blood. Rogaan breathed in . . . out . . . in . . . out, calming himself, focusing his thoughts and emotions so to call forth that thing he did to make the world slow. *Nothing.* Frustrated, Rogaan tried again to call forth the quickness. *Nothing.* Looking at the warriors who now looked at him with curious eyes, Rogaan felt a swell of concern. He needed to stall them, give himself more time to call *it* forth. So, with a raised hand and index finger he made to make light conversation, "Just a moment . . ."

Before he saw it coming, Rogaan felt the sandaled foot of the dominant warrior on his chest knocking him backward several steps onto the side railing of the ship before he stopped his momentum. Pain shot through his chest and back from the strike. Looking up . . . *Whack!* A fist across his jaw sent his head violently, painfully to the right, an agonizing punch to his right side threatened to take his air, a stinging kick to his right shin, a blow to his left arm as he tried to shield himself from the barrage of punches and kicks . . . blow after blow. Rogaan felt more pain and a growing fear that they would take his *Light*. Staggering blow after staggering blow landed all over his body making him disoriented . . . weakened. He felt his innards go ill from the remnants of the poison. Then, a blow to the side of his head hurt intensely as it drew blood. His head rang like a bell. Rogaan staggered on his feet. Fear swelled within him. *Am I to die here? Testing?* He caught movement on his left just before another stinging punch landed on his jaw. He saw the warrior to his right clearly moving as if almost as fast as normal . . . slower than just moments before. Rogaan blocked the warrior's left hook with his right forearm, then hit him with a fear-fired-by-anger, left-handed pile-driving punch to his face. Rogaan sent the warrior into an upending summersault with him landing on the deck, unmoving. Felt footfalls on the wood planks behind him, Rogaan ducked a swinging punch. Then, with a twist of his hips, rotating left, Rogaan punched with his full body at gut level where he thought the footfalls would put his target. His fist hit the midsection of the dominant warrior solidly, doubling him over. Filled with anger, Rogaan struck the warrior with a left uppercut straightening him up, now leaving him standing though swaying with eyes unfocused. Angry and without mercy, Rogaan drove his right fist into the face of the defenseless warrior. His fist painfully striking an immoveable open hand that just appeared in his path before he hit its intended target. The shock of the impact numbed Rogaan's arm to his shoulder.

"Enough!" came the even-toned command from the red-clad warrior. A big warrior a full head taller than Rogaan towered over them.

As the hairs on Rogaan's nape and arms bristled and the hair on his head itched almost painfully, he looked astonishingly at his fist in the *friend's* grasp. An eerie, multicolored vapor slithered around both their hands as Rogaan's arm tingled and started shaking. He jerked his hand back before he realized he desired it so. His skin felt as if biters crawled all over just before he shook uncontrollably head to toe. He knew it was only agonizing moments, the shaking, but it felt longer. With a willful effort, Rogaan forced the pain into the back of his mind making it endurable.

"That Tellen instructed you in open-hand better than expected," the red-clad, chiseled-faced warrior stated. "You can also endure punishment."

"What? Why?" Confused and fighting through the fog of pain, Rogaan barely managed the simple words from his mouth.

"What?"The red-clad *friend* asked rhetorically. "You're of the Blood!"

"I do not understand." Still confused about what was happening and in pain, Rogaan spoke with his teeth just short of grinding them to their roots.

"Your blood is of the Brothers."The chiseled faced, short, yellow-bearded *friend* stated as if his words should be enough of an answer. The big Baraan . . . *No, this one is something else . . . not quite a Baraan, but akin* . . . regarded Rogaan with his tilted, radiant green eyes for a few moments before glancing at his companions.

Near, the swaying warrior appeared to have recovered and swayed no longer. His brown face looked composed as his blue eyes regarded Rogaan with curiosity, lacking any hint of anger. It was then, Rogaan realized he felt anger at them for the beating he received. The warrior took up a guarding stance, feet spread shoulder-width apart, hands on sheathed weapons, his spear now laying on the deck. He stood stolid after backing a few steps away from Rogaan at a hand gesture from the red-clad *friend*.

"Roga of the Blood An . . ."the red-clad warrior turned away before taking up again his position next to the forward railing where his long spear lay across the rail, his back to Rogaan. "Ancient is the bloodline of your father . . . if he is your father. Mithra of the Clan Am. I don't recall giving the Bloodsign to that line. Is he not, Mithra of the Clan An . . . a chosen bloodline of the Turil Tellens?"

"Those are his relatives . . . from Turil . . . They are of the Clan An." Pains melted away as Rogaan offered memories of his cousins visiting Father in Brigum some years ago. What they were about, Rogaan never understood, but visit they did . . . with much revelry. Rogaan briefly spoke of the closeness his cousins had for each other and his father, in the hopes to convince this *friend* that Mithraam was indeed his father.

"The clans work not in that manner, youngling," the red-clad warrior offered with a stern tone that carried in it . . . irritation. "And neither does the Bloodsign blessed upon the Clan An. To be your father, he must be of the Clan An. Or you have another father."

"I have only known him as Mithraam . . . *my father*," Rogaan replied.

"Interrupt me no more, youngling," the red-clad warrior reprimanded. "My thoughts are becoming clear. Yes. Much is unknown still; yet, I can use this new knowledge."

Rogaan felt indignant at being reprimanded when there was no call for it. And his simmering anger at the others for making on him so many bruises grew with every painful movement. The warrior lying on the deck stirred. *Who are they? What do they want of me?* Rogaan wanted the guessing to stop and to have answers.

"My gratitude for you saving me from the island . . ." Rogaan offered words for his and Pax's and Sugnis's rescue as a gesture of his appreciation before demanding answer. "I have questions for you."

"Speak not in that manner to your—"The dominant warrior standing in his green-gray eur armor lashed out in an indigent tone at Rogaan before being cut off by the red-clad warrior's gleaming metallic left arm and open hand raised signaling "silence." All did fall silent for an awkward moment. Questions burned within Rogaan, but the body language of the *friend* and the attitude of his companion gave him pause in pressing further. In the silence, the second warrior companion lying on the deck staggered to his feet before taking up a guarding stance with spear pointing tall. His brown face just as neutral as his companion's, but with a hint of anger peeking through.

"I accept his ignorance." The red-clad warrior spoke not to Rogaan but to his companions. "And his impudence this time. He's of the *confused* in this land, not knowing his place."

The *confused?* Rogaan felt more so now than ever. *What is this one babbling about?* Rogaan just wanted to know what was going on with so many seemingly pulling his strings as masters would their puppets. His questions . . . he felt he must ask. Rogaan started off in a demanding tone before he decided to tread more carefully and softened it. "Why am I here?"

"The only question with significance," the *friend* spoke still with his back to Rogaan but offered no further answers.

"Why do you need my . . . blood?" Rogaan asked more carefully, fearful of what the answer might be.

"That is . . . complicated," the red-clad warrior stated in an even tone, as if contemplating something as he answered. An awkward silence fell between them as the red-clad warrior raised his long spear to his shoulder height, poised to strike at something below.

"I want to understand . . . Why did you save me?" Rogaan pressed.

"Which occasion?" the *friend* asked what seemed like an honest question.

Rogaan was caught off guard by it. Which one does he ask about? The Brigum Hunt . . . in the Valley of the Claw, or on his return to Brigum near Coiner's Quarter, or in the streets of Brigum when he and Pax were hopelessly outnumbered by Kantus and his gang and the Brigum *Tusaa'Ner*, or on the prison isle . . . the *ekur'Idagu*, or from the Beyond this morning? *Were there other times?* Rogaan started wondering.

"You have been keeping me from the consequences of those seeking me harm," Rogaan admitted to himself and openly, unsettling his sense of pride as he spoke the words.

"Many interests are involved," the red-clad warrior informed. "Some wish you dead and no longer a threat. Some want you as theirs to use. Surprisingly, you bested much of what they sent after you. I aided when there was need."

"Threat? Me?" Rogaan repeated, then turned his surprise into a question.

"To all held important by them," the red-clad warrior answered, his armor making dull, almost metallic sounds when his arm guards touched as he speared something in the waters below. He appeared in thought before speaking again. "You and the others . . . all keys."

"The prison isle . . . the Beyond?" Rogaan answered the *'friends'* previous question . . . which one, after thinking about all the *occasions*. "I did fall. I was being taken . . . to the Beyond. You did pull me back to . . . here."

"Why," the red-clad *friend* stated as if answering a question, cutting off more of Rogaan's words. He poked at something again, below in the water with his long spear. "Your blood and the blood of the others are the keys needed to unseal my kingdom. A great irony, my kin made entering Vaikuntaars impossible without your kind working together, with me, as if that would make right the earth."

"How can this be?" Rogaan asked with much surprise, even a degree of shock. He felt confused before. Now, Rogaan felt lost. Vaikuntaars . . . The forbidden City of the Dead, in the Blood Lands, was how his father described it when teaching ancient history. "How can my blood be a key to open . . . the City of the Dead."

"Yes, the City of the Dead . . ." the *friend* sounded amused. "Not of the *Dead*, but of the *Self-banished*. And a vault protecting . . . *items* of power that can be used against this world. I must secure it before *he* does."

"I still do not understand how my blood is special or important," Rogaan said with a bit of frustration and much denial.

"Yours and the blood of other bloodlines must be freshly spilt upon the altar before the Citadel of Vaikuntaars to unlock its seals." The red-clad warrior struck hard at something in the water below and out of sight from Rogaan's vantage spot. "Only then can Vaikuntaars' portal be opened, and the citadel be restored to its former glory."

Rogaan did not like the sound of "spilt blood" and "altars" and the blood being his. He quickly decided he wanted nothing of this, as it would mean his death. Shivers shot up and down his back. *How do I decline this "offer" to be used in such a manner?* Then, it struck him . . . Who was "*he*" that this "*friend*" spoke of? And despite Rogaan fearing the answer, he just needed to know for certain who this *friend* is. "Who is this '*he*' you speak of? And who are *you* that I would sacrifice my life for?"

His long spear raised to again strike at the unseen below, the red-clad warrior stood motionless as if surprised by the boldness of Rogaan and his questions. The tall, almost giant, warrior appeared in contemplation, maybe of how much to reveal or whether to kill this young Tellen outright. Rogaan felt certain he was no match for this one, but it appeared he was needed . . . at least his blood, and maybe that was worth a bargain for his father and Suhd. Maybe. Long moments passed. The two companions behind Rogaan stirred with shifting feet and whispers. Rogaan felt he had to show boldness and courage if he was to get answers and, hopefully, a bargain. He held his attention on the red-clad warrior, hoping his guardian companions would not strike him down from behind. The ship shuddered as if something large struck it just under the bow. The red-clad warrior looked surprised and frustrated at not noticing whatever it was and for not having speared it. Then just as quickly, he set his long spear back into the holds on the railing, appearing not to give it a thought.

"'*He*' is the scourge of this world." The warrior stood tall speaking with deference, but also with much hatred and a hint of trepidation. "A mortal Baraan who stole the drink and the food forbidden, consuming them . . . somehow surviving the transformation which should not have been. Then, learning the manifestations of the *stones* after stealing from the *Dingiir* their most sacred of Agnis. The One who grew in strength in the manifesting arts learning the forbidden from Enurta and his allies. Those traitorous ones aiding Qingu and his army of Nammu's wicked creations. The One who reaped much destruction on the old world in the *Shiarush War* . . . Dragon War, taking the *Light* from mortals and *Dingiir* alike. The One who made possible the destruction of the Celestial Halls. The One who became *Namerium-I-Emuku*, Sworn to Power, and of the *Marked*. Enurta's most powerful and deadly priests. The cause giving rise to the creation of the *Sentii*, the supreme warriors of the *Dingiir*, and the *Kabiri*, mortal manifesters of the Agni in the divine service of the *Dingiir*. The One spurring reason for the creation of the *Ra'Sakti*, the most powerful devices ever conceived for use by mortal hands. The One who dared challenge the *Dingiir* . . . the Father of the *Dingiir*, Ea, wounding the father. The One who escaped the grasp of the *Dingiir* in the final days of the war. The One who outshined all others of the *Marked* in power and desires for conquest. He is Luntanus Alum, the deadliest of the *Shunned*."

Dingiir . . . Ancients . . . the Sentii . . . the Marked . . . Shunned. Rogaan felt his legs weaken and his body shake. Fearing he could not keep upright, he dropped to a knee trying to steady himself and take a breath. The red-clad warrior turned facing Rogaan, and as he did, his armor glowed red along lines connecting glowing symbols of vertically entwined serpents about a staff on his breast plates. Rogaan's nape and arm hairs bristled. The serpent symbols intensely glowed before simmering down such that Rogaan did not need to shield his eyes to look upon him. *Who is he? Do I dare bargain with him?*

"Charged by the Ancients, I am to end this affliction on earth . . ." The glowing red warrior stood tall and commanding as his companions . . . His guardian servants behind Rogaan dropped to a knee. His voice now deeper and reverberating all about the ship, ". . . and vow to destroy this *Shunned* and all who aid him. I am *Vassal* to Vaikuntaars, Gatekeeper to the Realms of Heaven."

Chapter 12

Makara

D ark eastern skies and golden haloed clouds to the west told all that dusk was
almost upon them. Despite his great strides to the contrary, Rogaan still felt
anxious about the darkness and fretted about this cycle of night to come. Not only
would the moon be near renewal of another twenty-eight-day cycle providing little
illumination through the night, but the *Makara* would be close enough to battle
the three heavily armed ships of the Farratum forces . . . and evidently, one of the
fabled *Shunned*. So, Rogaan understood from the *Vassal*, before being dismissed by
him until the early morning. Rogaan now sat on a small barrel on the open aft
deck closest the entrance to his cabin. Next to him, sitting on another small ale
barrel, was Sugnis, now with better coloring in his face and in a better mood.
Having adjusted his sitting position relative to Sugnis to ensure the deck breeze
carried his mentor's odiferous aromas away from him, Rogaan spied about for his
troubled friend. On the deck above he found him, where Pax leaned over wood
railing talking with that dark-haired, blue-clothed sailor who claimed to know
Pax's father. They appeared to be getting along quite well. As jealous as that made
Rogaan feel, he felt better for Pax having someone to talk to instead of keeping on
with his brooding.

Earlier, when the cycle of the Ur's waters flowed back to the west, the *Makara's*
partially filled sails and oars were all it had to keep the ship moving down the river
eastward, though slowly. The crew was obsessed with doing so. Now, with the wind
dying down and the waters flowing eastward, the oarsmen below kept the *Makara*
moving toward morning faster than the waters. Learning the names and meanings
about ship things and their doings from the *Mu-Lusuh* . . . the water-thieves running
the *Makara*, Rogaan understood there would be one more cycle of the Ur's waters
flowing westward . . . with the incoming tide of the sea before they caught the trio of
ships. How the river and the sea were connected was something that hurt Rogaan's
head. All he understood of these tides and times was that they would assault the
three larger ships after the next cycle of water changes, after the waters first flowed
westward, then, again, eastward, toward the sea.

The sanity in attacking three ships . . . all larger, and Rogaan's assumption of them being more heavily armed, was a question he and Sugnis posed to both *Vassal* and crew. None even hinted a doubt concerning their plan. That unnerved Rogaan. Even Sugnis expressed misgivings of the *Makara*, a smaller vessel attacking these three ships that were previously owned by the Ebon Circle . . . owned by the Master Dark Robe himself, and that he took the ships from an attacking force of the Senthien some many years back. Warships. A shiver from butt to head shook Rogaan. *This is insane!*

The *Makara*'s gray sails had been dropped and tied down during the last cycle of the tide waters. Raised now were black sails, making the ship almost invisible against the night sky and dark waters. An order went out among the crew and given to both Sugnis and him to put out all lamps and for no puffing out on deck or in windowed cabins. The crew's discipline and matter-of-fact ways in making the ship run impressed Rogaan and gave him a hope that they might know what they are doing concerning this insane attack plan.

"Stay unruffled, young Rogaan," Sugnis's deep and grumbling voice almost sounded like his old self. "If things go wrong, it won't take but for a moment to have your *Light* swallowed by the behemoths of this river."

"*Water-dragons* do not have me worried . . . too much," Rogaan replied with a false bravado that he thought did not conceal well. He felt a bit put off about his mentor's casual attitude concerning dying. "It is this *Vassal* and the *Shunned* . . . the *Shunned*, he seeks. These things are of old tales, what my father told . . . taught me before I could properly use a forging hammer."

"Haven't you seen wonders enough in recent times to know your father's teachings were of history and not tales?" Sugnis asked with a reverberating belch, one he seemed pleased with.

For a moment, Rogaan thought his mentor might turn sick again, but it passed. He hoped the Tellen was over the worst of getting what the crew called his "water-legs." He feared Sugnis's fighting skills would be needed before the breaking of dawn and wanted nothing hampering him. As to the wonders . . . Yes, his eyes had seen many unexplainable things. Things told in tales of old, of villains and heroes and the great struggles for mere survival. *Still, how can these things be happening now . . . with me in the middle of them?*

Rogaan looked forward on the ship to where the *Vassal* and his companions still stood at the bow. Tirelessly, the *Vassal* continued spearing things in the water as his pair of warrior sentinels kept his blindside guarded. Pointing to them he asked Sugnis, "And what is that about?"

"He be keepin' da *mu'usumgal* from slowin' da *Makara*." A lean, dark-skinned

Baraan sailor dressed in dark grays, puffing a lit rod, spoke while approaching Rogaan. "When in waters dey claim, dey be challenin' da ship hittin' da bow. Da beasts see *Makara* as one of dem or worse and dey be defendin' territory. Sometimes da *mu'usumgal* damage da hull . . . da big ones, anyways. And when dey go ta kill a ship, dey do just like dey do da own. Dey rip da tail off. Ships . . . wreck da rudder. *He* . . . be obsessed catchin' dem Farratum ships and wants no slowin' of dis one. So, he keeps at teachin' da *mu'usumgal* who be da big one out here and off da hull."

Four quivers of arrows identical to the ones given him with his bow in the cabin were then laid at Rogaan's feet by the sailor. When leaning over near Sugnis, the Baraan's nose crinkled fiercely, but he kept to what he was doing instead of making an issue of the Tellen's odors. Rogaan suppressed a knowing smile as best he could. Quickly standing up upright and shifting his position more upwind, the sailor announced, "Da *Vassal* wants ya ta get comfy shootin' dat bow in da dark. Says *he* be needin' ya eyes ta tell out distances."

"What . . .?" Rogaan asked. "How?"

The dark-skinned Baraan's almost whitish smile contrasted brightly against his face in the fading light. The sailor took one last, long, pleasure-filled puff on the rod making its end burn brightly before flicking it overboard. "Soon, we be tossin' bait in da water from da bow. When da *mu'usumgal* go for dem, he wants ya shootin' dem eyeballs."

"In the dark?" Rogaan asked incredulously.

"Much talk of Tellen dark-sight . . ." The dark-skinned Baraan smiled big again. "Ya should be seein' da dragon eyes all right. Da question be, can ya poke dem out?"

"Who talks of Tellen dark-sight?" Rogaan asked wanting to know how so many folks knew of it and what they thought it was.

"It be well known ta us River Folk and da *Mu-Lusuh*," the sailor answered confidently as he looked about the ship while continuing his explanation. "Tellen port guards in Turil almost always see ya comin' unless ya be da *Makara*."

Without allowing another question from Rogaan, the sailor turned and was off into the gloom of dusk and the dark tones the ship seemed to be designed to make. It struck Rogaan that the *Makara* and its crew were not ordinary river-thieves. "Who are these people?"

"You asking me?" Sugnis asked of Rogaan with a bit of a surprise.

"Who are they?" Rogaan asked again. "I thought I knew much learning from Father and his books. Though the main substance of his teachings be sound, actually experiencing things is . . . more different."

"That is life, my young friend," Sugnis cryptically answered with a broad smile.

"That is no help," Rogaan rebutted.

"What we put in our heads when someone describes a thing or when we read a book is often not a complete picture of that thing . . ." Sugnis offered with his serious face, as he always wore when trying to explain a subject.

"You read books?" Rogaan asked half-seriously, half as a jibe. In all honesty, Rogaan just could not picture Sugnis, with his dirt-stained appearance and his hole in the ground living, a reader of books.

"Experiencing it adds details, substance, scents, textures, and those little things difficult to describe in words." Sugnis finished his thought while giving Rogaan a sideways glance. "Though it is a pleasure every now and then to read a good book . . . even in my homey holes."

"I still cannot picture you with a book," Rogaan admitted.

"A condition of my apprenticeship with—" Sugnis stopped talking dead in the middle of his explanation. He first looked as if he had accidently spoken secrets; then a grump came to his face. "Enough of this familiar talk."

Disappointed again in not learning who Sugnis was working for and knowing better than to press this issue, Rogaan decided to return to his question, "Who are they of this *Makara?*"

"The *Makara* and its crew are famous on the Ur," Sugnis explained with his voice low. Rogaan looked at him with a surprised expression at him knowing of them and at him not sharing this information earlier. "They thieve from other ships and ports both small and large. They are a smart bunch that seems to be as daimons in the night—here in a moment and gone in the next. And when killing is at hand, they have a solid reputation at doing it."

"And those three?" Rogaan pointed to the *Vassal* and his warrior guardians.

"You know more about the *Vassal* than anyone." Sugnis gave Rogaan a knowing smile and a tease about his fellow conspirators. "The other two. They are *Sentii.*"

"What!" More a statement of disbelief and denial than a question, Rogaan stared at Sugnis a moment before looking back to the *Vassal's* guards. "*Sentii?* How do you know?"

"I have . . . experienced them before," Sugnis explained in a serious tone. "A bunch not to be trifled with without your full attention. Deadly warriors. Though those two are young and without the hardened scowls of their elders. You surprised me holding your own with them and for soundly laying one out."

Rogaan felt both hurt in Sugnis's lack of confidence in him and with pride having surprised his mentor at surviving the two *Sentii* . . . even if they were young and without their scowls. It then dawned on Rogaan that Sugnis did not attempt to help him when he was getting his *Sentii* beating. "Why did you not aid me with the . . . *Sentii?*"

"They were not about taking your *Light* . . . this day." Sugnis cut him off as he stood up. He staggered back and forth with the ship for a moment before gaining his water-legs solidly under him. "The *Vassal* needs you for something and is not going to see you seriously harmed and certainly not killed. I thought you insulted one of them, and they were teaching you a painful lesson."

"No," Rogaan replied. "The *Vassal* was testing me. He said I was with the Blood or something of that sort."

Sugnis regarded him for a long moment before stepping toward the railing. He pointed to the bow where a group of the crew was gathering and setting a line of sailors with large fish in hand, each fish almost half the length of a Baraan standing. "Gather up those quivers. The *Makara's* crew is soon to toss that bait."

Rogaan quickly joined Sugnis at the railing, purposely positioning himself upwind of his mentor. Sugnis knowingly gave Rogaan another sideways glance before pointing to the first of the large bait fish tossed from the bow. As Rogaan strung his bow and positioned a quiver over his right shoulder and another on his belt at his left hip, a water-dragon . . . A *mu'usumgal* broke the surface of the water with part of its body length rising in the darkening night air as it savagely struck the bait from below. A splash not as large as he expected saw the water-dragon disappear beneath the waves. Seeing a small bit of its white underbelly made it easy for Rogaan to judge its body positioning along with its large eye shining brightly in the last of the day's light. Rogaan now understood. They had overly large, shining eyes. The *mu'usumgals* were creatures well suited for the darkness and for attacking from below. Nocking an arrow, Rogaan took several deep breaths and calmed himself. He felt his heart slow as he commanded his body so. He did not know how these arrows would fly or the true strength of the bow, but he did not want any unsteadiness on his part to be a reason for missing.

Another bait fish hit the water with a loud splash. Rogaan drew the bow anchoring his fingers to his cheek just at the right corner of his mouth. He strained just slightly pushing the bow out away from him with his left arm. The bow was at its maximum draw length and well suited for him. His eyes and mind focused on the sharp flint stone arrow tip placing it just under the bait as he followed the floating fish. His wait for another breaching target was short. As the beast rose from the water in another savage attack, Rogaan followed its rise leading his shot to the front of its nose and slightly high. Twenty-eight strides. He let loose the arrow. It passed high just above the water-dragon's head and a little forward of his intended target.

"Strong bow," Rogaan commented.

"The *Vassal* seems to know more of you than feels comfortable," Sugnis remarked.

Another bait fish hit the water. Again, Rogaan calmed his breathing and focused his eyes and mind on arrow tip and floating bait with the bow at full draw. Another water-dragon struck the bait hard rising almost vertical out of the water with Rogaan following the rise with his arrow tip. Thirty-one strides. Rogaan let loose the arrow. It struck just to the right of the beast's eye. The water-dragon twisted in the air exposing its white underside fully as it plunged back into the dark waters splashing in a swirl of foam before disappearing into the dark depths.

Another bait fish toss into the almost black waters. The last of the dusk light was fading. Again, Rogaan drew his bow, calmed his breathing . . . his heart and focused his eyes and mind on flint arrow tip and floating fish. A big water-dragon breached the surface of the waves at a flat and shallow angle. Thirty-seven strides. Rogaan let the arrow fly, striking the beast in its reflecting eye. Waters foamed white as the terror twisted and splashed with fins and tail before diving back into the darkness. Sugnis grunted, being impressed with Rogaan's archery skills and eye for distances.

"The arrows are well made and consistently weighted," Rogaan commented.

"Outstanding with a bow," Sugnis stated with pride. "He was not overstating your skills, after all."

Rogaan looked at his mentor with a questioning expression. "Are you ever going to speak of who you are working for . . . with?"

"No," Sugnis answered in his gruff grumble of a voice. "If you come to know of them, it means that things are grim, and that we are outmatched . . . badly."

"That is of little comfort," Rogaan disappointingly commented. He wished for all the help as possible in the hours ahead. Still, he survived not one, but two *Sentii*. Even if they are young ones in *Sentii* ways. Rogaan smiled at himself and felt pride in that and for quickly getting a feel for the gift of a bow.

Another bait fish splashed into the waters. Rogaan drew his bow again as he settled into practicing and demonstrating his impressive bow skills with a quiver and a half of arrows gone before no more bait fish were tossed to the black waters.

The crew of the *Makara* settled back into their normal routines on the dark decks. If not for his dark-sight, Rogaan would not be able to see anything more of the crew than shadows beyond his arm's length. Instead, he saw much of their goings about and preparations with ropes and hooks, ballista bolts, small catapult stones, and clay and glass jars of liquids being positioned around the ship's decks into holders, all that appeared to be made for just this kind of work. His unease of the darkness lessoned but never disappeared as he retired to their shared cabin where Pax was asleep. Sugnis checked on them before disappearing back to the decks before Rogaan settled into a fitful attempt at sleeping the few hours before his predawn summoning.

Chapter 13

Shunir'ra

The *Makara* creaked and moaned as it rolled slightly port, then starboard. More words of ships and sailing he learned from the crew. Surges of forward motion, ever so slight, came at even intervals in time with a drum beating somewhere below his cabin. The vibrations from footfalls and heavy objects being used or moved throughout the ship Rogaan also felt. It was in these times he cursed his sensitive Tellen perceptions. The scent of Sugnis was faint in the cabin, giving Rogaan a puzzle about whether the Tellen ever lay in his bunk this night. He guessed his mentor was about the ship learning everything possible so to take advantage of his surroundings in the coming fight. Rogaan felt guilty for not doing the same, but he needed to absorb the reality that they are about to go against a *Shunned* . . . the deadliest of beings in his father's old tales, except, of course, for the Ancients themselves. *How can I be in the middle of this?* The unfamiliar and strange surroundings of the *Makara* and his cabin made it even more difficult for Rogaan to sleep. A couple of short naps and small meals in between during the night were all he managed, but restful sleep eluded him. He envied Pax on the top bunk. His light snoring told Rogaan his friend soundly slept, surprisingly, the first time in a long, long time. What gave his longtime friend the peace to sleep so soundly Rogaan could only guess at, but he was happy for Pax that he did.

If Rogaan counted correctly the drum sessions used to keep the oarsmen rowing together, he calculated that it was near time for him to join the *Vassal* and his guards . . . his early-morning summoning. With begrudging trepidation of the morning and day to come, Rogaan rose and put on all his clothes, armor, and equipment. Nothing of his was to be left in the cabin, especially, he considered, if things went wrong. Which he feared would. Nothing except a filled chamber pot was left . . . except for a sleeping Pax. His friend of many years in Brigum, growing up together. Rogaan watched his friend sleep peacefully for a few moments, reflecting on their past and present situation from the cabin doorway. Pax from the poorer side of town and himself from a well-to-do stone and metalsmith. How unlikely and unwavering their friendship had been through many trials with townsfolk and families asking of and chasing after them. Pax even enjoyed playing matchmaker between his sister Suhd and Rogaan. That thought brought a smile to Rogaan. His success came late, when the forces of the world sought to cut a rift between them . . . him, Pax, and Suhd. Then, their struggles from the Valley of the Claw to the prison jails and Arena of Farratum. Their friendship started to be pulled apart. First, Suhd taken as a servant for laws broken Rogaan still did not understand. Then, in the arena, the *Lights* taken from Pax and Suhd's parents. Lastly, he and Pax being sent to the prison isle to serve sentences they did not think warranted for the crimes Farratum claimed against them. At every tribulation, their friendship seemed to fracture more as Pax blamed Rogaan for his parents' brutal plunge into the *Darkness*. Rogaan feared this was the last time he would see his friend, even if Pax did not consider him one any longer.

"Live well, my longtime friend," Rogaan spoke quietly, loud enough for Pax to hear, but not so loud to wake him. "May the Ancients smile on you and Suhd. You will always have my friendship."

Stepping from the cabin with tear-filled eyes, leaving his still-snoring friend to himself, Rogaan made his way to the aft deck. A breeze smelling slightly of salt and heavily of decay struck him when stepping from the narrow cabin's hallway. Also, on the breeze was a slight hint of burning oils, though he saw nothing burning about the ship. No lights at all. The night was almost pitch black, but his Tellen-sight afforded him a view as if the sky were with a half moon. Rogaan immediately tried to get a sense of where everyone was and the condition of the *Makara*. Her sails were full but not straining. The oarsmen and their drum below were working at a brisk pace. Sailors on the decks forward were all in hide and piecemeal metal armors standing at what Rogaan took for assigned positions. Most carried short swords or long daggers. Some had spears. Others carried crossbows.

Two catapults on each side of the lowest deck ahead were set in their positions with sailors tending them. On the deck where he stood, one to a side were placed heavy ballista with cocked bolts and tended to by two sailors each. In the high nest, up the main sail's heavy timber pole, Rogaan made out one sailor performing lookout tasks. *Yes. The Makara's crew is quite a capable bunch*, Rogaan admitted if only to himself. His hopes to survive the morning rose for a moment, and then just slightly in his thinking, before thoughts of the *Shunned* filled his head, dashing such folly. He murmured to himself before setting off to join the *Vassal*, "This is a bad idea."

On his way forward, Rogaan spied Sugnis watching him from the center main deck next to the timber mast, atop the roof of the cabins and storerooms. Sugnis also fully equipped for conflict, appearing not to have left anything behind in the cabin. The *Sentii* had eyes on him, watching him overtly as if he were a threat. As Rogaan walked, Sugnis gave him that look of his telling Rogaan to take great care in the words he spoke and actions taken.

After several sets of steps and ladders, Rogaan found himself on the forward deck of the *Makara* with the *Sentii* guardians of the *Vassal* glaring at him without really looking as if they were watching him. *What is all that about?* Rogaan pondered a moment before putting it to the back of his thoughts and stepping forward. He walked past the *Sentii* without them challenging him. He nodded at them. They just stared back. A twinge of angst uncomfortably shot through Rogaan. He did not feel safe around the *Sentii*. And he suspected they did not trust or respect him. Turning his back to them took some effort, but he needed to take a position to the right of the *Vassal*, who was still at the forward railing spearing threats to the ship. As to the *Vassal*, he showed no signs of tiring and his focus was . . . extraordinary. Obsessive, even.

"Rested well, young Roga of the Blood An?" the *Vassal* asked without taking his attention from the dark waters.

"No," Rogaan answered honestly. "Sleep did not find me this night."

"I see you befriended the Blood-Bow." A smile from the *Vassal* hinted to some victory or confirmed wager. "The finest bow of the *Sentii*. Made of three types of trees native to the Blood Lands. Light to carry, good as a staff weapon when unstrung, consistent in accuracy dry or wet, and strong delivering arrows. Though not as strong as your metal bow."

"Finest bow of *Sentii* making . . ." Rogaan repeated the *Vassal's* words just to make sure he heard him correctly. "Yes. It is well balanced and powerful. No. It is not a match for my *shunir'ra*."

"I understand your *shunir'ra* was made by your hands." The *Vassal* made more of a statement then asked a question, but Rogaan felt he sought him to reply.

"Yes, with a little help from my *father*," Rogaan answered, emphasizing his father's assistance.

"And your father's *imur'gisa?*" The *Vassal* tread in unfamiliar territory for Rogaan. "Was it not what Farratum sought because of . . . unpaid taxes? Petty fools."

"As I understand such things," Rogaan answered with bitter memories of the *Tusaa'Ner* and *Sakes* jailing him, his friends, Pax and Suhd's parents, and his father. Then there was the Arena. His anger flared at those memories. "It was the source of troubles that set all of us on this . . . cruel path. Farratum authorities claimed Father withheld payment of *required taxes* on objects of value. Said he hid it from them. The rod was not his to own. It belongs to his clan from Turil. They left it with him when

I was much younger after they visited us in Brigum. There was a ceremony about it before his Tellen kinsmen left."

"That fills in that piece of the tale." The *Vassal* seemed satisfied.

"What tale?" Rogaan asked. Not understanding how any of this fit together with him being jailed, Pax's parents now *lightless*, and now them about to fight with a *Shunned*.

"Before my . . . the Ancients departed this world," the *Vassal* started into an explanation carefully choosing his words and what he revealed, "they sealed Vaikuntaars by lock like none before. Stone obelisks requiring the use of keys . . . the rods . . . your father's clan's *imur'gisa*, the family treasure entrusted to the An bloodline, is one of them. Along with other *Sentii* clans, one each from the major races . . . the Baraans, the Evendiir, the Mornor-Skurst, and the Tellens, were all sent out into the world, away from Vaikuntaars and the *Sentii*. It was anticipated the wandering races would mingle with those of their kind not of *Sentii* heritage and become forgetful of their long ties to their gods. That they would grow apart along racial divides and not easily collude with each other against the Ancients and their *Sentii* protectors. At a future time, when a great need was at hand, the races, the old clans of the *Sentii* wandering about in the world, would find themselves brought together to open the City of the Council . . . Vaikuntaars. The rods are the *Isell-Dingiir*, the Keys of the Gods, requiring a blood sacrifice by each rod-bearer at the obelisk. Only then will the seals open, releasing the barrier keeping me . . . all from the city."

Rogaan stood slack-jawed listening to the *Vassal's* words explaining that all of this and his family was tied closely to the Ancients and happenings thousands of years ago. Rogaan thought first to deny it all, but too much had happened to him . . . He had seen and experienced far too much to question the words of this *Vassal* as to Vaikuntaars, the Gatekeeper to the Realms of Heaven, but he wanted to. Then, his memory of his mother describing the rod as the *Isell-Dingiir*, just before he found himself out of Brigum and on the run, caused him to exhale in defeat of his denials. *Mother also knew. She was part of all this*. Rogaan felt betrayed and then doomed to fulfill his expected part in this grand scheme. Still, he did not understand what was driving this *great need*. He saw none of it in his experience. "What is this great need?"

"Would you see the world with the *Shunned* ruling from the City of the Council and wielding the powers of the *Ra'Sakti*?" the *Vassal* asked simply.

"I know little of either to make a judgment," Rogaan replied. "Though anything with the *Shunned* ruling does not appeal to me."

"Then you understand, young Roga of the Blood An." The *Vassal* now wore a confirming smile while referring to Rogaan by some formal . . . something. It started to bother Rogaan. Partly, because it more than hinted at responsibilities not willingly taken on by him and that it firmly secured Rogaan's ties with things ancient and frightening. "This *Shunned* has forced the gathering of *Sentii* blood to protect the world from him and his kind. I see it in your eyes."

"What?" Rogaan suddenly felt guilt. For what he did not know.

"Your disbelief or desire to disbelieve," the *Vassal* counseled.

"It is all much to take in," Rogaan replied while looking into the dark expanse of the night, broken only by three tiny points of light far into the depths of the darkness.

"When your father accepted his *family treasure*, he accepted the charge of rod-bearer, bearer of the *Isell-Dingiir* for the Blood Clan An." The *Vassal* sounded as if he were proclaiming a great honor. "When he masterfully removed the black stone from his *imur'gisa* and placed it into your *shunir'ra*, and you somehow became bonded to it, he passed on the bearer-ship to you."

"What?" In a tone so flat Rogaan asked, truly in disbelief . . . and his body now tingling from head to toe with a feeling both cold and warm, causing his everything to shake. Rogaan found himself unable to breathe as he gripped the railing to keep himself upright.

"Breathe, young Roga of the Blood An." The *Vassal* attempted to calm him.

"That is not helping . . ." Rogaan shot back through gritted teeth as he endured the painful sensations. Then, with tear-filled eyes, he asked questions he never considered or knew existed in his mind before now. "Me . . . rod-bearer? It was enough that Father took on this obligation. How could he . . . Why would he do this to me?"

"To keep the *Shunned* from obtaining unstoppable powers and ruling over all with his dark-metal fist." The *Vassal* spoke as if all his words were obvious and rational to think. "Luntanus Alum thinks your father is the blood key he holds. The key as a rod is still needed to work the obelisk, but one that no longer holds the Powers to unseal Vaikuntaars."

"Powers . . .?" Rogaan felt confused, again.

"The black stone in your *shunir'ra* . . ." the *Vassal* hinted as if this too should be obvious. When Rogaan did not make the connection he sought, he continued his explanation. "The *Agni* of the *Isell-Dingiir* is the true key to the seals of Vaikuntaars and is now part of your *shunir'ra* and bonded to you."

Rogaan dropped to a knee as he maintained a solid grip on the railing.

Breath escaped him as he felt adrift, his head swimming in an endless expanse of nothingness. All his fears and joys and desires . . . Everything was gone. He felt numb . . . felt nothing as his mind tried its best to understand . . . accept all that he was told. Rogaan felt an alien hand on his shoulder and neck, something almost metallic, then the hairs his body over felt as if they all straightened at the same time as a wave rippled through him, causing him to shake and convulse painfully as a foul taste filled his mouth before disappearing. It felt as if it lasted a long time, but it was over in a moment. Rogaan opened his eyes to find himself on hands and knees on the deck. His head swam and spun for a few moments before becoming calm. The horrible taste in his mouth gone. It surprised him that he felt better than before the touch of the hand. Rogaan stood up with almost a bound. *I feel stronger . . . more alive.* Looking at the Vassal, he asked, "What did you do to me?"

"Far less than I desired . . ." the *Vassal* stated. "The powers of the Agni can be felt by those sensitive to it. Your skin and hair tell you when the powers are manifesting near you. The *Shunned* can feel it at long distances, so I used very little of the power to cleanse you of the last of the poison and to help you with more vitality."

Rogaan stood with a well-being he had not felt in a long time. He felt stronger and more alert and without worries than since before he left Brigum. *These Agni and their powers are not just the doom of the world the old tales tell of. They can be made to do for the good of things.* Rogaan looked at the *Vassal*. He put on a red helm taking a moment to settle it in place. When he lowered his hands, a slight glow following his armor's lines leading to entwined serpent symbols on his breast plate and helm all glowed red, then went dark.

"Is your armor . . . Agni—" Rogaan tried to sound intelligent about asking his question.

"No." The *Vassal* cut him off. His voice sounding off, reverberating a little and muffled, as if talking distant from a container. "It is something else."

"My thanks for doing what you did to me—" Rogaan expressed his gratitude to the *Vassal* for healing him.

"I have need of you at your best." The *Vassal* cut him off again before pointing beyond the bow of the *Makara*. "We approach the ships. See the lanterns lit on their decks and in some of their exterior cabins? They do not know we approach. Good."

Rogaan followed the *Vassal's* gauntleted fingers forward. The glowing lanterns were tiny, specks, but clear to his vision. Spots in the darkness got larger. Wanting to know how this battle would end before it got within an arm's length of him, Rogaan asked the *Vassal*, "How are you going to sink them?"

"Not before we find them," the *Vassal's* muffled voice answered cryptically. His red helm had an open vertical center slit in front under two slanted slits over his eyes. The *Vassal's* eyes were covered by a clear "glass" was the best Rogaan could describe it. On the glass, Rogaan saw tiny symbols moving about that he could not make out.

"Who?" Rogaan asked as he tried to keep from looking at the *Vassal's* eye slits to figure out what those tiny symbols meant.

"Not who . . . *what*." The *Vassal* became more focused on the ships by the moment. He appeared to be looking for something, even from this distance. The *Vassal* looked down in his helm, closing his eyes, and raised his left hand toward the flotilla. He seemed to be . . . *feeling* for something. When his hand lowered and helm raised again, he spoke. "I have need of your services, young Roga of the Blood An."

Rogaan wished the *Vassal* would stop with the formal title when addressing him. It was not necessary to keep reminding him of his bloodline and the bonds forced upon him. Sugnis's unspoken words of counsel filled his head, ". . . *care of your words and actions. Especially with this one.*"

"What can I do?" Rogaan asked honestly, though his knees and legs felt weak.

"I feel the *Isell-Dingiir* and their Agnis," the *Vassal* answered without taking his focus off the flotilla, "though I cannot separate them. I need you to find your *shunir'ra*."

"I do not know how to find my *shunir'ra*," Rogaan replied, almost sounding as a protest.

"I will teach you, Roga of the Blood An," the *Vassal* answered.

Chapter 14

Sacrifice

Calm my mind, he said. Rogaan stood thinking to himself leaning over the forward deck railing overlooking a trio of three manned, ship-mounted ballista more forward and slightly below him. Four of the *Makara* crew tended the mounted weapons, one at each ballista, port and starboard and center, and one assisting them all with loading and cocking in the dim light of an almost-new moon of the morning. On Rogaan's left stood the *Vassal* in his strange, almost metallic-red armor watching the approaching lights of the flotilla ahead of them. On Rogaan's right, Sugnis stood, dressed in his subdued toned eur armor looking ready for battle. At least that is what Rogaan thought of his mentor as he looked up to the night sky still dark except for the light from the sliver of moon and fields of stars and the tiny lantern lights of the three closing ships . . . their prey.

Calm my mind, Rogaan repeated to himself. Breathing in deeply and exhaling deeply multiple times until he felt calm, then reaching out with his mind, just as the *Vassal* had instructed him. He sought his *shunir'ra* . . . to feel it, or more specifically, the black Agni embedded in his metal bow. Nothing.

"I do not think this is working," Rogaan warned, trying not to sound as complaining.

"We need to be closer to the ships before you are able to feel your *shunir'ra*," offered the *Vassal* with an unshakable confidence. "I now have need of yours and your fellow Tellen's skills at distance telling."

"Judging distances in the dark is not best." Sugnis gave his own warning to all who would hear.

"Your sight is better than any Baraan aboard," the *Vassal* replied confidently and knowingly with his resonating voice. "The ballista is to be fired almost blindly using the lit lanterns of the ships to strike their hulls near rudders. To hit with accuracy, they need you Tellens to both call out distances to the rear most part of the ships . . . in strides."

"I don't see what a bolt from one of these ballistae can do against a Senthien-built ship." Sugnis sounded a little defensive and a lot skeptical.

"Jazmaat . . ." the *Vassal* called out as if expecting a need to answer questions.

B. A. VONSIK

"Yes, me Lord," the *Makara's* crewman assisting each of the three-manned ballista below answered. "Details of da me-made special bolts. Dey be carrin' scent of dem *mu'usumgal*. Not da biggest *mu'usumgal*, of course. Of good size . . . makin' da biggins see da ships as one of dem. It be simple once a biggin see it dat way. It bites da ship like a *mu'usumgal* it no like . . . at its tailfin ta make it move no more."

The *Vassal* looked at Rogaan and Sugnis as if the obvious had just been spoken. When neither of them looked to understand the tactics, the *Vassal* rolled his eyes. "Oh, Tellens. Jazmaat . . ."

"Explain like dem be younglings?" the Baraan asked, then continued with his explanation without waiting for the *Vassal* to answer. "Da rudders. Da rudders. Dat be what da *mu'usumgal* be bitin'. Dey rip dem ta pieces. Da ships can no be controlled after dat."

"You, young Roga of the Blood An . . ." the *Vassal* addressed Rogaan with a knowing tone. "You will then tell me if you feel your *shunir'ra* on one of the two trailing ships. If so, we board the ship you call out. If you have no feel of your *shunir'ra*, we attack both ships with fire as we pass and go onto the lead ship and do the same."

"How can you be so sure the *mu'us* . . . the water-dragons will attack so quickly?" Rogaan asked.

"The *mu'usumgal* are very, very aggressive," the *Vassal* answered with an overly satisfied confidence.

"Da *mu'usumgal* be a mean one." Jazmaat spoke with absolute confidence. "Dey no like da me-made scent. Dey bite and bite fast."

"This can work," Sugnis mumbled deeply almost under his breath and sounded concerned for it. Rogaan gave a silent "What?" look to his mentor when Sugnis no longer gazed at the deck. The Tellen just shook his head and turned his attention to the *Vassal*. "Who will board the ship with Rogaan's *shunir'ra*, and what will you have us do?"

"Roga is with me," the *Vassal* announced. He looked directly at Sugnis with an intimidating grin. "You will remain on the *Makara* with the crew, defending it from any who board her."

"Just you and Rogaan will board?" Sugnis made more of a disapproving statement than a question. "That is not—"

"Your troubles, Tellen." The *Vassal* cut him off. "Me and my *Sentii* are more than a match for the crew and soldiers. The *Makara* will break away as soon as we board and set way for the port of Anza."

"How do we return to the *Makara*?" Rogaan asked, now confused about how things were to unfold.

"Not your troubles, Roga of the Blood An."The *Vassal* was straight-faced while Rogaan winced at how the *Vassal* formally addressed him still. "I will take care of our passages.You . . . feel and find your *shunir'ra*."

They all stood on the forward deck, Rogaan, Sugnis, the *Vassal*, and his *Sentii* guardian-companions, watching the distance close between the *Makara* and the flotilla. Almost no talk between them as the battle drew near and the anticipation, and angst for Rogaan grew.The night kept from his eye the details of the two ships trailing until they were inside of three hundred strides' distance.The lanterns above and below deck on those ships became clear and defined for Rogaan at just over two hundred strides. Large were the ships.

"Are you sure the *Makara* and crew are not outmatched by these ships?" Rogaan felt compelled to ask.The *Makara* appeared half the size of just one of the ships.

"*Makara* with her crew and us are more than a match for them," confidently answered the *Vassal* found under his helm, though Rogaan long gave up trying to discern what those symbols on the *Vassal's* eye glass were. "Call out distances every ten strides once we get within one hundred fifty strides of the ships. Call out loud enough for the crew on the ballista forward us to hear."

Rogaan watched and waited. One hundred ninety, one hundred eighty, one hundred seventy, one hundred sixty. He spoke aloud concerning the ship they approached on their left, "One fifty."

"One seventy," Sugnis started calling out distances to the ship on their right. It was slightly ahead of the one Rogaan watched.

"One forty," Rogaan called out aloud.

"One sixty," Sugnis called out in his deep voice.

"One thirty," Rogaan called out. The heavy thump of a ballista reverberated in the air. Immediately, the crew started to recock and reload it. A stout thud combined with a pop Rogaan heard a few moments after the bolt's release.

"One thirty," Sugnis called out.The ballista on his side let out a heavy thump at the bolt's launch that reverberated in the air and around the ship for a moment. A few moments later, a repeat of the stout thud and pop rang out.

"Load catapults," came the command from somewhere behind Rogaan. "Load 'em with da burnin' stones."

"Distance . . . young Roga," the muffled voice of the *Vassal* sounded anxious.

"Ninety strides," Rogaan called out as his eyes started to make out the details of the ship ahead and on their left.That ship's crew was frantically moving about its decks while yelling unintelligible commands and orders. Remembering he needed to be calm and with an empty mind to feel his *shunir'ra*, Rogaan closed his eyes as he tried to rid himself of all thoughts except his masterwork blue metal bow. It took him a few moments to feel calm and with the image of his *shunir'ra* the focus of his thoughts. He stood oblivious to everything around him. There was only the bow. He waited . . . and waited . . . and waited, hoping to sense his *shunir'ra*. Nothing.

"I do not feel my *shunir'ra*," Rogaan announced. He opened his eyes to find the *Vassal* looking at him with a contemplative head tilt.

"Strike with fire the ship on port!" the *Vassal* command.

Echoes of the *Vassal's* command sounded twice more behind Rogaan as the *Makara* pulled up alongside the Senthien-built ship splitting the distance between it and its sister ship on the *Makara's* starboard side. Rogaan turned to watch the crew make a near simultaneous release of the port-side catapults, sending two, dark round objects arcing through the air toward the twice taller sailing ship. Immediately, the crew tending the empty catapults ran from one side of the *Makara* to almost the other, pulling ropes and resetting the weapons. In the distance, bursts of flame splashed across the larger ship in two locations; one on the side of the aft-raised decks where the command crew would be and one on the lower aft deck under one of the sails, catching both the deck and sail on fire.

"No . . ." Rogaan heard a pain-stricken moan from Sugnis.

Turning, Rogaan found Sugnis's pain-filled eyes staring at the burning ship, making Rogaan's head swirl in confusion. *What upsets Sugnis?* As Rogaan sought an answer, Sugnis desperately looked to the other Senthien-built ship starting to come alongside on their starboard side.

"Strike with fire the ship on starboard!" the *Vassal* command, this time for the second ship of the flotilla. The ballista commanders echoed his command.

A sense of dread filled Rogaan as he watched, with an almost expectation, Sugnis draw his crossbow and in one smooth move, nock a bolt into place and fire in the direction of the catapults on the *Makara's* starboard side. His Tellen mentor then dropped his crossbow as he burst into a sprint for the catapults, drawing his sword and long knife while leaping from their elevated deck to the one below where the weapons sat ready to launch their deadly fire stones. The individual catapult crewmen started echoing the *Vassal's* command for the second time when one of them fell to the deck with Sugnis's bolt in his neck, fletching on one side and the bolt's flint head on the other. Sugnis smashed into the catapult crew striking down several before the *Vassal's* *Sentii* companions tackled him. Rogaan had not even noticed them leaving their positions. Knowing his mentor's open-hand fighting skills, Rogaan expected the fight with the two *Sentii* to be over quickly with Sugnis the victor. Instead, *Sentii* and Sugnis rolled struggling on the deck as the one catapult untouched by the fight sent hurling in an arc its deadly payload toward the starboard ship.

"No!" Sugnis growled. The Tellen kicked free of one of the *Sentii*, then spun into a crouch and stood with the other *Sentii* wrapped about his shoulders. Letting Sugnis's neck go, the *Sentii* retreated a step from the Tellen as Rogaan caught a red blur of movement on his right. Landing on the lower deck near to Sugnis, the *Vassal* in one attack move kicked his booted foot directly into Sugnis's chest, sending Rogaan's mentor flying seven strides to the *Makara's* outer railing, crashing through the stout wood and into the abyss of darkness beyond.

Stunned, Rogaan stood. He disbelieved his eyes. *What happened just cannot be. A moment Sugnis was next to me . . . the next . . . gone.* His eyes looked about the ship, hoping to find his mentor. The port catapults launched another pair of fire-stones at their target, setting it further in flames as the ship listed and started turning sideways. The rudder must be gone . . . *mu'usumgal.* The crew finished resetting their starboard catapults, then launched a pair of fire stones at their target, the already-burning ship on its side near the aft command deck. Splashes of the deadly fire spread across the ship's main and elevated decks setting fire to both wood and sails. The port catapult crew was now reloading their deadly weapons for a third strike as the starboard crew ran their ropes, recocking their weapons. All this was happening around the red-armored *Vassal* who watched the efficient crew from the lower deck where he sent Sugnis flying overboard . . . to his death.

The port crew called out their firing cadence again, launching another pair of fire-stones to strike the forward decks of the disabled ship, adding the forward sails aflame to those center and aft, now in a full blaze. Uniformed *Tusaa'Ner* and the ship's crew were dropping rowboats into the dark waters. Others leapt from the ship, some on fire. Water-dragons immediately taking them as meals. Screams of agony came from all over the burning wreck. Rogaan felt . . . a disturbing sadness for the dead and the dying. The dreading anticipation of battle being a much-better feeling than the realities of blood spilt.

More ropes got ran as the *Makara's* port crews again made to reset and rearm their deadly weapons. With bellowing echoes of command, the starboard catapults once again launched a pair of fiery death stones toward the other ship, striking it center and slightly forward, sending the sails and much of the decks aflame. That ship too started listing and turning out of control on the gloomy waters. With the first of their battles all but won, Rogaan stared at the burning death traps as the *Makara* quickly left them behind.

So absorbed in the sorrowful reaping, Rogaan did not notice the *Vassal* and his *Sentii* guards climbing to the forward deck until the first of them dismounted the ladderlike stairs. They were acting as if nothing had happened, chatting amusingly among themselves. As if practiced, the *Sentii* strode to their previous positions taking up their at-the-ready stances while the *Vassal* returned to the railing next to Rogaan. Still stunned and even a bit in shock at everything, Rogaan simply stared up at the *Vassal*, him being a head taller.

"Am I to have issue with you, Roga of the Blood An?" The *Vassal's* reverberating words carried a sharp tone as he stood unmoving looking forward at the last ship of the flotilla.

Rogaan felt sick . . . angry. His heart pounded, and his breath came in rasps. Anger filled him. He wanted badly to strike the *Vassal*, beat on him until the Baraan, or whatever he was, lay bloodied on the deck. Then, a ripple of fear racked Rogaan as he did his best not to let it show. *This one so callous, so volatile.* Rogaan started realizing the full and deadly nature of the *Vassal*. He was on a quest, focused to a fault. *And I at the center of the Vassal's need.* Rogaan's thoughts returned to the image of Sugnis and the *Vassal's* kick. *So powerful. No hesitation.* Rogaan swallowed hard, not only of the spit in his mouth but for the uncontrolled anger he felt. He was on dangerous ground, or at least a deck. He needed to take care of his words and actions . . . and even his expressions as they might get him in a worse predicament, but he needed to know of his mentor, his friend. "Sugnis?"

The *Vassal* remained silent and unmoving. He simply stared forward at the lights and silhouette of the ship ahead, closing fast, as the first blue hints of dawn shown high in the predawn sky. "Water-dragons surround our ships . . . ravenous and vicious. Your Tellen mentor has no chance of living. He betrayed me. That, I will not allow. Now, tell me when you feel the *Isell-Dingiir* you take for your bow."

Chapter 15

Ancient Revelations

Many of the crew and more of the *Tusaa'Ner* on board leaned over the outer rails looking far behind the *Khaaron* at a scene of shocking destruction, the *Khaaron's* sister ships, the *Erebuus* and *Nyx*, burning and adrift. Hundreds of *Tusaa'Ner* and almost as many in support likely lost, if not already *lightless*. And the supplies for the journey ahead, also lost. A shadow of a dark ship with full sails periodically visible against the backdrop of angry flames burning the decks and sails of the wrecks. *Daimons*. An eerie silence fell over the decks of the *Khaaron*. Aren heard himself breathe as much as the rasping of those near who weren't holding their breaths, though Aren wished those around him would have bathed for the sake of his wrinkled nose. His hopes rose as he gazed upon the scene of death and ruin, concluding with two ships lost that the expedition was now doomed and that they wouldn't be traveling into the Blood Lands. He breathed a sigh of relief at that. Breaking the silence, above on the command deck, a female Baraan's voice rang out in shouts of rage at the ship's commander and everyone else near making accusations of their incompetence and collusions to thwart her expedition. Aren recognized and winced at the piercing screech of *Za* Irzal.

On the command deck with the *Za*, as best as Aren could make out, were the *Khaaron's* commander and first and several of their crew who steered the ship. *Za* Irzal's aides, Ganzer and his aide Lucufaar, kept to the outer rails of the deck, allowing Irzal to rant without them getting the brunt of things. Irzal's daughter, the *Tusaa'Ner sakal*, stood near her mother with a hand ready to draw her sword at anyone thinking to raise a weapon against the ranting *Za*.

Something pulled at . . . vibrated Aren, drawing his attention to the burning wrecks. Amidst the roaring flames, bluish lights swirled forming a mesh, like a fishing net around one of the ships, until all the fire was enclosed. Then, in an instant, the flames were gone on the left of the two burning ships. At first, Aren thought that the ship sank, but the bluish mesh remained with the moving ship then started fading away. *What did I just see?* he asked himself with his curiosity stirred. It was a simple pattern of what Aren reasoned as air, though he didn't understand why he thought it so. Shouts from the crew announced to all the sinking of the *Nyx*.

Should I tell them? Aren decided not to encourage their thinking of continuing this expedition with one of those ships surviving. *Besides, it'll be dawn soon enough for them to see the ship with their own eyes.*

With a surprise, Aren found himself moving his hands in a manner of the shaped mesh. *Yes. I see how that is the pattern of the net, but I still don't know how the air made the flames die.* With a little frustration, Aren looked away from his hands and up at the command deck, certain that Ganzer would have a task for him to attend. He caught Lucufaar staring at him with a look of something between surprise and concern. It was a quick moment before Lucufaar glaring at him with those dark, deep-set, squinty eyes, started yelling at him, "Dawdle no longer, Evendiir. Return to my cabin."

Aren didn't understand why he was to go to Lucufaar's and Ganzer's cabin. He felt as he did being sent to his room by his father as a youngling and made to challenge the aide of *Za* Irzal's aide. Before he could raise his protest, Ganzer, in his blue jacket and kilt, bore down on Aren with his contempt-filled eyes, scolding him. "Not another tongue of protest, Evendiir. To our cabin."

They'll pay for this! Aren promised himself as he trudged the deck toward the outer door leading to the narrow hallway within. Again, he cursed them, but Ganzer mostly for not allowing him boots or sandals so his feet didn't touch the splinter-rich deck. Aren felt a vibration sensation in front of him. He stopped. Whitish "sparks" of flames rapidly formed a Baraan-sized rotating, rainbow-colored circle above the deck ahead. Three individuals stepped from the circle before it collapsed into a faint trail, leading to the bow of the ship. The vibrations disappeared with the visible circle. On the forward deck of the ship, another rainbow circle opened wide again, allowing a single, red-armored being to step out before the circle vanished completely. Aren stood taking in the details of remnant trails trying to learn all he could. *I can use this . . . if I can figure it out.* The slamming of a door snapped his attention back to his deck. Looking back to the new arrivals, Aren saw the two Baraan-like ones, dressed in subdued browns and greens worked-hide armors and carrying spears and long knives, entering the hallway to the inner area where the cabins of the *Za*, her aides, and commander were, now unguarded. The third arrival was that Tellen . . . Rogaan, dressed in hunting clothes and armor, bow over his shoulder, short sword over his other shoulder, and long knife on his side, now standing with his eyes closed and arms outstretched. The Tellen then opened his eyes looking forward of the ship before noticing Aren standing only strides away. With eyes growing wide in surprise, he asked, "What are you doing here . . . Aren?"

"What are YOU doing HERE?" Aren replied with just as much surprise.

Pointing at the spot he and his earth-toned-clad warriors appeared through, "Who are they?"

"Fellows," Rogaan coyly replied.

"That one?" Aren pointed forward ship at the *Vassal*.

"Dangerous fellow," Rogaan honestly replied, though his response almost sounded like a question.

A bolt of lightning crackled above Aren's head making him involuntarily duck as if that would save him from the strike. Aren felt the lightning, the vibrations of its manifestation that came with it. Looking to its source, in the direction he felt the vibrations come from, he found the red-armored fellow directing lightning over their heads and at the ship's command deck burning marks into the wood and painfully knocking over one of the crew and Ganzer, leaving them down with smoking clothing. Ganzer's going down brought a smile to Aren's face. *You deserve worse.* The *Za, Khaaron* commander, and another crewman were not to be seen. From the deck above, he felt more vibrations, different, but just as powerful. Then, Aren's mouth dropped open in awe-filled surprise. Standing tall in his black pants and jacket and lavender shirt deflecting the lightning from striking him with something like a vaporous shield of air, Lucufaar's illuminated face framed by his light brown hair was one of supreme focus as deep shadows walked across his body. The bolts came one after another for what seemed a long time, illuminating the ship in the predawn gloom, until they and their waves of vibrations suddenly stopped.

"You have regained some of your strength." Lucufaar stood tall as he projected his voice loudly across the ship. The aide to Ganzer sounded no longer like himself, respectful and deferring. Now, he sounded as the Lucufaar of the cabin when he played dangerously with Aren and the ax-and-flame Agni stone. This new Baraan's attention was fully focused on the red-armored fellow . . . the dangerous fellow. "If this's the best you can do, our fight will be just as short as the last."

"Lucufaar . . ." Aren breathed out as he studied the remnants of the lightning and air shield manifestations.

"Is a Tellen *Sharur* aboard?" Rogaan asked Aren while they crouched low on the deck together.

New vibrations from the forward decks preceded a barrage of blue bolts of light sizzling over Aren's and Rogaan's heads. They both involuntarily ducked. Above on the command deck, the scene was still awe-inspiring to Aren with Lucufaar standing tall, effortlessly deflecting the bolts with vaporous shields in each hand.

"I have to learn these . . ." Aren spoke aloud studying to himself in wonder the visual patterns of fading powers while trying to understand what the vibrations meant to these manifesting. The Tellen's question to him finally sank in sparking an answer if he heard Rogaan right. Confirming the question, "What . . . a Tellen?"

"A *Sharur* Tellen," Rogaan corrected.

Aren at first thought Rogaan was asking of his father, an assumption making him not prepared for the *Sharur* part of what the young Tellen sought. Aren recalled there was a Tellen dressed in forest colors lying about on the first lower deck with another two Baraans, dressed similarly, watching over him. Aren had paid little attention to the Tellen during his coming and going from the cargo hold below, so he had no other details to offer, though he found this all curious with them all being in the middle of a battle of *The Power*. "Forward on the ship, one deck down. He didn't look well. Why him?"

"He has something of mine," Rogaan answered as he plotted a course to the forward deck area through the huddled groups of the crew and *Tusaa'Ner*. "Oh, and the one you call Lucufaar . . . his true name is Luntanus Alum."

Rogaan was gone as soon as he spoke the ancient name, jumping and sprinting forward on the ship's decks before Aren could raise a "what" or "who" at his assertion. New vibrations drew Aren's attention upward where the heat by an orange-red manifestation passing above bathed his face, the ball of flames Aren greatly desired knowledge of flying to the command deck. *This one's a treasure!* He immediately set to studying the manifestation while trying to lock into his memory the feel of the vibrations. The ball of fame's lines of the power structured to contain the heat released . . . A wave of heat pushed hard on Aren with a deafening clap of thunder vibrating through him as the ball of flames exploded. Aren fell from his crouching position to fully on his backside, never taking his eyes off the figure emerging from the flames on the deck above.

Black and lavender the figure stood tall as red-, yellow-, and blue-colored vapors swirled about him until they disappeared into wisps of flames, lighting up the whole ship in an orangish shade. He in the flames seemed unaware of the need to be burnt black by the fire, his tan skin its complexion before as now after the intense burst of heat. The deck and ship about him were bathed in flames as he stood within a mesh of scintillating vapor. He looked about him feeling disgusted. A bluish mesh, like the one Aren saw earlier engulfing an entire ship, swirled out from and about the Baraan, expanding until it enclosed all the burning fires. Quickly, darkness engulfed the command deck except for the blue mesh. Then too it winked out leaving all in the deep gloom of the predawn as a strong rush of howling air came from behind Aren. The vibrations of the manifestation felt similar, but a bit different from the earlier one on the distant ship. Looking behind him, Aren saw only darkness as a thick and overwhelming smell of burnt forest wafted over him.

"You're no match for me, wounded immortal!" Lucufaar bellowed loudly from the deck above. His voice deep and strong and now having lost all its tones of respect and courtesies. Aren saw the powers manifesting white-blue in the aide to the aide's hands even before the powers were visible and illuminating parts of the ship. All Aren's hairs stood on end, and his skin prickled at powerful vibrations preceding bolts of lightning arcing out from Lucufaar toward targets unseen forward on the ship. Mesmerized more than afraid, Aren sat while following the lines of Power, absorbing with his mind their patterns as he sought to remember how the vibrations worked.

An egg's throw in front of Aren, the door to the inner cabins slammed open. Emerging from the darkness, the two green- and brown-armored fellows accompanying Rogaan returned from the cabins now carried the medium-sized wood chest Lucufaar highly prized and coveted. Aren almost lost his breath at the sight knowing nothing good was about to happen. The two tall fellows trotted together with the chest between them for the stairs to the lower deck near Aren. Aren felt new vibrations. Strides before the green-armored fellows reached the stairs, Aren saw a nearly invisible manifestation from above formed into a wall of clear crystal barring their escape. He looked on at all the powers in awe. Lucufaar had made the barrier while maintaining his lightning strikes to the forward parts of the ship with one hand. Realizing the unseen wall was in their path, Aren raised a hand and was about to warn them when the two fellows slammed into the unyielding crystal structure, sending them both harshly bouncing back to the deck and the wood chest flying in Aren's direction. Time seemed to stop as he helplessly watched the wood chest, with lock and clasp now missing, hit the deck and spew across the planks four wrapped, rod-shaped things and that dreaded crystal, still in its red and black hide wrap. The wrapped crystal finished tumbling right at Aren's right hip.

"Marut, the *Isell-Dingiir* . . ." one of the two green- and brown-armored fellows spoke to the other in a dialect of Antaalin Aren's father had taught him years ago.

"Grab them, Harut, before all is lost!" the second of the two armored fellows ordered the first.

Both green- and brown-armored fellows scrambled for and grabbed up the wrapped, rod-shaped objects as Aren felt the red gemstone laying near whisper to him. *I'm not listening.* In the corner of his eye, Aren saw Lucufaar redirect his lightning at Marut and Harut, striking recklessly masts, sails, decks, and more as he did so. Aren sensed a familiar vibration rising anew. Between the two fellows and their prizes, whitish "sparks" of flames rapidly formed a Baraan-sized, rotating, rainbow-colored circle low on the deck. Neither of the fellows could avoid the rotating rainbow circle with all their momentum given to getting to their wrapped prizes. They disappeared through the circle just as lightning decimated and lit fire the wood deck they would have been on. In a wink, the rainbow circle collapsed into a faint trail toward the forward areas of the ship, leaving Aren studying the remnants of the Power for both circle and lightning. All fell silent and without vibrations as the last vestiges of Agni Powers disappeared from Aren's sight. The ax-and-flame Agni crystal whispered again to Aren. *I'm not listening*, Aren told it. Again, it whispered . . . calling to him . . . compelling him to possess it. *No!* "You've given me only pain and sorrows."

Looking up from the red and black hide wrap, Aren's eyes found the one above in black and lavender. He clearly saw the aide's eyes with a glow, as if consumed with the Power . . . and he was staring right at Aren, staring into . . . *through* him. An uncontrollable chill all over gripped Aren. Again, that whisper filled his head, calling to him to pick up the ax-and-flame, to possess it. A powerful urge to comply took hold of Aren. He reached out.

"No!" came a bellow from above.

Aren's fingers touched the red and black wrapping. Familiar vibrations quickly growing alerted him. A barrage of blue bolts sizzled at Aren, the first striking him in the right shoulder, stinging and burning like nothing Aren could compare. The second bolt hit him on his left side, sending waves of stinging pain throughout his body. The smell of burnt flesh made Aren angry . . . He knew it was *his* flesh that burned. He felt on fire, burning within. Agony made him desperate to stop more blue bolts. Sizzling sounds continued as the smell of burnt wood mixed with that of his burnt flesh, but no more bolts struck him. Vibrations swept over Aren's body, a strange sensation as he looked up to see his left hand raised with a vaporous shield projecting from it stopping the blue bolts of stinging light. One after another the blue bolts rained from the one in black and lavender. Aren felt the prickling of panic . . . felt it difficult to breathe and his blood draining from his everywhere. *Oh no. Oh no. Oh no. This is all wrong!* Black and lavender . . . aide to the aide . . . Lucufaar. Black and lavender . . . his ancient name, the one cursed by the gods, by the world, by the Ancients . . . Luntanus Alum . . . the most diabolical and dangerous of the Shunned! *And he wants to send me into Darkness.*

Chapter 16

Powers

*L*untanus Alum! *The Shunned! Me fighting a Shunned! With only a shield of the Power manifested between him and me. This can't be happening. This can't be real. This can't be happening.* Distraught with disbelief, Aren feared how long his raised left hand, now trembling and burning in strain, would last holding his vaporous shield against the strength of this *Shunned*. Aren didn't know what else to do. Dropping his arm and shield to run or even flee slowly would see him sizzled to a crisp before he could jump from the deck to cover. *What do I do? What do I do?* In desperation, Aren yelled out, "Someone . . . *Anyone*, help me! Help me!"

Fighting . . . against a *Shunned*, Luntanus Alum at that, Aren considered a quick journey into the *Darkness*. Worse, Aren looked at his right hand as he lay huddled on the planks under his manifested defense. The red and black hide wrap now open allowing Aren's fingers to touch the ax-and-flame red Agni. Something was different with this unintended touching. A presence whispering to him, maybe more than whispers in some way. Aren felt it, but he didn't know how. It was like someone crawling into his head, then speaking softly. Not like the spinning symbols . . . something worse. The whisper kept on with utterances too faint and distant for Aren to understand. His curiosity getting the best of him, Aren focused on the utterances, just for a moment. He needed to know what the whispers were saying. His left arm weakened, then started trembling terribly. Panic grabbed at him, almost taking his wits from him. *I won't be able to hold back the sizzle much longer. What do I do? What do I do?* Aren felt stuck in an impossible nightmare he could never have dreamed. His trembling and burning arm buckled, collapsing up against his body, causing him to growl through the pain to keep the vaporous shield deflecting the blue bolts. "They just keep coming . . . keep coming. Can't hold them back. Can't hold them back any longer."

Aren closed his eyes concentrating on his left arm and his vaporous shield . . . his only defense. Whispers speaking, telling him something. *Go away. Not now.* Aren felt himself losing the battle to the *Shunned*. *Too strong . . . The Shunned is too strong.* Strong hands grabbed his shoulders. Into silence the whispers retreated. A deep growl of pain came from someone near, followed by curses a street rogue would blush at while the strong hands pulled Aren. His eyes closed, concentrating on keeping the vaporous shield in place, Aren felt himself moving, sliding along the deck planks. Wafting puffs of burnt wood and flesh filled his nose. *Not my flesh?* More blue bolts struck his vaporous shield weakening it with each burst of light and heat. Aren felt the power of each new burning bolt weaken his defense. It was almost gone. Exhausted, he started giving over to his fate . . . accepting his *Light* to be taken by the blue bolts. He let go of his manifestation . . . his only . . . . Suddenly, he felt weightless . . . floating. His manifestation of the shield he let go of with his mind. Floating . . . feeling good . . . free. He no longer had a care.

Thud. Pain rippled through his jarred head, jaw, and shoulder. Aren's head spun in confusion. *What happened? Moving . . . no walking . . . something holding me up.* Bright lights. Warmth. Moving again. Bright lights. Dull stinging. Moving. Floating. His back and teeth rattled with a thud. Aren sensed he was finally lying on his back with pain from backside to head. Rising again. Moving forward, then sideways . . . then the other way. Spinning now. Floating, ending with a thud and a jarred left shoulder and side. Aren had no idea where he was or of his situation. He hurt as he lay on his back . . . somewhere. Spinning images in his head, seemingly nonsensical, forced Aren to lie motionless wherever he was.

"Wake up," a deep growling voice demanded.

Aren felt his chest and head being shaken. It all felt so distant, the voice and shaking. He felt exhausted and knew it but didn't understand how or why. Vaguely he cared, but his body just wouldn't cooperate with his mind.

"No place to lie around. Need to finish . . ." the deep voice made comments maybe to someone else.

"I know you?" Aren asked the voice with slow, deliberate words. The voice sounded familiar to him. Aren tried to open his eyes but found them very heavy and unresponsive.

"Kind of," the deep voice answered. "We helped each other in the Farratum Arena."

"You're that Tellen . . ." Aren's mind started to clear. Pains from all over his body made themselves known. He hurt. Groaning his words as he tried to sit up, ". . . Rogaan. Correct? Of course, it is. I never forget."

"Yep," Rogaan answered with a bit of a groan. Aren assumed the Tellen's groans meant he was hurt too.

"Why?" Aren honestly asked wanting to know why a stranger would risk his life for him. Aren just didn't have faith in folks to do such things without a motive, usually to get something they wanted. He forced his eyes open to his blurry surroundings. They were behind one of the small boats lashed in a cradle on the main deck.

"I do not know . . ." came the contemplative reply from the Tellen. "Just seemed the right thing to do."

Well, that didn't make any sense to Aren. He wouldn't have put himself in danger to save this Tellen. *He has something wrong in the head*, Aren concluded as he felt vibrations preceding the Power. He witnessed above them another barrage of lightning arcing from the forward deck where the red-clad fellow was on the aft decks of the ship. The *Shunned* resumed his attack on the fellow.

"Forgive me . . . I must retrieve my possession," Rogaan announced before hopping away to the stairs off to their left leading down to the decks below. Arrows peppered the wood deck and forward cabin walls, missing the Tellen as he dove down the laddered stairs.

"That's going to leave marks," mused Aren as he felt content to lie where he was allowing himself to regain enough strength of body to crawl out of this mess. *What tired me out so fast? I've never felt anything like that before.*

More lightning arced above, back and forth between the forward and aft decks, between the red-clad warrior and the *Shunned*. Aren felt their vibrations . . . He focused on memorizing them. Blue bolts and small flaming spheres too. Some exploding far too close to him making him nervous at the heat and that he might get burned. He tried to lift his head. Still, his body felt heavy and sluggish. *I'm an easy target if I draw attention to myself.* Assaulting his nose, wafts of sulfur and burning wood mixed with the scent of the air just after a thunderstorm. He felt and watched the battle go on under a bluing dawn sky as the exchanges of the Powers continued for what seemed a long time before the Tellen climbed up from the stairs with a black and tan hide case a half-stride long in hand. The other Tellen, the white-bearded one, followed him from below. Running, Rogaan slid on the deck planks into the spot he previously left lying next to Aren. He motioned to the white-bearded Tellen to follow.

Clad in greenish hunter's armor more robust than Rogaan's, the Tellen staggered to his boots and made his best effort to fast-walk that turned out to be more of a series of stumbles as if drunk from a day's festivities. *Two days of festivities*, Aren figured watching him. Arrows and flying parts of the *Khaaron* kept just missing the Tellen. *Great . . . one of those we now have*, Aren grumbled to himself. When the Tellen went down to the deck, all of his own accord, Rogaan was able to reach out and grab the stout fellow. With arrows sticking into the deck and exterior cabin wall, Rogaan pulled and dragged the white-bearded Tellen to cover behind the boats.

"My thanks, young Rogaan." The white-bearded Tellen expressed his gratitude before losing his stomach to the deck opposite him and Rogaan.

"Great!" Aren commented. "Can this get worse?"

"Time to go!" Rogaan suddenly announced waving his black and tan case to one of the fellow-warriors who arrived with him. That warrior made a hand sign to someone unseen atop the forward cabin.

A new vibration grabbed Aren's attention just before a multicolored light show erupted far above the sails of the *Khaaron*. *Who are they signaling?* Aren asked himself. *They seem to be following a plan . . . one evidently not meant to take the ship or kill the Shunned.* Aren didn't like that last thought . . . the *Shunned* living and him on the same ship. *They must have a plan to escape. I've got to leave with them.* He tested his arms and legs to see if they had strength enough to carry him. He wasn't sure, but he had to risk falling on his face or be left on this ship—*with Lucufaar . . . Luntanus . . . whatever in Kur his name . . . the cursed Shunned.*

"Get ready to move and quickly, Trundiir," Rogaan warned the white-bearded Tellen. This Trundiir, stouter and by almost a head a shorter Tellen than Rogaan, responded by swallowing hard as he raised himself into a crouched position. "You too . . . Aren. If you wish to leave this *Shunned* behind."

Aren felt it before he saw the white flaming sparks start rotating into a rainbow-colored gateway . . . a step-gate, if Aren recalled its name correctly from his father's teaching, as described in the legends of the distant past. It formed to their right, near the green-clad warriors. Aren needed to make sure the manifestation was meant for their escape. Someone needed to use it first before he dare step through it. Then, he wondered at Rogaan and the white-bearded Tellen not running to the rainbow circle. *What are they waiting for?* The crackle of flames followed something like clay pottery breaking somewhere forward of Aren and the Tellens and yelling by the crew and *Tusaa'Ner* about a fire. Looking in-between the boats, between the *Shunned* and him, Aren saw an area of the deck in flames, and the crew quickly fighting to put it out, some of them catching fire. A new vibration caused Aren to peek about the *Khaaron*. Lines of the Power caught his attention. They formed a barrier along the right side of the ship. Explosions of flames struck the almost-invisible wall in two places, then dripped down the barrier to the dark waters as if a burning oil of some kind.

A pair of blue-clad *Tusaa'Ner*, a male *sakal* and his subordinate, attacked the green-gray-armored warrior closest the gateway. The warrior easily held his own, quickly cutting down the subordinate *Tusaa'Ner* while keeping the *sakal's* blade from him. As that battle raged, Rogaan and the white-bearded Tellen took off for the gateway, the white-bearded Tellen clearly slower. Before they got to the rainbow circle, the door to the forward cabin swung open. Standing in the doorway in red-brown hide armor was the dark-haired *Subar* catching first sight of the chaos and looking at trying to make sense of it all. The white-bearded Tellen passed the slowing Rogaan, then paused in front of the rainbow-colored gateway, appearing uncertain of stepping inside. Rogaan shoved the Tellen through, then made to leap in when a desperate young voice, a familiar female Baraan voice, called out to him from the doorway next to the red-armored *Subar*. Rogaan froze, then turned with an unbelieving look on his face searching for the female Baraan. *This isn't good*, Aren worried. He planned to stay close to this Tellen for reasons that gnawed at him, but if the Tellen stayed or got himself killed, that would leave Aren on the *Khaaron* with the . . . *Shunned*. Aren shivered as he fought with his own body to rise so to escape the ship.

"Suhd . . ." came the surprised and lass-struck words from Rogaan.

Aren cringed as he struggled to his bare feet. *This isn't good.*

He recalled Suhd's rough treatment in the Farratum jails. How the *Sakes* and *Tusaa' Ner* mishandled her . . . or tried to until Rogaan broke one of them and killed the other. On the *Khaaron*, she sometimes helped Aren, or more accurately, she assisted the *Subar* in his doings, which meant fetching him so the *Subar* could ask more questions. She tried to run from the doorway to Rogaan, but the armor-clad *Subar* caught her gray tunic, pulling her back into him before wrapping his red-brown, hide-armored left arm around her. A desperate look in the *Subar's* eyes lit off a flare of anger on the half Tellen's face as Aren grew even more concerned. *The Subar is smitten with her too. Damn, this youngling's sway is strong.* Several times, Aren felt her scent seeking to make him compliant . . . even tried to make him enticed with her, but his Evendiir blood resisted the temptations. At first, Aren thought her deliberately doing what the worst of the female Baraans did, enticing and influencing others with their flirts and natural scents, but he observed Suhd not even to be aware of what she did. *Her mother's fault for not teaching young Suhd of her deadly potential*, Aren accused.

Then . . . A fight broke out between the red-armored *Subar* and Rogaan after Ezerus tossed Suhd back into the interior of the cabin, the two going at it with fists and long knives. The ax-sword on the *Subar's* back useless in such close quarters and in such a short scuffle that Aren almost missed. Rogaan, with a blurry of fast strikes, left the *Subar* rasping for air while disabled on a knee. Still, he reached for his ax-sword on his back. Suhd went running past him and into the half Tellen's arms. Their hug and short exchange of words were interrupted by a bellow above from the red-armored *Kabiri* warrior warning of approaching death.

Aren felt the spheres of fire coming from the *Shunned*. He shivered as the red-armored warrior on the upper deck parried away the flaming spheres with Agni Powers, away from Suhd and Rogaan and the rainbow circle. On protective impulse, Rogaan grabbed up Suhd and jumped through the rotating circle of colors. The green-armored warriors immediately followed.

Now, run, you idiot! Aren scolded himself for not already have gone for the rotating rainbow, the step-gate, and escape the *Khaaron*. He ran, but not as fast as he wanted . . . more of a frustrated hobble than anything else. Out of nowhere, someone grabbed him by his tunic and pulled him back and away from the colorful circle. It was the *Subar,* pulling Aren backward before making haste for the step-gate with his ax-sword in hand, all while wearing obsession and desperation in his eyes.

"You'll pay for that!" Aren promised his revenge as he recovered his feet and set off after the *Subar* in a wobbly run and his escape. New vibrations told Aren lightning was on its way. Fearing it focused on him, he cringed in a slight hunch as he pushed on toward the rotating colors . . . committed to escaping this ship while hoping he could beat the Power. Blazing lightning struck above and in front of him. *Not me!* Relief poured over Aren as he shielded his eyes from the sudden brightness. One step from the rainbow circle, the *Subar* intensely immolated white as he launched upward, ax-sword in hand, atop exploding wood planks of the deck beneath him. Overboard, he helplessly flew giving Aren only a glimpse of his burnt armor and pain-contorted face. Aren gave him not another thought as he leaped over the hole in the deck and plunged into the rainbow circle.

Chapter 17

Lasting the Shunned

R elief filled Aren as he felt himself floating inside a rainbow tunnel made of the Powers. Strangely, he felt no vibrations, heard no sounds, felt nothing . . . no movement, not even time. He found himself looking about in wonder in all directions, trying to figure out its structure. Its complexity breathtaking. Its beauty mesmerizing. But suddenly, without warning, Aren's peaceful moment interrupted with him tumbling, tossed from the comfort of the rainbow and onto hardwood planks, sending him butt-over-head until his legs and arm painfully stopped him rolling.

"Auch!" Aren yelled out in pain when a hard-soled foot bent his back awkwardly. He recoiled and curled up on the wood planks both as a means of stretching his back in a manner it was meant to be and to conceal the item surprisingly still in his hands . . . the red and black hide-wrapped red gemstone. How he still gripped it astonished him. When he regained his wits from the pain, he remembered the red gemstone . . . the Agni. Panic gripped him, making him want to throw the cursed thing away, but instead, he fought hard to remain still, not bringing undue attention to himself. *Must keep this Agni from everyone.*

Opening his eyes, Aren found himself lying at the far end and in the center of a semicircle of heavily armed, ratty-clothed Baraans. A musky odor . . . or sweat and worse assaulted his nose. *More unbathed Baraans . . . Really?* At the other open end of the semicircle hung above the planks the rotating sparks surrounding the rainbow circle. *Did I just pass through that?* Aren asked himself, not certain he experienced the mythical step-gate. To one side of the Baraan semicircle, Aren found the white-bearded Tellen, Trundiir, on his knees with Baraans holding a long knife at his neck and a spear poking his left side. He looked unhappy, even for a Tellen. On the other side of the semicircle stood Rogaan, still with bow and sword over his shoulders, amidst the Baraans, holding the dark-haired Suhd close to him. The Baraans were mixed, some not paying much attention to him while others stood, having spears, clubs, and blades at the ready in case he did something unapproved. The two green-clad warriors stood near the step-gate with spears ready for anything other than the red-armored one to appear. The surface of the step-gate shimmered suddenly, then appeared to expand, then contract. Everyone held their breath with attentions fully on the rainbow circle allowing Aren to stand and slip behind the semicircle of what he concluded were some of a ship's crew. Feeling near exhaustion, he felt himself trembling as he moved. A pair of pointy tips poked him not so gently in the back, stopping his planned withdraw and escape from the crowd.

A vibration with an odd feel coming from the shimmering rainbow step-gate warned Aren something was going to happen. He dropped to a knee and hunched down even farther to protect himself from the unknown. A shockwave of heat emitted from the rainbow circle knocking over almost all the Baraans, both the green-clad warriors, and Rogaan and his lithe, dark-haired friend. Only the white-bearded Tellen and the Baraan with the long knife at him stood, the Baraan evidently shielded from the blast by the Tellen's girth. When Aren felt he could open his eyes without getting hit in the face by flying debris, he found himself on his knees and small fires surrounding the red-armored warrior lying on the deck planks, his armor shredded in multiple places and completely gone in others. Then the angry-looking shimmering rainbow circle winked out.

Silence fell over the ship. Aren heard his heart beat rapidly as his body continued trembling. Then, a murmur came from the crew as Aren looked about to get his bearings. The ship he now stood on had triangular black sails and less width than the *Khaaron*. The ship felt different in its movements . . . quicker, faster. Beyond the crowd and aft decks and cabins behind them, blue filled the dawn sky to the northeast. Darkness still held the sky to the northwest providing him good contrast of two burning and smoking ships just visible over the railing on his left beyond the cabins and command deck. One ship floated totally engulfed in flames and looked to be sinking, the other with a fire blazing its center sails. The flames of that center sail were then snuffed out with another bluish net of the Power. Aren watched, trying to make sense of the Power as it faded away. Almost unnoticed until Aren caught it out of the corner of his eye, a third ship slowly spinning without guidance on the waters to his left, to the west, trailed dark smoke that grimly looked darker than the surrounding gloom of the dawn.

"It's over," escaped the relieved, yet trembling words of Aren he meant only for himself. Some of the crew and Trundiir gave him a quizzical glance. The rest looked on to the mess of the deck wondering what had happened. Most wore empty, confused faces, a sign of being disoriented by battle and the Power.

As if appearing from nowhere, the lean, dark-haired brother to Suhd ran to her, crouching down before embracing her with hugs and kisses while speaking words Aren couldn't make out. The half Tellen Rogaan lay raising himself up on his elbows, then just watched them. A sincere smile grew on Rogaan's face. If Aren wasn't mistaken, the young half Tellen had a tear or two in his eyes.

"All of ya get ta tasks!" boomed the words from a blue-clothed crewman up on the command deck. Aren assumed him commander of this ship. "We have da river and a city ta be gettin' ta."

The crew immediately dispersed for riggings and rope lines and other things Aren didn't know how to describe. The two green-clad warriors, who Aren now questioned their race as Baraan, tended to the slow-moving, red-clad warrior who still lay on the deck, his damaged armor smoking and with rising vapors as his two companions helped the big Baraan remove it piece by piece. Looking closer, Aren wasn't certain the big fellow was Baraan, either. His head looked slightly elongated, his complexion, though brown with touches of green and with facial features like Baraans, looked unfading. *Who are they?* Aren questioned. All three of their looks, their appearance, were . . . off. *What have I gotten myself into?*

A pair of pinching jabs in Aren's back reminded him there were those behind him of an untrusting nature. He slowly turned knees with his trembling hands clinging to his chest and the red and black hide wrap. Two rough-looking, sandy-haired Baraans, both barefoot and dressed in rags for clothes Aren was certain hadn't been washed in some time by the odor, poked long daggers at him.

"What ya got der?" one of the rough-looking, dagger-armed crewmen asked in a manner Aren took as threatening. "Hand it over ta us, and we not be pokin' ya."

Aren didn't know how to take the meaning of the demand. Alarmed the two wanted something more than the wrapping, he scrambled to his feet, then backed away. Bumping into something solid, Aren slowly and with a bit of trepidation raised his still trembling hand over his shoulder searching for what it was. Discovering a rock-hard face and jaw with a very short beard, Aren felt a sense of relief roll over him. He turned to confirm with his eyes it was the half Tellen, Rogaan.

"He is with me," announced Rogaan, as if that should settle everything.

"No before he be givin' over dat in his hands," replied the other rough-looking crewman. Aren's risen hope plunged at the words.

"He's not to be harmed or stolen from," the half Tellen accused and threatened.

"Ya no be givin' da word here," the first rough-looking crewman made his declaration. Their pair of long daggers then made at poking Aren again.

Strange the sensation that grabbed Aren's attention . . . the long daggers quickly forgotten, completely. Strange the vibrations to him both new and unknown. Aren saw the half Tellen sense it too but seemed confused about what and where to look. Aren glimpsed the lines of Power curving about them as vibrations increased. He felt his flesh being tugged at, pulled apart, giving him alarm. He barked at Rogaan as he grabbed the half Tellen's snapjaw hide chest protector trying to pull him down as Aren threw himself to the deck. "Down. Get down, you idiot!"

Rogaan resisted at first Aren's tugging but then gave in to the pull on his chest armor. Both landed on their sides, then rolled on their stomachs as Aren covered his head with a hand. A burning sound filled his ears while his skin crawled as if plunged into a mound of crawlers and biters. He fought to endure the horrifying sensations on his skin and an urge to jump up and run. Then, the crawling sensations disappeared. So too gone were the vibrations. With a peek above his arms, the lines of the Power were gone. Aren sat up looking about. The aft elevated structure of the ship suffered a stride-wide hole with the hole's bottom edge just a few hands higher than the deck. The timbers had been completely cut through from the stern of the ship to this side of the raised structure enclosing the cabins. Looking through the smoldering hole, Aren saw the waters of the Ur and the distant smoking *Khaaron* in the gloomy dawn, still drifting on the river's current, still without control. Whatever bore that hole in the big timbers and wood of the structure and cabins passed directly between the two green-clad warriors and over the now half-stripped red-clad warrior still lying on the deck planks. Both the green-clad warriors looked about with mouths agape at the damage to the ship and the several dead crew. Aren was certain the warriors both felt the Power before witnessing it too as they gave each other a fist-bump while wearing looks of relief.

Aren gasped as he looked to his right where the Power passed near him and the half Tellen. Standing erect were two pairs of legs. Near, Aren recognized the heads with upper chests of two crewmen laying on the deck. Both died with horrified expressions. The ship rolled slightly, toppling both sets of legs with dull thuds that ended up next to the severed heads. Aren let out his breath, relieved he too had not been in the Power's path.

"What was that?" Rogaan asked in a calm, even tone.

"I don't know its name . . ." answered Aren with a bit of frustration. A chill rippled up his back as he realized the reach and intensity of the manifested Power. Aren shouted out for everyone to hear. "It's of the Power, of the Agni . . . the *Shunned*. Must get away from the *Khaaron*. He can still touch us."

"What . . . Who?" Rogaan asked.

"Lucufaar . . . Luntanus . . . the *Shunned!*" Aren again raised his voice, now trembling. He yelled up to the command deck and the crewman dressed in blue. "We must get far away and quickly from the *Khaaron*!"

"Who be ya givin' me orders?" the blue-dressed commander rhetorically asked.

"Follow his guidance, Saalar," came a choking voice from the barely moving big fellow clad in red. The half-stripped warrior then attempted to stand but fell, collapsing back to the deck.

"Quickly . . . Saalar! Quickly, you idiot!" Aren yelled out again. "The *Shunned* still can reach out to us with his deadly ways."

Saalar barked orders right and left as he made sure Aren caught his threatening stare. A female Evendiir in an emerald dress appeared near Saalar's side also yelling commands. The crew responded in the gloomy dawn with sails elevating and riggings tightening and any number of things happening about the ship Aren was unfamiliar with. The sound above of canvas whipping on canvas told Aren the sails were opening. The ship lurched forward with newly puffed out sails above. Then, the ship started into a slow left turn, causing yells and more barked orders from the command deck.

"She be damaged!" Saalar bellowed out to the crew. "Da tiller trackin' partly ta da wheel. Re-rig da sails ta haul her close ta shore."

"What is happening?" Rogaan asked of whoever near could answer.

"We must get far away from this . . . *Shunned*." Aren repeated himself to the dark-haired half Tellen and his friends, Pax and Suhd, who now stood near listening to the goings-on. Awed by the expanse and might Luntanus Alum commanded the Powers, Aren's skin crawled and hairs stood with real fear for the first time since Farratum's arena. "Out of his reach with his Agni Powers."

Arguing drew Aren's attention to the green-clad warriors now half-carrying the big warrior between them. They passed by Aren and Rogaan for the stairs down to the main deck. Intensely at their task, none of the warriors gave the slightest glance at Aren or the others. The once red-clad warrior now with a bare chest and back with what appeared as scales and partial armor on his lower body was barely conscious and mumbling words. Aren only heard some of them, and of those he did not understand. The big warrior bore many scars of what looked to be blade slashes, stab cuts, and burns. Some of them fresh as the scent of burnt flesh followed him. "Help us take forward the *Vassal* to his cabin."

"*Vassal?*" Aren asked of no one.

"He named himself *Vassal* of Vaikuntaars," answered Rogaan.

"City of the Dead . . ." clarified Aren. A chill rippled through him as he stared at his trembling hands wishing they would stop.

"Yes. Place of the Ancients," answered the white-bearded Tellen, dressed in dull-green hunter's armor with dark brown hide boots. The thick-bodied Tellen walked by them on shaky legs. He offered his services to the two green-clad warriors who were lowering the *Vassal* down the stairs.

Rogaan grumbled something Aren didn't catch before dropping his bow and quiver of arrows, then went to help the warriors and Tellen with the big-bodied *Vassal*. The four of them worked together quickly getting the *Vassal* down to the main deck as the crew of the ship watched but offered no assistance. Pax and Suhd left Aren to join the group on the main deck as they half-carried the *Vassal* toward the forward cabin in the forecastle. On the *Khaaron*, Aren remembered the forecastle as a prison for the few unfortunates of use to Lucufaar . . . Luntanus Alum. Aren felt a pang of fear thinking of the *Shunned*. The stories of legend didn't measure up to what he experienced of the cursed one, he reflected. Aren looked about and found himself alone while still holding to his chest the red and black hide wrap and the Agni within. He suddenly felt alone. Normally, he welcomed such a feeling, but today's happenings made him fearful of both mortals and Ancients. While growing up, he dreamed of meeting such beings . . . the *Vassals* of the Ancients and those of legends and myths. They were never supposed to be. *Seems they're not just stories*, Aren considered as he ran after the others while trying his best to look as if he needed no one.

As Aren approached the group carrying the *Vassal*, he felt a vibration . . . intense and powerful coming from the direction of the adrift *Khaaron*. He calculated it several marches to the north adrift on the eastward flowing Ur. He turned seeing lines of Power carrying a large and intense ball of liquid red flames just strides above the waters of the Ur. It came straight at them from their port side with great speed spewing up volumes of heated vapor in its trail. Aren warned anyone who would listen, "His reach is upon us. Hide."

Aren dove for cover among crates stacked against the cabin wall. The heavy crates and boxes offered little cover, but it was all he could find with doom so quickly approaching. The rest of the group looked about searching, finally seeing it too, coming with great speed, a sphere of red, yellow, and blue flames. They all followed Aren's lead dropping to the deck, allowing the *Vassal* to plunk down on the wood planks with a thump.

Peeking through the crates, Aren couldn't take his eyes from the rapidly approaching flaming sphere, wanting to learn everything about it. It might mean their doom, but he didn't want to waste an opportunity to learn of anything that could give him his own power. The lines and pattern of the Power and the feeling of its vibrations left him with an intense curiosity of this manifestation. With a rumble, the burning sphere struck the port side of the ship near midship, exploding . . . sending a roaring concussion wave through the air and a great shudder through the wood frame and planks of the ship. Aren, crouching behind the crates, was knocked off his feet as heat rose instantly to a painful searing before dissipating almost as fast. Burnt wood and sulfur filled his nose as flames spewed over the deck touching sails, timbers, crates, and crew. Most of the damage seemed below where yells and screams from the crew came in numbers as the moments went on. A warm, salty mist covered the ship, putting out small fires here and there. Aren rose from the deck into a sitting position trying to get the ringing in his ears to stop by shaking his head this way and that. Looking about, he found everyone among the group and some of the crew doing the same. Somehow, he survived.

"We be takin' on water!" yelled voices from below. More crew across the ship echoed the danger with their loud yells. Many footfalls and more yelling below deck told Aren the crew was trying to repair the damage to stop from taking on water.

The blue-clothed commander bellowed orders from the command deck that Aren couldn't make out from the ringing still in his head. *Oh, what a head pain*, he moaned to himself. He felt terrible, as if his whole body and head had taken a beating.

Struggling with the *Vassal*, the green-clad warriors were getting him to his boots and toward the forward cabin. The two warriors reluctantly accepted help from the white-bearded Trundiir and dark, short-bearded Rogaan. The four of them carried the more than two-stride tall *Vassal* into his cabin leaving the door open behind them. Aren, curious of this *Vassal*, found himself at the cabin door looking in. Spacious by any standard of ship design, Aren now understood. The bed they placed him on looked as three crates set end-to-end with generous padding and more covers on top. The *Vassal* seemed awake, but only vaguely aware of his surroundings. *His battle with the Shunned must have taken a toll.* Aren looked down at his own still-trembling hands and understood a little, he imagined. Stepping into the cabin, he spied more red armor on the floor and several long cases. They looked stout, but not made of any metal or wood he was familiar with. *What in Kur are they made of?* Gleaming silver locks unlike any he ever had seen secured both. Next to the cases, a backpack of dark tanniyn hide appeared to be stuffed full. Nothing else worthy of noting or remembering caught his eye.

"What? Get out!" one of the green-clad warriors demanded when he caught sight of Aren looking around.

Aren stood unmoving. *I have rights to be here*, he confirmed to himself, feeling empowered now that he no longer suffered under the thumb of Farratum or Lucufaar . . . damned Luntanus Alum. *Who are these two to give me orders?* Indignant at their ordering him about, Aren made it a point to stand his ground—even if he still trembled while doing so.

Trundiir looked at Aren, then to Rogaan, then spoke, "We should take our leave."

Rogaan nodded in agreement at the Tellen. They both slowly backed away from the warriors tending to the *Vassal* as the Tellens scanned the room. Taking in everything, both Tellens glided over the wood plank floor trying to be quiet in their passing with each seeming to be competing with the other. If a contest, Aren had to admit, Trundiir was much better at the style of movement.

"Come join me, Aren." Rogaan made his request as he passed by Aren at the door.

"Would you point me to some sandals or better, boots, for my feet?" Aren half-asked, half-demanded of Rogaan.

Trundiir stopped in front of Aren presenting a challenging stare up at the Evendiir's face. Standing a full head taller, Aren almost laughed at the scene . . . *Little Tellen trying to intimidate an Evendiir—me.*

"They will cut off your naddles and feed them to you as soon as let you stand here gawking," informed Trundiir in his serious, deep voice.

"I have a right to stand wherever I wish," Aren proudly and arrogantly spoke with a hint of a shake in his voice.

"You have no rights with them," Trundiir stated in his deep rumble as matter-of-factly as Aren thought possible before he pushed past Aren. Stopping at the cabin door, Trundiir spoke. "They are *Sentii* and have little fondness for the rest of the races. Do as your pride and arrogance compel."

"*Sentii?*" An outburst of the name escaped Aren before he realized he spoke.

"And the one they attend to . . ." Trundiir's deep voice grumbled on as he walked away. "is far more dangerous to us than any *Shunned*."

Chapter 18

Scheming

"**D**a *Makara* still be takin' on water and soon be goin' ta ground near da shore." Pax explained what was told to him by the *Makara*'s second commander a few moments ago. Gone was Pax's brooding demeanor when Aren first boarded the ship. The dark-haired Baraan stood with the rest of the group on the slanting deck, though was the only one openly wearing a face of angry determination. The deck's listing raised the port side of the *Makara*. It was an attempt by the crew to slow the ship's taking on water, at least until reaching the shallows. "Da commanders say da ship be a dangerous place ta be after groundin'. Ship can sink bein' dragged out in da river when da current changes or be torn apart on da rocks or attacked in da shallows by tanniyn and *mu'usumgal* . . . da water-dragons."

"And this *Shunned* with his troops . . ." Rogaan injected a question into the conversation. It was clear to Aren the half Tellen was unsettled by Luntanus Alum and uncertain of what to do next. "How long before he comes looking for us?"

"Do not know about him, but we should go to the hills and forest once we get to shore." Trundiir's deep voice was almost a grumble while he visibly continued holding back an unsettled stomach. Aren noticed the Tellen's skin coloring to be still a bit greenish.

"What of da . . . *Sentii?*" Pax inquired. "Dey be ownin' da wilds there."

"Not this far north," white-bearded Trundiir flatly answered, then belched with a sour face.

"How do you know that?" asked Rogaan in disbelief.

"Hard lessons learning with the *Sentii* here before . . ." Trundiir answered, then belched again. Aren wondered how long it would be before the Tellen made a mess of the decking, again. "They are a hard people. Dedicated to the Ancients unlike any temple *Kunsag*. And they are fierce protectors of their lands beyond Anza . . . violently so."

"So, we keep away from da mountains and stay in da hills." Pax announced the group's unagreed upon decision. When no one protested, he continued. "How do we get back over ta da other side of da river . . . back to Farratum and Brigum?"

"Is that a good idea for us?" Rogaan asked. "We just broke out of that prison isle. And the *Vassal* left it a mess. Where can we travel north of this river and be without Farratum or Brigum's Ensi wanting to put us back in manacles?"

"We can no go with da *Vassal*!" Pax protested. "In da Blood Lands? No. I no trust what he be schemin'."

"You can make a life out here . . ." Trundiir belched his offer of a resolution to their situation, "in these hills. At least until you figure something different."

Aren didn't like where the discussion was going. He wanted to get back to Windsong and its familiar hills, and to his father to learn more of the Agni and of the Power. A whisper somewhere in his head taunting, compelling him into wanting different. *No. You're not telling me anything*, Aren warned off the whisper.

"What of ya father?" Suhd asked with a concerned tone. Pax, Rogaan, and Aren all looked at her thinking she was talking to each of them. She avoided her brother's tearing eyes and solidly fixed her gaze on Rogaan.

"Father?" Rogaan repeated.

"He still be on that ship," Suhd announced as if everyone was aware of what she spoke.

"On the ship . . . the *Khaaron*?" Rogaan asked, shocked and astonished.

"Yes," Suhd answered with a bit of frustration.

Rogaan stood silently for moments as everyone watched him. Aren felt a twinge of fear accompanied by a smaller twinge of guilt for not speaking of Rogaan's father being present when the half Tellen was on the *Khaaron*.

Rogaan turned his attention deliberately and directly onto Aren. He looked unhappy in every way. "You said nothing—"

"You asked of the other Tellen . . . a *Sharur* Tellen, exactly." Precise in his memory and argument, Aren didn't flinch when answering Rogaan. "I answered about what you asked."

"Truly." Rogaan looked at Aren as if he had horns . . . that he was about to rip from their roots. "You spoke nothing of him. Did he not save you in the Farratum court?"

"Would you have had the *Shunned* and the *Vassal* put a hold on their scuffle so that we could *chat* of everything of concern in your life . . ." Aren rhetorically shot back at Rogaan in an attempt of getting control of unpleasant their conversation. Rogaan fell silent staring at Aren with fuming eyes. Everyone else shifted their attentions back and forth between the two while holding their tongues. Awkwardness filled the silence. It was plain to see the half Tellen was more than angry . . . likely all at Aren and certainly of the situation. The question present in everyone's awkward silence was . . . would Rogaan have the self-control to act . . . fruitfully or be brazenly reckless? Aren hoped for the first as he bit his lip holding back a much-desired and -deserved scathing rebuke about this whole situation . . . and Rogaan. Instead, he locked stares with the half Tellen mustering as much courage as he could marshal. Long, silent moments passed in the dawn hour with only the fluttering of sails, the lapping of water against the ship, and the mostly faint voices of the crew trying to keep the *Makara* afloat.

"We stay with the *Makara* as crew." Solemn words came from Pax breaking the silence, sounding as if he reached a best of all decisions.

"Father needs to be rescued," Rogaan announced with heat in his voice.

"Ya father be in da hands of an ancient killer," Pax countered Rogaan's heat with an attempt at reason. "Told so by da worst . . . bloodiest stories tellin' our history. Legends should no be real. Dey be frightenin'."

"Words of ya father before seeking . . . Mithraam, it is." The blue-themed, well-dressed second commander spoke as he approached. "Ya father wanted to see with his own eyes a livin' legend. Yes. Da Tellen be known even out here. He be well thought of by da River Folk as a champion of da *free ways*."

"Then, help us rescue him," Rogaan asked with a frustrated tone.

"A fool's task," the dark-haired, clean-shaven second commander of the *Makara* answered in an unexpected way. The Baraan stopped his sure-footed steps on the listing deck to be standing next to Pax and Suhd. "We be damaged and need sailin' ta da shallows before takin' on much more water. And dat ship, da *Khaaron*, da *Makara's* crew knows now it be carryin' an Ancient One. No one be helpin' ya . . . or even me with such a task."

"Rogaan . . ." Pax almost sounded as if pleading by his tone, "ya can no be askin' us ta give up our *Lights* tryin' ta save him. No with him in da hands of a *Shunned*. Dis be da stuff of legends, and we should be readin' and hearin' of it. No livin' it."

Rogaan's eyes were instantly wet, and Aren thought he saw a thunder cloud forming over him. Rogaan made to argue but was cut off.

"Ya father no wanted dat for ya, Roga of da Blood An . . ." the second commander spoke with compassion in his eyes. When Rogaan's face twisted at the *Vassal's* given title of him, the second commander pursed his lips, then continued. "Such a seeker of da *free ways*, as ya father, would no be wantin' his only son ta fall ta da blade or be made *lightless*. Not even ta free him."

"We need ta be stayin' with da *Makara*," Pax restated his desire.

"Ya father no wanted dat for ya, either," words of prudence directed at Pax and Rogaan came from the second commander. "He be wantin' ya away from da water-thievin' livin'. Wanted much more for his family. He said so before he ever held ya in his arms. He heard da stories of Mithraam in da civil war, fighting by da side of da Ebon Ones ta beat tyrants back and make Shuruppak da lands of men . . . not rulers. He and da Ebon Ones made da lands free . . . until a handful of years ago when darkness be startin' ta poison Shuruppak, again."

Rogaan looked stunned and angry, all at the same time as his eyes darted from the second commander to each of those around him. When his eyes fell on Suhd, they softened and then became wet again.

"Listen ta them, Rogaan . . . please," Suhd pleaded with her own wet eyes.

Aren found himself agreeing with the young Baraan. His head felt a little light and swooning, and he held a desire wanting to please her . . . wait! Aren shook his head. *That damning scent of sway of hers. It's strong.* Shaking his head again, he recalled the group's arguments and found himself agreeing with Pax and the best for them was staying with the *Makara*. But that seemed unlikely. He looked at the half Tellen to see what he was to do.

Rogaan's demeanor softened, but his frustration at knowing his father a prisoner of Luntanus Alum and with a purpose unknown, didn't diminish. "For now, we keep ourselves safe. Seems we stay here with the *Makara* or hide in the lands on the southern shore of the Ur."

"Da *Makara* be no good for ya all," the second commander continued with his explaining of their situation. "Dey will no be welcomin' ya. Crew is small and tight with each other. And when we ground, we be in da shallows where *mu-usumgal* and more will be lookin' for meals, makin' a ruckus as dey do. Not long after, da walkin' jaws and claws will be drawn ta da shore and shallows. Da south shore is ya only way."

"I am good with that . . ." Trundiir's deep-sounding words trailed before he let out a loud, foul-smelling belch. He then continued with a look that he might not keep his stomach down. "More sooner . . . more better."

"But we——" Pax's attempt to negotiate was cut off.

"We talked of dis," the second commander reminded. "It be ya father's wishes. It be firm land for ya."

"How do we get to shore if we are grounded in the shallows?" Rogaan asked with a solemn sincerity, but clearly to cut off further protests by Pax.

"Ya be given passage in one of da rowin' boats," answered the second commander. "It be ready now."

A strong urge to leave the ship for the shore welled up within Aren. Surprised at its powerful draw, he looked south to the thin beach. It was sparsely peppered with snapjaws, featherwings, and leatherwings, and a mix of land-dwelling tanniyn both small and large. Then, there were the shallows as they neared shore . . . Would there be more of those water-dragons? A dangerous place. Still, it allowed them an escape. This strong urge to head south almost made Aren yearn for it. Confused at this sudden desire to head in that direction, he asked himself, *Is this more of Suhd's scent of sway?*

"Leave . . . now?" Pax asked of the second commander in a tone that made Aren think Pax felt a sense of abandonment.

"Da . . . *Vassal* be in da forward cabin with his *Sentii* tendin' him," the blue-clad second commander explained. "It be some time before he be recovered enough ta be lookin' for ya. We be keeping the *Makara* off da grounding as long as we can to give ya time."

"Time for what?" Suhd asked innocently.

"Time ta disappear," the second commander made his offer clear in purpose. "Give da boat back ta da waters when ya get ta shore. It be makin' it harder for his *Sentii* ta find ya. I fear da *Vassal's* plans for ya all be no good its end."

Yes . . . came the whisper from within. Powerful now the desire came at Aren. His mind protested at the dangers on the shoreline they had to overcome. *Away from the Vassal . . . from the Shunned*, the inner whisper kept urging Aren.

"Yes!" Aren burst out. Quickly recovering from his momentary sense of surprise and embarrassment, he continued with less than the sincerest motives. "His offer gets us away from this fight between this *Shunned* and the *Vassal*. On shore, our white-bearded, belching friend can lead us into the wilds where we can hide from the *Sentii* and their master and the *Shunned*. We can figure through the rest once we get safe."

"I am for it!" belched Trundiir with a closed fist bump to his chest, his greenish complexion worsening.

"I am too," added Rogaan with less enthusiasm and lacking the fist bump.

Pax held a fierce protest in his eyes until his sister gently took hold of his arm and made a pleading case to him. "Brother, ya all I be havin' anymore. This *Shunned* and *Vassal* scare me ta darkness. We need ta be gettin' away. Father's friend be givin' dat ta us."

Emotions rippled over and over on Pax's lean face. Fierce protests formed from the sorrows of a determined brother . . . the protector of his sister. Aren watch in curiosity wondering which side of Pax would win. When moments passed with all watching in silence Pax's contortions, he finally spoke. "We will be leavin' da ship."

"Now, someone fetch me some weapons," Trundiir grumbled through another smelly belch.

"And a pair of boots . . . and some clothes and a walking stick," Aren added, now that everyone was listening.

Chapter 19

Serpent's Awakening

Desolation. A world aflame in the rain of stars falling and exploding in the moment of union between that above and what is below. Alone. A lone survivor standing on slick footing among heaps of human carnage spread across a fresh wasteland . . . Fetid leftovers of war. No. Not a survivor. Regrets and disgust filling the rancorous air spoiling all in the clash of beliefs between those of mankind and those above. The initiator . . . The cause holding a crimson blade stained in wet crimson in hand while suffering the putrid wafts of burning flesh mixed with stinging clouds of acrid death. Sickening the smell. Horrifying the gaze. Repugnant the touch. Haunting to the *Light*, tainting it. *A vision—but of what?* he asked of no one. Recoiling from its experience, he needed to know.

What am I seeing? Where am I? he asked both himself and the haunting presence besieging him.

"You serve me," the presence declared.

I am the Subar serving only the Supreme—he defiantly countered, attempting the declaration of his own allegiances before being abruptly cut off.

"Very well," the presence emotionlessly uttered, yet with a certainty of outcome to be.

Ezerus suddenly realized he felt suspended and adrift . . . cold. Opening his eyes, he confirmed himself submerged in gloomy chill waters atop dark depths. The dawn sun's rays were only able to penetrate the surreal immediately surrounding him. *How did I get here?* he asked himself, still disoriented. *Where is here?*

A large shadow passed at a distance beneath him. He felt it in the water as much as caught it in a glimpse. Then, another passed, smaller, closer, but no less dangerous. Alarmed and wanting an escape, he forced himself to look up, finding the *Khaaron's* keel near though appearing unreal through the watery distortions . . . his liquescent burial box. Drifting away, the *Khaaron's* top decks continuously lit up in the blues, oranges, reds, and blinding whites of the Powers. He shivered, not of his cool, watery embrace, but of being so close to the Powers of Agni. *Must get to the surface to breathe,* Ezerus both told and warned himself. His breath was starting to wane, and his chest hinted at that inner burning that would command him to gulp at his surroundings for air. Something teased his mind to turn and look around. Without warning, out of the darkness, a massive shadow emerged from the depths bearing down on him with jaws agape displaying its outer and inner rows of deadly spikes.

Nowhere to go, no means to defend himself, Ezerus braced for the imminent impact. He reflexively tensed his whole body and shut his eyes tight, not wanting to know the exact moment the beast and darkness would take him. He swirled about violently on powerful currents of churning water before the spikes closed on him, painfully, then forcefully propelling him through the waters at speeds not of his abilities. He expected the bite to drive the tooth-spikes deep into him, but they only pushed into his light armor compressing his ribs. Opening his eyes, he met the open hand-size orb of the beast's left eye. It looked at him yet appeared more interested in the waters beyond. The water-dragon jerked him back and forth, forcing Ezerus's breath out . . . It was almost gone, hastened by the beast's instinct to thrash before pitching upward toward the water's surface. Fighting to keep from gasping for the air that was not there, Ezerus struggled against the burning growing pain in his chest. He knew what was coming. The water-dragon would break through the surface of the water, then swallow him brutally. The race between needing to inhale air or water was near its end. Ezerus knew he couldn't will himself not to breathe much longer. Still submerged, darkness started its final embrace upon him as the burning in his lungs grew unbearable.

Then, the darkness gave way to brightness as he and the water-dragon broke through the watery surface. Ezerus sucked in air as deeply as he could while being propelled above the water. The toothy-spikes released him, but a glance confirmed they were all around him . . . four terrible rows of white spikes in the top and bottom jaws. As he reached the peak of his slowing airward travel, Ezerus felt a moment of being weightless, suspended in air. It felt pleasant, the bliss before the pain. That presence surrounding him in the water felt stronger now, swirling about his body. It grabbed him, violently, painfully, before jerking him through the air in a blink. A sense of both weightlessness and of being dragged about, Ezerus tumbled when his feet raked through the water. His tumbles found him headfirst in the water, taking in the liquid up his nose, causing him to gag and cough as he continued tumbling—a left arm and shoulder in the wetness. Then, his back. Then, his left leg and back. Then, his right, before his head plunged back into the waters. Ezerus held his breath for the moments this time upside down in the waters. His tumbles continued until slamming painfully into something with a dull woody "*thunk*." His head a swirl, Ezerus looked about trying to shake off his disorientation. He floated just above the waters in the gloomy dawn. Scintillating vaporous tendrils held him firmly in a painful embrace, almost crushing him. *What in Kur . . .?*

A glimpse back to the river caught sight of the massive water-dragon still chasing him at the surface. It sped through the waters leaving a trail of foamy white. Almost upon him again, the beast's aggressiveness gave Ezerus a panic. He felt himself an easy target—prey—for the beast to finish what it started in the waters below. Unable to move or will himself in any direction, Ezerus yelled out in a bellow of fear as he shut his eyes tight again. The intense pain of his neck wrenching accompanied a jerk of his whole body upward as the red vapors coiled and tightened, propelling him vertically along the hull of the *Khaaron*. A splash and horrendous "*thud*" beneath him found the water-dragon slamming into the side of the ship, splintering and breaking hull planks above the waterline as the beast shook its massive head at the water's surface. Ezerus watched the huge black-and-white-armored hide of the beast sink back into the waters before starting a lethargic swim off to unknown destinations.

Clearing the ship's rails in his ascent, Ezerus's upward motion ceased. Now, hanging suspended above the deck by scintillating vaporous tendrils, his skin prickled at being touched by the Powers while simultaneously feeling relieved at not having been a morning meal. His thoughts turned to the irony of his situation. *I never wish to experience this again.*

"Neither I," the presence reverberated in his head.

"What?" His skin prickling and his hairs standing painfully, Ezerus looked urgently all about him. "Who . . ."

"It is I," the presence filled his head as the vaporous tendrils rotated Ezerus upright before setting his boots to the wood deck.

Standing near Ezerus, a familiar lean, clean-shaven face, now half-blistered and burnt. The face's always neatly combed light brown hair mussed about revealing a singed left ear that almost had the slight point of an Evendiir. Struggling not to gawk as he took in the aide to the aide, Ezerus observed the wiry Baraan's black and lavender clothing peppered with gashes and burnt spots. The lavender fabric on his left shoulder completely ruined by fire revealed burnt, blistering flesh. Despite the wounds, Lucufaar approached Ezerus with only a slight limp that was new. The Baraan held his demeanor strong and focused, ignoring what Ezerus thought painful injuries. Now noticeable to Ezerus, the color of Lucufaar's hair slowly turned from light brown to silver-streaked gray as his lean face took on slight wrinkles and folds of a Baraan of latter days. A chill rippled through Ezerus. Standing in front of him, Lucufaar took on a dangerous aura as Ezerus's eyes watched in disbelief and a growing uneasiness. Most unnerving were the dark, squinty eyes of this new Lucufaar, strong and focused on Ezerus.

"Give me your hand," the presence commanded him.

Ezerus heard the words in his mind. Lucufaar's lips had not moved. Ezerus hesitated to comply out of pride and a fear of the unknown. *What is happening?* he asked in his mind. Lucufaar's dark, squinty eyes turned crossed with a slight furrow on his brows, convincing Ezerus to raise his right hand. Those dark, squinty eyes then took on a demeanor of disgust.

"Your left hand," the presence commanded.

Again, Lucufaar's lips did not speak the words Ezerus heard in his mind. The once-frustrated, subservient-postured Lucufaar was no more. A new Baraan stood in his place, forcing another chill to ripple through Ezerus. Then, an angry disgust in himself gripped Ezerus, being a strong Baraan of a high position in authority within Shuruppak, as the *Subar* he was compelled to challenge this presence and Lucufaar. "Tell me who you are so I know the name that shall answer—?"

"Answer to no one." Lucufaar spoke as the idle vaporous tendrils came alive, painfully constricting Ezerus. "I am Luntanus Alum . . . your master."

That chill turned to icy cold terror. Ezerus's mind panicked with embarrassing fear that he no longer cared who saw or reported. *Must get away! Must flee this monster!* Ezerus struggled against the vapors as he growled with exertion and frustration. Losing all sense of his surroundings and dignity, he fought against the red vapors coiling about his body with every move he made. In horrid crushing pain in ways he couldn't describe, Ezerus let out a bellow begging for help from anyone . . . everyone, while looking skyward to the heavens. "Help me, Ancients of Old!"

"Silence!" the presence commanded in a cold tone. "They dare not challenge me."

Ezerus stopped struggling. He succumbed to the futility of his situation . . . in the hands and unexpected mercy of the most dangerous and ruthless of history's *Kabirs*, the *Shunned*. Wondering how this can be, he settled his mind trying to block out the pain subjected on him by the scintillating vaporous tendrils. His eyes regained their ability to focus, allowing him to look upon his surroundings. Luntanus Alum stood before him focused and determined in an unknown purpose. Ezerus felt the vapors pulling at his left arm, raising it to the *Shunned*. The daimon of daimons, worst of the *Shunned*, reached out and took hold of the red gem-encrusted ring on Ezerus's right hand. A horrible chill ripped through Ezerus. The signet ring of the *Subar*, giving Ezerus his unchallengeable authority to go where he wished and do what he wished to ensure loyalty to Shuruppak, vibrated and turned warm, then hot . . . painfully hot. Ezerus growled at the new pain, but unable to move his arm or hand to remove it from the pain-maker. He could only endure as the *Shunned* pressed on the red gem, forcing it deeper into the now soft metal of the ring until the gem touched the skin of his finger. The *Shunned* spoke words Ezerus didn't understand, a different tongue and knowledge from his. The red gem glowed. *No! An Agni Stone!* Ezerus's mind went wild with fear and disgust as he tried to pull away from the ancient daimon so that he could rip the ring from his finger, even if it meant ripping his finger from his hand. A deep chill spread through his body. He instinctively knew this sensation would take his life if he didn't stop it or flee from it. Ezerus futilely struggled against everything . . . the red vapors coiling him, the ring, the Agni Stone, the *Shunned*, the feeling of his *Light* slowly being drawn from him. It was over in an instant. All the pain gone. Ezerus fell to the wood deck in a relieved and gleeful thud.

Looking up from his prone sprawl, Ezerus saw a renewed Baraan standing over him. The *Shunned's* lean face and shoulder still bore scars, but the burnt blisters and skin were no more. His hair now dark gray with streaks of silver, but unburnt and combed straight. The *Shunned* stood taller in a manner, and his dark, squinty eyes took on a dangerous confidence.

"You are bound to me, *Subar*," Luntanus Alum announced. "Your *Light* is tied to mine, to serve me, as I will."

Ezerus didn't fully understand what the *Shunned* meant by "bound," but it didn't sound a good thing. Trying to sit up, Ezerus found himself weak and in pain with every move.

"Why me?" Ezerus asked not expecting an explanation.

"You may be able to endure my needs," the *Shunned* answered.

Chapter 20

Tightening Coils

I am Subar. I am Subar. My word is unquestioned. My orders are heeded. There is no station higher beyond the Supremes. I am the Subar, Ezerus told himself over and over again in his mind, trying to believe . . . trying to convince himself. His conviction of his place in the world shaken by the binding and the presence. Looking at the deck planks between his knees, he sat, trying to convince himself but failing despite his chanting. In the depths of his mind, *he* was there . . . The presence, sensing him, watching him, working his influence on him, judging him. For what he was being judged, Ezerus could only guess. *How do I free myself from this . . . harness?*

"He has hold of you as well," a deep voice speaking deliberate words sounded out.

Ezerus looked up from his deck planks, then about the room of the forecastle seeking the source of the words and finding it in between a sleeping male Baraan and female Evendiir. The old Tellen with a boldly braided, gray-touched beard stared back at him. Dressed in a worn gray tunic identifying him as a lawbreaker in bondage, the Tellen sat bound in manacles secured to the far wall. Yet, he stared with eyes that told his spirit had not been broken. Unsettled, Ezerus met the Tellen's gaze and made his best effort to sound still the authority, "Silence, stoner."

"Never did find that title appealing," the Tellen challenged.

"I am one that cares little of what appeals to you," Ezerus shot back while being taken aback at the Tellen's boldness.

"He will use you and discard you," the old Tellen kept at annoying Ezerus. Not speaking of it, Ezerus feared the old Tellen spoke truth.

"I said SILENCE!" Ezerus demanded with raised heat in his tone and now his own anger-filled gaze burning. No reaction from the Tellen. No fear. *Why is he not fearing me?* Ezerus asked himself.

"He is dangerous to all you care of," the old Tellen kept at Ezerus.

"You know nothing of what I care for," Ezerus replied in a sneer.

"Your beloved Shuruppak," teased the Tellen. Ezerus did not know what to think of the Tellen's words and so remained silent as the Tellen kept on about things. "That is his goal. Though, he must first achieve something in the Lands of the Ancients before making for his prize."

"You see things that are not, stoner." Ezerus chided, hoping his insult would put the Tellen off and make him silent. "He has no need of the ancient relics or knowledge to take Shuruppak for himself."

In days of old, the *Shunned* were the power and authority of the lands where the *Dingiir* did not tread. Not understanding how he knew such things, Ezerus searched his thoughts and memories. *Where did that knowledge come from? How do I know such things?* The presence teased at him from somewhere deep in his mind, whispering words he could not hear, yet gave him knowledge. At that realization, Ezerus suffered an uncontrolled shiver he hoped the Tellen and others did not see.

"He will use you in your station . . . sully your name," the Tellen kept at Ezerus in his even, measured tones. "Sully the name of the *Subars*."

"No . . ." Ezerus started to challenge defensively but caught himself and stopped. Getting himself under better control, he stared at the Tellen with disdain for his boldness and fascination at his insights . . . even if his conclusions were difficult to see as predictions. "The *Subars* are independ—"

"Are of Shuruppak," the Tellen both interrupted and finished. "They are the shadow hand of quiet authority in Shuruppak. The hands that guide and shape the decrees of the *Zas* by fear of what can be accused, of secrets threatened revealing if defied, by lies when the truth does not serve their purposes . . . spread for the good of Shuruppak."

How does this one know of such things . . . of the Subars? Ezerus's instincts and loyalty to the empire compelled him to respond and deflect, shade the truth to ensure good governance was maintained . . . for the good of Shuruppak. He fought an urge to counter the Tellen's conclusions. *This Tellen's understanding is far beyond most . . . especially for one so far removed from the centers of authority.* Ezerus felt exposed. Desiring a dismissal of this Tellen . . . and that presence, and a return to the shadows of authority he felt comfort in, Ezerus abruptly stood, knocking over his stool. "One from the wilds of Brigum doesn't know the goings-on of Shuruppak!"

Ezerus spun on his heels turning his back to the Tellen before striding for the door . . . his escape. He opened the door hoping to make his getaway without comments. This just wasn't to be.

"You must fight the *Darkness*, or it will consume you—become you," the old Tellen pronounced a foretelling.

A shiver rippled through Ezerus. The *Darkness* . . . in his thoughts . . . his mind . . . his heart, desiring to consume all of him. His entire life the *Darkness* journeyed with him, teasing him, goading him, tempting him, causing him to lose his self-control in fits of frustration and rage at the unfairness of things denied or not rightly offered. The *Darkness* held him firmly in his younger days until he was taught to accept the inequities and to focus on changing the slights of living by an unassuming elder who lost his *Light* at the hands of free-marketeer ruffians. A traumatic loss for Ezerus, fatherless from when he could remember and motherless not so long before meeting the elder. Ezerus focused his pains and sufferings into a strategy to change the world. So, formed the goal, then the plan, and then the achievement of *Subar* where his hand offered stern guidance to the powerful and a stiffer hand to the unruly. Quiet, the *Darkness* remained in recent times, at least eleven cycles of the *Dur'Anki*, allowing him the self-control and disciplined social skills to enter service in the *Sakes* of Ur where he quickly climbed the ranks of profession earning the favor of those above him and of the more ambitious and ruthless Houses. Then, in his boldest of moves, uncovering a plot of disloyalty among those serving the *Zas*, exposing them with accusations, flirting with the truth to ensure judgments favoring their guilt. The execution of the Disloyals brought a sense of safety to the *Zas* who sponsored Ezerus's appointment to the *Subars*. A beginning. The *Darkness* quiet but never gone as long as it felt satisfied, even if only a little. Now, the presence of the *Shunned* in his mind threatening the loss of his self-control and self-discipline, his ability in keeping his focus on what mattered . . . that which mattered to him, Ezerus, the *Subar*. Looking back at the old Tellen, Ezerus offered a confession. "My lurking companion is the *Darkness*."

Admitting the sways on his heart and thoughts made the first step toward Ezerus accepting his darker nature. He denied it most of his life, the beast inside, but this morning's turn of fates increasingly gave him courage, strength to care less of other's thoughts of him and to embrace himself. Contemplating his newfound self and unclear fate, Ezerus walked the busy decks in the late morning as the *Khaaron* continued its voyage drifting without steerage on the Ur River. Scattered clouds and a slight breeze carrying the faint scent of blossoms, salt, and decay spoke of a calm day that he was thankful for, allowing him his solace without suffering tilting footing. The limited number of oars available on the ship was of little use with the missing tiller and against powerful currents flowing eastward, then westward, dominating and determining where they went. The sails, all either heavily damaged or destroyed by fire and the Powers, were being pieced together by the crew. His hairs uncomfortably prickled at the thought of the Powers. They unsettled him. They were kin to the *Darkness*, though much more dangerous. Pushing away such thoughts, he returned to his stroll. A waft of burnt wood mixing with the salty air filled his nose as he slowly maneuvered around bustling workers as he sought a way to make the most of his situation. *Accept the inequities. Change the slights.* Some of the crew gave him less-than-favorable glances and some full disapproving looks as he passed. Obviously, they expected him to pitch in with repairs. *That is beneath my station.* Much of the *Khaaron's* crew and many of the *Tusaa'Ner* were now busy repairing the ship as a small gathering at the stern, carrying large planks of wood, looked in the attempt of providing enough tiller to at least point the ship in a direction desired. Others piecing together enough fragments of surviving canvas to make one large and one small sail that the deckhands started installing to the masts. Two of the badly damaged masts had reinforcing structures of wood and chains constructed around them. Where they got that much wood was a mystery to Ezerus. *Accept the inequities. Change the slights. Accept the inequities. Change the slights.*

A distant whisper, barely noticeable, teased and taunted his thoughts. *Not again.* Louder the whisper rose until Ezerus almost heard what it was telling him. The whisper spoke again. Still, Ezerus didn't understand it as it drew him, pulled at him. *What is it saying?* His head down, he found himself looking at the stairs to the aft cabins. A glance around the ship allowed him to spy the outer area around the cabins and command deck. *No Luntanus Alum.* A great relief swept over him, though he didn't know why. The *Shunned* wanted him alive. For how long, that was a different question, but at least for today, Ezerus felt safe. Louder spoke the whisper. "Enter."

Realizing he had climbed the stairs from the main deck to the cabin deck without remembering doing so made Ezerus a little unsettled. Try as he did, he couldn't recall climbing them. *Am I day-walking?* The loud whisper spoke to him again. "Enter."

Ezerus looked around once more at the crew and *Tusaa'Ner* busy with repairs. Nobody was close enough to speak to him so. He felt an unseen tugging at him, toward the cabin's hallway door. *Enter it says . . .* Ezerus felt what lay beyond the door to be where he should be. He entered. A step inside brought him to a halt as his eyes adjusted to the lamp-lit narrow hallway. Three doors, one to either side of the hallway and a set of double doors at the end of the hallway were all stained in crimson. A body, once in *Tusaa'Ner* armor, torn apart limb from limb and head from chest lay all about with freshly split blood soaking the decking. Shocked at the unexpected scene, he stood looking at the mess trying to make sense of it. The scent of blood and spilled innards filled his nose and for a moment, made him gag. Ezerus didn't recognize the poor fellow laying in pieces as he fought an urge to back away and return to the exterior decks. Despite the gore, he felt to be in the right place . . . almost. The door to the left cabin swung open.

"He wishes your attendance," an out of sorts Ganzer announced to Ezerus. The aide to one of the most powerful *Zas* in the outer lands of Shuruppak looked frightened and sickly. Not so frightened and more curious, Ezerus stepped inside the cabin.

The spectacle inside was almost as chaotic as the hallway but without the gore or obvious violence. Ganzer with his uncharacteristically messy, short black hair and rumpled clothes, stood uncomfortably close to Ezerus keeping silent and with his once-mean brown eyes screaming to be somewhere else. To his left sat a frightened *Za* on a small, disheveled bed. She displayed reddened eyes and tearstained cheeks. Her eyes spoke of disbelief and bewilderment. Her revealing blue gown clung to her almost curvy body in a soaking sweat. Standing across the room, dressed in a lightly built blue *Tusaa'Ner* armor and with long knife drawn, stood immobilized *Za* Irzal's daughter, Dajil. Framed in red-yellow hair, her light brown face held an expression of determination in the presence of horror. Curiously, she stood immobile. To Ezerus's far right, sitting behind a desk built small to fit properly in the cabin, was Lucufaar . . . Luntanus Alum, the infamous ancient *Shunned*. A shiver ripped through Ezerus looking at the *presence*.

"Maybe you desire to spare the wretched lives of their honor guard?" Luntanus Alum spoke without looking at Ezerus, though Ezerus knew he was being addressed.

An awkward silence filled the room as Ezerus's mind went in many ways trying to think of a proper . . . correct response. The scarred *Shunned* looked up at Ezerus acknowledging him being in the room with his expecting dark, squinty eyes. Ezerus knew he needed to answer the danger . . . knew he needed to show subordinated strength. "Why?"

A smile spread across the *Shunned's* scarred face as he waved his right hand around the room. "Seeing all that is about you and still having the orbs to ask me *why*. I favor your spine."

Fear mingling with relief filled Ezerus as he forced a swallow trying to make his parched mouth moist. Luntanus Alum stood, his silvery dark gray hair pulled back in a tail and wearing a lavender tunic with a wide black tanniyn hide belt fitted with a bold silver buckle. The *Shunned* took in Ezerus for long moments before speaking, "Men-at-arms are needed where we go. These disappointments and that belligerent *sakal* in the hallway are not trustworthy to lead. You are *Subar*. In the rankings of Shuruppak, you have the authority to assume leadership. Either you direct these miserable guardsmen, or I will subdue them, likely killing half or more."

An unexpected twist of fates. By Shuruppak laws, where a *Gal* is absent to decree who commands in such situations, a *Subar* possesses the authority to assume any position of rank in all things except making legal decrees, including the daily acts of a *Za*. Ezerus started to understand Luntanus Alum's false play as an aide to an aide of a *Za* to achieve his ambitions . . . whatever they are. The cunning and discipline required to act so, the pride swallowing and pretend subordination to inferiors, Ezerus was uncertain he could have endured it. Still, the question remained to be answered of his commanding the *Tusaa'Ner*. Ezerus felt uncertain of his ability to command guardsmen in mass, but to refuse this *Shunned* would be a fool's act.

"I will command the *Tusaa'Ner*."

Chapter 21

Thorns and Strife

The *Makara* limping off to the east along the shoreline with what remained of her sails stirred mixed feelings in Rogaan. It was midmorning with a strong sun making it difficult to see the ship with any detail now that was sailing just under the yellow ball of brightness to the east and north. Relieved to be off the ship, as any respected Tellen would, Rogaan turned his worry to their small boat and that it might not survive the dangers of the shallows ahead. The southern shores of the Ur River offered scattered beaches both small and of dark sands, rocks really, where water-dragons liked to congregate, or so he was told by the crew. The swirling waters, strong currents, sharp rocky formations, and the beasts were all dangers to overcome—with no guarantee of succeeding—but they had to take risks to get away from forces and beings beyond them, most near the *Vassal* and his *Sentii* guardians. Rogaan and his companions launched their rowboat in secret from the *Makara* with most of the crew thinking it was being prepared for when the ship grounded itself in the shallows somewhere downriver. The *Makara's* second commander saw to the spread of the misinformation. Their launch was not without troubles in the choppy waters as Trundiir fell into the Ur when trying to board the rowboat from the *Makara's* rope ladder. A stroke of luck, he grabbed the rim of the rowboat keeping himself from plunging deep into the dark waters. In a desperate scramble, Rogaan and Pax pulled the heavy Tellen into the rowboat before a water-dragon got a bite on him.

With everyone and their supplies in the boat, they let the *Makara* sail away, leaving them the task of paddling to shore. They paddled hard to fight the strong eastward current aiming their boat for one of those tiny landing spots tucked in between outcrops of craggy rocks. Only a few of the smaller water-dragons were visible there sunning themselves at the water's edge. That gave them their best chance at surviving and making land. Four of them paddled hard, a still-greenish-skin Trundiir, a not-so-enthusiastic Pax, a complaining Aren, and a focused Rogaan all worked their way to firm land. Rogaan could not shake off the feeling of being exposed on the water and a meal for everything he could not see in the dark depths beneath them. A chill struck him with every look and glance into the water . . . the deep unknown with dangers lurking within unnerving him.

"Da boat be leakin'," announced Suhd from the rear of the rowboat.

"Seriously . . ." Aren complained while looking into the wet beneath his bench seat at the front of the boat, one he shared with Pax. The situation allowed him an excuse to take rest from paddling. Looking down, Aren appeared captivated by the rising water soaking their packs and gear.

"Keep da paddles goin', mystic one," Pax calling out Aren at not keeping up with the paddling put an angry face on the struggling Evendiir. His red face contrasting deeply with his brown tunic gave a sign he found the paddling straining. Aren darted an unfriendly glance at Pax, but after a few unpleasant moments, his paddle went back into the water.

"What ta do about da water?" Suhd asked with more than a little concern in her voice.

"Use da tin pot ta bail it out," replied her brother in an urgent tone. Suhd searched Pax's pack for the tin pot. A quick success found her flinging water everywhere with it, though mostly out of the boat.

Rogaan stole a quick look back at Suhd when he thought it would go unnoticed. *She is as beautiful as ever.* Rogaan found his gaze lingering longer than planned as she half-splashed, half-dumped water over the side of the rowboat, her dull yellow tunic growing wetter with each scoop and throw of water. Ripping his eyes from her found a smirking Pax looking back at him catching his old friend longingly gazing at his sister. Rogaan found it impossible to suppress a smile when Pax, dressed in a dark blue tunic and black pants and boots, kept smiling. Heat flushed Rogaan's face at being caught so blatantly with his attention not on paddling. *Things are starting to feel as they used to*, Rogaan noted to himself with a relieved sense of hope. The strengthened hope gave him new vigor and stronger strokes with his paddle. Trundiir, in his stout hunter's armor covering a dark red tunic and part of his brown hide pants, sat with his dark boots in rising water opposite Rogaan on their bench. The white-bearded Tellen only grunted at noticing Rogaan sneaking looks at Suhd, causing even more heat to flush Rogaan's face. Pax and Aren used their paddles more to guide the boat than anything else with Pax matching Aren's weaker strokes. Positioned behind Aren, Rogaan curiously noted the lean Evendiir laboring at the physical work yet still found the energy and breath to complain about his sufferings.

Aren, Pax, and Suhd were close to exhaustion by the time they neared their intended landing spot. The beach was indeed between treacherous rocky formations on the southern shore that functioned as perches for diving flocks of featherwings and leatherwings. Occasionally, their boat heaved upward or sideward from waves

. . . or worse when it felt as if something bumped them from below. Everyone became alarmed and paranoid about what lurked beneath after the first couple of "bumps," giving motivation to all to be done with these deep waters. Motivated to push past the pains in his arms, shoulders, and back, Rogaan began paddling hard to get them to shore as quickly as possible. The rowboat nosed up, then down on the small waves near the shore as Suhd kept at bailing the water out. Up again, then down. Trundiir's complexion took on a deeper green that Rogaan feared could become permanent, but the white-bearded Tellen kept on paddling, matching Rogaan stroke for stroke as their rowboat closed within a stone's throw of the beach.

Suddenly, their rowboat lurched forward, then backward as screams from Suhd filled Rogaan's ears. The rowboat creaked and shuddered. Looking behind to Suhd, he found a large-eyed water-dragon beyond her with jaws clamped on the back of the boat . . . its head massive to Rogaan's eyes. The toothy beast somehow bit down on the stern of the boat without breaking it apart, though it had a strong enough hold on them to start dragging the boat—and them—backward and under.

"Get away! Get away!" Suhd yelled as she jumped forward from her seat and into Rogaan's arms. Rogaan could only smile at her body touching his, though Suhd just gave him a wide-eye look before jumping forward into the front of the boat with Pax.

Disappointed at Suhd forsaking his embrace, Rogaan looked about to find a grumpy, greenish-colored Trundiir glaring at him. Trundiir spun on his seat while grabbing a spear lying between them, then made to stand while somehow keeping his balance. Rogaan grabbed the other spear, lying atop his Blood Bow between them, and whirled into a low crouch hoping to keep the boat from rocking worse than it already did. He glanced at Trundiir to see what he intended. Trundiir's acknowledging glance back, along with his slight hefting of his spear, gave Rogaan confidence the white-bearded Tellen was going to attack. Almost in unison, each sank their spears into the upper snout of the water-dragon. The beast struggled in pain against the spear tips before releasing the boat with a mad hiss as it aggressively pulled itself from the pointed metal tips. The black-headed beast stared at them for a long moment with what Rogaan took as malevolence before sinking into the watery darkness.

"That head was larger than the boat," Rogaan said in awe.

"Let us make haste to shore," Trundiir demanded in a low, calm tone.

No one argued as Trundiir quickly returned to his seat and plunged his paddle into the water. Rogaan joined him, soon matching the Tellen's urgent pace. Aren and Pax too increased their paddling efforts almost as if they were mad with fear. They quickly found themselves within a dozen strides of the dark, rocky beach. Featherwings swirled the air just above them while leatherwings circled higher. Rogaan hoped the winged creatures would leave them be and that their "spot" was far enough away from several smaller, sunning water-dragons so not to provoke an attack as a blending swirl of fear and hope filled him.

Almost there . . . over the underwater drop-off. Rogaan's fear dissipated as they nosed the boat over the submerged steep ledge separating the vast deep waters from the thin rim of shallows lining all the shores of the Ur. *We made it.* A reverberating thud below sent the boat lurching upward. Driven down into his seat, then to the bottom of the boat, Rogaan lay pinned as an explosion of fear consumed his thoughts. He gripped his seat and a near rail to keep himself from falling out of the boat just as the wood of the hull breaking loudly filled his ears with a moaning creak. A moment later, the boat splinted apart under him sending Rogaan rising in an arc toward the beach flying wildly while he and his companions yelled. Moments later, the unsettled feeling in the pit of his stomach ended in jaw-jarring agony as Rogaan impacted the solid sands of the beach before painfully bouncing and tumbling over dark rocks until he flopped and rolled to a stop.

"*Aaauucch,*" he moaned as he lay unmoving, not knowing when his pains would go away. With his eyes looking up at the sky, he saw that dark-colored featherwing circling high. The place he lay smelled faintly of salt and heavily of pungent decay. A loud cracking of wood and a deep, reverberating hiss forced Rogaan's eyes open and head up to see it. Looking from his prone sprawl, he found the large water-dragon wading in the shallows violently tearing apart what remained of their boat. When the animal seemed satisfied at having dominated its rival threat, it silently slipped its massive black-and-white body backward off the shelf of the shallows and into the watery dark depths where it resumed its throne as king of its domain.

"Dung!" yelled Aren while rising to his feet not far away from Rogaan. As he did, he danced, scraping off something from his left foot with a stick.

"What?" Rogaan asked the Evendiir.

"I stepped in dung," Aren answered while focused on his sandals and looking for a stick to scrape away the dark substance sticking to his foot. "Of all indignities, stepping in a large pile of it."

"It won't be killin' ya," Pax snidely sniped at Aren from the other side of Rogaan.

"It's in between my toes," Aren described in detail with revulsion, signifying the seriousness of the situation. "It feels disgusting and stinks."

"Den, wash it off in da water," Pax spoke in a disrespectful, dismissive tone. Aren stopped his scrapping efforts to glare at Pax with his hostile eyes clear to see. Pax returned Aren's glare with his own unfriendly stare.

"All stay clear of the water,"Trundiir growled from somewhere behind Rogaan. "We have need to collect what we can find of our supplies and equipment on the sands and rocks, then get to the tree line."

Trundiir seemed on edge to Rogaan. Looking about beyond their immediate disaster of an area, both of the young water-dragons to his left were watching them from their sunning spots more than thirty strides away. Both looked curiously at them, in a "scary meal" kind of manner. To their right, Rogaan spied open, dark, rocky beach and craggy rocks with white-colored featherwings covering them. Looking back to his left, Rogaan concluded the water-dragons presented little danger to them while on land. *What is Trundiir so concerned of?*

"What has you troubled?" Rogaan asked Trundiir as he got to his feet. "I thought this side of the Ur, just to the evening side of Anza, isn't well traveled with few beasts of the wilds drinking the Ur's salty water mix. At least, that is what the *Makara's* crew spoke of."

Trundiir gave him a quizzical glance, then went on to gathering their scattered things. Pax and Suhd too were collecting everything they could find. Suhd . . . Rogaan's eyes lingered on her for a long moment before ripping them away from his heart's desire. Aren still was cleaning the dung from his foot, now using the large rock he sat on. Trundiir spoke. "We are on the south side of the Ur River. The kind and friendly Wilds of the North are not these lands. Everything here is more . . . meaner . . . the animals, the trees and bushes, the folk, and the soil is rockier and difficult to traverse."

"Aah," Rogaan replied as his eyes glanced back to Suhd. *She is beautiful.* A throat clearing from Trundiir brought his attention back to the Tellen.

Trundiir gave Rogaan another disapproving look. "And a contingent of *Anubda'Ner* are to join the *Tusaa'Ner* from those ships. They crossed the Ur by barge two days ago. I think they will join somewhere north of Anza, maybe in Haven. Now, they are anywhere along the road between Shores Landing and Haven or in the small Di'Tij between them. If we are where we think, the small Di'Tij is south by a handful of marches. We must avoid it and all towns. There will be eyes watching for anyone not known to the townsfolk . . . and they will seek favor of the troops by informing on us."

Rogaan's eyes and attention trailed away from Trundiir as he spoke, instead, finding and becoming focused on Suhd, in her yellow tunic held to her waist by a wide black belt as she walked about collecting their equipment on the rocky beach. *Beautiful*.

Whack!

"Auch!" Rogaan immediately rubbed his head where Trundiir hit him with a stick. "Why strike me?"

"Did you hear *any* of my words?" Trundiir asked rhetorically, now standing close. He tossed away the stick he hit Rogaan with then scented the air taking note of the wind's direction. "You need to focus your thoughts on what I have told you. You must puzzle together things to understand your surroundings and what we are to contend with."

Rogaan thought to argue over how much attention he did give Trundiir, but instead, remained silent to mask his embarrassment at not having put the parts of this puzzle together. He decided to swallow his pride a bit and start picking up their scattered belongings. In a short time, all that was salvageable and not in the water, they had. Even Aren decided to join them in collecting their belongings, though he did so while grumbling in large words about the stupidity of sandals and the merits of boots. To Trundiir's visible relief, they left the beach heading through broken bush over red-brown rocky soil heading toward the forest more than a march away. Aren could not stop grumbling about the rocks in his sandals and the smell that still followed him as they went. Trundiir took the lead, setting a hard pace. He appeared to have all his equipment from the boat, including his carry pack, a one-handed ax, a long knife, and the metal-tipped spear with blue-green feathers he used to stay off the water-dragon. Rogaan lost one of his two quivers of arrows and the other good spear matching the one Trundiir carried. Instead, he had a stone-tipped spear the *Makara* crew decided to throw into their boat as they launched from the ship. Aren seemed to have everything as well, a small carry pack he insisted on when they were being given equipment for this journey and the wood walking-stick he took without permission from the equipment rack in the ship. Pax had his carry pack and a long knife on his side. Rogaan suspected he had tucked away more than a few daggers or knives under his clothes. Suhd . . . *so beautiful* . . . She lost everything in the water-dragon attack except for the blue, brown, and red long scarf one of the crewmen gave her. A twinge of jealousy—no more than a twinge—rippled through Rogaan when the smiling and smitten crewman presented it to her. He still felt the jealousy but did not understand why it held him strongly now that the crewman was far off.

They moved quickly through the broken bush with Trundiir, avoiding the clumps of bushes except to put one or more of them between them and something ahead he attentively spied at a distance before motioning them to move away from and around. Aren followed the Tellen, though with complaints about not having boots until Trundiir said something to him that Aren did not like much. Suhd . . . *so beautiful* . . . in her yellow dress and red scarf and hide sandals, those last given her by another smitten crewman, made her way without complaint over the rocky ground. Jealously, again, rippled through Rogaan at the thought of the crewmen smitten with her and wanting to give her things. One even offered his long knife and to cut out his heart for her. *Insanity*. Rogaan was about to throw fists with the crewman on his offer, but the barefooted Baraan was slapped and chased away by the second commander before Rogaan could act. That memory and others like it on the ship harshly lingered in Rogaan's mind making him angry and with feelings he could not comprehend.

The ground suffered a prolonged shaking, causing Rogaan to trip over a fair-sized rock and had him almost falling. His thoughts returned to the now. Pax looked back at him with curious concern before returning his following of his sister. *So, enjoy watching her walk . . . so graceful*, Rogaan thought as he followed at the rear of their line with a primitive stone-tipped spear in hand, guarding them from things Trundiir described as meaner than anything on the north side of the Ur. *Meaner than a raver. That is hard to believe.*

The broken bush filled with fighting *tur'usumgal* . . . little-dragons and chirping featherwings of all colors gave way to increasing numbers of pine and small-leaf thorn trees. Here, the chirps and squawks from the small animals and the featherwings started to sound like those back home. Rogaan found himself feeling more comfortable with these familiar sounds of the wilds and the trees, except for the thorny branches, especially when they passed by one able to provide a moment's shade from the warm sun. Aren continued to complain of the rocks and his smelly sandals. Not far after the broken bush gave way to sporadic stands of trees, they found themselves in a forest of tall pines and dense, thorny trees with large-leafed trees in places where it appeared to be wet most of the seasons. Some of the large-leaf trees were just now starting to turn colors. Trundiir led them around the thorn-rich trees and bushes as best he could, but they were everywhere and seemed to reach out and painfully grab any and all passersby. Everyone except Trundiir soon found themselves bleeding from cuts and thorn picks and their exposed clothes ripped and torn. Aren found the thorns to add to his complaints. Not soon enough for Rogaan and the others, they came to a reddish-brown-packed dirt road where Trundiir stopped the group with a raised hand. The Tellen stood motionless, though Rogaan knew he was alert as ever. He soon motioned for them to follow him across the road.

"Keep walking in a line in each other's tracks," ordered Trundiir in his deep voice as they approached and crossed the road. Spots were all over the road where it was obvious workers filled in holes and ruts with the reddish rocks of the broken bushlands.

They continued forward and slightly uphill fighting the thorns until Trundiir appeared wavering in decision. Songs of featherwings with their chirping and squawking throughout the forest were undisturbed in their passing and as they stood waiting for their white-bearded Tellen guide to end his visible thinking. After a few moments, he selected a thick grouping of thorny bushes that sat under a large stand of trees offering dark shade. They all followed the Tellen, quietly moving to the uphill-side of the thorny cover where they could see the road, but where Rogaan thought it would be difficult for anyone below to see them.

"What is it?" Pax asked first.

"Not certain," was all Trundiir answered as he looked for a position to spy through the thick thorns.

"How can you not know what you're hiding from?" criticized Aren.

"I felt the ground quiver," answered Trundiir matter-of-factly.

"I felt nothing," challenged Aren.

"I no feel da ground shake," added Suhd.

"Tellens feel quiverings and shakings through the ground and stone," Rogaan answered Suhd's unasked question. She turned her radiant blue eyes on Rogaan, making his heart skip. *So beautiful.* She cocked her light brown face slight, allowing her long, black hair to fall over her shoulder. *So beautiful.* Rogaan became lost in Suhd . . . until he felt a bop on his head. When he looked for what hit him, he found Trundiir with another disapproving, almost angry stare.

"What?" Rogaan asked.

"Finish answering her so she will fall silent," demanded Trundiir in a low, frustrated tone.

Rogaan glanced about to see what the others were thinking of him. All of them were staring at him with confused looks. Except for Suhd, who wore a mix of concern and frustration on her brown face.

"Well . . . Do ya feel da ground and stone shake?" she asked, evidently for a second time.

"Yes, though I have to touch it with bare hand or foot," Rogaan answered.

"Did no know dat of ya," Suhd commented with a knowing smile that melted Rogaan's heart and sent a tingle rippling through him.

"Would you just stop that!" Aren burst out in frustration.

"What?" Rogaan asked, this time of him.

"Your swooning over her," answered Aren, as if what he spoke of was obvious to everyone.

"Swooning?" Rogaan did not understand what Aren spoke of as anger welled up within him at anything that might get between him and Suhd. Aren's accusation at "swooning" was something.

"It's been stomach-turning watching you swoon and make-eyes every time you look at her." Aren continued with his description of how Rogaan carried on concerning Suhd. "It's going to get our *Lights* taken from us."

"Dat be enough from ya, mystic." Pax attempted to stop Aren's harassing of Rogaan.

"I do not swoon!" Rogaan sounded more defensive than he wanted.

"He no swoon . . . over me," declared Suhd.

"Enough?" Aren finished Suhd's thought then focus on Pax. "You've been sulking and blaming Rogaan for your parents' end since the arena. Saw it then, and I still see it now. So, why defend the Tellen brute, now?"

"I no be sulkin' . . ." Pax sounded unusually unsure of himself. With his voice cracking, he denied Aren's accusation. "I no blame Rogaan for me . . . ma and pa's *Lights* bein' taken."

"I am not a brute!" Rogaan denied.

"Rogaan is no ta blame!" Suhd defended him.

"All of you . . ." Aren started to say something but stopped when he received a whack on the head with a spear haft. "Auch. Why did you strike me?"

"Silence!" Trundiir ordered. "Of all days, the four of you choose this moment to argue. Something approaches. Now, be still and do not speak."

Rogaan crouched in silence, as did the others. Despite anger and frustration on everyone's faces, all kept quiet, if for no other reason than Trundiir might do more than whack them with his spear. Satisfied, Trundiir returned his attention to the road some one hundred and twenty-two strides away, at its closest, by Rogaan's estimate. Rogaan noticed the featherwings had gone silent. Was it because of their squabbling or of what approached? Their wait was not long before the faintest noises could be heard of large beasts snorting and stomping at the soil, chains chiming, and the creak of wheels turning under strain. Rogaan pressed his hand to the dirt and rocks to feel what approached. It was large and coming from their left . . . from the west, a caravan with more steeds, wagons, and folks than he could make out in the jumble of quivers felt on his fingers and palm.

"Who are they, Trundiir?" Rogaan asked.

"It must be the *Anubda'Ner* . . . I know of no other force so large," answered Trundiir as he kept watch of both the road and behind them to their left.

"Why ya be watchin' our left?" Pax asked.

"Scouts," answered Trundiir while alternating his gaze between the road and the hillside to their left. "I hope we are far enough from the road for them to pass below, but I cannot be certain."

"Why not keep moving deeper into the forest?" Rogaan asked.

"Moving creatures are far easier to see than ones sitting in the bush and shadows," answered Trundiir as if he was teaching an apprentice.

Rogaan sat silently for a moment thinking on Trundiir's words. All made sense from Rogaan's experience stalking animals and tracking wounded prey. It was much easier seeing them when moving than when they bedded down, or worse, when they did so in the deep shadows.

"Ready your bow, Rogaan . . ." Trundiir spoke calmly yet with a sense of urgency.

Rogaan hesitated a moment trying to see what had his fellow Tellen concerned, but then readied his Blood bow with a nocked arrow.

"Do not hesitate if I tell you to kill." Trundiir's words sent a wave of discomfort through Rogaan. "Shoot for the heart or head as you would any creature of the wilds. Take the scout quickly so he cannot sound an alarm."

Rogaan made to protest Trundiir's request, but then saw his friends' faces. Pax, Suhd, and even Aren wore looks of concern. And then the sadness in the eyes of Pax and Suhd made firm Rogaan's decision to hold his protest and do as Trundiir said. He swallowed hard. Other than the *Saggis*, he never thought in plan to take another's *Light*. This was different than back home in Brigum. Few seemed helpful since they left the safety of their home. Most proved unfriendly and hostile. Rogaan readied his bow, but more importantly, he readied his heart and head.

Chapter 22

Mighty Guardians

The five of them quietly sat among the thorny branches of the underbrush concealed from the road below waiting for the worst kind of luck yet hoping trouble to pass them by. All about them, the scent of chalky metal mingled with old flowers. Rogaan realized the metal smell came from the reddish dirt. *A strange thing*. Only a few little-dragons remained in the open blustering and fighting with each other over territory and mating rights. Silent were the featherwings. If not for the distant snorts, chiming, and creaking of the approaching caravan an eerie silence would have fallen over the place. Rogaan had his *Sentii* Blood Bow ready with a nocked arrow. Memories of his practice at the breaching water-dragons gave him confidence he could hit the small mark of anything within seventy to maybe eighty strides. Though, he had mixed feelings at planning the taking of *Light* before it was needed.

Trundiir motioned low with his empty left hand for everyone to be alert and to be still and quiet. His right hand clutched the haft of his spear tightly, sending Rogaan's heart racing both with excitement and unease at what he might be asked to do. Through the thick thorns, Rogaan spied beyond and below movement passing from their left to right, but not much more. How far away…he could not make an accurate guess. The movement stopped slightly to their right as low undiscernible voices spoke for a moment. Then silence, except for the snorts, chiming of chains, and creaking still at a distance, but closer than before. Rogaan's heart now loudly started beating in his ears as his chest tighten and his mouth went dry. After what felt a long time, Rogaan spied motion below moving off to their right. He breathed a sigh of relief. *I will not be asked to do…that, today*.

Pax, Suhd, and Aren also started breathing again as they looked at the ground and each other with smiles of relief. The snorts, chiming, and creaking grew louder. Another noise mixed within the rest came to his ears . . . off to their left, one Rogaan was so familiar with . . . the drawing of a bow. A tingling surge exploded through his body with his hairs everywhere standing painfully on end as the world nearly came to a stop. The greens and browns and grays of the trees touched with the reds and yellows of some of the turning leaves and the greens and cinnamon-browns of the bushes exploded vibrantly to Rogaan's eyes, and so too the whites of the thorns, as did the reds and browns of the soil and rocks, and the blues and whites of the sky above. Standing out brightly, his companions sat with their colors boldly displayed, almost glowing to Rogaan's eyes. That scent of chalky metal from the ground and rocks forced on Rogaan a memory of being in the smithy with his father when a youngling. And the flowers struck him as powerfully sweet. Looking left, Rogaan found a Baraan, dressed in gray-blue eur armor, thirty-seven strides away, his nocked arrow just released from its bow. Rogaan watched the arrow in vivid detail come directly at his head. He forced his upper half back and down, making the arrow pass a hand's span beyond his nose. A vivid royal blue shaft on the arrow Rogaan clearly saw. Colors not of the *Anubda'Ner* and not of the Farratum region.

Looking back to the scout, the Baraan slowly displayed an expression of unbelieving surprise. From his back-leaning position, Rogaan raised and drew his bow so that the string just touched at the right of his lips. In the air coming from his right, a steel-tipped spear wobbled and flexed on its way toward the scout. The scout attempted to dodge the spear but was too slow. His chest took the full brunt of the steel tip and heavy wood haft, staggering the scout backward. Rogaan hesitated to release his arrow. *Is it needed?*

"Finish him!" came Trundiir's words so slowly Rogaan almost did not understand them.

Looking back at the scout, he found the Baraan trying to rise to his feet. Rogaan did not have a clear kill shot and held his arrow's release, again.

"Finish him or he will us!" came Trundiir's words slowly again.

Rogaan watched the Baraan scout get to his feet on shaking legs before placing his hands on the spear haft trying to pull it free. Rogaan focused on the side of the scout's chest under his arm, not where the spear struck and through which the front and back of the eur armor buckled together . . . its weakest place. He let loose his arrow. It flew slowly yet true, striking the scout in between the chest and back pieces of armor and passing completely through him. The scout staggered, then fell. The vivid colors and textures of Rogaan's surroundings turned pale and less appealing as the slight breeze suddenly felt normal on his skin. Rogaan then felt a hand on his midsection shake him. It felt like a normal touch of a hand and not one of slow movement. Looking, it was Trundiir clutching Rogaan's hide armor while grasping in his other hand Pax's shirt. Trundiir let them both go as he prepared to sprint off toward the scout.

"Chase down the other, both of you, and end him before he can signal his companions," Trundiir spoke quick and direct as he ran off. "I will finish this one."

Trundiir drew his long knife as he sprinted off uphill, not allowing Rogaan a word of questioning or answers of reassurance.

Pax exchanged questioning glances with Rogaan before putting on a resolved face, then went sprinting off after the other scout. A loud grumble from Rogaan's stomach announced his sudden sense of intense hunger. *Not now!* He argued with his own body, not wanting to be slowed or distracted. Worried they would be found out, Rogaan quickly rose and chased after Pax with bow in hand. Going downhill over loose rocks so fast caused Rogaan to trip often and fight not to fall with just about every step. Pax quickly outdistanced him as they ran after the scout who had already made it down the hilly slope before turning left back toward his caravan. The scout was swift footed—too fast for Pax to catch him.

Rogaan stopped and set his feet as he pulled an arrow from its quiver. He nocked the arrow and drew the bow as he raised it, so the bowstring and his fingers touched just to the right of his lips. He focused on the running scout, his target. Sixty strides, sixty-two strides, sixty-four strides. Rogaan let out half of his breath as he focused on the scout's hips. Seventy-two strides, seventy-four . . . Rogaan let loose his Blood Bow's arrow. It arched up slightly in the air, then down, striking the scout in his left thigh, sending him tumbling to the rocky ground. Rogaan nocked another arrow and drew. Pax, still running, was closing the distance to the scout. Rising from the ground, covered in reddish dirt, the scout continued limping off toward his approaching caravan. Rogaan focused again. This time on the left side of the scout's chest. Eight-three strides, eighty-four . . . Another arrow went arching through the air. It struck the scout in his back, but the Baraan went down so quickly Rogaan was unsure if the arrow hit in between the eur armor pieces.

Rogaan set off running down the hilly slope of red rocks directly to the scout. Pax reached the downed Baraan first as Rogaan made his way as fast as he could over the loose red rocks. Looking up from the treacherous terrain, he watched Pax raise one of his blades to strike the fallen scout. Pax held his strike. When Rogaan caught up with them, Pax still held his blade high looking down at the bleeding scout now struggling to breathe. He looked young. They were some thirty strides off the road and thankfully, still in the trees and thorny underbrush.

"He be only as old as us, Rogaan." Pax sounded distraught with indecision. He lowered his blade, then put a hand on the scout's chest. "He still be breathin'."

Looking up, Rogaan caught sight of the caravan's lead warriors in gleaning bronze sitting atop their sarigs as they approached. He spied them through the trees far down the road. *More than half a march away.* Another unwanted grumble came from his stomach as he felt the ground tremble through his boots. He did his best to ignore both and hoping his midsection would stop making the uncomfortable rumblings.

"We cannot leave him here." Rogaan spoke the obvious as he fought with himself. He knew the scout was a danger to them, but he was so young and innocent. "I will carry him. You, cover dirt over his blood and our footsteps."

Rogaan did not wait for Pax to agree. He grabbed the wounded scout and hefted him over his left shoulder, then took off up the hilly slope of rocks holding the scout in place with one arm while using his Blood Bow in his right hand to give him a third point of balance. Rogaan relentlessly climbed the rocky and thorn-thick slope, fighting to keep his balance while making his way upward. Halfway up the slope, Rogaan felt the scout reaching for his long knife, trying to pull it free of its sheath. He squeezed down hard on the Baraan with his arm to give him a warning. "Enough of that."

The scout went limp as Rogaan went on climbing the slope. Pax caught up as they neared their bushy hiding spot. Trundiir met them just in front of the thorn-rich bushes that still concealed the rest of their companions. He guided Rogaan and Pax to where the other scout lay motionless, his bloodstained throat cut and his eyes still open. It looked that the scout's eyes no longer held his *Light*. Rogaan noticed a sorrow on Trundiir's face as he lay the younger scout down next to the older. Rogaan took in a deep breath of mixed, unsettled relief after carrying the Baraan uphill so far as Trundiir felt the young scout's chest and neck for life and his mouth for breath.

"This one is *lightless* as well," announced Trundiir with both satisfaction and melancholy in his voice.

A sadness rolled over Rogaan at the results . . . not his intentions to make *lightless* this young Baraan. He hoped the scout to live so his troop folks might find him later when Rogaan and the rest of his companions were far away. Rogaan looked to Pax who did not share sadness on his light brown face or in his tired slate-blue eyes. Instead, his friend's eyes were sizing up the scout's belongings for looting.

"Anything good on dem?" Pax asked with a bit of excitement and anticipation in his voice. "Anything we maybe can use?"

"Not the colors or equipment of the *Anubda'Ner* of Farratum's region or of Anza," Trundiir announced with a nervousness in his voice as he held in his hand a sash from the older scout. "The younger scout looks too young for the *Seb'Ner*. Likely a local guide. One who came to be in the wrong place today. The older one . . . royal blue, his sash and arrow shafts. He is *Seb'Ner* . . . from the Royal Guard of Ur."

"Not the Guardians of the Empire?" asked Rogaan with both disbelief and a growing unease.

"Da Mighty Guardians of Shuruppak?" Pax asked with a nervous cracking in his voice.

"That be them," replied Trundiir in a manner mocking Pax.

"I not be touchin' or takin' anythin' from dem," declared Pax as if touching them was poison. "Findin' guardian stuff on us be our *Lights*."

"Yes, it will be." Trundiir agreed. "But what is done is done. Their armor, weapons, and stuffs can mean the Light of Life or the Darkness of Death out here in the Blood Lands. We take everything of use and hope their bodies are not found soon."

"The caravan of . . . *Seb'Ner* is almost here." Rogaan was hoping for an answer of what to do.

"We keep watch for more scouts as we take what we need from these two . . . while the caravan passes," declared Trundiir. "Pax, keep with your sister to make sure she is safe and an eye on that Evendiir."

"Ya no trust him?" Pax asked suspiciously.

"I do not know him," grumbled Trundiir as he started to drag the younger scout's body and things to another thorny tangle of bushes above where Suhd and Aren sat quietly talking. "And he complains too much."

"Ya got dis?" Pax asked Rogaan pointing to the body of the older and larger scout.

"Yes," answered Rogaan with an increasing realization that they would never be going home, at least not as they knew it.

"Keep them quiet and still," Trundiir ordered of Pax just before he disappeared behind a thorny tangle of bushes. He then spoke from behind the thorns. "More scouts are likely to be about, but hopefully, not this high up the hill."

Rogaan and Pax parted, Pax returning to Suhd and Aren to inform them of the plan and likely of their new danger. Rogaan carried the scout's body and equipment to Trundiir's second hiding spot, setting down the body next to his *lightless* companion.

"There was enough room to do this with the others?" asked Rogaan.

"I do not know how strong your Baraan woman is," Trundiir replied matter-of-factly.

"She is strong and has kept up with us," Rogaan defended Suhd.

"I mean of stomach," Trundiir continued. "Has she ever dealt with the *lightless* before this?"

"Not like this that I know of." Flashes of memory of the underground arena and him taking *Light* from one of the guards came to Rogaan. Despite him saving Suhd from their taking her against her will, it is what sealed his fate forever as a lawbreaker in the eyes of Shuruppak. Yet, Rogaan felt no regret at the happening. He saved Suhd . . . at least, then.

Trundiir motioned for Rogaan to strip armor and items from the other scout. Rogaan complied, working in silence for a time until the lead warriors and their stout sarigs of the *Seb'Ner* caravan started passing on the road below. Rogaan then sat watching them through holes in the thorns, hoping Pax covered signs of their fight well enough for the Mighty Guardians not to notice. The ground vibrated with their passing. He could feel it through his hands, boots, and backside when he closed his eyes. A light smack on his left arm by Trundiir startled Rogaan out his intense focus on the ground and the forces below. Exhaling, Rogaan realized he had been holding his breath.

"So, her *sway* on you only happens when in her presence or in trail of her," Trundiir stated in his matter-of-fact deep grumbling manner.

"What . . . What are you speaking of?" Rogaan asked, not certain where Trundiir was going with this.

"Tellens are more strongly influenced by Baraan *sway* than the others," explained Trundiir. "Your *swooning* is a danger to everyone, including Suhd."

"I care for Suhd . . ." declared Rogaan louder than he intended.

"Quiet," Trundiir demanded. "I am certain you do. I mean you no ill will where she is concerned. She is beautiful, strong in will, and pure of heart. It is simple. When you scent her *sway*, you become drunk of her. You do not think right and become easy to surprise and make poor choices. You are a big bag of uselessness for the rest to carry along and protect—or worse, a ball of flame spreading like wildfire seeking to protect her. You cannot let that happen out here. Animals in these lands are not so . . . tame as around Shuruppak. We will have all our *Lights* taken from us."

Rogaan made no reply; instead, sitting in silence thinking while watching the *Seb'Ner* caravan pass. Royal blue and gray flags, pennants, and covers numerous with the moon atop a winged sword everywhere. Powerful niisku were pulling heavily loaded wagons that creaked in strain of what they carried. Rogaan was surprised at how many of them passed. He lost count. Kydas carrying all sorts of large, crated equipment were also used as steeds by the larger warriors while the rest of the troops used sarigs. He lost count of them too. And sarigs carrying bronze-chested eur-armored warriors, over two hundred of them when Rogaan lost count. They kept on for a time and some, walking and wheels rolling by, making Rogaan wonder if these troops and steeds were endless. When the final sarigs bringing up the rear of the caravan passed, it was midday under a cloudy sky. The clouds keeping the sun from baking the lands and all traveling it.

The cloudy day made him think of family for some reason. Then, another random thought . . . *Father. I thought I had saved him from the Tusaa'Ner. That Im'Kas would see him freed after the arena*, Rogaan recalled with frustration and angst. Then, he remembered his father's resolve in remaining in the jails as a prisoner of Farratum when the Dark Ax offered to get them free. *So strange Father's doings.* Rogaan pondered his father's behavior and his words while they were captive in the Farratum jails. ". . . I need you to keep strong your trust in me and what I am to tell you. You will be tested, and harm will likely find you . . . You will need to endure . . . because of what I cannot give them." *What can you not give them, Father . . . and who?* Rogaan still did not understand all of his father's part in these affairs. His father's words kept reverberating in his head of when the Shuruppak civil war ended, and he and the Ebon Circle battled the Houses against their keeping rule over the peoples. Helped by the Tellen Nation, they were victorious in defeating the Houses and then in forming an alliance with the smaller Houses. The smaller Houses then taking up the cause for the peoples who fought with the Ebon Circle . . . and Father . . . against a cabal of the Great Houses. In the end, distrust and lack of cooperation between the Great Houses were as much a cause of their defeat as was the Ebon Circle's-led opposition.

A negotiated peace was agreed upon between the Houses, the Ebon Circle, the Tellen Nation, and the leaders of the commoners throughout the lands. All would be governed by laws, made by the *Makers of Laws*, the *Ksatra'Za* in Ur and the *Anubda'Zas* throughout the city-regions of new Shuruppak, along with the Chosen of the Peoples . . . called *Bartam'Eadda*, the Noble Houses . . . the *Niral'Eadda*, and the guilds . . . the *Dagas*. Some thirty seasons of *Roden'ars* this system of governing, in a style used in the Tellen Nation, succeeded.

An unsettled peace took hold throughout Shuruppak with the Councils of each city, town, and village choosing those to represent them in the law making as *Zas*. By the new laws, protectors, *Servants of the People*, were formally organized . . . the *Kiuri'Ner*, *Tusaa'Ner*, and *Sakes*. They were limited in numbers and duty-bound to serve and protect the people . . . no more. *Lawmakers* and *Servants of the Law*, the courts, were independent and to watch and thwart any attempt at consolidating power. They were beholden to the people and received their coin from the people. All worked as designed until the last handful of *Roden'ars* passed when a corruption crept into the fabric of their ways, the Servants of the People and the

Lawmakers. They started growing their own authorities and no longer steadfastly served the people. Instead, they sought to rule by picking and choosing the laws they enforced . . . a justice of social causes that found the peoples whipped up into mobs, to rally behind. The repeating cycle of governance brought about by the failings of people, his father instructed him of long ago. *Father was a central figure in the shaping of the Shuruppak I knew*, Rogaan came to realize at this moment. Rogaan further recalled his father warning him of the growing corruption in the western regions of the Shuruppak, then spreading out into the rest of the nation. *I did not take his words and warnings seriously*. Rogaan regretted his lack of understanding of his father's words then and not thinking of things other than himself.

"I still do not fully understand Father but cannot let him pay the gold for my failings." Rogaan spoke aloud, though his words were only meant for himself. Returning his attention to the here and now, he breathed a big sigh of relief. The *Seb'Ner* had not discovered them. Rogaan looked to Trundiir for any indication they were to move. The Tellen just sat quietly watching the road and hillside. Rogaan looked about. No soldiers or scouts. The songs of featherwings started to pick up as increasing numbers of the colorful flying creatures started darting about the trees and brush. Off in the distance, on the road, small leapers appeared looking nervously about. Trundiir remained still even as Rogaan looked expectantly at him several times. Rogaan grew anxious to move, to leave this place. Trundiir continued his watch over their surroundings.

"I think you understand him more than you admit," the Tellen spoke softly like rocks grumbling. Rogaan stared at him with heat in his cheeks. Trundiir obviously paid heed to his spoken aloud thoughts. "Mithraam is respected by many more than you will ever know. His causes are noble, just, and with purpose. At least that is what I hear spoken of him by those who have knowledge of your father. He is not so much a secret as you believe."

"What purpose in keeping himself prisoner?" Rogaan asked more of the air than of Trundiir.

"The *Zas* sent all of Farratum after him . . . by my understanding," hinted the white-haired Tellen at something more. "He sent you away on your hunt to keep you safe."

"How is my story known by so many?" asked Rogaan in a frustrated tone before dropping his eyes to his boots and losing himself in his own pool of melancholy . . . at the truth. "Father did not consider me ready for . . . this."

"Whoever is?" Trundiir offered a point of view, then answered Rogaan's earlier question. "Kardul spoke of your hunt."

"Traitor." Rogaan declared the big *Kiuri'Ner* something most would find difficult to believe.

"Traitor to you and your father," Trundiir spoke calmly. "Not so to Farratum."

Rogaan glared at the white-haired Tellen trying to figure out if Trundiir was defending Kardul. *Does he have loyalties to the Kiuri'Ner?* Rogaan asked himself in silence.

"To the good of the lands . . . and the people within Kardul is a traitor," Trundiir declared with a finality in his voice. "He has misguided loyalties and a cruel nature he considers necessary."

"Let us not forget my mother," Rogaan added before continuing with a flare of indignance. "And Pax and Suhd, their *lightless* parents, and folks from home to wherever the traitor is now."

"He rode with the *Seb'Ner* when they passed," Trundiir informed with calm, even words.

"What?" Rogaan sat gawking.

"Yes," Trundiir reaffirmed. "Your father and his captors will be joining Kardul and the *Seb'Ner*. Likely in Anza."

"What are you up to, Father?" Rogaan asked the air aloud again.

"By what my eyes have seen," Trundiir spoke calmly as he scanned the hillside and road below, "he battles malevolence to keep worst things from taking hold."

"I cannot leave him captive," Rogaan flatly stated.

"I know," the Tellen replied to Rogaan's statement.

They sat for a little time longer simply listening and watching the animals return to their daily routines, though the small brown leapers made Rogaan nervous as they slowly worked their way at the side of the road in their direction.

"Keep your distance from the Baraan woman," offered Trundiir.

"Her name is Suhd," Rogaan shot back, unable to decide if the Tellen's words were advice or a demand.

"Take notice . . . There is that anger protective of her I spoke of," explained Trundiir. He then continued. "Keep upwind of her as well until I can find what is needed to make an old family fix that may help you resist her and all other Baraan females who have *sway* as potent . . . as Suhd's."

Rogaan stewed for a time at the Tellen's words while Trundiir watched him and the hillside. Wanting to defend Suhd, Rogaan tried several times to speak of her to convince Trundiir his observations were wrong, but something stopped his every attempt. He eventually huffed a defeated sigh and put his head in his hands.

"Ready to go?" Trundiir asked as well as announced. "Needed to ensure no scouts lagged behind the column and for you to get your head right."

Trundiir rose, then collected the rest of the group. As they gathered around, he and Rogaan distributed the equipment taken from the *lightless* scouts, whose bodies laid stripped of everything except their underclothes.

"Try these on." Rogaan handed Aren a pair of black, soft-soled boots taken from the smaller of the two scouts.

The Evendiir gleefully accepted the boots, then tried them on, jumping up and taking a short walk, then a dance that brought curious smiles to everyone. "A little large, but they'll make for better travels over these rocks than those blasted sandals."

"Good," Trundiir stated with a tone of finality. "We are going to a place I know on the dusk and mountain-side of Haven. I found it when I was here a long time ago."

"Ya be here before?" Pax asked.

"As I said, many *Dur'Anki* ago," Trundiir answered sharply and dismissively.

"Where be ya takin' us?" Suhd asked.

"Caves where we will be safe from the *Tusaa'Ner* and *Seb'Ner* . . . and hopefully, this *Shunned*," answered the white-haired Tellen. "At least until they leave Anza."

"You're taking us east . . . is that not the same direction the *Seb'Ner* traveled?" Aren more stated than asked.

"We will keep away from roads." Trundiir pulled out a folded leather map of Shuruppak showing everyone the place he was taking them with a big finger pointing to a spot northwest of Anza. It lay on a direct path over the hills from Anza to where they now stood. Haven and the roads servicing it sat marches north and east of the caves.

"What of my father?" Rogan asked. "He is still prisoner of the *Tusaa'Ner* and this *Shunned*. I fear what they have planned for him."

"Da *Tusaa'Ner*, da *Seb'Ner*, and what else be . . ." Pax offered a line of reasoned thought concerning Mithraam making the case not to rescue him. "What else be in Anza ta take us? It be ta much. I be all Suhd has."

Rogaan stood silently battling with his own sense of duty to his father . . . and mother and this overshadowing sense of guilt for his part and responsibility in the *Lights* of Pax and Suhd's parents being taken. *They only have each other as family now. How can I ask any more of them?* Rogaan chastised himself for his disregard of their fears and wishes.

"I say we go to Anza," Aren offered his opinion. "It's less dangerous than staying out here."

"No!" Suhd exclaimed. "Pax . . . We can no go. So many of them. *Sakes* and others."

Pax hugged his sister to him as he glared at Aren. Guilt swept over Rogaan, powerful and demanding. He shook his head trying to clear it. No good. He still felt heady. In the corner of his eye, Trundiir stood holding a leaf just above his waist, the wind blowing it lightly. *WIND!* Rogaan looked at the leaf. The wind blew from Suhd to him. *I am downwind.* As Pax and Aren argued in a verbal sparring match, Rogaan quietly moved from where he stood walking around the group until the wind no long blew her "*sway*" onto him. Immediately, his light-headedness started to improve. *Wow! That really does work*, he concluded as Trundiir smiled and nodded in approval.

"We can no go ta Anza or anyplace dis side of da river . . . until dey leave," Pax declared.

Rogaan did not know what to say. His friendship with them cost them almost everything, and his guilt for their suffering just continued growing. Rogaan looked to Trundiir for help, for him to say . . . Rogaan was not sure what he wanted the Tellen to say.

"I still say we go to Anza," Aren offered again as he squarely looked at Pax. "You two can keep to the wilds. It's not for me."

Trundiir looked up from his boots after long moments staring at them. He appeared to be avoiding Rogaan's gaze before looking his fellow Tellen eye-to-eye. His face looked long with regret, and his eyes were glassy. "We figure out our future days by keeping out of the cage of the *Tusaa'Ner* and *Seb'Ner* and this *Shunned*. We live off the hills until they leave Anza."

"Where?" Pax asked of Trundiir with a mix of concern and anger. "Where . . . da caves ya talked of?"

"There is plenty of water near the caves," Trundiir offered a reason to follow his plan.

Rogaan remained quiet as a bit of anger swelled up in him at Trundiir's back-walking words. *He all but told me to see my father free when we talked.* Rogaan mulled over where this talk was going. He looked around to the rest of the group. Trundiir held a sad expression but showed no sign that he was to change his last words. Aren looked impassive, as if the conversation was no more than how blue the sky is. He even looked a bit bored. Pax looked everything conflicted but unwilling to take Suhd near those who had harmed her. Suhd simply looked miserable with tears streaking her dirty cheeks as she tried to avoid Rogaan's gaze.

"We go to the caves," announced Trundiir. Aren gave the Tellen a half-foul look, then returned to his passive appearance. Trundiir looking squarely at Aren, "You can remain here. The rest . . . plenty of game small and bigger to keep us fed. And these rugged thorn-covered hills offer protection from larger teeth."

Rogaan stewed over the plan as they all traded and balanced their scavenged equipment among one another. He said nothing to the rest of the group about Trundiir hinting that he should seek to rescue his father. That was not going to happen sitting in a mountain cave. Looking at the new equipment in their possession, especially the scout's armor, an idea sparked.

Chapter 23

Insight

The sun sat just above the Spine Mountains far to the northwest by the time they stood in front of Trundiir's cave entrance. Night would soon engulf them, causing Aren a slight shiver. For the moment, it was a spectacular view from the hilltop across the Ur River valley and to the Spine Mountains where Windsong sat guarded by great vertical timbers surrounding the town. *Home*. He longed for it and felt the start of regrets for his choices bringing him here. Not long ago, the Tellens set off to make the cave safe to live within, leaving him with brother and sister. Not wanting conversation, he turned his attention to the view as he recalled the group's day trials getting here. Admittedly, the white-haired Tellen knew his wildscraft, keeping them from running into a hand and some herds of tanniyn, most the plant-eating kind, though they can be dangerous without eating you. The two meat-eating packs, one leapers and the other something he never saw before, Trundiir successfully maneuvered them, avoiding likely death. He considered their not being the interest of the packs more luck than skill as the claws seemed more focused on hunting other tanniyn than the two-legged prey Aren and the others were.

As he watched the sun sink to touch the distant mountains, he searched his mind for any sign of those troubling symbols. *They're not here*. Relieved at it, he turned his thoughts to what so suddenly made them silent. *Something to do with that half Tellen. I must understand this.* He reviewed his memories of every encounter and interaction he had with Rogaan and also the times the half Tellen wasn't around that the symbols fell silent. Recalling the ship and several other times, he looked up into the sky. Orange-red-highlighted clouds touched by the last rays of the sun peppered the sky. Near him, the sky was clear of high-flying leatherwings, and the low-flying featherwings were strangely quiet as well as absent from the air, except for one dark-feathered flier. A moderately sized featherwing that flew as if it owned the sky. *I've seen him several times while on the* Khaaron. *Something with this creature, too.*

"Aren!" Pax in a hush tried to get the Evendiir's attention.

"What?" Aren asked, irritated at having his thinking disturbed. He looked at Pax who appeared frustrated in his unblinking stare.

"We be needin' ta get wood ta keep a good fire burnin' for da night," Pax announced, then stood in an awkward silence Aren allowed. When the Evendiir didn't respond, Pax turned in a huff, shrugging his shoulders at the air as he almost stomped off to go looking for dried wood. Joining her brother, Suhd gave Aren an unhappy glance before the two started the bending down and standing up with growing piles of wood in their arms.

Aren returned to his much-desired thinking, rereviewing his memories for any details he might have missed. So much had happened from his days in Farratum with the half Tellen and his Tellen father, Mithraam . . . *He respected me. Not this brother and sister twosome now lightless of parents.* Then there was that Dark Ax and the *Subar*, Ezerus . . . *strange mix of peoples.* The thought of Irzal gave Aren a shake. He knew not if it was from being desired or from the loathing he felt at being forced under threat to indulge her cravings. *She'll pay for her abuse.* At least her daughter, Dajil, made no attempt at hiding her disapproval of her mother's attentions on him. Ganzer . . . *What a fool. He'll pay for his mistreatments against me.* Aren shivered at the next name in his review. *Za* Irzal's aide to her aide, Lucufaar . . . *Is he truly Luntanus Alum?* Aren didn't want to believe he shared presence with a *Shunned. The Powers he commanded . . . manifested . . . overwhelming.* He shivered again. *What am I to do other than run from him?*

"Approach . . ." a whisper came to Aren's mind, causing him to freeze with a chill so strong he feared his bones would break. *It's him!* Sweat poured from Aren soaking his clothes as he fell to his knees trying to breathe. He felt this presence before, but not so strongly. *It has to be him! He's searching for me. How is this possible?*

Fighting the chill racking his every muscle, Aren forced words out, commanding himself, "Hide, you fool! Hide your mind!"

The presence faded away, leaving Aren on his hands and knees gasping for breath and fighting not to sick up. At the moment, he almost wished for those symbols to return to obscure the vague yet disturbing images left in his mind by the presence. They were indiscernible but provoked a power sense of danger and foreboding in him.

"What be in Kur happen ta ya?" Pax's familiar voice broke into Aren's thoughts.

Aren felt a pair of hands support him as he rolled into a sitting position. Looking up to a pair of female Baraan eyes, he fought confusion and a sense of not really being there. "I don't know."

"Look what we have," the rough voice of the half Tellen was unmistakable. Rogaan stopped at the mouth of the cave when he saw Aren; then he just stood there with a long knife in his right hand while holding high by the tail a dead dragon in his left. A moderately sized, greenish-skinned dragon, its head just scraping the rocky ground. "What happened to you?"

"Nothing." Aren tried to deny anything of importance happened, though the half Tellen's skeptical look told him he failed. Aren's body revolted against his attempt to stand, putting him back down sitting on his backside. After holding Suhd off at arm's length, he made a second attempt, finding himself standing on shaking legs. He hurt all over.

"Do you need a hand?" Rogaan asked him.

Aren waved off Rogaan's offer of help. *I'm not about to let them think me feeble.* He struggled with each step but managed to walk himself near Rogaan as Pax and Suhd returned to building up a pile of firewood just outside the cave as the last light of the day cast deep shadows all about them. Finding a rock at the front of the cave to sit on, Aren watched as Trundiir, a little farther inside, prepped shavings, sticks, and small logs before sparking a fire with his flint and steel. Just outside, on a low-hanging branch of a thorny shrub-tree, Rogaan used vines to hang the dragon by its hind feet for skinning and cleaning before it would get a good cooking. The half Tellen also hung a thick, two-stride long serpent he must have also killed in the cave. Aren suffered a powerful shiver at the sight of it. He never liked those things or the shivers it gave him looking at one.

Soon, the cave's interior glowed with flickering flames that Trundiir then gave over ownership to Suhd to keep fed the fire. Rogaan finished his gutting and skinning of the dragon and serpent, then turned sticks into skewers with chunks of their flesh, all the while, Trundiir dragged in a large felled tree that looked dry, then started breaking it up with stomps and leveraged branch twisting then cut by a sharped-edged chain he pulled from his pack. Soon, the Tellens and the siblings had things prepped for a night in the cave and a good meal.

Each in the group carefully selected a place around the fire to sit, first looking for things that might bite or sting before settling. The Baraan brother settled himself next to Suhd, across the fire from Aren. *Smart fellow.* Trundiir sat deepest into the cave with his back to the darkness. He seemed least bothered by their accommodations. Rogaan chose to sit closest to the mouth of the cave, sitting with his back against rocks allowing him a sidewise glance and view of the inner cave as well as the night sky and approach to the cave. Aren observed each one noting their mannerisms, decisions, and choices they made even concerning the smallest of things such as which fingers they used to hold the skewers of dragon and serpent meat, who they watched, and with whom and what they shared.

"Would ya stop dat!" Pax eventually spoke after many uncomfortable glances at Aren.

"Stop what?" Aren asked innocently, though with a hint of impudence.

"Lookin' at us . . . watchin' like ya plannin' ta cut our necks." Pax replied.

Aren sat quietly for a long moment considering how to respond to this pretentious Baraan youngling. *I want to take this one's mind apart to teach him he isn't my equal, but I need this bunch to survive and get back to civilization.* "I have no intentions as such. Cutting your neck would not increase my chances of surviving these wilds."

"But ya would, if it did?" challenged Pax.

"Pax!" Suhd objected with a disappointed expression.

Her brother immediately looked only a little regretful and tried his best to put on a friendly face. It worked for Suhd, but Aren knew better watching Pax. Aren surmised the rogue didn't like or trust him and still held hard feels about his friend, the half Tellen. *He's selfish and too wanting to be wounded by his own losses to trust . . . or even like. I don't know why the half Tellen keeps trying to be his friend.*

Aren set his skewer into the dirt propped up with several good-size rocks allowing his dragon meal to cook slowly and completely. Pax fell silent focusing on cooking his skewered meal of dragon over the fire Suhd kept well fed with thick sticks and small logs. Rogaan too kept quiet as he cooked well his skewered serpent meat. In between her tending the fire, Suhd minded her skewer or let her brother hold it when needed. Trundiir set both of his skewers leaning from a set of stacked rocks he placed near the flames, allowing him to pull out of a sack from his pack herbs and what looked to be freshly picked fruits, then pass them out to everyone. Aren didn't expect any generosity from the white-bearded Tellen, but accepted herbs and fruit when offered. They waited for their meals to cook and cooked well at Trundiir's insistence. He spoke in his grumble of a way of illnesses suffered by under cooked meat before he brought in an armful of broken branches that he proceeded to cut and sharpen into straight-cut stakes while his dragon and serpent cooked to a blackened condition.

They ate in silence, nearly emptying the water bags each was given for their journey. Aren watched and learned as much he could from what they weren't speaking of. Pax and Suhd appeared to be enjoying their moment and freedom from being chased speaking to each other in their hushed whispers. The ground and cave shook several times as Trundiir kept at making stakes and contraptions of sorts from vines, stakes, and sticks. The Tellen seemed unconcerned at being in the cave during the often-felt tremors and seemed he was preparing for a long stay in this place. Rogaan was a different tale. He looked preoccupied with his inner thoughts and unsettled ones at that, if Aren was reading him well. When not looking inward, the half Tellen inventoried his equipment while eyeing the things each of them had taken from the *Seb'Ner* scouts. *He's thinking of something. What? What is he planning?*

Rogaan added dragon meat to his empty skewers, then laid them across several of the heated rocks surrounding the fire. Trundiir added three more skewers to other heated rocks. He said it would dry out the meat, giving it a start to being made into marching-food in the day's sun, tomorrow. Aren was familiar with the process and purpose and decided to follow their example with dragon meat on his skewer, making it a point not to touch the serpent flesh. *That flesh is just not right to eat*, he retold himself.

"How can we keep safe from da nasties of da night?" Suhd asked without a prelude.

"Most large tanniyn are quiet in darkness," Trundiir offered with his rock-grating grumble. "So are featherwings and leatherwings. Fur-diggers and climbers and serpents and dragons like we eat own the night. Those are harmless and more fearful of us than we are in danger of them."

"Will da fire keep dem away?" Suhd asked with a hopeful look on her face.

"Should help," answered Trundiir with a confident tone. "Little furs may seek warmth near the fire. Serpents too, though I have not seen many that could harm any of us."

"Serpents . . ." repeated Aren such no one could hear him. A shiver pulsed over him at the thought of one of them crawling around him. Then, a whisper teased at him. It was somewhere in his mind. He at first dismissed it as his imagination, but the whisper came again, and again, and again. It was there, but so faint his mind couldn't hear the words it spoke.

They all made places to sleep where they ate or nearby. Aren settled in lying length-wise with the fire that Suhd placed two more logs on. By his observation and count, they had three more logs for the fire and that they would not likely last the night, so he hoped the rocks would stay warm enough for him until morning. Despite his reluctance to do so, he eventually used his pack with the ax-and-flame Agni Stone within to rest his head on when he couldn't get comfortable. Sleep eluded him for a while as the ground shook several more times, though less intensely than during the day. *I hope the cave doesn't fall on us. It's been here longer than I've been breathing . . . So, stop concerning yourself with it.* With the dangers of the shakings put out of this mind, he hoped to doze off into an Evendiir trance, at least, but as the fire burned down, he realized he was too tired do so, and that sleep would eventually take him. So, he gave in, hoping to get enough rest in the night that would allow him to wake before the others so to be ready for anything the half Tellen might try to do.

Chapter 24

Woes and Revelations

A ren found himself suddenly awake standing somewhere deep in the cave, standing before a large wheel of stone and steel guarded by four thick, shaped, rock pillars. Colored metal wove around and through each of the pillars . . . metallic white-silver, green-pale, red, and black. To Aren, it looked that the door could spin in its place inside the rock wall, but no means were obvious allowing it to be opened. Engraved on the door were rings of symbols that changed as he stared. Three rings in all. At first, Aren found what he looked at confusing. Then, symbols previously tormenting him started appearing and disappearing on the rings. *A puzzle. A lock. Seals. But to what?*

His growing curiosity about the device was too much for him to resist. He approached the pillars but stopped when he felt his skin prickle. He looked down at himself to make sure biters were not crawling all over him as he felt they were. He thought to the manifestations he observed on the *Khaaron*, searching for one that could shield him from the crawlers, even if only imagined. A vaporous shield immediately formed in front of him. Still he felt his skin crawling. The pillars and symbolled rings blurred, then became sharp to his eyes, then blurred again as Aren adjusted the vapors trying to block the sensation. *Nothing.* Frustrated, he dismissed the shield. Looking at the pillars, he realized they formed a barrier wall filling the cavern's girth. His eyes barely making out blue and white sparkling following the invisible wall passing through the pillars when looking at darker areas of the cave. *Shielding myself doesn't work. Then, remove them.* Aren shot sizzling blue bolts of light at the pillars. They flashed blue and sparked lightning across their metal weaves as the cave loudly vibrated. Aren's skin crawled painfully, forcing him to back away until the sensations became tolerable.

Deeply frustrated, Aren stared at the pillars seeking a way past them to the large wheel of ringed symbols. He noticed slight impressions on each of the pillars. The impressions . . . looked like handprints at near the height of his chest. Shadows suddenly appeared in front of him giving him a start and a skip of his beating heart. Then, he watched as they took the form of people . . . a male Baraan, Tellen, Evendiir, and Mornor-Skurst. The shadows glided across the cave floor taking positions at the pillars; the Baraan at the green-pale metal-wrapped stone pillar, the Tellen at the white-silver, the Evendiir at the black, and the Mornor-Skurst at the red. Glowing rods of gold, talisman came to Aren's thoughts, appeared in each of the shadows' left hands just as they placed their right hands into the impressions. Aren's skin started crawling all over, unpleasantly, then painfully. At the peak of his pain, he felt his skin stripping from his sinew as he threw up his arms shielding his eyes from a blinding flash of power from the four pillars.

Aren found himself lying on his back, panting. Opening his eyes, he only saw painful flashing explosions of white and black. *What's happened? Where am I?* Panic rising in Aren tightened his chest and throat recalling memories of his youngling years spent in fear of so much. He closed his eyes and concentrated on his beating heart. After a time, he felt his heart slow, then become calm. Spinning symbols flashed in his mind. *No.* They stopped. Opening his eyes again, he was relieved to find the explosions of white and black gone. Looking about, he found himself lying in the cave where he fell asleep, next to a now-smoldering fire. His hands were still raised, blocking the first rays of the morning sun sneaking through rocks and trees and shining on him where he lay his head. *What in Kur did my mind see?* Aren didn't move from where he lay in sweat-soaked clothes wondering what he experienced in his dreams. More strange pillars flashing with lightning brightly came to his mind, followed by more spinning symbols and pain. He tried to pay them no heed. *Was it real?* He then denied them telling his mind it was only a dream. More symbols spinning violently flashed in mind. *Rogaan!* Aren looked up with a start to find the half Tellen and his things gone. Pax and Suhd still lay sound asleep in the shadows across from the smoldering fire. Trundiir was also gone, but much of his things remained where he had left them last night.

In a panic, Aren rose and collected his belongings, including his skewers from the warm stones with mostly dried dragon, and set off to the mouth of the cave where he stood, allowing his eyes to adjust to the growing brightness of the new day sun. Scanning the hillside leading up to the landing in front of the cave, Aren saw nothing of Rogaan . . . or Trundiir. *My plans are in ruin*, he chastised himself for sleeping so long. Panic welled up within him before he forced himself into calming down and deciding what he had to do next. Vibrant-colored symbols spinning violently filled his mind until he shook his head hard enough to hurt. *That half Tellen is off to see his father free. I must brave the wilds of these hills to get to Anza to get close to that cursed half Tellen.* Resolved to act so boldly despite being ill prepared for it, Aren spied off into the direction he thought Anza to be. *I'm not certain*, he admitted to himself. *I could get lost . . . and eaten.* He stood arguing with himself . . . when he saw it. The lone dark flying thing in a part of the sky. The featherwing from last night . . . and from the river when he was on the ship . . . and even before that, he thought. He now more than suspected it, the featherwing, playing a part in this "adventure," though he was uncertain how. It soared at a distance, what Aren guessed as to the southeast, at a height just below where the leatherwings usually flew and above where any featherwing dared to climb. "Follow that one. If I'm thinking straight . . . and I always do, I'll find that half Tellen somewhere below it. And that leads me to Anza and to be rid of these torments."

Aren rushed off after the featherwing. He was not fond of the wilds despite being taught by his father how to live in and survive it. *Many unpleasant things an Evendiir needs to do to survive*, Aren reminded himself as he trotted down a somewhat used path leading him in the general direction of his soaring sign. He calculated Rogaan only had a short start ahead of him, and as he recalled, this half Tellen didn't seem to run fast. *That should allow me to catch him . . . and make these symbols sleep*. Aren trotted the path hoping not to run into tanniyn, or worse, and wishing the bushes he continuously brushed against had shorter thorns.

The hills relentless with thorn-rich bushes and trees pricked and cut at Aren's clothes and skin, drawing blood and discomfort in so many spots. Aren even found himself ducking low-hanging branches also thick with thorns as he made his way along the path. The number of times and intensity of the symbols appearing to him seemed to lessen. *I must be closing on the half Tellen*. He calculated he covered more than a march of these hills when he lost sight of the featherwing when the path took him into heavy tree cover. Stopping to catch his breath and hoping to reorient himself, Aren realized he was in a low hollow with a trickling stream and thick vegetation. *Oh no! I need to remove myself from here*. Panic surged in Aren at his recall of Father's teachings that low hollows, especially ones with water, are preferred hunting areas of leapers and other predators. Squawks, snorts, and distant bellows filled his ears, causing him more angst. Aren jerked his head left and right trying to see everything about him all at once. Immediately, the wilds became confusing and disorientating as his ears filled with the pounding of his heart. For a time, he couldn't think well enough to pick a direction to go as spinning symbols came to and went from his mind. Stray thoughts told him to calm himself. *Breathe . . . breathe*, Aren told himself. With an effort, he took a breath and closed his eyes. He repeated this calming ritual just as his father taught him. Aren opened his eyes after some time. The low hollow remained around him. To his relief, the squawks, snorts, and distant bellows didn't set upon him anything intending to eat him. Now calmer, he looked for his footprints leading back to the cave. Having found them, he picked a direction opposite them that went uphill in a direction he thought to be on a line he was traveling.

In a short time, Aren topped a ridge allowing him to survey the surrounding hills. He spotted the featherwing aloft, maybe a march away over the next ridge in the direction of the rising sun off to his left, as it had been when he left the cave. More spinning symbols flashed painfully in his mind. Aren did his best to ignore them. They then disappeared. In the small valley below, the trees gave way to a lake. The area was alive with animals and beasts of many types, though the leatherwings he saw kept high and distant from the featherwing as the other featherwings, many vibrantly colored, kept low and close to the trees. Several small herds of tanniyn, colorful shieldbacks, and longwalkers surrounded the water. *Where are the teeth?* Aren asked himself as he scanned the valley and surrounding hills. To his relief and concern, he spied only one pack of predators . . . a pack of blue-colored leapers trotting up the next ridge in the direction of the lone featherwing. *Dung!* Aren fought with himself at what to do. The leapers were likely after Rogaan, a lone "animal," unprotected by a herd. *What to do?* Aren asked himself. *Go back or try to help Rogaan?*

"Go back to the cave and keep safe or . . ." Aren struggled with his sense of self-preservation, strong as it was. But then, there was Rogaan, who, so far, had shown Aren kindness and respect. *I should help him*, Aren decided. *No . . . I'll have my Light taken from me*, Aren undecided. Painfully, spinning symbols filled his mind. Aren breathed deeply trying to calm his mind. Success, partly, as the symbols dimmed but stayed in his mind this time. He became angry with himself for his indecisiveness. A faint whisper wove around the symbols in his mind. It called to Aren filling him with a desire to head south. He felt lost in the chaos in his mind. "Make a decision . . . Aren."

He took a step down the ridge, then quickly started chopping his feet as he descended the hill in a hurry, reluctantly filled with the intent to help Rogaan, *if possible*. Aren wished his motivations were purely unselfish, but he admitted to himself that they were not . . . entirely. Running as fast as he could keeping a pace allowing him to run long, Aren raced across the northern edge of the lake keeping his distance from and an eye out for tanniyn. There were big beasts in the valley and dangerous despite not being the type of teeth to be afraid of. Up the opposite hill Aren ran, slowing as he did. Fatigue was becoming his enemy, though the symbols had disappeared to his relief.

Topping the ridge, Aren saw the featherwing, from its high place, dive into the valley below. Aren looked for Rogaan through the trees of the valley. At first, no sight of the half Tellen until a cloud of dirt and dust kicked up at the base of the opposite ridge in between two stands of trees. Aren saw Rogaan rise from the cloud of dirt and dust, letting loose arrows rapidly at the unseen up the hill. A dull hum . . . vibrations touched Aren as the featherwing swooped down just in front of Rogaan then around him left to right in a half circle . . . A sparkling wall of fire stood in its trail. Aren stared in awe and confusion. *How?* The featherwing climbed back into the sky coming level with Aren before rolling over into another dive.

Below, Rogaan let loose more arrows, striking blue-hued leapers, all two to three strides long, standing angry and confused at the sparkling wall of flames. One of the leapers fell to the ground from an arrow to its head. Four remained by Aren's count. Squawking grunts came from one of the leapers, spurring the others into motion circling around the wall of Agni Power. Aren felt another hum soak into his body as the featherwing swooped at another of the leapers striking it on its head. A blinding flash of lightning exploded at the moment the featherwing struck the predator. The tanniyn went wildly rolling about the hillside shrieking in pain. The featherwing climbed again. Rogaan let loose two more arrows at an unseen tanniyn to his left. Another humming sensation told Aren the featherwing was about to strike. This time, it missed its intended target as the leaper ducked the talons of the featherwing. Three remaining by Aren's count. *No! Two more sneaking up at Rogaan's back.* Aren saw Rogaan was unaware of them, and the featherwing was still climbing . . . most likely also unaware. The leapers closed on Rogaan in a fast trot. *They're going to be on him in moments!*

Aren summoned his memories of the Agni Powers manifested on the *Khaaron* and fashioned in his mind the "song." He felt his body humming as he formed the shape of lightning bolts in his right hand. Strange how the crackling lightning about his fingers did not hurt as an almost euphoric feeling spread throughout his body. Concentrating on the trotting leapers, Aren formed in his mind the "song," adjusting it, before sending the bolts of blue and white streaking at the tanniyns. They fizzled out only strides from him. Embarrassed at himself and happy nobody saw his failing, Aren called forth the "song," again, then unleashed the lightning. Failing now meant the leapers would be on Rogaan. Two bolts struck the deadly animals on the left and one the tanniyn on the right. Another bolt struck the ground in front of the leapers, all releasing blinding white flashes upon striking with the one hitting the ground, kicking up a puff of dirt. The left-most leaper stumbled and fell to the ground as the right-most leaper stopped in a defensive crouch looking around for its attacker.

Whoa! Aren just realized he manifested Agni Powers and tossed them hundreds of strides. Yet, he was unsure how he did it. The featherwing dove again, striking its intended target on this passing swoop as Rogaan took notice of the leapers Aren struck with the Powers and sent an arrow into the one rising from the ground. The leaper reeled from the arrow to its chest before limping off into the trees. A new series of squawking grunts stopped all the leapers in their moments . . . all with snouts high as if waiting or listening for something. More squawks sounded causing them to turn and run off to the south. Aren watched as the leapers departed, their pack now smaller and with a few struggling behind trying to keep up. Then, Aren stood in shock and with a sense of awe looking at his hands. *What did I do? How did I do it?*

A caw from above drew Aren's attention high. The dark-colored featherwing passed over him before turning back toward Rogaan. Aren noted a sparkling glint from the featherwing as it turned, allowing the sun's rays to strike it just right. Below, Rogaan held his *Sentii* Blood Bow high above his head and waved it at Aren. Wanting not to waste any more time than necessary out in these wilds, Aren quickly made his way down the ridge and across the narrow valley to join up with the half Tellen. As he trotted, Aren realized the spinning symbols were gone from his mind as too the whispering had stopped.

As he got close to Rogaan, Aren spotted a leaper lying prone under a pine tree. Its chest unmoving. Arrows, one in the chest and another in its head, appeared to have ended its life. Rogaan approached the down leaper. A swooshing sound drew his attention to the dark featherwing making a low and near pass before it climbed back into the sky. Glancing at the half Tellen, Aren found Rogaan frozen in place holding his Blood Bow watching the featherwing to the exclusion of everything else.

"Does it do that often?" Aren asked Rogaan of the featherwing.

"What?" Rogaan asked as if realizing he was being spoken to. "No. The black one has been watching me for some time. Never has it done anything like . . ."

"Manifest Agni Powers?" Aren completed the half Tellen's words.

"Yes," Rogaan answered with a visible shiver. When he looked to have recovered from it, he asked Aren a question. "Do you do that often?"

"What?" Aren wasn't certain about what Rogaan was referring to.

"Send lightning," Rogaan clarified.

"It's new to me . . . just happened." Aren found himself answering honestly despite wanting to sound as if he knew what he was doing. Wanting to change the subject, he pointed at the *Sentii*-made bow in Rogaan's hand. "You're good with that."

"You should see my *shunir'ra*," boasted Rogaan.

"Are there any more of those leapers?" Aren sincerely asked, hoping that they were all gone.

"I think not," answered Rogaan.

"*Shunir'ra?*" Aren didn't understand the reference.

"My blue metal bow . . . my masterwork according to Tellen traditions." Rogaan attempted to describe without a long explanation. "I made it to demonstrate my skills for my acceptance into the Tellen clans."

"Yet, you live in Brigum . . . in Shuruppak?" Aren asked, not completely understanding why Rogaan was seeking acceptance into Tellen clans. "Aren't the Tellens and their clans in Turil?"

"Yes, though my father holds true to the Tellen traditions, and if I am ever to walk among the clans, I must receive *Zagdu-i-Kuzu*," explained Rogaan. When Aren put on a confused expression, Rogaan further answered. "My recognition . . . my Tellen Coming of Age."

They then stood awkwardly looking at each other for a short time. Aren decided to remain silent in their uncomfortable exchange of stares to see what Rogaan was thinking.

"Why are you here?" Rogaan finally asked.

". . . I'm not going to stay in that cave," Aren answered, hoping it would be enough for the half Tellen. Rogaan just stared at him with an impassive expression. Aren could tell Rogaan was mulling over something in his head. *Likely if he thinks I'm speaking the truth, and if so, what to do.*

"Dung," was all Rogaan said as he walked to a fallen blue and gray leaper where he retrieved his arrows.

"Pardon my understanding . . ." Aren retorted.

"In Farratum's jail . . ." Rogaan continued. "This Lucufaar wanted something from you. Tormented you for it. You kept whatever your secret is from him. Then, on the ship, he threw Powers about as if a Black Robe. Someone powerful. What I have been told is he is Luntanus Alum, one of the *Shunned* . . . one of those legends that should not be."

Aren remained silent at realizing this half Tellen to be more intelligent and observant than he thought. And . . . Rogaan knew more than he could know. He must have learned from someone with knowledge of the Ancients and the Old Times.

"You should be cowering in that cave . . . hiding from him," concluded Rogaan. "Instead, you are running about these wilds chasing after me. You obviously know where I am going, and that means getting closer to that *Shunned*. Why are you here, and what do you want?"

Much more intelligent than he appears, Aren acknowledged to himself. Being the untrusting kind, he wasn't about to share his inner secrets with the half Tellen. *I must give something to this one, or he's going to push me away.* Aren considered what to say as the half Tellen pulled more arrows from several more leapers, then preceded to cut claws from the tanniyn arms and feet. Surprisingly, Rogaan cut into but not through the flesh of fingers and toes of the leapers, then used his strength to rip each of the claws from the flesh, grunting as he did. The claws came free, almost bloodless, trailing sinew that the half Tellen then easily cut away. Aren used Rogaan's distraction to mull over what to reveal. *What? How much? Rogaan's been honest and respectful with me as much as I can tell. Hmm . . . Let me test his openness with me.*

"What is that featherwing to you?" asked Aren seeking an answer he wasn't certain of. "It clearly is intelligent, and it possesses the Powers of the Agni."

"It has been flying around me ever since they placed me on that ship to the island." Rogaan appeared to be sincerely answering. "It sits high on perches watching me at times or takes to the sky up high circling about me. It flew by distracting several *Lugasum* cutthroats and a *Saggis* Light-Takers while on the prison isle. That kept my *Light* and me one. What it did moments ago is the first I have seen, and now that I have, I think it has one of those . . . Agni Stones, as *he* named it, harnessed to it. I dismissed what I thought was a gem on it before, though now, much sense it makes that it is one of those Agnis."

"Who is 'he'?" Aren asked of Rogaan's reference to the "naming" of the Agni Stone.

"The *Vassal*," answered Rogaan. "That is what he calls himself . . . the warrior in red armor we carried to the forward room on the *Makara*. The one who did battle against the *Shunned* on your ship."

A chill swept over Aren. *Too many powerful ones suddenly revealing themselves. And these cursed symbols and whispers in my mind. Something large and dangerous is to happen . . . soon.* Aren started warming up to Rogaan being one of few people who was honest and trusting toward him, and the half Tellen didn't even want something from him. "Why are you speaking so freely with me?"

"I have no reason not to trust you," was Rogaan's simple answer. "You still owe me."

"Owe you?" Aren was genuinely caught off guard and surprised at somehow owing this half Tellen when he just saved Rogaan's life.

"Why are you here?" Rogaan asked again.

Aren mulled over what to reveal, then considered how he would speak it . . . the truth. For the first time . . . ever, Aren decided to take a chance sharing a secret with someone. "I have symbols I see in my head. They torment me with their puzzle, and they often come with pain. For some reason, when I'm near you . . . They go away."

"Do you understand why?" Rogaan asked.

"No," Aren answered honestly and without hesitation or reservations. *That felt good to speak honestly with someone.*

"I need to be getting to Anza . . ." Rogaan changed the subject of conversation. "I am going to see my father freed."

"How will you accomplish that . . . alone?" Aren asked with a slight bit of concern for the half Tellen.

"I will work out a way," answered Rogaan.

"Why not have your friends . . . Pax and his sister help you?" Aren asked curious to why he separated himself from the others.

"They have already paid too high a price being my friend," Rogaan answered with what sounded like a tightened throat as he turned to start making his way up the next ridge. "They will be safer with Trundiir in that cave . . . away from me."

"Well, I'm glad not to be one of your friends." Aren spoke with a mix of sarcasm and honesty.

"You might want to keep yourself that way," Rogaan offered as he climbed the hill, cleaning his arrows, then returning them to their quiver as he went.

Aren hesitated, reconsidering to follow or not to follow this half Tellen. It was only a few moments, but his internal conflict between looking out only for himself his entire life and now giving this stranger trust, was painful in its own way. The ground shook. At first, Aren thought it from the largest of tanniyn but realized it was the ground itself. *The Tellen seems confident in what he's doing.* He eventually took a step . . . up the hill. A hope. Then another step and another until he found himself catching up with Rogaan while still wondering if he could truly trust this half Tellen.

They soon topped the ridge where they both crouched low between groups of thorny bushes and a stand of pine trees, spying on the rising smoke of civilization a little more than two ridges away. High above, owning the sky to itself, that dark-colored featherwing soared. Aren wondered what that creature really was . . . and if to be afraid of it. It had only shown him indifference until it drew Rogaan's attention to him on the ridge. *That must mean something.*

Rogaan soon was off, down the hill. He kept a good pace with Aren easily keeping with him. Rogaan led them through the wilds down, then up forest-covered ridges spotting and giving wide space to plant-eating tanniyn small and huge, and when he found predator tracks, moving quickly away from where they headed.

Past midday, they found themselves under gathering storm clouds as they hid among more thorny bushes and trees at the top of the last ridge looking over a city a little smaller than Farratum. Aren thought Anza was more of a large town. Keeping low and concealed, they spied over the ridge to get a good look at their surroundings. The city wall was unlike Farratum's heavy stone and more like his hometown Windsong, made of tall, thick timbers, except at the gates, both on the north and south sides of the city's western approaches. The gates were of gray stone block construction with tall timbers used for large double doors. Atop the gates flew equal-sized flags; one bearing a scarlet wing and sword symbol on a gold background and the second a gold scepter on a silver background. A low ridge rising beyond and above the timber walls was populated and dominated by seven gleaming stepped pyramid temples and their gardens, each temple brandishing unique-colored flags lazily blowing in the wind; the northern most blue and tan, the next south blue, next the gold scepter on silver, next brown and black, the next one green, next red and black, and the southernmost white. To his frustration, the ridge and large stone temples blocked Aren's view of the rest of Anza. Of the "city" he could spy, were stables near the gates, tightly spaced stone and timber-constructed dwellings and shops with colorful street-side canopies, log and stone homesteads, and crop fields in between. Cooking fires wafted from many of the dwellings. The streets Aren could spy showed busy with peoples, carts being pulled by either small niiskus or Baraans, and Baraan-carried sedan-chairs Aren assumed carried the well-to-do. Strange the consolidation of temples inside one wall, Aren considered. In all his readings and teaching from his father, only one temple typically sat within the limits of a town or small city, dominating it.

Another odd feature of Anza was a lone gleaming temple with fortress like circular stone walls sitting on a rise of terrain just outside the "city" near the northern gate. Gold and red flags around the temple were many. On them, Aren could just make out a symbol of a dark circle or golden disk. This temple bore much activity both inside its walls and in the surrounding hillsides of what appeared to be silver-clad warriors with red and yellow coverings and sashes. A number of sarigs, some with mounted warriors, stood alongside the kydas bearing equipment, and niisku attached to several wagons. It appeared the rabble had only one water wagon among them. *They're not going far*. It appeared to Aren the temple was amassing a militia for some purpose close by.

"Your thinking?" Rogaan asked.

"About your unworkable desire to see your father free of the . . . *Shunned*?" Aren made more of a statement to the half Tellen than question before being helpful. "Or how to get past the gates and guards without having us taken to Anza's jail?"

Rogaan gave Aren a half-scowl, then returned his attention to Anza. The half Tellen appeared to examine every aspect of the "city" with intense focus before speaking again. "Would you not do the same for your father?"

Aren didn't expect to be challenged in such a manner. The question bothered him as his first instinct answering it was . . . *no*. Aren felt more unsettled by his unspoken answer the more he thought on and felt about it. And he felt . . . selfish and . . . unworthy of his father. "Curse you, half Tellen."

"Curse me?" Rogaan asked in a not-so-a-surprised tone. "Did not my father help you in Farratum when they took you before the *Za* and *Gal*, and did you not help us in the arena?"

"That was different . . ." Aren tried to deny he felt some kinship for father and son. He admitted to himself that it was mostly because they treated him with respect while not demanding anything from him. Aren wanted to tell himself that he was just using this half Tellen until he could find an escape from his situation, but he felt safer being around Rogaan than not. "We were all kept prisoners in the grasps and under the boots of others. Our only means to survive was to aid each other, work together. To get free of them."

"Do you feel free now?" Rogaan asked simply.

Aren thought on it for a few moments. *Curse this half Tellen. Is he swaying me with some Baraan ways?* Aren reflected on his own sense of self and concluded he didn't suffer from a weakness like Rogaan suffered from his Suhd. *He's "swaying" me with words and thoughts. Clever he is. Making me feel . . . guilty.* Aren didn't think that was possible, nor did he want to admit it, but this half Tellen was more challenging than others of either of his races. And he was right. "No."

"No to freeing your father or feeling free?" Rogaan sought clarity.

"Feeling free," answered Aren. "We are all trapped within these happenings. Some by choice. You . . . by kin and blood. Others by friendship and associations. And me . . . curiosity and now . . . need."

"You have something in your head that you want to stop?" Rogaan asked.

"I want it out, but I want what it means . . . it's secrets" admitted Aren before realizing he spoke so freely of his inner thoughts and wants. "Curse you. Why is it so easy talking with you? I want the knowledge that's in it."

"I have much practice with difficult folks." Aren assumed the half Tellen spoke of his friendship with Pax. "We will likely need that knowledge. Something very bad is soon to take place. I cannot rid myself of that feeling. And we are part of it, despite our desires."

"Yes . . . I have that feeling, also," Aren found himself agreeing.

"Im'Kas and my father both told me I needed to endure," Rogaan continued explaining. "I am. Father too hoped for me to carry his burden after he no longer could, that burden being so important for him to involve family."

"Endure what?" Aren asked.

"What has been thrust on me . . . by all of them . . . all of it," Rogaan spoke in a reflective manner. "That was at first, nothing of my doing and my blaming everyone for what was happening. I held no responsibilities in what was happening to me. Though, now, I understand all my desires and choices made my today what it is. 'Endure' truly was of my own conflicting desires, my uncertainties and . . . cowardice. I once wanted to be a *Kiuri'Ner* but did not see or understand all of what it means to be one. My father wanted me in the Ebon Circle, away from all of this. Now, I simply want to see my friends and family safe and free, and that means for me gaining the knowledge and skills of a *Kiuri'Ner* . . . and more, if I am to have any chance at success."

"I think you have unseen friends aiding you." Aren looked to the darkening sky, finding comfort in seeing the featherwing still circling above.

"And I do not even know who these *friends* are." Rogaan spied the featherwing before returning his attention to the city and temple. "Im'Kas, *lightless* Sugnis, Trundiir . . . even a little from that Dajil in the *Tusaa'Ner*, all have aided me. And you. My gratitude for striking with lightning the leapers at my back. I could not defend myself from them all."

Aren remained quiet at Rogaan's expression of gratitude and of what he experienced in recent battles. Aren recalled what he observed of Rogaan and what he saw and felt earlier with the *Shunned* and *Vassal*. How he easily turned that knowledge into manifestations, and then the almost euphoric feeling as the Power flowed through him. *I want to feel that again.*

"I felt miserable and unworthy of my father and family, of my friends, and of me when blaming everyone for these enduring sufferings," Rogaan confessed. His face and voice turned to resolve. "I cannot spend my days living in such a way. We are caught up in this, and until it is resolved, my family, friends, and I are not free to live our lives."

"It may cost you much," warned Aren. *And, it may cost me much . . . It has already.*

"You are likely right, and there are obstacles . . ." Rogaan agreed but sounded resolved despite the hardships past and expected in the days ahead. "My father being prisoner is one of them. My family not being free from threat of blade and bars is another. My friends and their losses with no sight of freedom in their days ahead are another. Plans this *Shunned* and this *Vassal* have entangled us in and what it might mean to everyone . . . It cannot be a good thing. Your freedom has been lost by who chases after us and what you say is in your head."

Silence is all Aren could offer Rogaan. He did feel trapped and somehow compelled by whispers in his mind. *I do want this to end*, he admitted to himself. "I offer we take advantage of the assembling crowd at the temple. I think they mean to go into the city. With your *Seb'Ner* colors and armor, we should be able to take advantage of the chaos enough to gain entrance."

"Then we learn the city and find a spot where we can wait for the *Tusaa'Ner* and this *Shunned*." Rogaan started to lay out a plan as the ground trembled under them. Waiting for it to calm, Rogaan stood silently. "We find and free Father from his bonds, and then, maybe, he can provide insight on all of this and the growing feeling I need to be in these mountains. Something is calling. A feeling I cannot explain."

Aren stared at Rogaan for a long moment at his revelation of feeling as being *called* into the Blood Lands. *It's not just me.* Relief spread through him that he was not alone in this calling. Then, concern at their lack of means to live in a city. "How will we live inside? We have no coin."

Rogaan rolled, then reached into his carry pack. He pulled out two hide pouches bound up with hide cord. He tossed one to Aren. A pitched clatter sounded when it struck the ground. "I took these coin pouches from the *Seb'Ner* scouts. They have balkas, ingots, and a few gems, each."

"Does Trundiir know of these?" Aren asked with a smile at the roguish act by the half Tellen.

"I think he encouraged me to follow this path," Rogaan offered more of an explanation than answering the question as the first drops of rain started falling. "I cannot be certain, though I know he purposely gave me the opportunity to leave this morning."

"Sly Tellens . . ." Aren didn't realize Tellens had any capacity in being devious. *Take heed of this*, he noted for future times. "Let's see to resolving these woes upon us."

Chapter 25

Him

A light rain kept the dust of the road from kicking up by the boots, sandals, and feet of the column. He found relief in the dust's absence and for the cooling clouds and rain. A welcome change in the weather, though dangerous for this time of year if the temperatures continued to drop. He noted the ground trembled more often here than north of the Ur. *Does it mean something?* Sitting upon his stout sarig, in his red-brown armor now adorned with the Farratum *Tusaa'Ner* red cape of command, he led at the front of what remained of the *Tusaa'Ner* and support provisioners; ninety-some survivors from over two hundred and fifty boarding the three ships in Farratum a day ago. The losses were a disappointment at best, though their survival was a wonder, crediting the commander and crew of the *Khaaron* with their makeshift riggings aided by winds from the Powers getting them on the Dukkha River and into port. It was there in the port of Haven they met with facilitators, sent ahead of the expedition, with prearranged supplies, wagons, and steeds. Immediately setting to the road the *Tusaa'Ner* and provisioner survivors, with steeds and wagons filled with water and supplies a-plenty . . . enough for double their numbers as planned, the guardsman column remained largely on foot as the steeds were meant for officers and not the ranks who were mostly unskilled at riding such beasts. What they were short on were weapons and guardsmen, having lost two of the expedition's ships in battle on the Ur. *So much for the Za's personal guard being strong.*

Now, tamed by their master and riding in a fume nearby on a smaller sarig, sat Dajil in blue-padded leather armor with red cape and red-plumbed helm bearing the new rank of *seergal*, first commander. A promotion borne of both her being next in the chain of command to the wrecked first commander, after his unsuccessful challenge to *him*, and for her being the daughter to the *Za;* now, a well-kept face to legitimize *his* authority. To his disappointment and frustration, Dajil sat slightly slumped over and with a rage burning in her eyes. He had to change that. "Sit tall, *Seergal.*"

"Yes, *Ar'seergal,*" Dajil reflexively replied to his authority over her as defined by Shuruppak law. Her words were high-pitched, bringing a grimace from the *ar'seergal.* She set her back stiff with her chin a bit high.

"Remain silent when we stand before Anza's North Gate, and then when we're within," he instructed his second in command. *To my utterance and no more will she follow my commands*, he noted and cautioned himself. "Do so in matters where I speak and ensure the ranks comply."

"Yes . . . *Ar'seergal*," she replied with heat in her high-pitched voice.

That will have to do, he told himself as he reluctantly accepted her defiant compliance. Looking down to his right hand, the red-jeweled signet ring of his legal authority seemed to glow. *Not my true authority, but enough for all else to understand.* "You shall address me with the title of my greater station . . . not that of a lowly *ar'seergal*."

"Yes, Ar's . . . *Subar*," Dajil more submissively replied, her words in a pitch a little lower.

Ezerus felt a curled smile come to his face with the *seergal's* improved obedience. She and her mother didn't yield to his legal authority when they were in Farratum, as Shuruppak law affords such authority to the *Zas* inside civilization walls. In the wilds and away from the *Zas'* elected city, the *Subars* carried greater authority over both the *Zas'* militias and the *Zas* themselves. Yet, this *Za* Irzal knew well Shuruppak law did not hold sovereignty here. Something more held it out here. Ezerus felt it in the back of his mind . . . always there. Always watching.

Scanning the countryside with its abundant low-flying featherwings and thick forests of thorny trees and underbrush brought memories of his previous visit to Anza. Not yet a *Subar* but in the service of Shuruppak, he learned of this place of treachery. In these unhallowed lands, he learned the unrestrained use of authority. The road they slowly traveled followed the river's western banks rising from the docks some marches ago and toward Anza. Anza, the gateway city to the Blood Lands or more appropriately named "Gateway to the Ancients." Ezerus thought then and even more so now that Anza was more accurately a gateway to the lands of the forbidden . . . the *Sentii* and death. *Am I truly going into these lands?* he asked himself. *Yes*, answered another voice with absolute conviction. A sense of unease grew in Ezerus at the intrusion into his mind. *I don't think I'll ever become used to this. I don't want to become used to it.* Silence gave him a sense of hope the presence in his head would be gone someday.

The light rain made the packed dirt road slick and messy for the *Tusaa'Ner* column, slowing them even more than just being on foot; yet, they pressed on knowing safety after the sun went down was always best inside of walls, the larger, the better. Their midday departure at the docks and the twelve-march journey to Anza would put them at the city near nightfall . . . without the slick road. Ezerus grew more concerned as the afternoon dragged on with their slow pace that the night would engulf them before they could meet up with the *Anubda'Ner* at Anza. The *Za* had arranged for the *Anubda'Ner* to join this expedition as their main militia under her authority. They were to bring experienced *Kiuri'Ner* and *Sharur* to lead the way into the Blood Land mountains and to the City of the Dead . . . the Throne of the Ancients, Vaikuntaars. Three dangerous encounters so far with shieldbacks, longwalkers, and a pack of small leapers found Ezerus wanting those *Kiuri'Ner* and *Sharur* with them—now. Disdain filled his thoughts for some reason he didn't understand. The thoughts remained in his head for a short time before disappearing. He looked around nervously to the covered wagons with the extra sarig steeds in trail, eight wagons in total with the leading one at the center of the column where the *Za*, Ganzer, and *he* rode.

In the late afternoon, it became obvious to the ranks they would still be out in the wilds after sunset. A stir rose through the *Tusaa'Ner* such that Ezerus grew concerned of panic and desertion. Looking to his brooding second in command, he ordered, "Stop to the column."

Dajil gave him an "I told you so much" look before giving orders to the flag-bearers to raise red flags as she yelled in her high pitch the command, "Column, halt!"

In uneven fits, the column of city-experienced *Tusaa'Ner* stopped their movement. With a grimace of irritation from her screeching, Ezerus urged his sarig to the side of the column where he planned to address the ranks but still wasn't certain what he would say to bolster their confidence. The ground shook a few moments, then stopped. Ignoring the repeating trembling, he sat up tall before filling his lungs to project his words, when Ezerus spotted through the drizzle a pair of large blue and black leapers running up on the rear of the column. It took him several blinks of his eyes to grasp the horror of the moment, then pointed to the pair as he yelled as loud as he could, "Leapers!"

A moment of shocked silence descended upon the *Tusaa'Ner*. Moments later, yelling and screaming erupted from the rear of the column as chaos consumed the once-orderly ranks. The rest of the *Tusaa'Ner* started to break ranks when hollering from the columns' *kunza* gave them pause. Spears met the two leapers at the rear of the column, but with little success, as Ezerus watched with fearful disappointment concern two provisioners now in the jaws and claws of the beasts. In the corner of his eye, Ezerus caught more movement. Three more huge leapers jumping from the tree line high into the air now descended on the center of the column. A tingling sensation started in his right hand, then spread throughout his body in the time needed to take a long blink of his eyes. The three leapers landed on *Tusaa'Ner* at the side of the column, scattering those reaming ranks nearby. Smoke puffed upward from the canvas hide at the side of the wagon just before three bolts of lightning from the kyda-drawn carriage struck each of the leapers, illuminating the beasts while burning their feathers and skin. Stunned silence fell over all, allowing Ezerus to hear the drizzle piddling on his head. Another prickling tingle and a glow from the wagon told Ezerus *he* was going to strike again. Before more lightning could be unleashed, the three leapers retreated into the trees, screeching as they ran. Ezerus looked to the rear of the column where the remaining two leapers were also running, but in their jaws and claws dragging off the two flailing provisioners. Relief washed over Ezerus at *his* powerful intervention and the limited loss of lives. Dajil started yelling commands to retrieve the provisioners as she made to break ranks on her sarig.

"Hold, *Seergal!*" Ezerus commanded with a raised voice.

Dajil pulled up reins, bringing her sarig to a halt. Those making to follow her also stopped in their places when they saw her unmoving. Ezerus observed she was again in a fume now with eyes straining in danger of popping from her head. She screeched. "Those provisioners need to be rescued."

"They're *lightless*," stated Ezerus.

"They're alive!" hissed Dajil as she snapped reins spurring her steed. Her steed made to burst into a run but went nowhere as it snorted with frustration.

Tingling filled Ezerus as he watched the sarig restrained in place by an unseen hand much as Dajil had been in the *Za's* cabin on the *Khaaron*. Ezerus knew what was happening and expected she would provoke harsh wrath. Dajil let out a growling scream of frustration as she turned her attention to the first wagon. Ezerus followed her gaze. On the wagon the driver sat motionless with eyes wide with fear. Standing just behind the driver's seat *he* stood in dark colors that mingled with the shadows of the hide canvas cover making it difficult to see him clearly. Next to *him*, *he* held a terrified Irzal as he waggled a finger at Dajil and himself.

"*Seergal!*" Ezerus spoke in a harsh voice.

She completely ignored Ezerus with her eyes fixed on her mother and captor. Ezerus feared she was about to commit to actions that would see many *lightless*. He softened his tone, "Dajil . . ."

"What?" she snapped at Ezerus in her high-pitched voice, bringing a grimace to her *ar'seergal*.

"Take your place," Ezerus ordered in an even tone.

She glared at him for a long moment, then screamed in frustration as she returned her sarig into her position before the attack. Ezerus quietly joined her as a cloak of silence fell over the *Tusaa'Ner* column. Ezerus held up his right hand, then waited for his *seergal* to follow protocol. It took a few moments, but Dajil relented, shouting commands to move the *Tusaa'Ner* column again forward.

Chapter 26

Nothing as Planned

Night engulfed the *Tusaa'Ner* sooner than Ezerus wanted as drizzling gray clouds continued to hang low over the foothills of the Anza region. The clouds and wet continued to keep the temperature low though everyone's relief, but just above getting cold and uncomfortable all day. Now, with the early nightfall, a chill filled the still air as it started feeling uncomfortable. Ezerus wondered if this was normal for these mountains, and, if it were to get colder, meant they would need more clothing and blankets for the days ahead. Those ground tremblings occurred less often now, with the sun down, though they seemed to cause a stir among some with each happening. *Everyone is edgy*.

Earlier, the *Tusaa'Ner kunzas* saw to placing torches in the hands of strategically located guardsmen throughout the column. Now lit with smoking trails, the torches did little in illuminating the road for their travel, but it felt strangely comforting to Ezerus having the fires to stay off the teeth and claws of the wilds.

"How much further?" Dajil asked in a high-pitched grump.

Ezerus wasn't certain she meant her question for him. If she did, he would need to see her disciplined for continuing to display disrespect openly. Ezerus thought about when and where best to make the show of it. *Now would be too dangerous with all the screaming she would do. Too many hungry creatures in the wilds would be drawn to her suffering. Waiting until they were beyond Anza and into the Blood Lands would be worse. That leaves . . . Anza, it is!* he decided.

"Another couple of marches should be," answered a grizzled, gray-bearded Baraan walking beside the sarigs, outfitted in *Tusaa'Ner* blue hide armor and armed with a long knife, cudgel, and whip. Ezerus recognized him as the senior most guardsman, the *kunza*, one who answers to the *sakal*, who then answers to the *seergal*. The *sakal*, a rival male of Dajil to Ezerus's understanding, was wounded earlier by a leaper and now received tending in the healing wagon. So, for the present, the *kunza* answered to Dajil, who acted as both *sakal* and *seergal*.

"How are you so certain?" Dajil asked the gray-beard, her pitch low.

"Spent days here when young . . . before I took to the *Tusaa'Ner*," he answered with an experienced, even tone. The *kunza* expression changed to one of uncertainty.

"Do we have one of those *Shunned* with us like the rumors saying? I mean . . . the mess we cleaned in the hallway on the *Khaaron* and lightning fight on deck . . . and here on this road . . ."

Dajil appeared stunned and frozen atop her sarig with fear almost radiating from her forward stare. Ezerus noted her condition and what looked to be her realization of things. *Good. I can use this to keep her and her moods in order.*

"No, *kunza*." Ezerus address the question. "He is *Kabiri*. A powerful one aiding the *Za's* expedition."

The *kunza's* silence didn't give Ezerus confirmation the gray-beard believed the explanation. He needed to put down rumors of a *Shunned* . . . the infamous *Shunned* of legends, at that, among them, or there would be desertions.

"I know of him from dealings in Ur and with the Supreme *Zas*," offered Ezerus the *kunza*, trying to get the rumors put to rest. Silence fell upon the *kunza* and the *seergal*. Both were in deep thoughts, though Dajil's near-horrified expression concerned Ezerus if he was to make the rumors go away. Before he could think of how to break his *seergal* out of her unresponsive state, the *kunza* spoke.

"Should be seeing city lights at the top of this hill climb," he offered.

"Thank the Ancients," Dajil grumbled with a sense of relief in her voice.

"The Ancients have no care for you or any but themselves," Ezerus snarled. He didn't know where that came from. He placed little faith in the Ancients or the many of stories about how they ruled humanity. Ezerus felt disdain for the ancient gods since a youngling, but never with the fierceness he now felt.

All fell silent as the column climbed the road in the slowing drizzle to the crest of the hill, where the torchlights atop a large block stone twin-tower gatehouse came into view less than a march ahead. With a new surge of vigor, the column, *Tusaa'Ner*, provisioners, and steeds, picked up their pace to get to Anza and safely within the walls of the city. Passing a side road on their right, they saw a red flag hanging almost limply with what looked to be a golden solar disk on it. *Mark of the Ancient Marduk*, Ezerus commented to himself. Another growing feeling of disdain flowed through him, though not as intensely as before. *I can't wait for the day these sensations cease.*

The column was ordered to halt by Ezerus with a raised fist when in front of the gatehouse. All immediately complied with a rumble of murmurs from the *Tusaa'Ner* ranks. Double doors under a stone bridge spanning the two circular stone towers, were of stout timbers banded with metal top, middle, and bottom. Torches illuminated a trio of lightly hued flags bearing the scarlet winged-sword symbol high on the ramparts above. *The symbol for Anza . . . and the Ancients of old.* The latter came to him from knowledge not learned in his memories. *What is happening to me?*

"I demand again, who asks for entrance to the guardian city, Anza?" a voice from atop the ramparts almost yelled.

Ezerus blinked, finally seeing the guardsman above dressed in a combination of hide chest and metal shoulder armor and metal helm. A scarlet sash hung from his belt matching larger versions hanging from each of the towers left and right. Ezerus felt many eyes staring at him and looked about. Everywhere he looked, he found eyes waiting for him to answer the guardsman. Embarrassed at being caught up in his thoughts . . . and everyone seeing it, Ezerus growled at himself before answering. "This is the *Tusaa'Ner* guard of the *Za* Irzal. You should have word of our travels to your city."

"You're expected . . . enter," the guardsman announced, then waved his right arm.

The sound of heavy metal clasps and a bolt preceded both doors slowly swinging open to the inside. Ezerus raised his hand to signal for the column to move forward. Shouts from Dajil and the *kunza* echoed his signal announcing for their *Tusaa'Ner* and provisioners to enter the city. Ezerus noted the construction of the gate's stonework, well fitted large blocks of granite with no gaps in between. Open slots on both walls of the inner sides of the towers showed a metal portcullis that could be slid or rolled on a stone trench they passed over. The design had the metal bars on the outer side of the timber doors when everything was closed, making the gate extremely difficult to breach. *This has to be the work of Tellens, and by the look, very ancient*, Ezerus took note. Inside, he noted the rest of the walls surrounding the city were not of stone, but larger, three-banded timbers, like the doors, set in massive stone platforms. At evenly spaced intervals . . . about one hundred strides, block stone towers rose to the height and some of the timbers providing stout lookout posts that would be hard to take down. At intervals in between the towers, additional timbers were set as braces to the walls. *Strong . . . simple . . . able to absorb tanniyn assaults*. Ezerus found himself admiring the work and design.

Half-filled stables with fenced animal yards lined the left of the stone-paved road to the timbered wall. To the right, another paved road went off that appeared to follow the timbered perimeter wall as far as his eyes could see in the darkness. Past the perimeter road and at the right side of the road, more stables, and in between them, several large, stone-walled inns with slate roofs and chimney smoke . . . *from hopefully cooking fires*. Standing at the right side of the road, in front of the fenced pen, were a rabble of thirty-some citizens waving lit torches and red flags, some being no more than rags. Their chant sounded like street noise to Ezerus as he could not make out their words. As the *Tusaa'Ner* column passed the rabble, he noted they were all Baraans, mostly males . . . and young, except for a couple of elders in their midst. At seeing Ezerus, one of the elders, dressed in red and yellow temple robes, stepped forward, silencing the rabble. In the torch glow and with a purposeful gaze focused on Ezerus, he spoke in a deep voice filled with pride and conviction. "He has risen! His names are fifty! Behold our new protector and savior!"

Confused at the elder's gleeful proclamation, Ezerus proceeded onward with the *Tusaa'Ner* column as a sense of urgency welled up inside of him. *What in Kur is this?* he asked himself. On the road ahead at a spot where a packed dirt path leading right off to the inns met the paved stones, stood what appeared to be two groups of sarig-mounted officials flanked by torchbearers. On the right, three Baraan males dressed in hide body with gleaming metal shoulder armor and helm and scarlet sashes were what Ezerus assumed to be Anza *Tusaa'Ner*. On the left, five mounted officials on stout sarigs, each in dark-padded eur armor with bronze chest plates and helms, and royal blue sashes. Their standard of the moon atop a lightning bolt on a royal blue flag was held tall by a young soldier sitting upon his sarig next to a more stoutly built and older Baraan who wore a helm with the royal blue feathered crest and a red cape of command. *No Anubda'Ner . . . and what in Kur is the Seb'Ner doing here?* Ezerus asked himself with alarm that things were not going to plan. Then, he reflected as well as reminded himself . . . *Nothing has gone to plan, now that I think on things.*

He raised his right fist high when he was within a rock throwing distance to the eight on the road ahead. Shouts from the *seergal* and *kunza* brought the *Tusaa'Ner* to a halt. Ezerus urged his sarig on with his steed obeying in even steps forward. Sarig footfalls and a snort from another steed behind him told Ezerus Dajil fell in trail and would accompany him with the parlay in greeting from the eight. He and Dajil brought their steeds to a halt in front of and in between the two groups with her to his right. Ezerus realized the *kunza* also accompanied them on foot, on his left, bearing a lit touch.

"Greetings the great city, Anza," spoke the center official on the right.

"Greetings from the guardians of *Za* Irzal," responded Ezerus.

Ezerus's gaze shifted to the five on the left. They remained silent. *This is not going well*, he thought. He decided to push on the silence as he moved his right hand to allow the torchlights to touch his signet ring. "Greetings to the *Seb'Ner*."

The *Seb'Ner* with the blue feather-crested helm and red cape simply nodded in acknowledgment. A moment of awkward silence filled their space until the *Tusaa'Ner* broke it.

"I am Darvaar . . ." The *Tusaa'Ner* removed his helm, revealing shoulder-length black hair and a scarred face under a scruffy dark beard. His helm tucked under arm, a gesture of friendly greetings. "You will have these inns and the pens surrounding them for your stay."

"I am Ezerus . . . *ar'seergal* of this *Tusaa'Ner* troop of guardians," announced Ezerus in polite tones as he removed his helm, then tucked it under his arm in a way that his right hand and *Subar* signet ring sat high for the torchlight to dance on it. "Your offer is generous. We accept."

"When you have settled, there is much to discuss and plan for the travel into these mountains." Darvaar spoke with a nervous tone as he glanced toward the *Seb'Ner* commander. "Send word by one of my guardians when you are ready."

Ezerus looked to the *Seb'Ner* commander who remained silent. *Nothing . . . Something is off*, Ezerus noted to himself. Tipping his head to the *Tusaa'Ner*, he placed his helm on, then urged his sarig, turning it back to the column. Dajil and the *kunza* followed.

"That went well . . ." Dajil cynically commented with a hint of satisfaction in her high-pitched voice.

"Take care, daughter of Irzal," cautioned Ezerus with a menacing grimace. "Push on me no more or you will be put to discipline *and* the Question. See to your *Tusaa'Ner*."

Dajil held her tongue and kept her face passive at Ezerus's unveiled threats. After a long moment of reflection or lacking something snappy to say, she urged her sarig forward, shouting orders for the *kunza* and the guardsmen to follow. Ezerus watched them herd what remained of the *Tusaa'Ner* and provisioners into the space and pens around the inns. As the wagon carrying Irzal and *him* passed, Ezerus felt that sense of urgency flare powerfully, causing him a ripple of discomfort climbing his spine. *I'm missing something*, Ezerus thought to himself. *What is it?*

Chapter 27

Discipline

Yawing deeply, he tried again to shake off the drowsiness that seemed to cling to him. Sleep was evasive most of the night, despite the respectable bed he had been provided by the innkeeper. *What am I missing?* he asked himself for the countless time. When he did manage to sleep, his dreams were filled of *him* and *his* thoughts, though Ezerus remembered few of the details. That frustrated him as much as he felt relieved. Yet, that sense of urgency lurking in the back of his mind . . . He was uncertain where it came from and what the urgency was about. Still, he acted on it before sitting for his meal by sending off one of the Anza *Tusaa'Ner* guardsmen assigned to their inn. Now, he waited.

"Another drink?" asked the attractive, dark-haired Baraan barmaid.

Ezerus looked down at his plate and mug that was his morning meal. Remaining, a half-eaten leg of tanniyn, of what he didn't know, though it ate well, a few berries, and some pieces of flatbread. His mug of ale almost empty. "Another . . . yes."

Transfixed on the barmaid swaying her way back to the bar with her knee-length green dress flowing to her movements, Ezerus watched. Stepping into his line of sight and spoiling his view of the barmaid approached Darvaar in his *Tusaa'Ner* armor uniform with its scarlet sash. Annoyed, Ezerus did his usual best at controlling his outer demeanor, putting a smile on his face. He made a mock attempt to rise from his chair in a show of respect that Darvaar waved him off from completing.

"Enjoying our fresh mountain tanniyn?" Darvaar asked, breaking the silence.

"It's some of the best tasting I've had," Ezerus replied politely. The scars under the Anza *Tusaa'Ner's* shoulder-length black hair and scruffy dark beard were deeper and more pronounced in the light of the day.

"A chair?" Darvaar held his open hand pointing at the unused chair at Ezerus's table.

A nod from Ezerus found the local *Tusaa'Ner* sitting across from him. Ezerus expected to be summoned and escorted to Darvaar's defender hall. Instead, the *Tusaa'Ner* was alone, sitting with him in the tavern. In the spirit of his usual tactics dealing with others, Ezerus kept silent waiting for Darvaar to reveal the purpose of his visit.

"Are you getting all needed to prepare for your journey?" Darvaar asked.

"Your people are helpful," Ezerus replied. "I am told we will be ready to depart tomorrow morning."

"Blankets are being added to the supplies with the air turning cold . . ." said Darvaar with a hint of something more needing talked of. He looked a Baraan in a dilemma, and an uncomfortable one at that, struggling to speak, but only after a few attempts before managing to overcome that keeping him silent. "I was paid well to see all of you quickly prepared for travel into the Blood Lands despite protests by the local guilds and by the privileged."

Ezerus knew of the local resistance against anyone traveling into the forbidden lands and of the payments made by Irzal in balkas and gems . . . and his recent discovery, younglings, all bypassing both the local *Ensi* and citizens and into this one's secret chests or chambers. Noting the unsettled manner of the Baraan, Ezerus's curiosity climbed as he nodded to his "fellow" *Tusaa'Ner*, hoping he would continue.

"I was told the *Anubda'Ner* would be providing final payment," Darvaar continued. "Yet, these *Seb'Ner* appeared . . . and no *Anubda'Ner* . . . and not knowing anything of our agreement. Worse, how do you know of them and their *antaal'sagkal?*"

"The *Seb'Ner?*" Ezerus asked, wanting to be clear of which group Darvaar was talking.

"Of course," Darvaar shot back with a hint of frustration. "Their *antaal'seergal* means not to let you pass into the wilds beyond. He's already placed some of his guardsmen on the bridge."

An uncomfortable flash of urgency swept through Ezerus. *This isn't the missing, though is not planned for.* He needed as much information as this Darvaar would give up and that was best possible if he wasn't on edge. Ezerus decided to give him assurances with a mix of truths and lies. "Your final payment is safe in my hands. The *Anubda'Ner* is no longer part of this, though I didn't expect such a large contingent of *Seb'Ner*. I need details of where they are and how many. And what of my supplies?"

"I will tell of their places," agreed Darvaar. "Yet, I must have payment—"

"Payment will be provided when my *Tusaa'Ner* are beyond the bridge," Ezerus interrupted with his unnegotiable position. "The supplies?"

Darvaar looked a Baraan who had eaten dung. He struggled with not getting what he wanted but eventually agreed after looking into Ezerus's unyielding eyes. "Your supplies are split up. Half are in the outer storehouse of the home behind the Anza Halls. There are niisku with wagons and sarigs there for you, as well."

Darvaar fell silent, appearing to consider the merit of holding back on all information about their supplies. Ezerus simply stared at the Baraan. The silence became uncomfortable, then deafening to the scarlet *Tusaa'Ner*. Ezerus then shifted slightly in his chair leaning forward with his right hand resting atop his left hand on the table. "I will see you put to the Question if you keep anything to bargain with."

Darvaar looked to Ezerus's unblinking eyes, then to his tapping finger. It took a few moments before the *Tusaa'Ner* authority of Anza recognized the signet ring of the *Subar*. The Baraan's eyes shot wide as sweat began pouring from his brow. He swallowed . . . hard.

"Forgiveness . . . *Subar* . . ." Darvaar's demeanor turned fearful in a blink.

"The supplies?" Ezerus repeated.

"At an old mine not more than several marches into the Blood Lands," Darvaar spoke rapidly trying to get everything out in one breath. "A trusted patrol keeps it guarded. It can be found in the east foothills. I put a few more sarigs there with the supplies."

"What else?" Ezerus asked while fingering his signet ring. That sense of urgency remained, though Ezerus sensed a feeling of satisfaction that wasn't his own.

"Nothing more except those followers of Marduk entering the city just before you arrived and marching on one of the other temples chanting something about rising to fifty," Darvaar offered.

A flash of fear rippled through Ezerus, then was gone. *What in Kur was that?* Unsettled and not wanting to show it, Ezerus made to get up from the table.

"Your ale," smiled the dark-haired barmaid as she presented a fresh mug to Ezerus.

Ezerus settled back down into his chair as she set the mug on the table. She was pleasant to the eyes and had a way about her that Ezerus found favorable. She quietly stood demurely waiting for something. At first, Ezerus was not knowing what she wanted, then realized payment was expected for the meal. "Ah. How much?"

"A silver balka for the meal and mugs," she replied.

"A bit steep . . ." He thought to negotiate lower, but then thought better of it wanting to watch the barmaid sway about. He plucked a silver and several copper balkas from his belt pouch and gave it to the smiling woman. She nodded slightly before turning toward the bar. Transfixed on her swaying in that green dress, Ezerus forced himself to look down, then to the Anza *Tusaa'Ner* to break her charm. The urge to take one more peek at her found him glancing back to where he expected and wanted to see her again. His innards clenched. Approaching was the red-blond-haired Dajil with clenched fist and another fume on her slender face. Without looking at Darvaar, he spoke dismissively. "Get me details on the *Seb'Ner*. We're done here."

Darvaar spotted the hostile Dajil, dressed in her blue armor and red cape, stamping toward them. He made sure to disappear before she arrived. Loosing what was left of this calm, even enjoyable moment, Ezerus became annoyed. Subduing his exasperation, he met Dajil's green-eyed gaze as she closed the distance to him. *She continues with her displeasure.*

"Why am I kept from Mother?" her radiant-green eyes in a fume, Dajil demanded in a huff. She stood with fists on hips before the *ar'seergal's* corner table. She seemed not to care that many *Tusaa'Ner* sat in the tavern area of the inn, also eating and some heavily drinking their morning meals.

Ezerus maintained his calm exterior despite his growing annoyance as he relaxed back into his chair, his eyes shifting from the angry *seergal* to his unfinished meal. *A waste of food with all these troubled ones around*, he thought.

"My mother . . ." Dajil spoke impatiently in her irritating, high-pitched tones and anger-filled eyes. Ezerus raised his right hand, extending his index finger with the intent to get her controlled with his own dismissive display.

"Correct your ways." Ezerus controlled his growing anger, though his grimacing at her voice was not.

"My ways?" Dajil indignantly replied in her irritating, high-pitched voice. "What's he doing to her—"

In a single move, Ezerus stood and grabbed Dajil by the throat, locking his fingers around her slender tan neck, her skin only a few shades lighter than his own. Her radiant-green eyes went wide in complete surprise. His action surprised himself as well. It was unlike anything he had done before. Ezerus preferred to manipulate minds and emotions. It took longer in achieving yet was more effective and more satisfying. This urge to strangle the *seergal* was something new that both shocked him as much as gave him satisfaction, especially if it made her not talk.

"Your disrespect is at an end!" Ezerus growled, his anger on display for everyone to see. Dajil struck at his arm with her fist to no effect except for making the *Subar* angrier. Ezerus yanked at her violently, increasing the strain of his grip on her throat while dragging her along toward the front doors of the inn. Choking sounds replaced her words. Then, the sound of a blade sliding from its sheath alarmed as well as angered Ezerus. He stopped and yanked forward Dajil with more strength than he thought he had, lifting her boots off the wood planks and slamming her to the floor on her back. A painful gasp came out of her mouth. She let out another gasp when Ezerus closed his left hand around her arm stopping her from driving the blade of her long knife into his midsection.

"Release her!" loudly demanded an experienced, even-toned voice.

Ezerus looked up from the struggling Dajil to find the grizzled, gray-bearded Baraan standing tall in his armor in a ready-to-fight stance with hand on the pommel of his long knife. Several others of the *Tusaa'Ner* found the courage to stand with their *kunza*. Ezerus took his hand from Dajil's throat and grabbed her long knife as she choked breath into her lungs. The *kunza* half-drew his blade, causing Ezerus to raise his eyebrows in an unintimidated manner. He then tossed Dajil's blade to the floor so that it was out of her reach. Standing, Ezerus met the *kunza's* challenging stare. "Prepare the rack, *kunza*. This insubordination by the *seergal* is to be addressed."

"*Ar'seergal* . . ." the *kunza* left incomplete his question as regulation called for a confirming of a "discipline" session. This was to be her fate. When he grasped the fullness of the situation, he fully sheathed his long knife, then tried not to carry out the command. "That discipline is only for the lower ranks. Never has a—"

"She *is* my lower rank," Ezerus stated the obvious, emphasizing "lower" in his words.

"*Ar'seergal*, she is the daughter of—" the *kunza* started pleading.

"Prepare the rack, *kunza*, or you'll also find yourself on one," promised Ezerus. "I won't speak this command again."

Ezerus lowered his gaze to his subordinate still lying on her back rubbing her throat. His face now felt impassive as he regained his usual composure. Yet, that sense of urgency grew hotter in the back of his mind telling him there was not time for this, but he had to set the order of things within the *Tusaa'Ner* and with this *seergal*, now, before they entered the Blood Land. Besides, he needed to give Darvaar time to collect the detailed information on the *Seb'Ner* while he looked for himself the state of things concerning their supplies, wagons, steeds, and the Guardians of the Empire. He needed a distraction. *Never let a predicament be squandered.* Dajil tried to rise, but Ezerus's boot on her chest kept her on her back. "Either this fixes you, or you bleed *lightless* before your *Tusaa'Ner*."

Chapter 28
Temples and Spears

The air felt cold as a chill rippled through him, his breath almost forming a mist when he exhaled. Gray clouds dominating the dawn bestowed a patchy pattern while moving low over the city on a light breeze. Entwined in the ghostly patchwork was the blue-gray sky above. The dim morning light on the wet north-south running cobblestones made the street seem as flowing water as it grazed the wood steps nearest him as he stood. A sign in front of the tavern-inn identified it as the Ringing Bell. The morning sun, not yet high enough to shine through the cloud deck, gave light enough for his eyes to make out the street's stonework and shadowy forms on it, the few merchants up early moving their goods with niisku and kyda-drawn carts. A mix of smells, both pleasant and not so much, played with his nose, making it difficult for him to decide if he liked the place where he stood.

"This is uncomfortable," Aren complained.

"Just put it out of your thoughts." Rogaan dismissed his complaint.

"Maybe you can . . ." Aren continued complaining. "I don't have muscle as you do. Evendiir are built for warmer places."

Rogaan assessed Aren's outfitting. His black, soft-soled boots looked warm enough. The green woven pants and brown tunic with sleeves to the elbows also seemed warm enough. That wide snapjaw hide belt kept everything in place and the wind out. The forest-green hide carry pack Aren would not let leave his grasp was slung over his right shoulder. Rogaan thought strange the Evendiir's platinum-brown hair. He was lean and wiry in body and face with a hairless chin and green eyes, Rogaan saw him truly for the first time. And Rogaan agreed, Aren was not built to keep his warmth. "You are true on that."

"Why are you seeing me like that?" Aren sounded accusatory.

"Like what?" asked Rogaan, not understanding the question.

"As you look at me now," Aren clarified, but still with an accusatory tone.

"Just considering your words against your appearance," explained Rogaan.

"Well . . . Don't keep your eyes on me that way," Aren demanded. He shivered noticeably. "I suffered enough of that last evening with all those in the tavern. Too many leering eyes. And . . . I didn't care for the groping I saw on you."

"Do you have to speak of it?" Rogaan felt unclean at the recall of last night's time in the tavern. All he wanted was a meal and to be left alone. Instead, an incessant clique of Baraan males asking if they could sit with him was uncomfortable enough. Then, the touching started with attempts by friendly "accidents," then to the outright grabbing of his parts. Not wanting to draw attention to himself or Aren . . . who sat by himself at a corner table, Rogaan thought only to give foul glares at his accosters. It mostly worked, but several were insistent on pestering him until he removed himself to his room . . . with his room chair propped against the door it to keep out the unwanted. *So . . . Aren had noticed. This is embarrassing.* "It was . . . unsettling. It would have been acceptable, even flattering from the few serving maids. From the young Baraans . . . males . . . unwanted."

"Were they taken by your sway?" Aren asked, curious about that aspect of the Baraans.

"My sway?" Rogaan asked incredulously, then added with indignant denial. "I have no sway. That is a female thing. And a cruel thing . . . for me . . . for males."

"Well, I think it was your sway." Aren sounded as if he was teasing. "Strong from the way they pursued you."

"Would you stop this?" Rogaan half-demanded, half-pleaded. When he looked to Aren, the Evendiir wore a friendly smile and had good-humored eyes but said nothing. "I did not like their . . . groping."

"Is that why you hit him?" Aren asked about the young Baraan this morning that Rogaan upended over a table just before they departed.

"Yes," answered Rogaan. "He asked me to stay the day, then grabbed me where he should not have."

"I thought leering eyes were uncomfortable enough . . . but those hands." A smile grew on Aren's face with his teasing tone.

"Enough of this, friend," Rogaan forcefully pleaded. "This inn will not see my coin another night. Besides, the coins they demanded for meal and bed were robbery."

"I wouldn't worry about them allowing you back in," Aren mused. "I thought you shouldn't have hit him so hard. Now . . . His feet in the air seems fitting."

"We should go before more of them wake," Rogaan recommended.

"Agreed." Aren fell in stride with Rogaan as he stepped down to the street and set off toward the North Gate. "I think we should seek a high place to see the city and watch for the *Tusaa'Ner*."

"Agreed," Rogaan concurred as he pointed to a pair of stone block temples sitting atop a rise to their right. "Maybe on the other side of that hill?"

"It could work," agreed Aren, looking up at the cloudy sky as they made their way up a well-kept stone pathway lined by trees and shrubs with leaves browning. "No sign of the featherwing. Do you know who it serves?"

"No," answered Rogaan honestly as the pathway started serpentining right and left as the hill became steeper. "I wondered at it, but no face behind the wings comes to me."

They both stopped when they heard arguing ahead and above on the pathway. Spotting them was easy through the trees from the ruckus they made exchanging words. One group in blue robes with feather adornments and the other in red and yellow robes like the followers of . . . Marduk, they saw last night on the streets. Rogaan and Aren quietly waited for the arguing to get resolved. It did quickly with the blue robes ushering off to the south the red and yellow robes. Down the hill they went following another pathway through crop fields that had already been harvested, across a cobblestone road winding east into the heart of Anza. The red and yellow robes then took another pathway through more crop fields working their way up to a grand stone temple siting alone on its rise. Red and yellow flags bearing the golden solar disk fluttering slightly all around that temple.

"I thought that temple had different colors yesterday when we arrived," Rogaan asked after noticing it this morning.

"Gold, silver, and white were its colors yesterday." Aren commented from the image in his mind of what the temple looked like just before dusk yesterday. Returning his gaze to the temple above them, "The blue robes are no longer in our path. Let's find a place to do your watching."

As the ground trembled for the first time today that he recalled, they quickly made their way up the stone pathway under cover of groomed foliage while keeping sharp eyes out for the blue-robed temple *Kunsag*. A sense of dread grew in Rogaan the closer they approached the stone temple and its fluttering blue flags. Flashes of the intimidating dark robes' temple lit with the torches of Kur came to his mind, causing his skin to prickle and his neck hairs to stand painfully. Shaking off the eerie feeling, Rogaan found a pathway circling around the temple. They set off to the right, then left following the hillside back to the north where they found themselves overlooking crop fields below, some harvested and others being harvested by bare-chested Baraan younglings, a number of homesteads, and a set of inns surrounded by pen-yards and stables, now filled with the sky-blue colors and the crossed spears and towers of the Farratum *Tusaa'Ner*. The place looked bustling.

Rogaan and Aren found a secluded spot below the temple with a set of stone benches surrounded by more groomed trees and shrubs. *At least these things do not have long, sharp thorns pricking me every time I get close.* Rogaan pulled a seeing-glass from his carry pack, something the *Seb'Ner* scout gave up when he lost his *Light.* Rogaan searched the inn, stables, and the *Tusaa'Ner* for any sign of his father. At under two hundred strides distant to the inn, he could make out many faces through the seeing-glass and the equipment each face carried. *Nothing,* Disappointment filled him. He continued searching, systematically looking at each building and wagon. While doing so, he and Aren started bickering a little at the Evendiir's paranoia about being caught by the temple *Kunsag,* or worse, their *Kabiris.* The subject went unresolved.

After a time of several mild ground shakings and them switching using the seeing-glass to search for Rogaan's father and studying the *Tusaa'Ner,* Aren started looking to the right at the greater Anza. While the Evendiir gazed away, Rogaan noticed a ruckus at the inn. Squinting to see more clearly, he saw that red-blond-haired *sakal* being pulled out of the inn against her wishes by two big, blue-clad guardsmen and tied to a set of stout poles in the courtyard. "What is happening down there?"

"What . . . What do you see?" Aren asked while trying to look around a tall shrub to see the inn.

"Remember that female *sakal* in Farratum with the reddish hair and screech of a voice?" Rogaan asked Aren, expecting him to know who he was talking of.

"Dajil?" Aren perked up as he tried to get a better view of the inn and Dajil. "She treated him fairly despite the disrespectful guardsmen she commanded and her mother's atten . . ."

"That is the one . . ." Rogaan confirmed her name as he watched the *Tusaa'Ner kunza,* under the cold direction of that one who tried to take Suhd from him on the ship. The *kunza* prepare Dajil to be lashed. "They mean to whip on her."

"What?" Aren sounded shocked and incredulous, now looking through the seeing-glass at the scene. He lowered the seeing-glass and stared unfocused off into the distance. "Dajil . . . no. That can't be. Her mother protects her from those she oversees."

"It looks that the *kunza* is being commanded by that red-armored fellow I struck on the ship to save Suhd." Rogaan described the situation he was observing.

"This can't happen," Aren grumbled as he again set the seeing-glass to his eye, then fell into silence as he took in the scene. He winced.

Rogaan heard the distant crack of a whip followed by a painful scream. Then, another and another and another, each time Aren wincing before Rogaan heard the whip. Looking with his unaided eyes, Rogaan could make out the courtyard happenings. The whipping and her screaming were interrupted only by the red-armored fellow talking to Dajil. She shook her head in defiance six times before she could no longer lift her head because of the continuing lashes. At the end of the sixth set of lashings, she hung from her bound wrists on the poles with her head slumped to her bare chest. Aren started grumbling some more, then turned to rant in a language Rogaan did not understand. It was clear to Rogaan that Aren strangely cared about Dajil and held hatred for the red-armored fellow. Rogaan felt his neck hairs prickle, warning him as if someone was doing something with one of those stones. Looking about, Rogaan found the air around Aren's hands glow different colors before returning to normal.

"Ezerus . . ." Aren's tone grew heated as he watched through the seeing-glass Dajil being dragged to the eastern inn. "I don't know how yet pay you will . . . *Subar* or no *Subar*."

"Do you think her *lightless?*" Rogaan asked. He too felt an odd fondness for the *sakal* after she showed him a strange compassion when he was being sent to the pit under the arena.

"I don't think she is . . ." Aren dropped the seeing-glass from his eye. He was visibly shaken and angry. "Things are strange that he had her disciplined . . . in front of her guardsmen. *Tusaa'Ner* rarely do such a thing as I've observed. This makes no sense."

Aren raised the seeing-glass again. Now, surveying the *Tusaa'Ner*, he appeared to be tallying up their numbers and supplies with great quickness. Rogaan squinted at the brightness of several heaven rays breaking through the clouds as he tried to make his own counts and hoping to find his father, alive.

"What are they doing here?" Aren blurted out in surprise and frustration.

"Who?" Rogaan asked.

"Your Baraan friends and the Tellen . . ." Aren answered Rogaan while handing him the seeing-glass. "They're on the road walking past the *Tusaa'Ner*."

Through the seeing-glass, Rogaan soon found Pax and Suhd and Trundiir walking the road beyond the inns and *Tusaa'Ner*. *No! They should not be here! Unbelievable!* A wave of worry washed over Rogaan, not wanting his friends to suffer any more for him. "I left them in the cave to spare them more pain."

Rogaan watched his friends walk the lightly congested main road of cobblestones past the inn's stables and half-filled pens, then past another block stone temple on the far side of the road sitting atop a small rise. Something about the temple felt familiar to Rogaan. His nape hairs prickled.

"Ah . . . we have . . . You need to look this way." Aren fumbled with his words.

Odd . . . Aren stumbling with words, Rogaan mused. He pulled his attention away from the seeing-glass and turned around. Three bronze metal spear tips nearly poked his eyes. Focusing beyond the bronze blades, he found three leather armor-clad guardsmen with blue and tan tunics, all wearing the symbol of a storm cloud with lightning bolt, and headbands trailing with colored feathers. The three held their spears ready to plunge them into him and Aren. *Temple guardsmen?* Rogaan asked himself. More surrounded Aren with the same unfriendly ways of pointing their spears at the Evendiir.

"Surrender yourselves in the name of Kishar!" demanded a stout Baraan with a deep voice.

Chapter 29

Revealing

Surrounded by blue and tan tunics and spear tips in his face, Rogaan weighed his options . . . surrender or fight. *If we surrender, they will take both our equipment and day. That cannot happen if Father is to be freed. Fighting could mean injury or worse . . . though we could get our day.* Rogaan resigned himself to having to fight his way out of this. Looking to Aren, the Evendiir saw it in Rogaan's eyes and shook his head "*No*" to a confrontation, as he too had spear tips at his face and belly.

"Friends . . ." Aren spoke in a tone unthreatening to the guardsmen, "we are peaceful travelers looking for guidance from the Ancients. I . . . We understand this place may be what we seek."

"Quiet, Evendiir!" growled the stout guardsman.

"I mean no offense, kind guardian . . ." Aren attempted flattery while continuing in his nonthreatening tones. "We—"

"Why steal looks at the inns and dwellings?" asked the guardsman with an accusatory tone.

"There are new ones in the city, and we were curious about them," Aren answered honestly, but still with his forced friendly tone. "They could be meaning harm and—"

"Silence from you!" again growled the stout guardsman who held his spear tip at Rogaan's face. "You speak as if we're fools."

"When the sandal fits—" Aren kept his pleasant tone as he insulted the guardsman.

Trying to summon his Wild Spirit, Rogaan made straining grunts that caused the guardsmen to look at him with uncertain, worried eyes. Then, he recalled his moment with the *Sentii* companions when he fought them at their speed. He then was angry but had removed it from his mind while keeping it in his heart, replacing it with resolve as he did now, replacing his fear with resolve. Colors exploded with vivid details and vibrancy as the world and the guardsmen slowed and his nose suffered assault from the trees, shrubs, and incense from where he knew not, and the unwashed guardsmen standing in front of him. In a single move, Rogaan dropped his seeing-glass, then grabbed in his right hand the three spears pointed at his face just behind their bronze heads as he spun to his left, pulling the spears from the guardsmen. He continued his spin until facing the guardsmen where he stomped his foot to a halt and spears in hand and haft butts stamped to the ground. Rogaan stood looking at the shocked guardsmen as their colors faded and movements became normal. *I am hungry*, Rogaan's stomach grumbled a little.

"We are not foes." Rogaan made to calm the moment while hoping he could convince the temple guardsmen, they had nothing to fear from them.

"He's one of the Quickened!" another guardsman fearfully blurted out. The rest stole nervous glances at each other, then started to back away. The stout guardsman was the last to follow.

"Do you want these returned?" Rogaan asked the guardsmen holding up their spears. They turned and scurried away a short distance in the direction of the north most of the nearest two temples, the step pyramid temple high on the rise to Rogaan's right. Rogaan looked to Aren who held just as a confused expression as he felt.

Footfalls approaching from the other temple on the shared rise to their south alarmed the scurrying Kishar guardsmen who moved still closer to their temple as the footfalls grew louder. Aren looked to Rogaan with questioning eyes.

"I think we should disappear . . ." recommended the Evendiir.

"Agreed," Rogaan replied as he and Aren jumped from their lookout left to the pathway they followed earlier. "Let us hurry."

They ran south back on the winding pathway that circled around the temple rise, the garden shrubs turning to small trees on their right as they went. On their left, a drop-off of some four and more strides to uneven dirt and rocks below. After they turned a bend with still heavy greenery for this late season, they slid to a halt. Before them, at the first crossroads they came to on the path . . . a three-way intersection seven strides ahead, stood two handfuls of spear-carrying guardsmen . . . these dressed in scale armor and feathered plumed helms and as covers blue tunics bearing a scroll held in a fist mark.

"Halt in the name of Nunamnir!" a big, burly guardsman demanded as he stamped the butt of his spear on the ground.

Rogaan looked to Aren with questioning eyes. The Evendiir glanced to the left side of the pathway where the drop-off offered them a dangerous escape. Rogaan glanced, assessing it. Over five strides here. He shook his head "No" to Aren as the drop was high enough, they would almost certainly injure themselves.

"Surrender or what?" Aren asked Rogaan. "We can't run, and fighting isn't my thing."

"Can't you do that . . . stone thing?" Rogaan asked Aren, hoping his new friend had abilities not yet shown.

"Stone thing?" Aren looked at Rogaan with incredulous, insulted eyes.

"Yes . . ." Rogaan returned Aren's eyes. "Use that large one you carry with you."

Aren's eyes and face turned alarmed, surprising Rogaan at the intensity of the Evendiir's reaction. Aren then just straightened his back and stood tall with an odd, calm expression that seemed to imply he accepted Rogaan finding him out on something he kept secret. "It doesn't work that way. I don't have control—"

"Are ya two just going ta keep with ya private talk?" the burly guardsman sarcastically asked, then demanded in a harsher tone, "Or are ya ta surrender ya weapons?"

"Would you give us a moment?" Aren asked the guardsman with a hand wave.

The entire troop of guardsmen dropped into an aggressive crouch with spears raised at Aren's wave. Revealed behind the crouched guardsmen was an average height Baraan dressed in blue robes with a circlet of gems on his head. Aren froze not completing his wave. He stood for a moment assessing what just happened.

"This isn't good," Aren commented as he felt the unfamiliar vibrations of a manifestation in the making. "The temple's *Kunsag*."

"We have a manifester!" The *Kunsag* announced before barking. "Guardians . . . advance!"

"What now . . . manifester?" Rogaan sincerely asked.

"Run back down the path and look for a place to jump down," Aren offered.

"Agreed," Rogaan replied as he turned, then stopped. Behind them some eight strides were more of those in blue tunics and armor acting in the name of Nunamnir with spears pointed at them. Both groups of guardsmen now deliberately advanced on them. "Have anything else?"

"Nothing helpful," replied Aren with a hint of resignation in his voice.

A screech from above brought everyone to a stop. Circling high was that dark featherwing. A second screech from somewhere over the southern temple came another featherwing, a brown and white one, flying directly at them. The brown and white predator swooped low over the head of the *Kunsag*, forcing the Baraan to duck. The featherwing then turned and landed in the pathway separating the guardsmen with the burly commander and Rogaan and Aren. The featherwing fluffed up its feathers while spreading its wings wide, then squawked as it stamped its talons. The guardsmen paused their advance at the aggressive display by the brown-and-white-one-stride-tall featherwing.

"Kill it!" ordered the *Kunsag*.

"Not an act that will go well for you," an unknown male voice announced from somewhere on the unexplored pathway near the *Kunsag*.

Everyone hesitated with most looking to the pathway branching south down the temple rise. Rogaan spotted in between the trees two figures approaching at a measured pace. Emerging on the cobblestones from the garden trees came two darkly dressed Baraans. The bigger of the two stood a guardsman dressed in layered leather eur armor with leather helm, a sheathed short sword, a long knife on his belt, and dark metal spear in hand. The second, almost a head shorter, seemed familiar to Rogaan with sand-colored hair, a lean build, black leather armor, loose dark pants, and leather boots. A short sword and sling on his belt appeared to be his only weapons. Prominently on display was his dark metallic pendant hanging from a dark metal chain about his neck. It was a symbol that sent a shiver rolling through Rogaan. A circle enclosing a staff with entwined serpents. Atop was set a smoldering black gem. Rogaan's hair stood on end as his skin prickled. *They must be using that Stone Power.*

"Ebon Circle!" Several of the guardsmen spoke in unison as an alarm.

"*Kabiri* . . ." the *Kunsag* recognized. "Why have you trespassed?"

"To give warning . . ." the *Kabiri* spoke with confidence. "These two are wanted by the Circle."

"They have trespassed against Nunamnir and will suffer their fate," the *Kunsag* declared.

"Only if you wish to suffer my master . . ." the *Kabiri* looked up to the sky to the featherwing. Then, he looked to the brown and white featherwing in fierce display. "And his ax."

The *Kunsag* turned visibly nervous as he scanned the sky then looked at the featherwing in hostile display between him and his trespassers. He appeared to be uncertain and with fear, struggling to choose between what he was commanded to do and what the Ebon Circle *Kabiri* demanded. In that moment, Rogaan saw on the *Kunsag's* face a change in his demeaner and a decision of a new path. "Guardsmen! Reform!"

The blue tunic-clothed guardsmen stood, then gathered in orderly formations in front of Rogaan and Aren as well as behind. When in formation, they held their spears pointed up by their sides. Relief swept over Rogaan. *No fighting or jumping from high places trying to escape.*

"Take them, *Kabiri*, and never return." The *Kunsag* announced his chosen path.

"This way . . ." the dark clad *Kabiri* motioned with his hand at Rogaan and Aren. Without waiting for them to comply, he and his armed escort turned and started walking down the pathway they arrived on. "I encourage you to follow."

Rogaan gave an asking look to Aren who shrugged his shoulders. The featherwing in front of them gave an ear-piercing screech before taking off in a loud flutter. Rogaan thought he spotted a harness on the creature. Aren first moved with Rogaan quickly following. As they went by the guardsmen, Rogaan kept his eyes fixed on them. The burly guardsman and the *Kunsag* both stared back at him with eyes filled with frustration and anger. They quickened their steps to catch up to the two from the Ebon Circle. *I cannot believe I am doing this . . . the Ebon Circle, of all places and peoples.*

The *Kabiri* and his guardsman quickly led them down the cobblestone pathway and out of the garden just short of an east-west running road of cobblestones with crop fields to their right and storefronts lining the road on both sides to their left. Across the road ahead of them, on another rise surrounded by crop fields, stood a large block stone temple that appeared to be changing its colors. It had a mix of flags, silver with gold scepters being lowered and red with golden solar disks being raised. Circling above in wide arcs under the low gray clouds remained the dark and brown featherwings. Their presence started growing on Rogaan a sense of safekeeping when he viewed them. The *Kabiri* stopped just short and behind the merchant houses waiting for Aren and Rogaan to catch up while the *Kabiri's* guardsman looked about the rear of the merchant house ensuring all was safe.

"I must get you safe in the Temple of Sinn before the city sets upon you," the *Kabiri* explained. "There, we wait out all those seeking you until we can steal you out of Anza and back to Brigum."

"No!" protested Rogaan. "Father must be freed."

"Mithraam doesn't need saving," the *Kabiri* stated.

"What . . . maybe not by your hands but . . ." Rogaan further protested as he noticed the *Kabiri* looking as much Evendiir with his slender build and fingers and slightly slanted eyes as he did Baraan with a shadow of facial hair and hair to his shoulders.

"This was always the plan . . . Rogaan," the *Kabiri* revealed, obviously trying to get the half Tellen to follow him to this Temple of Sinn. "You were never to be here. In Brigum or on *eKur'Idagu*, yes, but not here where you put everyone in danger."

"What . . . no." Rogaan felt confused and growing angry.

"And, you . . . Aren . . ." the *Kabiri* put stern eyes on the Evendiir. "You have something you shouldn't and need safe haven in a secret place, so *He* can't find you."

"I have no idea what you speak of—" Aren denied the *Kabiri's* words.

"The ax and flame," the *Kabiri* stated. "You carry it."

Aren suddenly appeared to suffer pain with a visible grimace. Concern filled

Rogaan as his Evendiir friend seemed in more pain than any he had seen before. Looking to the *Kabiri* for help, he saw the Ebon Circle envoy intently studying Aren.

"Our worst fears . . ." the *Kabiri* told his guardsman with a measure of alarm. "He's bonded, and the Agni fights us."

"What does that mean?" Rogaan felt the growing angst in his gut. "And what did you mean of my father not needing saving?"

"To keep the world safe . . ." the *Kabiri* appeared to struggle with what he would reveal. "Your father is the trick fooling this mad *Kabir*. You and your bow can't go to Vaikuntaars."

"He's not just a *Kabir* . . ." Aren spoke distracted with pain.

"Then, who is he?" the *Kabiri* skeptically asked.

"He's Luntanus Alum . . ." answered Rogaan. "The worst of the ancient *Shunned.*"

The *Kabiri* stood stunned with disbelief. He had no reaction other than to stand motionless staring off at nothing. Rogaan grew more concerned as the moments passed. He looked at Aren. His Evendiir friend seemed to be shaking off the pain he suffered but was still not focused on the present. Rogaan looked at the big Baraan guardsman. They met eyes causing the guardsman to accept he needed to act, though it would seem reluctantly.

"Kabiri . . ." the guardsman tried to gain the half Evendiir's attention. "*Kabiri.* Daluu!"

The half Evendiir blinked once, then a couple more times several moments later. He looked around with a nervousness he did not have before he heard the name *Shunned*. He blinked again, then looked at Aren and Rogaan. "How certain are you of this?"

"I heard him, and others admit it," answered Aren. If still in pain, he no longer showed it. "He tortured me and played with my fears as Lucufaar. The things he's done with Agnis convinces me."

"The *Vassal* knows much of him and harbors a hatred for this *Shunned*," added Rogaan.

"Who is this . . . *Vassal?*" asked Daluu as disbelief grew on his face and in his eyes.

"I know you now." Rogaan stared at Daluu with new recognition. "You fought him in the forest plains with the Dark Ax. You had control of the ravers for a short time. I wish you could have kept that control. He knows everything about this *Shunned*, about me, and much about your plan with my father. He also hinted that my father would have his *Light* taken once this *Shunned* learns my father is not the 'blood key' he thinks he is."

"This explains and changes . . . much." Daluu, *Kabiri* of the Ebon Circle, wore great concern and a growing fear on his face. He raised his left arm in the air and held it there unmoving. He gave an order to the guardsman. "Scribe this message to the master. 'Mad *Kabir* is *Shunned*, Luntanus Alum. *Warrior-Kabir* battled on fields with ravers is more than thought. Names himself *Vassal*.'"

The guardsman scribed on a small piece of parchment with a wood stick that left dark gray marks. Rogaan used one of those sticks once when young after he had taken it from his father's desk. He recalled getting in trouble for doing it. Loud flapping drew Rogaan's attention to the *Kabiri*. Now perched on his left arm was the dark featherwing. A large animal almost half a stride tall, with black feathers, twin tail feathers that trailed it in flight, and a solid dark beak with teeth. Its eyes showed intelligence and an alertness of its surrounds unlike any animal Rogaan ever came across. Buried in its chest and back feathers was a leather harness that stoutly held a smoldering black gemstone. *Is it one of those Agni Stones?* Rogaan asked himself.

The guardsman placed the parchment into a scroll message carrier on the featherwings right leg while Daluu talked to the animal as if he talked to an intelligent other, explaining their situation. As quickly as it came, the featherwing was gone, flying off to the north.

"This *Vassal* . . ." Daluu asked of Aren and Rogaan, "where is he?"

"He had command of the *Makara's* crew," Rogaan answered. "The ship was damaged, and he was wounded in his battle with the *Shunned* on the other ship."

"The *Khaaron*," Aren added.

"Was the *Makara* sailable?" Daluu asked.

"Yes," answered Aren with an almost bored tone. "And . . . yes, he could be here, by now."

"Changes . . . everything." Daluu seemed genuinely in angst, and a bit of panic showed in his eyes.

"What now . . ." Rogaan started to ask.

A reverberating horn sounded from the temples behind them. Long and deep, Rogaan felt it almost as much as he heard it. A second blast of the horn sounded after a moment's pause after the first. Then, a third blast, just as deep and reverberating. Then silence. No talking. No street din. Not even featherwings' chirping or squawking.

"What was that?" Rogaan asked.

"A warning of a kind . . ." Aren spoke with a worry of trouble. "Let me presume . . . that was for us?"

The *Kabiri* nodded his head in confirmation, then exchanged nervous glances with his guardsman. "Hoping they wouldn't do this . . . challenge the Ebon Circle. Horns alert the *Tusaa'Ner* something against the city has happened. *Tusaa'Ner* lock the gates at the horns. They'll watch the bridges, patrol the streets, and learn from the temple it's us to be hunted."

"They'll search for us first at your temple," Aren contemptuously spoke the obvious.

"Hunt us they will." The *Kabiri* resigned himself to their circumstance. "We must see you both out of Anza . . . quickly."

Chapter 30

The Heat

The third sounding of the horn gave warning something was wrong in the city and with the temples. Maybe those followers of Marduk speaking nonsense of fifty names were at hand. Reports from his scouts of the red and yellow robes taking over the temple of Anu had already reached him. *That could be it*. Still, more was happening. He felt it. The *Tusaa'Ner* prepared to be moving immediately.

"*Kunza*." He barked at the grizzled, gray-bearded Baraan in what was loosely named the courtyard of the inns. The Baraan snapped to almost attention at being addressed.

"Yes, *Ar'seergal!*" the *Tusaa'Ner kunza* responded.

"It's time to leave," Ezerus declared. "Prepare the troops."

"Yes . . . *Ar'seergal*," hesitated the *kunza*. A hard glance from Ezerus removed any lingering hesitation in the Baraan.

Ezerus's *Subar* robes needed put away in exchange for his armor to travel . . . and for any trouble that would find them or get in their way. He entered the stone-walled tavern on his way to his room in the inn section. His orders were already being echoed to the guardsmen surrounding him at tables and leaning on walls, hoping to have a restful morning eating, drinking, and getting nothing done. Climbing the stairs at the back of the tavern, Ezerus saw the large room already half-emptied with the other half picking up their equipment and things preparing to leave. Most grumbling, filling the air with their complaints. Ezerus found he didn't care about their discomfort. They were all . . . expendable. He paused and shook his head. Never had he felt so intense about so many being such. Dismissing the thought, he entered his spacious room from the upper level hallway where he found two female dark-haired Baraan servants dressed in clean gray tunics and low-strapped sandals. The room already immaculate, both were arranging his clothing and armor. Thoughts of enjoying them last night filled his head, though it didn't bring a smile to his face. Images of the youngling's face filled his mind's eyes. A long moment of anger and frustration swept through him at memories of that half Tellen taking her from him. He did his best to put her out of his mind as the two females stripped him of his white robes and donned red armor upon him. While dressing, her face and body kept filling his thoughts.

A tingling, like many biters crawling over his right arm, took him by surprise. It quickly spread over most of his body, leaving him weak and breathing heavy. *What has grip of me?* Since his dunking in the Ur River, this experience struck him several times, every time leaving him weak and ill. He feared whatever it was it not a good thing for him. That sense of urgency filled him again—this time, stronger than ever. Forcing himself to straighten and stand tall while dismissing the concerned looks on his attendants, he ordered them to finish and to have his belongings packed for travel. A light knock came from his room door.

"Enter," Ezerus spoke loudly.

A woman of aged beauty in white *Za* robes entered his room. Her practiced impassive demeanor broke into anger after the calm closing of the door behind her. Ezerus anticipated this would not be a pleasant moment as she came alone instead of sending her lackey Ganzer. "What have you done to my daughter?"

"What needed to be done," he dismissively answered. "She has too much of you in her blood."

"Whip her . . . in front of . . . *them* . . ." Irzal sounded as if she was heatedly reprimanding a child.

"Speak to me again in that manner, and I'll have *you* whipped as well," he promised. "I'm fairly certain *he'll* agree to let it be done."

Silence filled the room as the servants were done dressing their master and had returned to organizing and packing his clothes and things. Irzal's full figure under her still dirty-blond hair shifted several times as she worked to control the heat of her emotions. Regaining her practiced *Za* demeanor, "He wishes for you to move faster getting the *Tusaa'Ner* beyond Anza."

"They control the lone bridge giving access to the Blood Lands," Ezerus informed the *Za*, though fully expecting this knowledge to have already reached *him*.

"He says to leave the unworthy to *him*." Irzal had his answer for the anticipated question.

"I see . . ." contemplated Ezerus. *His* strength of the Powers granted that arrogance as Ezerus felt certain the *Seb'Ner* were of no consequence to a *Shunned*.

"Dajil . . .?" Irzal asked in a heated appeal.

The scent of her beauty filled the room. Ezerus felt it swooning him. Despite knowing what she was attempting and his best to resist her, he found himself becoming compliant to her . . . wishes. A spiky tingle flashed through him from his right hand, ridding him from the influence of her *sway*. Anger filled Ezerus for his inability to resist Irzal as much for her attempt at making him compliant. He looked into her sharply green eyes with even more heat than Irzal's. "If she continues her disrespectful mannerisms, I'll feed her *lightless* body to the guardsmen and whatever companions they have. Now, fetch me the *kunza*."

Chapter 31

Against the Chorus

T he four of them quickly made their way along the outer garden trails of packed dirt of the southern cluster of temples. High and to their right, fluttering flags in the light breeze of midmorning bearing the symbols and colors of the Ancients identified each stone structure's followers: a staff of brown identified the followers of Enuru and the horn-headed staff on green the followers of Ea for the first two temples they made their way around. From his observations yesterday beyond the walls, he knew three more temples were yet further south on this rise. The *Kabiri* had hope that the South Gate would not have so many *Tusaa'Ner* and *Seb'Ner* surrounding it as had the North Gate and his Temple of Sinn. Evidently, that temple was the seat of this Ebon Circle he had heard so much about though his years. A secret order that most feared. *Why are they truly caught up in all this?* Aren wondered.

They kept to the eastern slopes of the plateau the block stone temples dominated above, allowing them to see the happenings on Anza's main street and across the ravine to the Coiner's District. Three high bridges spanned the water-filled ravine joining the Temple District to Coiner's. The two northern bridges were simple constructions of stone and timbers. The southernmost bridge appeared to be a double bridge with a walkway of timbers below the upper level with the street. Being the longest of the three, the southern bridge had a center tower of old, large, block stone on a rising strip of land where deep rushing waters of two rivers from the Twins Mountains merged here in Anza. The center tower where the three spans of bridging met, east, west, and south, provided the only way to the Blood Lands not through treacherous snapjaw-filled waters. Safe passage was over a set of southern bridge spans and more towers branching off that center stone tower.

The cobblestone streets below were now alive with the scarlets and royal blues of guardsmen, most on foot and some on sarigs, who now certainly were hunting them. Most of the city folk cleared the streets and closed their doors and shuttered their windows at the sounding of the first horn. As the *Kabiri* had led them to the Temple of Sinn, the merchants retreated to their shops and boarded doors and windows, not wanting to be part of the events ahead. As the ground trembled sharply, a second set of three horn blasts came from a group of three large stone and timber buildings flying the colors of Anza. The buildings were in the center of Anza east of the north-south running main street and west of the deep ravine separating the two districts of the city. A strategic location for those wishing control of such a population. Most other city folk disappeared at that second sounding as scarlet-colored Baraans in various states of armor came running from their homes and some shops.

The *Kabiri's* guardsman brought them to a halt with a raised hand as soon as they rounded enough of the hillside to see South Gate. After a long moment to take it in, the *Kabiri* appeared frustrated as he grew ever angrier at their situation.

"*Tusaa'Ner* and even more *Seb'Ner* also surround South Gate," Daluu announced with a little growl.

"Where to . . . now?" Rogaan asked as he scanned the partly cloud-filled sky above. Disappointment washed over the half Tellen's face before it turned to that famed Tellen scowl of resolve.

"East Gate or a lesser-known passage out of the city from Coiner's District," Daluu revealed.

"Across the river?" Rogaan sarcastically asked.

"Where else would it be?" Aren asked with a bit more drama.

"Yes," Daluu simply confirmed.

"I am *not* swimming!" Rogaan made sure everyone understood his boundaries.

"Let's just get to the bridge," Daluu asked of the group with obvious hopes he could get everyone to agree.

"Across the main street?" asked Aren with raised brow. "Or do you have another lesser-known path?"

"Yes. There is a lesser-known path," Daluu smiled at Aren.

"Lead on!" Aren swept his open left hand toward the bridge. As he did, a point flash of white light sparked into existence, then was gone. Everyone stood silent looking at Aren.

"Did you do that?" Rogaan asked him.

"I don't know . . ." replied Aren staring at the place the light had sparked and his hand.

"What did you feel?" asked Daluu as he stepped closer to Aren while peering into his eyes.

"Nothing . . ." Aren lied. Daluu kept looking directly into Aren's eyes searching for something. Aren realized Daluu's eyes were brown and held a mix of both wisdom and uncertainty.

"You lie," Daluu challenged Aren.

"I do not!" Aren shot back instinctively. Whispers in his head were unlike any before. How many whispers he knew not, yet they reached out to him wanting something. Aren instinctively recoiled and shut them out of his mind.

"I see it . . ." accused Daluu. "Your eyes hold the misty touch of *Kunsag*. This only happens when more than one is mind-touching the Temple Agni. No . . . the Agni you carry. It's the lost Agni of his temple."

"What does that mean to us . . . exactly?" Rogaan asked as he fingered his long knife.

"That we need to make all haste out of this city," Daluu announced as he turned, continuing down the packed dirt trail they had been traveling. "Follow. Quickly!"

Rogaan gave Aren a concerned look that appeared filled with as much friendly empathy as fear of the unknown. Aren gave back to the half Tellen a smile meant to reassure Rogaan that he wasn't to have the "stone thing" harming him.

"Go," Aren told Rogaan. "I'm directly behind you."

The four ran a short distance through the browning gardens along the packed dirt path curving to the right around the hilly rise. Three more block-built stone temples came into view above, the last obscured by the second, preventing Aren from seeing it clearly. The second temple flew flags of red with a black sword and gem symbol on them. Rogaan stopped at a branching of paths just ahead of Aren. The half Tellen stood motionless, mesmerized at the red and black flags of the second temple. As Aren caught up to the half Tellen, his new friend hadn't taken his eyes from the block stone structure of the modest-sized temple.

"What is it?" Aren asked, now curious at Rogaan's loss of focus. His curiosity began turning to concern when his friend didn't move a muscle. "Rogaan, what disturbs you?"

"I know those colors and that symbol," Rogaan absently replied. "I have seen it. It cannot be."

Aren took a quick look down the path the *Kabiri* and his guardsman ran thinking he may need help with the half Tellen. They were halfway to a large residence in a stone-fenced compound of multiple stone building with reddish tiled roofs. Wanting Rogaan to get moving as Aren didn't feel right about this place, he reached for Rogaan when he heard a shuffling of sandaled feet on fine rocks to their right.

"Greetings from those serving the Great Ancient, Enurta." A Baraan dressed in red and yellow temple robes stepped forward from a group of seven bald males standing on a shelf of stacked rocks about waist high to Aren. Several others lingered behind the seven that Aren could not see. "We have felt its approach."

"What's approach?" Aren asked as he shook Rogaan. The half Tellen pulled his eyes away from the second temple to find himself staring at a group of temple servants from the block stone temple directly above flying flags of red and gold bearing the symbol of an ax enwrapped in flames.

"Now what?" Rogaan asked dejectedly.

"Now . . ." the robed Baraan spoke calmly but with a hint of excitement in his voice, "we rejoin with our Bonding Stone and to 'He Who Protects All.'"

"We do not know of what you speak." Rogaan tried disassociating them from this situation.

"He knows the truth." The red and gold robed Baraan pointed at Aren.

"Me?" Aren disingenuously replied.

"Him?" Rogaan asked, confused.

"Yes. Him," calmly answered the red and yellow-robed Baraan. A wave of the robed one's hand gave cue for the seven to begin a chant in a language Rogaan did not understand.

Aren felt the vibrations first, powerful and focused. Before he could summon his thoughts at defending against these seven, light like tendrils reached out to him and took hold of his head. Fingers of thought reached into his skull and into his mind demanding of him. What, he didn't understand. He pushed back with his mind as his half Tellen friend spoke to him through a cloudy veil.

"Aren . . ." Rogaan spoke as he kept his eyes on the *Kunsag* to ensure they were not to attack them in surprise. "We have need to get away from these—"

"*Kunsag*." Aren felt himself speak as if he no longer controlled his words. "Of He Who Protects All."

"Aren?" Rogaan spoke with growing concern and frustration. It was quick that his friend decided his words proved unless, so he reached out. Aren felt him being shaken. "Aren, wake up. Come back."

Aren felt his eyes roll into his head as another's sight replaced his vision. Disoriented, Aren tried to determine where he was . . . what he was looking at. Then, he realized he saw himself and Rogaan through the eyes of the *Kunsag*. One voice carrying the strength of seven struck his mind. "Deliver the Bonding Stone. Return it to us and the temple where it will protect the world."

Aren pushed back again against the seven finding no weakness in their hold on him. He watched helplessly as Rogaan half-pulled his long knife, then sheathed it before spinning around Aren . . . *me*. When he emerged on his other side, Rogaan had his *Sentii* Blood Bow in hand as he drew his nocked arrow aiming it at himself . . . *no, the Kunsag*. A cry of seven in unison painfully deafened his mind. *Defend . . . Shield of Air*. Instantly, a wall of swirling air grew in front of him . . . *no, the Kunsag*. The half

Tellen let loose his arrow. *It will deflect.* So certain the shield protects. *Pain!* The arrow did deflect but . . . *It cut through me . . . the Kunsag's left side.* The half Tellen already nocked and was drawing another arrow but glanced at his friend . . . *me. Attack . . . Vengeful Hands.* Bold tendrils of the Power reached out grabbing the bow of the half Tellen. He felt it as if his own hands. A powerful sensation. Most satisfying. *Pull to us. He is strong and still holds the weapon. Pull right. Still strong in his hold. Break the bow.* The Power's tendrils shifted over the surface of the bow. *Another arrow flies!* He watched the arrow approach at great speed and deflect from its intended aim. *Pain! One of the chorus is struck.* Pain rippled through his thoughts. *I . . . continue. Break the bow.* Fighting through the shared pain, the *Kunsag* struggled fighting Rogaan. *The half Tellen resists . . . He is strong. Concentrate. Break his bow.* The shared mind ignored all other things, concentrating on a single goal. *Success!* The voices cried out in unison as they watched the splinters of the strongest made bow known tumble to the dirt as the half Tellen . . . *no, Rogaan*, watch in disbelief. *My chance.* Aren sought out the one wounded by Rogaan's arrow. He felt him . . . and much pain in his left leg. Aren summoned his thoughts focusing on this one . . . distracted by his pain. With all he had, Aren struck!

Pain in his shoulder and left leg caused Aren to wither for moments until he realized he had no wounds and he breathed. His vision now clear. Looking up, he found Rogaan half-smiling and half-grimacing.

"We must go . . . must go . . . must go," the half Tellen . . . Rogaan spoke as he helped Aren to his feet.

"What happened?" Aren asked Rogaan, realizing his pains were not his own and now disappeared.

"I do not know but let us not stay here . . ." Rogaan tugged on Aren down the path toward the approaching Daluu and his guardsman.

Aren started down the path as he looked back to see six stumbling red and yellow-robed *Kunsag* and one lying on the ground withering in pain as he held his leg. Turning away, he decided to flee as his mind continued letting go of those fuzzy memories of being linked to all of them, the *Kunsag* of Enurta. Strides down the path, he and Rogaan met with the *Kabiri* and guardsman, both looking up beyond their companions to the *Kunsag*. Daluu's face was one of growing disbelief.

"Seven . . . I count seven . . . in Chorus . . . against you?" The *Kabiri* looked at Aren with utter disbelief. "How could you defeat them?"

"I had help from my half Tellen . . . friend." Aren answered Daluu, feeling good about himself, and too he believed he had a friend . . . one maybe he could trust. "We shouldn't dawdle; they'll recover soon."

Chapter 32

Anza and Wonders

The *Kabiri* gave lead to his Baraan guardsman as they entered the stone-walled compound through a side entrance. They bypassed the rear entrance for some reason as they seemed to be listening for something specific. It was a large estate for being in the middle of town, he thought. *Almost as big as my home.* A main house of two levels, and likely a cellar . . . with many stored and prepared foods for the cold season to come. His stomach grumbled. *I am hungry.* Another single-level house, maybe for guests or where business was conducted, and a stable big enough for storage and a few sarigs or kydas. The well-kept grounds were littered with playthings, giving a hint that this was a place where younglings spent much of the day in addition to the working tools in a couple of spots used in the upkeep of the place.

The guardsman led them directly into the stable where they gathered. The stable was bigger on the inside than he thought from the outside. *Strange how that always seems to be.* Two of the stalls were in use by sarigs, one a big male and another a modest-sized female. They snorted at the newcomer's presence but otherwise kept undisturbed. The guardsman gave his *Kabiri* an uncertain glance, clearly uncomfortable with revealing what they were about to. Daluu calmly nodded his head. His guardsman then entered an empty stall on the far side of the stable and pulled up a chain that appeared to be holding in place an anvil-like object, though he was uncertain exactly what the object was used for. The stone wall opened, allowing them entrance to a narrow shaft down with ladder rungs built into the rock wall below. The guardsman descended without hesitation.

"After both of you." Daluu held out his hand pointing to the shaft.

Rogaan decided to go next. He looked down into the darkness. Noise from below he hoped was the guardsman lighting a torch. A few moments passed before Rogaan's vision adjusted, allowing him to see much more of his surroundings. The place was dry. *This is a good omen.* He mounted the first couple of rungs, then descended the eleven-stride-deep shaft. As he went, a stiff breeze grew as the air moved the musty dirt smell of the passageway up to him and out into the stable. It felt good when he placed his feet solidly on the ground. Light from the shaft above was enough for Rogaan to see clearly his surroundings in a gray vision. The chamber they were in was almost five strides in diameter. On the walls hung stocked items . . . tools for digging and traveling. Elevated crates around the chamber had simple markings indicating what each held, though his dark sight was not good enough to read them from where he stood.

"Hold this," the guardsman half-asked, half-commanded Rogaan to hold a torch.

Complying with the "request," Rogaan held the torch while the guardsman attempted to make sparks to light it. After several attempts, the torch remained unlit. The guardsman grew frustrated at his failure when an orange point of light appeared at the end of the torch. It hung there for a moment with Rogaan uncertain what it was. Then, it grew a little and became hotter, hot enough for Rogaan to consider tossing it to the floor of the chamber. Then, the torch caught fire and started burning forcing Rogaan to shield his eyes until his dark sight adjusted to the reddish light. A hum of satisfaction came from behind. Looking, Rogaan found Aren pleased with himself as he blew breath over his fingers as if putting out a candle. The Evendiir smiled to Rogaan and bowed his head. Rogaan gave him a knowing smile back. Soon, the *Kabiri* started inspecting crates. He pulled wrappings filled with dried goods, sun dried and salted meats and gave them to everyone.

"We're going to be in the wilds for a time and will need these," Daluu explained, pointing to a side covey. "Water and containers are over there. If you need carry packs, they are in that crate over there."

"This is well organized and stocked," Aren commented. "As if it's used a lot."

"Anza has problems, Aren of Windsong." Daluu sounded confident and informed. "It was a place of great adventures and wealth for many years back before the Shuruppak civil war. Since the declaration by Shuruppak that no one is allowed travel into the Blood Lands unless sanctioned by the *Zas* of Ur, it dwindled. Being important to Shuruppak in keeping the Blood Lands closed, Ur started sending coin to keep the city alive. At first, it was almost a paradise. A place to visit and experience at least once in a lifetime . . . a better place to live if you liked not to work hard. The coin paid for many servants to the ruling and lesser Houses. The people became used to the coin given without need to work. Then, they became demanding of it and convinced themselves it was deserved for their hardships in the long past and for their importance as the gateway. Ur and the other cities of Shuruppak then shared the burden of coin and gave Anza even more. Many were drawn to the free coin. They flooded into the city and surrounding areas. It looked and felt to be a rich place, but it wasn't. Little was produced. Much was brought in by ship and cart. With it came the water-thieves, smugglers, gamblers, the depraved, those seeking to hide from Shuruppak, and many more looking for coin that was not earned. The streets became dangerous. The *Tusaa'Ner* and *Sakes* fought it but then became corrupted by it. The guilds and Houses bought the leaders, and those they couldn't were lied about in the square and pushed out of Anza. Those who endured it were found *lightless* if they caused trouble for the guilds, the Houses, or the law.

"Then, Shuruppak reduced the coin it paid to Anza. It dwindled again as the good folks left the corruption and dangers here, except for a few of the lesser Houses. This House is one of them. The Ebon Circle helps it and the others survive, hoping there will be a day Anza returns to the prosperous city it once was, a city without the given coin destroying it, the corruption, and keep all those that prey upon the rest from making their own law on the street."

"We endured some of what you spoke of last night and this morning," Rogaan interjected. "We saw less of it today."

"The taverns now fill with the unsavory and others looking for pleasures even when those they wish it from do not want it. They all think the taverns and streets are theirs to govern . . . and they do, except when officials *visit*. Farratum's *Tusaa'Ner* and the *Seb'Ner*, today. The trouble hides on such days. At least they're smart enough in that way."

"The temples . . ." Rogaan wanted to understand what they were to his place seeing several of them were now all but hunting them along with the corrupt others. His father taught him most of this about the true history of Shuruppak and Turil, so Rogaan understood.

"They have their own interests." Daluu offered a less-than-blissful explanation. "Most have keen eyes on the Ancients, our gods of old, carrying out rituals to keep the Ancients appeased, so their wrath goes other places. We are in the season of the *Dur'Anki*, and the rituals of *Roden'ar* are about to begin. That gives some relief to usual lawlessness in the streets and from those preying on others. Seems even the wicked, corrupt, and depraved can behave righteously when they fear accounting for their deeds. Makes me wish for *Roden'ar* every cycle of the moon."

"And the Ebon Circle?" Aren asked, looking Daluu directly in the eyes.

"We are evil in the land . . . haven't you been told?" Daluu mocked the common word across Shuruppak.

"Did not the Ebon Circle cause the civil war and sufferings of many throughout Shuruppak before its ending?" Aren asked, seemingly genuinely curious of what this *Kabiri* of the Ebon Circle held as truth.

"We need to get both of you out of Anza." Daluu changed the subject. Then, he thought a moment before speaking again. "I will leave you with this. *Our Charge by the Ancients* . . . keep all things of the Ancients from the hands and hearts of humanity. Knowledge and things Agni that seem to corrupt all but the best of hearts and, sometimes, even them. The masters of the featherwings aiding you are the two who were at the heart of events all those years back. They were young . . . like us, then. They fought the Crimson Cabal, House Lagash, and others seeking power and dominion over the people of the lands through lies to the peoples of their intentions. For their battles keeping the peoples free, the 'Dark Ax' was hunted by the *Urmuda'Sa* and had his *Light* taken from him in the Grand Arena of Ur. His execution commanded so by the emperor and his loyal Houses. Executed by cowards seeking a lie to live their lives on. The master 'Dark Robe' too was hunted by the best of the *Urmuda'Sa* and captured. He was taken before the blood-lusting crowd in the Grand Arena to be executed as was his *Kiuri'Ner*. He then killed his executioner and the emperor from the belly of that beast as they made to execute him. It was precise. Many of the people, even the ones enticed into wanting to see his blood, he left alive. He did it with the Power, then escaped with the 'Dark Ax's' body and returned his *Light* to him. Since then, they have dedicated themselves to *Our Charge* and to protecting the weak and aiding those unable to fight well enough for themselves."

"You expect us to believe all of your words?" Aren clearly did not believe everything Daluu had spoken.

"Judge the Ebon Circle on our deeds," the *Kabiri* stood tall and resolute. "Not by the words others speak of us without merit."

Aren appeared conflicted to Rogaan, the Evendiir standing in the middle of the chamber with his mind racing, thinking on all he had learned in his past and what he now was experiencing. Rogaan understood most of what Daluu revealed as his father taught him well much the same. All through his years, he had heard much the opposite on the streets and from friends and neighbors. He regretted even falling to fearing the Ebon Circle. *Still, some of it I harbor.*

"And that dark featherwing that has aided Rogaan and kept watch over even you, Aren," Daluu, the Ebon Circle *Kabiri* spoke, not as a better, but as an attempted friend. "It is the hand of the 'Dark Robe' himself reaching out."

"It was exciting the battle we had with those leapers," Aren recalled looking at Rogaan with immense satisfaction.

"Exciting . . . Speak for yourself," Rogaan interrupted as he walked by with his carry pack full. "I am still cleaning stuff out of my pants from that one."

"You may have need of these before the day is out." The guardsman held out a quiver of arrows and a short bow in Rogaan's path. Rogaan stopped short and stared at them for a few moments before he pulled from his back the half-stride-long black and tan hide case he had been carrying since he retrieved it from Trundiir on the *Khaaron*. He opened it and began assembling his *shunir'ra*, his masterwork . . . blue steel bow. He fit together the *nisi'barzil*, metal-blue limbs to the blue metallic handle section. The recurved limbs fit snuggly into their mounts where Rogaan then tightened them with a turn of a threaded screw and knob with his fingers and a grunt. *Locked*. He locked the second mounted limb in the same way. The handle grip wrapped in the best black and red raver hide available made the bow an attractive weapon. He pulled a blue metal cable out of the case and strung it to the bottom limb notch, then wrapped his leg around the lower limb. He took a breath, then grunted as he bent the bow limbs enough to attach the cable to the notch in the upper limb, then let the cable hold the straining power. A few drops of sweat dripped from his brow, though he did not know if it was from his straining or his prideful excitement. He looked at his bow with regrets for not having completed his *Zagdu-i-Kuzu* ceremony . . . his coming of age in the Tellen Clan. Turning the bow, he looked at the embedded gems he had put in the handle, five of them the size of his thumbnail. Four of the gems sparkled as light struck them . . . a red ruby, a blue sapphire, a yellow topaz, and a green emerald. Alone, they would make the bow worth a king's ransom. A gift from his mother's family, the House of Isin. Yet, the blue metal was priceless beyond the stones. A gift from his father he insisted was leftovers from a temple project that Rogaan now guessed was a gift from the Ebon Circle. *It could not have originated from any other*. And then the center gemstone, Rogaan now knew as a black Agni Stone, from his father's *imur'gisa* . . . the rod-shaped talisman of his father's Tellen Clan. *Useless as one of the keys now*. Holding his bow, Rogaan understood. *This is the fourth key, and . . . evidently, so is my blood*.

"If we are to face trouble like no other . . ." pondered Rogaan, "then let it be with a weapon like no other."

"I've only heard of this bow and started to think it just a false tale." Daluu looked at it in wonder. He stopped when he gazed at the black Agni Stone. "Should you have revealed it? Should it not stay concealed?"

"The best wood bow made . . . by the *Sentii* just broke in my hands against those *Kunsag*." Rogaan put rational thoughts to his actions. "I will not have it happen again.

"I do not even know your name." Rogaan looked to the guardsman.

"Esizila," answered the big Baraan guardsman.

"Esizila, hold this for me." Rogaan offered him his blue metal bow. "Take it. Hold it for me."

Esizila's face appeared drained of life as he looked to his *Kabiri* for guidance. Daluu simply nodded to his guardsman with his eyes pointing to the blue bow, the most prized bow in known existence sought after by *Shunned* and Ancient *Vassal* alike. Esizila reached out with slightly shaking hands taking the bow from Rogaan, then held it with a fear it would break—or take his *Light*.

Rogaan pulled out one of several small cases inside his larger case. He then pulled from his large case two steel reinforced wood shafts with fletching. Taking a blue metal broadhead from the small case, he mated it with the shaft. They locked together with a very carefully done twist. He did the same with a second arrow, then placed both arrows in special slots on the outside of his black and tan case where the broadheads were protected from unintentional contact. Replacing everything into the larger case, he slung it back on himself. Then, Rogaan held out his hand to Esizila. The guardsman handed Rogaan back his *shunir'ra*, then exhaled with great relief before starting to breathe again.

"Solid name," Rogaan looked at Esizila. Looking to the guardsman's weapons: a short sword, long knife, and metal spear. "I hope you are good with those."

"Indeed, I am," Esizila confidently answered.

"We all good to go forward?" Rogaan looked at Daluu and Aren.

"I can't top that," Aren replied having been slightly humbled by the bow.

"Neither can I," Daluu replied. "Let's depart this unwelcoming city."

Chapter 33

The Wrong Side

Under a partly cloudy sky void of all but two featherwings, the Farratum *Tusaa'Ner* column closed on Anza's Blood Bridge as reports from his scouts about disturbances around the city came to him. Sorting through what was important to consider and what wasn't was less a discipline and more a guess. Of his guesses, several close to Blood Bridge interested him most and seemed likely to be what he and his . . . master sought.

Riding next to him on her sarig was his *seergal*, Dajil. In her blue armor the pain she endured with each shift in her saddle was obvious by her numerous grimaces and breathless exhales she managed. *Let her suffer. Maybe her mouth will be more respectful.* Still, Dajil succeeded in giving Ezerus a lazy eye roll timed with another painful breathless moan. *If only I can get those rolling eyes to be respectful.* Behind her, riding a sarig, Farratum's *Za* of ambition and failure, Dajil's mother. Behind her mother, in the niisku-drawn wagon sitting next to the driver, was Ganzer trying his best not to be noticed. Next to Dajil, and behind himself, rode the . . . master. Ezerus felt the Power swirling about *him* and through himself. Difficult to feel and even more difficult to understand and yet much more difficult to control, the Power felt as if it was always there. Where the *kunza* was, Ezerus didn't know. *He* . . . the *Shunned*, directly tasked the *kunza* and a small group of their hardiest and off they went on the perimeter road. Their independent tasking didn't sit well with Ezerus as he didn't like being left out of things he was to have command and control of. *Rules get remade.*

Having just passed the Halls of Anza, large block stone constructions said to have been in existence since the Ancients walked the world, where city affairs were now conducted, Ezerus wondered how many of the Anza *Tusaa'Ner* would "escort" his column to make certain it didn't pose a threat to the city or its schemes. As the Farratum *Tusaa'Ner* column made its way down the main street, Ezerus noted the closed storefronts and those still on the cobblestones and plank walkways seeking to disappear at the column's approach. *Fearful people*, he concluded. Passing an empty cross road leading left to the middle of three bridges spanning the central ravine of Anza and right to the temples to the Ancients of Anza, Ezerus started preparing himself for what he would say to the *antaal'sahkal*. The commander of a *Seb'Ner* force was a high official and someone with knowledge of Shuruppak and her laws. He must have been sent here in place of the arranged *Anubda'Ner*. *Likely to stop us. Maybe to destroy us.* Ezerus held no illusions about the reason the *Seb'Ner* was sent. He thought making the attempt invoking his station as Shuruppak *Subar* superseding the *antaal'sahkal's* command and hope the commander would not fully understand that by the laws he could only do such a thing outside the walls of Shuruppak cities. More vacated streets told Ezerus he was right in anticipating a block and a fight they dared challenge it. *We'll . . . He'll challenge it.*

At their approach to the southernmost city bridge . . . the only means of accessing Blood Bridge and the Blood Lands, Ezerus noted that many of the royal blue guardians were present either on the bridge or on the road leading to it. Glancing back, he saw no sign of the city's *Tusaa'Ner*. *A lost opportunity to place forces on opposite sides of their enemy*, he thought darkly. More closed storefronts, inns, and taverns lined the street around the street intersection ahead as were no citizens outside here. Beyond the intersection lay South Gate and what Ezerus could see, many royal blue guardians. *They truly don't want us traveling south*, Ezerus observed.

Sitting atop sarigs in the intersection was as if a memory from the previous night. Two groups of mounted officials flanked by foot-bound guards. On the right, three Baraan males dressed in hide body armor with gleaming metal shoulders, helms, and scarlet sashes were Anza *Tusaa'Ner*. On the left, five mounted officials on stout sarigs, each in dark-padded eur armor with bronze chest plates and helms, and royal blue sashes. Their standard of the moon atop a lightning bolt on a royal blue flag held tall by that same young soldier sitting upon a sarig next to the more stoutly built and older Baraan who wore a helm with royal blue feathers and a red cape . . . the emblems of command.

"Come no farther, *Tusaa'Ner* of Farratum!" shouted the Anza *Tusaa'Ner* commander.

"So, this is where you choose to be, Darvaar?" Ezerus taunted.

"One must know which facing success lies," Darvaar replied pragmatically with much confidence.

"*Seergal* . . ." Ezerus issued his command.

"*Tusaa'Ner* . . . Column, halt!" Dajil screeched with a groan ending the issued command.

Ezerus saw his grimace reflected in those facing him atop their sarigs five strides away. The Farratum *Tusaa'Ner* column came to a halt. Ezerus surveyed the guardsmen in the intersections and along the road on the left to the bridge. *We're outnumbered*, he concluded.

"*Za* . . ." Ezerus offered his introduction for Irzal.

An awkward silence followed until Ezerus felt the anger flash. Not his, but he felt it all the same. Irzal spurred her sarig into moving in between Ezerus and her daughter. She looked all the part of a *Za* with her bright white robe, gold collar necklace, and gem-inlaid gold and silver tiara arched atop her dirty-blond hair. Ezerus made note of the wind . . . swirling, but generally from their back. *It will have to do.*

"By order of the *Zas* and sanctioned by the Shuruppak Grand Council, you are commanded to stand aside, then take up position as escort to the ancient city of Vaikuntaars." *Za* Irzal spoke in her best *Za* mannerisms, full of arrogance and condescension.

Nothing. No guardsman moved a booted or sandaled foot. Ezerus felt the heavy, awkward silence and the heat building up in Irzal. *So, there she is . . .* He wondered when she would show that side of her again.

"I said—" *Za* Irzal was cut off by the stoutly built Baraan in eur armor wearing the royal blue-feathered helm and red cape.

"I am *antaal'sahkal* of the Shuruppak *Seb'Ner*," the commander of the *Seb'Ner* spoke loudly and with absolute conviction. "You are ordered by the Grand Council to return to Farratum where you will face discipline for actions against The Peoples."

"How dare you—" *Za* Irzal spoke with vexed rage at the insubordination of the *antaal'sahkal* but was again cut off by him.

"I am ordered . . . by the Shuruppak Grand Council to take you, *Za* Irzal, into custody if you refuse." Again, the *antaal'sahkal* spoke with absolute confidence and certainty.

No. The Subar trickery won't work on this one, Ezerus concluded. *He's a formidable leader, and by the looks of him, will be difficult to defeat with a blade.*

"A mistake has been made," *Za* Irzal started glancing nervously to Ezerus and Dajil. "Send word to the Grand Council to have them confirm our permissions. It must be quick."

"A mistake *has* been made . . . *Za* Irzal," the *antaal'sahkal,* harsh and unbending, offered an explanation. "You have been lied to. No permission has been given for you or your . . . horde to anger the Ancients or the *Sentii*."

"This cannot be . . ." A shocked and desperate expression contorted Irzal's face as she looked around. Finding her aide, she paused. "Ganzer, what is this about?"

"I must defer to Lucufaar, my *Za* . . ." Ganzer spoke loud enough for Irzal to hear, then went back to trying not to be seen.

Ezerus felt the Power growing, surging. He lowered his hand to his sword attached to his saddle. Looking and assessing, he saw the *Tusaa'Ner* were completely unaware of the danger they were in, but the *Seb'Ner* commander and his guardsmen sensed it. Lucufaar reigned in his sarig next to Ezerus. Dressed in a new set of black and lavender tunic, pants, and black leather boots, the "aide's" lean, wiry build did not diminish his dangerous aura. Ezerus was a little surprised at how well his lean, clean-shaven face and silver-streaked gray hair looked . . . almost completely healed. Sensing the surging of the Power in the aide, Ezerus looked at Darvaar. "My fellow *Tusaa'Ner* . . . you chose the wrong side."

"If I may . . . I might be able to clear up this misunderstanding," Lucufaar offered to the group before them. "It is by my authority we shall enter the ancient lands, and you shall do as I will it."

The *antaal'sahkal* at first looked surprised at the words, then amused. The rest of the guardsmen in the intersection took to looking at each other to confirm they heard correctly.

"Would you put your advisor in his place," ordered the *antaal'sahkal* of Irzal.

"He . . . is not what you think . . ." Irzal's shaking voice cracked.

As the *antaal'sahkal* started to raise his hand to give an order that would not be favorable to the Farratum *Tusaa'Ner*, Ezerus felt the Power lash out from the *Shunned* and grab the *Seb'Ner* commander. Barely visible to his eyes, a vaporous tendril wrapped itself around the Baraan, lifting up out of his saddle into the air, then smashed him to the ground. Everyone stood in shock at the violence of the attack. The commander's limp body lifted into the air and again was smashed violently to the ground where he lay unmoving and broken.

"You chose the wrong side," Ezerus spoke to the *antaal'sahkal*.

"Guardsmen!" Another *Seb'Ner* officer, likely the *sakal*, took up command. "Atta—"

The *Seb'Ner sakal's* words cut short by the vaporous tendril wrapping itself around his chest and throat, choking him *lightless*. A stir among the *Seb'Ner* turned into a ripple of orders as the well-disciplined guardsmen all drew arms and took up defensive and offensive formations as each thought best, all under a sky with darkening cloud filling with thunder. Darvaar and his *Tusaa'Ner* bolted in several directions, leaving the *Seb'Ner* to fight the battle and the Power by themselves.

"*Tusaa'Ner!*" Ezerus found himself yelling at the top of his ability. "Defend the *Za* and her aide and cut down any who attack."

Ezerus watched as Luntanus Alum dismounted and started walking toward the bridge. As individual *Seb'Ner* guardsmen rushed him in attack, the *Shunned* struck them with bolts of lightning or lashed them with that vaporous tendril, now looking more like a nimble, flaming, whip like rope of great length. Regardless, the results were the same . . . *lightless* guardsmen, either by burning or from severing their parts. A volley of arrows arced at the *Shunned* from the *Seb'Ner* on the bridge—all deflected away as if blown on strong winds. Pieces of stone walls and tiles from roofs went flying when his burning whip slashed the hardened structures to get at guardsmen seeking protective cover. Small fires ignited everywhere from the dried wood, tinder, and clothing that touched the flaming whip. The *Seb'Ner* and Anza's *Tusaa'Ner* gave no heed to Farratum's *Tusaa'Ner* as Luntanus Alum slaughtered all before him as he strolled the cobblestone street.

Ezerus stole a look at a pain-stricken Dajil, finding her eyes now fixed in awe on the wrath of destruction in the street. Not certain how she would react, he gently tapped her shoulder with a long reach from his sarig. Dajil snapped out of her daze and recoiled from Ezerus causing her intense pain and whimpers escaping her lips.

"Order the guardsmen in advance," the *ar'seergal* calmly commander her. His *seergal* looked at him oddly, not seeming to understand who he was for a long moment. Her eyes then focused on him holding an anger that wanted to be unleashed.

"*Tusaa'Ner!*" she screeched loudly with a grimace. "Battle formation. Advance on the *ar'seergal's* decree."

The *Seb'Ner* gave up on their attacks against death walking toward them, deciding to retreat to the bridge using orderly formations of three and more. There, they took up and stood in a royal blue line of defensive . . . a wall of guardsmen with shields, swords, and spears bared. *Little help that will do against this Shunned*, Ezerus thought. Luntanus Alum just kept at his casual pace, slicing and slashing everything in his path. Ezerus thought of the useless loss of guardsmen taking place that could otherwise be consumed into his *Tusaa'Ner*. He waved his arm in command for the column to move forward with him. The Farratum *Tusaa'Ner* advanced.

Chapter 34
Blood Bridge

The underground passages followed a main tunnel with several side tunnels too deep for torchlights to penetrate. Everyone ignored them as they followed Daluu's guardsman. He noted the walls and mostly even floor of the tunnel to be dry and not musty, as he expected. *These tunnels must be used quite often.* Counting his paces at sixty-six, the four of them stopped at Esizila's raised left hand. He and Rogaan peered right around a turn in the tunnel. Esizila tossed his torch to the tunnel floor, then kicked dirt on it to extinguish. The tunnel trembled. Everyone looked above to see if the earth was to bury them. Satisfied the tunnel was solid, Esizila motioned for the same to be done with the second torch Aren now carried. With both torches dark, Aren saw that the tunnel around the corner was dimly illuminated with natural light. A wave of the guardsman's hand put them in motion, the guardsman, followed by Rogaan, then Daluu, and Aren following at the rear. When Aren cleared the turn, he had to shield his eyes from the glare of the tunnel opening ahead. As they slowly approached the tunnel opening, Aren's eyes adjusted to the brightness, allowing him to see it led to a long bridge made of great slabs of gray stone left and right reinforced and locked together with their shapes and metal braces that had knobs spread across them. The knobs looked similar, though much-larger versions, to those of Rogaan's bow. In between the stone sides laying across, at their feet and also some three strides above, great timbers that must have been cut from large trees, all fitted carefully, making a strong structure that would sway with the shaking of the ground, which happened often . . . More often than Aren was used to or felt comfortable about.

Stealing a look around the others down the length of the bridge was found a hallway like appearance with vertical windows evenly placed along it, letting in the morning sun from the left. *A very long bridge*, Aren thought to himself. It made him nervous, a set of spans so long. *How has it stood since all this time?* At a distance . . . Maybe more than eighty strides stood the circular large stone walls of the tower he observed above when he was taking in Anza from their temple garden perch. The tower had an arched walk-through opening on this side and on its opposite side where it led to another long span of bridge completing the distance across the ravine of Anza. *Even longer than I thought.* Aren felt even more nervous about being out on this bridge.

"The path looks clear," the eur-clad guardsman with his deep voice motioned for them to get moving.

As they stepped onto the timbers, each made a test of sturdiness with small hops to ensure the bridge would hold their weight. Aren thought their actions ridiculous but found himself doing the same to make himself feel better. They moved quickly after taking glances out the vertical slots they wished they hadn't. *Oh! We're so high.*

"How old is this bridge?" Aren asked, not knowing if he really wanted someone to answer.

"Since the time of the Ancients," replied Daluu as if reciting a book.

"Tellen built," Rogaan added. "It will hold up long after we are dust."

"I'll wager it's Evendiir designed," Aren added.

"Yes, on both accounts," Daluu confirmed with a questioning tone. "How did you . . . your fathers have taught you well, Roga of the Blood An and Ar of the House En."

Rogaan turned and looked at Daluu with scrutinizing brows. He seemed to be studying, examining him as if he were trying to decide something important. "Why call me in that manner?"

"That *manner* is the formal title used by the Old Blood," answered Daluu.

"You sound as the *Vassal*," pried Rogaan while intensely staring at the *Kabiri*.

"I don't know of him," Daluu replied.

"You certain you are not keeping anything from me?" Rogaan challenged.

"Yes, I am." Daluu stared back at Rogaan. "Though nothing concerning this . . . *Vassal*."

A long moment passed with each simply staring at the other. If he had been Baraan, the long silence might have bothered him, but as it was, Aren just pondered at his formal title while waiting for the two to see who would blink first. Shouts and footfalls above broke the silence as each looked to the others with a sense of alarm.

"Must get moving," Esizila insisted in his deep tone before turning back toward the tower in a brisk walk.

Daluu made to go around Rogaan to join with his guardsman, but Rogaan turned first, then trotted after the eur-clad Esizila. Daluu and Aren followed closely. From the timbers above, many footfalls, muffled commands to take up formations, and terse orders to launch volleys of arrows filled their ears. The crackling of lightning and consuming flames accompanied painful screams of anguish followed as more yelling and footfalls felt as much as heard made Aren anxious at the unknown happening around him. Aren wrinkled his nose of the waft of burning flesh. He felt the Power being used, but the vibrations were slight or maybe distant. He hoped it meant *Kabiri* or those *Kunsag* were battling the *Seb'Ner*, instead of hunting them.

Their group almost made the tower when a large handful of royal blue-armored guardsmen poured from the arched entranceway. Everyone stopped, surprised to see one another. A guardsman with a red cape and blue-feathered helm shouted, "That be them! Take them!"

Almost in unison, the handful of *Seb'Ner* drew their swords and readied them alongside those pointing spear at the Ebon Circle guardsman and Rogaan. At the red cape's command, the guardsmen started a methodical line abreast advance, making it impossible to get past without bloodshed.

"We'll hold them," Daluu told Rogaan. "Find a safe place in one of the side passages in the tunnels."

A nod was all Rogaan managed before turning back the way they came, looking at Aren, then past him with widening, frustrated eyes. "You need to look that way, behind you."

Expecting to see guardsmen with spears in his face, Aren turned. Relief washed through him. Though guardsmen were there on the bridge behind them, they were still at distance. Thinking of what he could do to stop them, he recalled the featherwing's manifestation that shielded Rogaan from the leapers. He watched, heard, and felt in his memory the elements needed to re-create it. Then, calming his mind, he focused on making the shapes, sounds, and vibrations he remembered. He felt the Power sparking and waning . . . that sweet feeling surging through him, then gone, sparking and waning . . . surging, then gone. When he felt he had it, Aren swept his arms left to right anticipating manifesting a wall of fire in the place of his choosing. Bursts of tiny flames formed in the air across the walkway but then disappeared in small, black puffs. *That's embarrassing.* Aren felt his face warm, and not from the fear of getting stuck with a spear. The three royal blue and two scarlet-sashed guardsmen stopped advancing. They looked at each other, hesitating at what they saw between them and their goal.

Again, Aren recalled his memory of the wall of flames made by the featherwing in the wilds . . . seeing and listening and feeling the composition of the manifestation. A blue object passed in front of Aren's face along with the cracking ring of metal striking metal. When he refocused his eyes on the here and now, he found Rogaan standing slightly right and in front of him nocking an arrow as he drew his bow.

Yells of pain and surprise ushered from several of the five guardsmen. Aren felt confused as Rogaan had not fired but held his bow at full draw. Two of the *Seb'Ner* fell to the timbers bleeding out as the other three turned in surprise at finding a Tellen, dressed in *Seb'Ner* scout armor, swinging a one-handed ax at them, and alongside, a tall, lean Baraan with dark hair striking with a pair of daggers to another's throat. Their strikes just missing their aims, Trundiir and Pax found themselves in a desperate fight with skilled swordsmen. Before Aren could call upon another manifestation, Rogaan released his arrow with a melodic metal ring. It flew true, striking the head of the scarlet-sashed guardsman about to cut down Pax with his blade after the half Tellen's friend missed with a too aggressively made dagger attack. A dull thwack saw the arrow pass completely through the scarlet-sashed guardsman's unprotected head, then clattered off stone further down the bridgeway. The guardsman collapsed *lightless* to the timbers with a thump.

Rogaan was already coming to full draw with a second arrow, then released it in another breath. The arrow flew as a low ringing melody filled Aren's ears, the stone flint-tipped shaft passing through the guardsman's neck who was swinging his large sword at Trundiir. Stopping his swing at the impact and passing of the arrow, the guardsman raised his hand to his throat, but not before large spurts of crimson started pumping uncontrolled from both sides of his neck. Gurgles emitted from the bronze-chested guardsman as he fell to his knees, now holding his throat with both hands as his large sword fell. The last guardsman about to strike Trundiir, a scarlet sash, let out a painful howl as his face turned to one of astonishment. He fell to the timbers. Behind him stood Pax with a wicked smile holding a pair of crimson-dripping daggers. A swing from Trundiir's ax lodged itself deep into the *Tusaa'Ner's* head. The *Light* in the Baraan's eyes winked out. Trundiir put his boot on the Baraan's chest to pull his ax out, allowing the limp body to join its companions. The last guardsman, a royal blue sash, wobbling on his knees, fell over *lightless*.

"A little help!" came the cry from behind.

Aren and Rogaan turned together, finding two royal blue-sashed guardsmen down unmoving on the timbers and Daluu grappling with two more while Esizila fought desperately against blades of the red-caped commander doing everything he knew to keep the blades from taking his *Light*. Aren quickly recalled his memories of another manifestation, one with more precision than the lightning. As Rogaan released another singing arrow, this time at the red-caped, blue-feathered helmed guardsman, Aren smiled, now knowing how to re-create the sounds and vibrations of his planned manifestation. It took a moment to form in his mind before an aura of blue light grew, engulfing his hands. He wanted more blue light . . . wanted this to hurt the *Seb'Ner*. It grew with an exalting sense of power surging through him. *It feels good, great!* He looked up, finding the red-caped guardsman staggering back from the panting Esizila. Appearing unable to put his full weight on his left leg and knee, the Baraan was unmoving. Another singing arrow from the half Tellen punched through another guardsman's bronze chest armor in the area of the Baraan's heart as broken flint flew, peppering everyone and everything. The commander looked at the fletching sticking out from his chest, then directly at Rogaan with shocked astonishment coming from under his helm. The guardsman fell backward with a thump on the timbers.

"Help!" came another cry came from Daluu as he lay on the timbers under a guardsman fighting back the arms and a blade a hand's width from his neck while kicking back another royal blue-sashed Baraan with his right boot.

Aren focused on the guardsman he thought most dangerous, pointing his hands and fingers at his bronze chest piece. He let loose the blue streaking Power, striking the guardsman near driving his blade into Daluu. As a blue aura rippled over chest armor, head, and arms, the guardsman shook while screaming out in pain. The shaking guardsman no longer attacked, instead allowed Daluu to push him up and away before waving his hands as if they were burned. The last standing bronze-chested guardsman recovering his feet from Daluu's kick quickly surveyed his downed companions, then made to run back into the tower. Before the panicky *Seb'Ner* could move, Aren felt the vibrations before he heard the sound and saw the lines of Power of a vaporous whipping tendril snap out from the timbers and grab the guardsman. Holding the other end of the tendril was the prone Ebon Circle *Kabiri*, who didn't look at all pleased. To Aren, the manifestation felt weak compared to that he sensed before by the *Shunned*, even at a considerable distance. The frantic guardsman now futilely fought the tendril, slashing his long knife at it. Daluu held the manifestation with considerable effort, then growled as he manipulated it, lifting the guardsman off the timbers and throwing him out a vertical window and from the bridge. The Baraan's screams ended suddenly without a splash. A moan escaped one of the bronze-chested guardsmen lying about, the Baraan that Aren struck with the Power. As he tried to rise from the timbers, a blade from the Ebon Circle guardsman driven through the neck put an end to his pains and the *Seb'Ner's Light*. Aren watched as Rogaan let off his drawn arrow, disarming the thing while the half Tellen looked upon the scene with a sense of satisfaction.

"A very good effort . . . all spoken," the Ebon Circle *Kabiri* commented after his guardsman helped him to his feet.

A dark-haired, yellow streak ran past Aren, slamming into a surprised Rogaan, hugging him as she gave out a little squeal. Rogaan looked as much surprised as everyone else, then hugged her back. Aren watched as the warrior fell away and that dangerously distracted half Tellen returned. Trundiir and Pax approached with earnest, though nothing to match Suhd's display.

"I thought I left you in the cave . . . where you would be safe," Rogaan spoke to Pax as he buried his face in Suhd's hair.

"Your friends convinced me otherwise," answered Trundiir. "I suspected your plans. Seeing to freeing your father, while I kept these two hidden from it all. When they realized you had gone, they insisted on helping you, despite my best efforts."

"Well, your help was timely," Daluu interjected himself into the conversation. "Though I must insist we get moving. A battle rages above, and who knows how many more are seeking us."

"Speakin' of dat," Pax pointed back the way they all came from the tunnel, "some of da red locals be tryin' ta follow us into da tunnels. Not be knowin' how long it takin' dem ta get past da secret stable door."

"Grab what's needed," Daluu told the group.

"Already did." Trundiir held up a large hand and a half sword the *Seb'Ner* attacked him with. It looked like a great sword in the Tellen's hands.

Aren surveyed the downed guardsman. *What a mess.* The numbers were remarkable. All the guardsmen down and no one in their group hurt. *Impressive.* Searching, Aren found a wood spear with a short metal tip to use as a staff. He stole a look around before rummaging for pouches and things of value. *I can't have them thinking me a common luzub.* To his amusement and relief, the others were already at looting the downed guardsmen of anything valuable, or that could be important to their survival. All except Daluu and his guardsman, who looked upon the activities with a bit of a high nose. Both stood apart from the collecting of "valuables." Aren then caught the guardsman, Esizila, holding his left side where it appeared his eur armor was wet with blood. *So much for everyone without injury. I hope he lives long enough to help us escape.*

"We must go!" Daluu insisted.

As things were being stowed in belts, pouches, and carry packs, noise and gruff voices from the far end of the bridgeway alerted them. Emerging from the west tunnel was a troop of scarlet-sashed *Tusaa'Ner*. When they saw the aftermath of battle, they paused, taking in the scene. With a shout from their leader, they raised their crossbows and fired wildly at the group. Suhd screamed as Rogaan threw her to the timbers. The bolt flying for her struck his scout armor in the back, deflecting off and finding Pax, cutting his left shoulder.

Before he thought what to do, Aren summoned the Power manifesting fire, then shaped it into a wall. He set it near the *Tusaa'Ner* across the bridgeway. He then wondered . . . *How do I maintain this without concentrating on it?*

"Everyone, this way to the other side of the bridge," Daluu directed.

"If I stop concentrating on this, the wall will fall." Aren partly informed, partly complained that he didn't want to be left behind.

"Everyone . . . go!" Rogaan ordered. "I will stay with him while you escape."

"Seriously?" Daluu questioned. "Both of you are more important than the rest of us. Noble you want to stay behind. Yet, it will be my *Light* if I let that happen."

"Suggestions?" Aren asked nervously, fearing that there was no way out of this for him. More guardsmen gathered behind his flames as Daluu and Rogaan *discussed* their situation.

Aren felt it. Vibrations. This time coming from Daluu. The vibrations were different than those he previously felt—*something new he's manifesting*. A tiny ball of swirling flame appeared in the Ebon Circle *Kabiri's* palm, then grew to the size of his hand. Sizzling, Daluu threw . . . no, more *pushed* the ball of flames toward the *Tusaa'Ner*. Clear for Aren to see, a trail of the Powers appeared in the wake of the flames as it passed through Aren's wall of flames, through the throng of guardsmen, and into the tunnel. It flashed brightly inside, followed immediately by a thunderous boom shaking the bridge and causing debris to fly every which way as the *Tusaa'Ner* everywhere were thrown to the timbers . . . several unlucky ones even tossed from the bridge.

"Drop your flames and start running," offered Daluu.

Aren didn't need to be told twice. He stopped concentrating on his manifestation, allowing the wall of the Powers to fade away, but the flames remained. *Oops.*

"By all of Kur!" Daluu sounded exasperated. "You set fire to the bridge."

"That's a good thing . . . isn't it?" Trundiir asked.

"This bridge is ancient . . ." the *Kabiri* explained. "It could burn quickly, trapping us into jumping in the waters below."

"It would take our *Light* . . . the fall," Pax stated, looking over the side of the bridge. He now held his sister's hand, ensuring she would stay close.

"Not the fall . . . the snapjaws," Trundiir answered for Daluu.

"This way, everyone," Daluu demanded as he swept his arm in the direction of the tower. "Follow Esizila to the other side of the river."

"My father?" Rogaan took hold of the *Kabiri's* right arm with his own.

"He is where he and the master need him," the *Kabiri* answered. Not what the half Tellen wanted to hear, but maybe what he needed to.

The seven of them ran east through the tower and onto the mirror bridgeway to that they just left. It would take them across the ravine splitting Anza, to the Coiner's District where Anza's wealth resided. Daluu was leading them to what he named the East Gate allowing them to escape the city. Aren felt strongly mixed emotions about traveling in that direction. As he passed through the circular block stone tower, he looked to the narrow stone-shaped steps built into the wall on the south side of the shape leading up to the street level. In his mind, *it* called to him to travel the steps. Aren paused, fighting with himself but only for a moment before he resumed chasing after the others, convincing himself he still could satisfy the whisper in his mind and make the travel . . . just from the East Gate. Aren, following Daluu, saw the other five run into each other, bunching up behind the Ebon Circle guardsman. He stopped for some reason. A quick look around the jumbled group found royal blue-sashed, bronze-chested guardsmen running at them from the opposite end of the bridge length. Many of them. Quickly realizing he could satisfy both his . . . needs, Aren felt the Power surge and flow through him. It felt so soothing and exciting all at once as his mind and body tingled. Everything around seemed more vivid . . . more alive. Remembering what he needed to do, he manifested another wall of flames, placing it halfway down the eighty-some-stride bridge length. Daluu immediately turned with glaring eyes on Aren.

"What . . .?" Aren questioned the foul-eyed *Kabiri* as he concentrated on making the flames as hot as he could. "You have a better idea?"

Daluu and Aren stood glaring at each other exchanging unspoken challenges. The *Kabiri* was clearly angry but didn't have an answer to Aren's question. Rolling his eyes, Daluu then yelled out, "We're trapped with one direction to go. This way, everyone."

The seven of them reentered the stone tower with Daluu in the lead. Once inside, Aren concentrated one last time on making the flames hot. They flared as the *Seb'Ner* yelled in retreat. Dropping his concentration, the Power now gone and the flames remaining burning the timbers and giving Aren an agreeable sense of satisfaction. Daluu mounted the foot-wide stone steps in the tower, then carefully made his way up keeping his body against the stone wall. Rogaan followed. Aren decided to hop in the line just behind the half Tellen. Trundiir grunted at Aren, then followed just behind him, making Aren feel as protected as was possible in their situation. Daluu paused at the top of the steps before climbing onto the street level. Rogaan did the same with only the slightest pause. Aren stopped with his head just exposed enough for him to take in his surroundings. *Only Daluu and Rogaan. Good.* He climbed the last steps with a sense of relief.

His relief evaporated when he peeked out of the arched doorway to the east. A troop of *Seb'Ner* accompanied by Anza *Tusaa'Ner* were making their way from Coiner's District toward them. *Too many!* though the smoke billowing from the lower level gave him hope fire would soon engulf the bridge length. Maybe another wall of . . .

"What in Kur is that?" Rogaan sounded dismayed.

Aren turned. His heart felt as if it stopped as his sensing of the Powers struck him hard, disoriented him, as a flaming whip . . . A tendril went slicing through a *Seb'Ner* formation at the other end of the bridge length. *Where'd that come from?* Aren wasn't knowing it, but if felt familiar. *Lucufaar . . . Luntanus Alum.* Smoke from the flames below billowed out and around both sides of the bridge not far behind the routed *Seb'Ner* formations. Everyone within their group crowded around to see while doing their best not to expose themselves to the happenings at both ends of the bridge crossing Anza's ravine.

"Fellows!" Trundiir almost calmly called out.

Looking at the other bridge length, the guardsmen were starting to cross where billowing smoke from below almost completely obscured Aren's view of the full bridge. *Too many . . . not going to happen.* Aren considered and decided as quick as that as he calmed his mind and reached out, allowing the Power to flow through him making the world vivid . . . alive . . . desirable. At his thoughts, another manifested wall of flames swept across the bridge width at the same spot where the smoke billowed from below. Screams from guardsmen caught in the fiery wall brought a sense of satisfaction to Aren. Only three guardsmen made it through.

"You two should be able to handle them . . ." Aren pointed at Trundiir and the Ebon Circle guardsman as he concentrated on making the flames hotter. The continued screams from those caught in his wall brought a smile to his face. Aren turned back to their *Shunned* problem, finding Daluu staring at him with a contemptuous gaze.

"We gravely need to talk," was all the Ebon Circle *Kabiri* said before returning his attention to their trouble coming from the west end of the bridge.

Aren watched as Trundiir and Esizila joined battle with the three *Seb'Ner*. A singing arrow zipped past Aren's head striking the center guardsman in the chest where the fletching remained protruding out from the bronze chest plate. A second singing arrow cut through the guardsman's throat, sending him to the timbers with his life spurting from his neck. Aren looked back at Rogaan, giving him a harsh gaze at the arrows passing so close to his head. "A little close, wouldn't you say?"

Rogaan returned a friendly smile that seemed a little too playful for Aren. Aren was about to chastise the half Tellen, but over Rogaan's shoulder, Aren spotted through billowing pillars of smoke most of the routed *Seb'Ner* lying about the west end of the bridge. A few of them still alive and attempting retreat and escape found their *Lights* burnt from them as the *Shunned* lashed them with his flaming tendril by his right hand or blue light bolts from his other. A ripple of fear uncomfortably washed through Aren. Nothing was to stop Lucufaar . . . Luntanus Alum. Aren suddenly felt sick for having been so close to the ancient legend. Vibrations new drew Aren's attention back to the *Shunned*. He watched as lines of the Power formed a ball on the west length engulfing the bridge where he had set fire to it. The smoke from the bridge fire lessened over the long moments he and everyone else watched in awe the awesome display of the Power.

"He stilled da fire." Pax made an anxious comment at what they all just saw as his sister hugged him with fear-filled eyes.

"We have need to leave from . . . *him*." Aren's gaze remained fixed on the approaching *Shunned*.

"I agree with your insight, Evendiir." Daluu sounded shaken and anxious while alternating between looking at Aren and the approaching *Shunned*. "You both saved us and gave us but one choice. Everyone . . . to Blood Bridge."

"Blood Bridge?" Trundiir asked returning to the tower. Both he and the Ebon Circle guardsman were splattered in blood, the guardsman now visibly limping but alive.

"Our only escape if we are to keep our *Lights*," stated Daluu as he stepped to the southern tower archway. Surveying the three lengths of bridge and towers to the south, he saw what he hoped he wouldn't. "More *Seb'Ner* in this direction. They approach over the bridgeway."

"We have more . . . companions with that *Shunned* this direction," Rogaan announced, watching the west bridgeway.

"*Shunned?*" Suhd asked as she and Pax peeked out of the same archway as Rogaan looking to the west. "What be that?"

"The bridge is ablaze to the east," announced Esizila in his deep voice.

"More *Seb'Ner* on the lower bridge to the east," Daluu sounded aggravated on the way to desperate.

"Jump from da bridge?" Pax recommended seeking a path not including fighting.

"Too high . . ." Rogaan dashed that idea.

"And . . . a large number of snapjaws now gather below," added Daluu as he returned from the side of the bridge just outside the southern tower archway.

"I say we take the path with least opportunity of becoming *lightless*." Aren laid out his rational thoughts that hid his inner desires while watching the approaching *Seb'Ner* on Blood Bridge. "We go south . . . big fellows in front."

Chapter 35

Consumed

The Farratum *Tusaa'Ner* kept to their formation as they followed their *ar'seergal* and *seergal* down the cobblestones. Before them, an ancient legend that all feared in their youngling years from tales told to them by fathers and mothers, was destroying wagons, carts, and wood and stone structures as he sought to kill all those who opposed him. Fires small and growing were all about them. A wake of annihilation.

He looked to his *seergal* to see if she was still able to do her duties or see her replaced. Sitting stiffly tall in pain, the grimace she wore spoke of her toughness or stubbornness, he didn't know which. Regardless, his discipline of her appeared to be working. How long . . . He didn't know that either. *When will she turn on me?* he asked himself as he kept his eyes looking for stragglers the *Shunned* missed. There were none. A chill rippled through Ezerus at the totality of death and destruction at Luntanus Alum's hand. *The legends spoke true of him.*

Ahead, the *Shunned* neared the royal blue and bronze line of defense at the bridgehead. Repeated volleys of arrows intended for him the *Shunned* waved away as if the wilds and winds were at his command. Smoke started billowing up from the bridge behind the *Seb'Ner* defenders. *What's happening there?* Suspecting something amiss, Ezerus started to issue the command to advance at a run. His words were drowned out by the yells and screams of his *Tusaa'Ner* as he felt the hairs on the back of his neck stand on end. Looking back, he found lightning arcing all about the column, from somewhere near the crossroads. Then, a brief series of orange-red balls of flames struck the column, setting afire a wagon and several guardsmen. Everyone was scattered, in chaos. In the distance through the destruction, Ezerus spotted a group of red and black-robed Baraans accompanied and protected by those two green-armored *Ursan* who attacked the *Khaaron* with the red-clad warrior.

Needing to reorganize his guardsmen, the wounded *sakal* now riding a sarig within the column raised a battle cry and set off to doing so without command from either his *ar'seergal* or *seergal*. *Maybe a good Baraan leader after all. If he saves the day, he needs promoting.* As the *sakal* rallied the *Tusaa'Ner*, the *seergal* turned her sarig to the rear of the column and made to charge into the fray.

"Hold, *Seergal!*" Ezerus commanded.

"What?" She looked at him with pain and dismay.

"The important battle is at the bridge," he told her not knowing how he knew that.

"But . . . Mother . . ." Dajil's face twisted in pain and agony, and not from her lashes.

The *sakal* had already gotten the column partially together as the niisku-drawn prisoner wagon, no more than a covered wagon with anchor mounts to attach leg chains to, moved away from the fight and toward Ezerus and Dajil. Sitting next to the driver was *Za* Irzal, in light chains. When Dajil saw the chains, her angered flared and her pain-stricken grimace turned to hatred as she glared at Ezerus.

"You had her—" Dajil screeched at Ezerus.

"Your lashings were merciful!" Ezerus cut her off. "Don't provoke more. Irzal's usefulness is waning. Consider if yours wanes as well. Your duty is to protect the *Shunned*."

His *seergal*, Dajil . . . daughter of *Za* Irzal, slumped in her saddle as she held defeat in her eyes. Tears flowed and dripped from under her helm. Ezerus felt disgust for her, but he needed his *seergal* to keep the *Tusaa'Ner* loyal. Then, her tears and whimpering stopped. Ezerus placed his hand on his long knife pommel, not certain of what his *seergal* would do. She looked up to the prisoner wagon and held a long moment of eye contact with her mother. Then, Irzal made a series of hand motions. Dajil shook her head, resisting the unspoken words. Irzal made the hand gestures again. Ezerus, concerned at this secret talk going on right before him, made to break in.

"*Seergal* . . ." he started.

"I have my orders!" Dajil declared with hotly determined slits for eyes. She spurred her sarig at the prisoner wagon.

Surprised at Dajil's reckless action, Ezerus spurred his own sarig in the hope he could catch her before she did whatever she was about to do. His sarig burst into a fast run, but he wasn't closing on his *seergal*. On the run, Dajil snatched a spear sticking up from a dead sarig in the street, the spear likely one of the objects the *Shunned* waved away when being attacked and charged the prisoner wagon.

"No . . . the driver," Ezerus feared. *She's trying to get the wagon to run wildly.* Then, he saw his *seergal* shift her point of aim with the spear. "No! She means to end her mother's *Light*."

Ezerus spurred his sarig on but realized he couldn't stop this daughter from taking her mother's *Light*. Dajil passed to the right on her mother's side of the wagon and continued on. *Is she seeking to attack the robed ones?* Ezerus followed, now confused about what she was up to. Dajil turned her sarig left at the rear of the wagon. Ezerus followed and turned too but found his *seergal* to be nowhere. Clearing the wagon, Ezerus spotted his *seergal* heading back in the direction they came. Either she was about to attack what remained of the *Seb'Ner*, or she was going to . . . *No!*

Ezerus spurred on his sarig with everything it had. Ahead, the *Shunned* had already made *lightless* all but a few disoriented *Seb'Ner* stragglers and now simply looked at the bridgehead watching the flames and smoke in front of him diminish and die. At this distance and with her head start, Ezerus knew he wouldn't reach her in time to stop her. He concentrated on *"Behind you."*

The *Shunned* twisted and turned around with his flaming whip lashing out in a wide-arcing sweep back at Dajil and her steed. She was on him . . . a thousand stones of charging sarig, spear, and sheer desperation. The flaming whip slashed under the animal taking two of its legs, sending the sarig tumbling and Dajil flying forward in an arc with spear still pointed at her target. Luntanus Alum dodged the spear but put himself in the path of the sarig. The thousand stones slamming into him hurled the *Shunned* into the stone wall at the side of the bridge. Dajil hit the wood timbers, then went tumbling past the burned and smoldering section of the bridge where she lay still.

Ezerus immediately made for the down Luntanus Alum. He wasn't certain, but he felt that the *Shunned* was still alive. He urged his sarig on stepping through and on the motionless *Seb'Ner* lying in his way. The crunching sounds under his steed's feet he knew were their bodies breaking. Dismounting, Ezerus found the *Shunned*, his black and lavender tunic and pants torn in places, trying to sit up against the stone wall, his wiry build struggling to make himself vertical. Blood matted his silver-streaked gray hair and ran down his now lightly scarred face. Those from the old scars from the *Khaaron*. A groan from the ancient legend told others he was in pain. Ezerus didn't need to hear the groan to know he was hurt. He felt it . . . all of the pain, though somewhat dulled. Thankful the pain wasn't his, he realized truly how connected he was to this *Shunned*. It frightened him. His growing thoughts of ending the legend's *Light* and being revered a hero for it caused him concern that He would know his thoughts.

"Yes. Taking my *Light* will bring you pain . . . fatally," Luntanus Alum told Ezerus with a slight groan.

"I wasn't considering such things . . ." Ezerus lied. *Did he know my thoughts?*

"Not important at present," the *Shunned* interrupted. "That little disobedient *karkid* of a *sakal* . . ."

"*Seergal* . . ." Ezerus corrected before he thought better of it. He didn't like playing word games, though titles were different.

"Also, unimportant," the *Shunned* corrected Ezerus with a warning glare. "She dared to take her best at me. I want her for *questioning*. Though first, and most important is that Tellen with his bow and that Evendiir with what he carries."

"I know not where they are," Ezerus replied.

"Trapped on the bridge," Luntanus Alum informed him, then grimaced. "I have a strange choice. Consume you this moment to restore my body so to remove them away from him and likely take your *Light* or do what must be done through your eyes."

Stunned by his words, Ezerus could only stare at the *Shunned*. He felt a dull numbness all over and a moment as if his life were held fragilely in the balance. He thought to flee. *He would . . . consume me? Make him . . . consider it not. Retreat with him to a place where he can recover.*

"You would be *consumed* in your cowardice," the *Shunned* confirmed. "And retreat is not a choice. The Tellen and Evendiir and what they carry may allow him entrance to Vaikuntaars."

"They have the rods?" Ezerus asked.

"No, those are about to be taken from his temple," Luntanus Alum informed him. "The ones on the bridge have other Agni Stones. I feel them. It is easier to see and act through your eyes when you submit. Resist me, and you will experience pain and injury."

"Not a choice, is it?" Ezerus stated.

"No." Luntanus Alum replied. "We must be quick. Help me stand."

Ezerus took hold of the *Shunned's* right arm and helped him to his feet. Luntanus Alum immediately set himself examining the burned area of the bridge and beyond, finding that Tellen now with a blue metal bow helping the traitor to her feet. Luntanus Alum looked at the Tellen with dark, narrowing eyes as Ezerus felt from him a powerful lust for . . . Agni.

Ezerus recognized the Tellen as the one who took Suhd away from him on the *Khaaron*, spurring a rage of jealousy in Ezerus before he took hold of it and forced a calming of himself. *I must not show that to him.* Focusing on the condition of his *seergal*, she was injured, weak, and staggering even with the Tellen's help. It was then the Tellen locked eyes with the *Shunned*. They held it for a long moment, so long Ezerus started to grow concerned. *Unsettling.* Then, in an act of extreme quickness, the Tellen let go of Dajil and raised his blue metal bow while drawing an arrow from his quiver in a single move, the quickness in which he moved was surprising to Ezerus. *How fast is this one!* In his next breath, the Tellen released the arrow. It came at them with great speed, faster than anything he had seen before—*no time to move.* A flash of orange-red from the *Shunned's* hand found bits and pieces of the arrow clattering against his armor and the *Shunned's* clothing. Before Ezerus could take in all that happened, the Tellen snatched another arrow, this from a tan and black case at his side and nocked it. That arrow sped at them also at great speed, and the *Shunned* struck the arrow with another burst of orange-red. The arrow remained whole, striking and passing through the *Shunned's* right shoulder, then cutting through Ezerus's hide and metal armor at his upper left arm. His armor fell away to the ground where the arrow passed through it. *How sharp is that thing . . . slicing through metal?* Ezerus asked himself as he felt the sting and wet of blood running down his left arm from the shoulder. *By Kur, what is this Tellen?*

A vaporous barrier exploded into position in front of them, protecting them from that Tellen. Ezerus felt a moment of fright mixed with pain in Luntanus Alum before he controlled it . . . or hid it, replacing it with rising anger at his new agony.

"My shoulder . . ." Luntanus Alum grumbled. "I must *consume*."

Fear gripped Ezerus at the *Shunned's* words. He felt it—a tugging at his innards, his head, his everything. His normal driven self grew tired and lethargic, so not like himself. His vision blurred, and his head started to swim as the bridge and smoke tilted. Ezerus dropped to a knee. Then, the unseen hand on him saw it all gone. He breathed, filling his lungs with needed air. He felt a hand on his left shoulder and arm. The stinging went away. Looking up, Ezerus found the *Shunned* standing tall with a hand pulling his hand from his cut arm.

"I can't have you *lightless* . . . yet," the *Shunned* declared, speaking of business he intentionally left undone.

"Have you . . . enough?" Ezerus found himself strangely asking. *Why did I ask that when He takes what he wants?*

"For the moment," the *Shunned* answered with an unexpected weariness. He let loose blue-white lightning at the Tellen, striking near him and the limping Dajil, both slowly making for the tower. Both staggered and fell to the timbers at the explosion of splinters from the close call of lightning. Ezerus felt the *Shunned*, his frustration, and self-anger at missing his target.

Looking over Ezerus's shoulder and back toward the temples, the *Shunned* set his dark, narrow eyes on something of an annoyance. Ezerus turned to see many of his *Tusaa'Ner* lying in the street with the last of the able guardsmen slinging arrows and spears at five red and black-robed manifesters of the Agni powers, still in the intersection, lashing out at guardsmen with light and lightning and fire. The

Shunned now stood by him and started muttering something unintelligible. A light appeared in his right hand, then grew into an aura of flames engulfing his hand in a reddish glow. It grew brighter as Luntanus Alum concentrated and muttered. The flaming aura grew more intense . . . hotter, yet it did not burn him. The *Shunned* then pushed the aura toward the red and black robes. The flaming ball constantly adjusted its approach, then struck the five, engulfing them in an explosion of flames. When the flames and smoke cleared, Ezerus saw the robed ones staggering about with his remaining *Tusaa'Ner* guardsmen charging them.

"That should draw him out." The *Shunned* spoke more to himself than for others, refocusing on his immediate surrounding.

"Him?" Ezerus asked as he struggled to his feet. Despite feeling fatigued, Ezerus no longer sensed the burning shoulder wound.

"Their Ancient hunter seeking my fall," the *Shunned* revealed.

Ezerus felt his strength returning as his skin color recovered to its normal brown. Relief and a hope at living were his once again. The continued ruckus back at the cobblestone intersection found those green-clad warriors in an exchange of arrows with his *Tusaa'Ner*. Somehow, Ezerus's *Tusaa'Ner* were losing. The robed *Kunsag* now counting four rejoined into their *Igal* . . . their Chorus. Soon, they would be manifesting to wipe out those that remained of his *Tusaa'Ner*. Disgust trickled into Ezerus's feelings. It then changed to a determination to end insolence. He knew its coming before he saw it, the reddish glow engulfing the *Shunned's* hand. Ezerus reeled back from the heat as the glow grew . . . hotter and blue-white. The *Shunned* unleashed the exalted flames at the Chorus, striking an unseen barrier in front of them, obliterating it, and sending the Chorus and their green-clad protectors tossed in various directions.

The *Shunned* stood with a satisfied grin. "Now . . . Let us seize this haughty Tellen and that irritating Evendiir as we put in chains our traitor. Stay close in defending me."

Chapter 36

Powers Elevated

Aren watched as dark-haired Rogaan, dressed in *Seb'Ner* scout's armor and carrying his blue metal bow, retreated to the tower almost carrying the *Tusaa'Ner* commander Dajil. Her torn blue tunic over hide armor and darkened metal shoulder guards scraped and dented, the *Tusaa'Ner* commander's red-blond hair whipped freely in the light wind. Her hip, leg, and shin guards looked as badly scraped and damaged as the rest of her armor making her severe limping understandable.

"Ya be losin' ya mind!" Pax complained loudly when he went to look for Rogaan after he disappeared from the tower and finding him in the open on the bridge. Rogaan half-carried Dajil at over twenty strides from the tower, making their way to his friends, his progress slowed by the *Tusaa'Ner* commander from her constant collapsing every few steps. "Ya know who she be?"

"He knows," Aren spoke for Rogaan, admitting to himself that he more liked Dajil than not. *At least she treated me with respect.* But Aren reminded himself too about the danger of her scent when she had a favorable word for you. *Powerful sway . . . Be careful.* "She's difficult to forget."

Aren saw and heard a second distant explosion of flames far to the west, near where he estimated the *Tusaa'Ner* prison wagon to be. Each time, he felt the vibrations of the Power before seeing manifested lines created by the *Shunned* at the bridgehead. *No need to tell Rogaan of the danger to his father. It'll only make matters worse . . . for me.* A new feel of vibrations grabbed his attention. *Where?* He looked about as he felt . . . *lightning* . . . focused toward . . . Rogaan! Searching past the half Tellen and Dajil, Aren found him, the *Shunned* . . . manifesting and exalting a powerful weapon. Without thinking of how to do it, a shield of something other than vapors manifested into existence beyond the tower wall, a wall of something like glass in the shape of a round shield and slightly glowing white. Made of the Power, Aren wondered at what it was and hoped it able to stop . . . lightning.

He thought it to move and found it responding to him. Elated and fascinated, all at the same time, he wondered at it. *What did I create?* An intense wave of the Power focused in his direction gave alert and alarm to him. Instinctively, Aren commanded the shield in the path of the Power. Almost instantly it went where he wanted it . . . directly behind Rogaan and Dajil. A brilliant bolt of lightning struck, deflecting off the manifested shield and striking the tower above and left of Aren, obliterating blocks of stones in a deafening clap of thunder. A cloud of dust swirled and descended on them as he and the rest of the group dodged flying rock debris, some sizeable enough to do serious harm. Aren felt another focused use of the Power directed at them again. Once more, he summoned the shield and put it in the path of the Power giving Rogaan and Dajil some protection as they entered the tower. Another brilliant burst of light exploded from the lightning bolt as it struck . . . Power against Power. Aren felt the heat of the lightning bolt as it deflected down into the timbers just outside of the tower. The old wood exploded in another clap of thunder throwing sizeable splinters everywhere, several hitting him.

Agonizing pain from the wood splinters took all Aren's focus. One of the splinters struck him in his right leg, the other in his arm. He fell to the timbers where he sat looking at the splinters sticking out from his body wondering how to remove them. Neither bled, which he guessed was a good sign, but the pain . . . *unbearable*. Someone started dragging something behind the stone tower wall. Looking up from his sitting position, Aren found the Tellen already examining his wounds. Trundiir pulled a folded white rag from his carry pack, then grabbed the large splinter in Aren's arm and gave him an "I am sorry for this" look just before he ripped the splinter out. Aren yelled out in pain, loud enough for the whole city to hear him. He didn't care. *That hurts!* The Tellen started wrapping his rag around Aren's now-bleeding arm when Daluu placed a hand in the way.

"I'll take care of him," the *Kabiri* told Trundiir. "Can you get everyone ready to run for the next tower?"

With a nod, Trundiir was off as Daluu kneeled to exam Aren's arm. Aren made to protest any of his aid, but he had already felt the vibrations . . . very different from any he felt before. He watched the lines of Power stretch out from Daluu's hand surrounding his wounded arm. His arm and then his body felt cold from the power and what it was doing to him. Before Aren could pull away, the wound felt less painful as he watched in slight awe his wound mending itself. Daluu grabbed the splinter in Aren's leg without any pretext or warning and yanked it out. Aren howled in pain. "Curse you!"

Tossing the splinter aside, the *Kabiri* quickly used his Agni Powers to start healing Aren, sending an intense chill through his body. Again, the unique vibrations and lines of the Power became etched in Aren's memories. In moments, the cold sensation passing through him disappeared, leaving his leg mended and pain soothed.

"You should be able to run," Daluu informed him.

"Run?" Aren looked at him not understanding.

"He's almost upon us." Daluu's eyes darted to the archway and the bridge. "We must go. Now!"

Aren understood Daluu's concern. *The Shunned.* Daluu helped him to his feet; then they joined the rest of the group. Trundiir and Esizila were already at the south archway eyeing the *Seb'Ner* on the bridge beyond the next tower. Six of them. Evidently, the guardsmen had decided not to come any closer to the Agni Powers raining on them all.

"What are they waiting for?" asked Suhd looking at the *Seb'Ner* guardians.

"Us," Trundiir answered in a grumble without taking his eyes off the royal blue-armored lurkers lingering just beyond the next tower.

"Well, we can't wait here." Aren felt anxious at the soon-to-be arriving *Shunned* and Ezerus. "Really. We must go, now!"

"I be agreein' with da mystic," Pax added his encouragement to depart their tower urgently. "Master Lightnin' almost be here."

"Trundiir and Esizila," Rogaan laid out a strategy he considered sound and easy to follow, "rush the *Seb'Ner*. I'll strike as many as I can with my bow before anyone can swing a thing. Pax . . . you and Suhd look after our *Tusaa'Ner* and keep her moving with us. Aren and . . . Daluu, you two do your Agni thing."

There was a moment's pause when everyone seemed to be weighing Rogaan's words. Then, in silence, everyone nodded in agreement. Trundiir and Esizila immediately set off running at the royal blue guardians. Daluu and Aren followed, but at a slower pace. Rogaan stepped onto the bridge and veered left, drawing an arrow as he did. Pax and Suhd followed with Dajil, still wobbling and hobbling.

Aren heard the singing of the first arrow from Rogaan's bow as it whizzed past his head. *Not so close*, Aren wished of Rogaan's arrows. The second arrow sang as the first arrow struck one of the *Seb'Ner*, sending him staggering off out of view. The second arrow struck another guardsman in the head, dropping him immediately. The remaining four guardsmen ducked around the tower walls for cover. Trundiir and Esizila were close to the tower's north archway when Aren felt the Power. A familiar feeling of vibrations . . . all focused ahead, as a rainbow of colors fell around Baraan-shaped shadows cast on the timbers at the tower's southern archway. He slowed, allowing Daluu to continue in front of him seemingly unaware of the Powers manifesting in front of them.

Several more *Seb'Ner* came into view in the tower's archway, backing away from the colors, as Trundiir and Esizila neared the north archway. Another *Seb'Ner* fell from above with a thud as a motionless lump in between his other guardsmen in the archway. *What in Kur is happening?* Aren started wondering what he was in the middle of as a pair of white lightning bolts struck from a concealed area beyond the tower. Both guardsmen shook and reeled in pain at the white light, then went staggering backward and out of view to the left of the archway. Rogaan passed by Aren in a run, as Aren realized he now stood some fifteen strides short of the tower preparing to summon a shield as soon as he needed it. Pax, Suhd, and Dajil went stumbling past Aren's right, as well, both brother and sister giving Aren an odd look, not knowing what to think of him having stopped.

Inside the tower and running into the southern archway, Trundiir suddenly jumped into the air and side-kicked Esizila on his right, knocking him off balance and down onto the timbers. A large, curved blade whistled over Esizila's head as he fell. The blade struck stone, cutting into it deeply. Trundiir fell to the timbers and rolled past the red and black metal-armored arm, now pulling the blade free of the tower's stone. Rolling to his feet, Trundiir held the *Seb'Ner's* sword he had won earlier now in two hands, facing this dangerous adversary. Rogaan stopped inside the north archway with an arrow drawn. He fired with that ringing sound echoing in the tower and the arrow disappearing beyond the south archway. Aren heard a *clunk* as if the arrow hit metal it couldn't penetrate. Having regained his feet and with sword drawn, Esizila made to launch himself into the fight at a target concealed from his eyes by the stone. Rogaan made a motion with his bow and head warning him off, then fired another singing arrow that sounded as ineffective as the first. Strangely, the guardsman complied, readying himself to strike in surprise. Somewhere in the tower, Daluu manifested something Aren felt but was unfamiliar with, except for it had an element of lightning. The *Kabiri* had not only just manifested but now was exalting, building it in the Power.

Ignoring Trundiir's raised sword charge, Esizila's ambush, and Rogaan's careening arrows, a tall red and black-armored figure stepped into the archway filling it. The armor looked similar to eur armor worn by those who could afford such, with a partially closed face helm that darkly concealed the eyes of the wearer. Both the arms and legs of the warrior were covered in the scale like mesh with feet booted and hands gauntleted. All the red and black armor appeared to be made of red and black-colored metal scales and plates. The warrior's only exposed flesh was his jaw and that behind a short, yellow-white beard.

Trundiir's sword landed on the warrior's back with a solid *clunk* as Esizila's sword struck the warrior's midsection with another solid *clunk*. The warrior, taller than the Ebon Circle guardsman by a head, backhanded Esizila, sending him off the timbers and backward where he landed unseen to Aren. Rogaan had drawn his second and last specially prepared arrow and had it at full draw; yet, the half Tellen appeared hesitant to fire.

The inner tower suddenly lit up brilliantly with lightning dancing all about the red and black-armored warrior. The *Kabiri's* Agni Powers attack caused discomfort to the one in the red and black armor, enough to cause him to step backwards into Trundiir's incessant grunting attacks with *clunk* after *clunk* of futile sword strikes at the warrior's back. Aren felt the new vibrations, but they manifested so fast he couldn't yell out in alarm. As the warrior raised a hand at the *Kabiri*, Rogaan decided to act, sending a singing arrow at the red and black armor. The arrow sank into the chest of the warrior, who stood motionless, staring down at the half-primitive arrow with the broadhead punched through his armor.

"Ahhh . . ." the red and black warrior spoke out in a deep, rumbling voice. "You surprise me again, Roga of the Blood An."

The warrior then pulled the arrow from his chest with a grunt, deforming the arrow shaft in his gauntleted hand as he did. He examined the bloodstained blue metal broadhead. "*Nizi'barzil*. You and your father need to be made smiths for the gods.

"Such little gratitude for my bringing you back to this *Light*," the warrior chastised Rogaan as he tossed the broken arrow and blue steel broadhead at the half Tellen's boots. While the warrior parlayed, Aren sensed the vibrations of him healing himself. Turning his attention on Aren, he gave warning to Rogaan. "I'll trouble with you in moments."

Oh, dung! Oh, dung! Aren in reflex manifested a vaporous shield between him and the warrior and then exalted it with everything he had. He felt the Powers being summoned by the warrior, and it almost frightened Aren into not being capable of thinking.

"I cannot allow you to see him freed!" the warrior announced as he unleashed the Powers on Aren.

Aren felt the Power just before seeing it come at him in waves of blues, violets, and reds. Pushed in front of the wave, the air seemed to resist the Powers, then . . . annihilation with tiny strokes of lightning riding its front. In the moments it traveled the twenty and more strides to him, Aren felt it as powerful and terrible. One last time Aren exalted his shield . . . his only defense but feared it was no match for this attack. The waves slammed into Aren's shield with a physical force knocking him back. Struggling to stay standing, he managed to keep his feet, as the air around him felt alive with lightning, stinging him everywhere as he watched in horror his shield being gnawed away. The waves kept pushing on him. Aren pushed back as much as he could but felt he was losing, as the sound of his Agni-created shield being annihilated deafened him in a roar of crackling. Aren closed his eyes, waiting for it to do the same to him. Silence took hold on the bridge except for the light swirl of the wind. The force pushing him gone. Aren opened his eyes to see the timbers beneath his feet sizzling much the same as his tunic and pants. Painful blisters rose in spots on his wrists and hands where directly exposed to the Powers. *I'm Alive!* Having exerted so much defending himself, Aren felt exhausted, dizzy, and out of breath.

Looking up, Aren found the red and black warrior standing in the tower's northern archway as if surprised the Evendiir remained alive. With a frustrated growl, the warrior made to attack him again. Aren felt it . . . the same as the last. He tried to defend himself by manifesting another shield. His concentration failed him . . . nothing. Desperation started filling him while Aren watched helplessly death, in this red and black form, staring him in the face. Slower came the attack. The warrior's Agni Powers manifesting this time seemed slower than the last. *He's exalting it.* Aren realized with horror the warrior meant not only to make him *lightless* but annihilated. *I can't withstand it. Where to go?* Aren looked about finding no cover. Blades striking and dancing off metal drew his attention back to the warrior where he found Pax striking him repeatedly. The red and black warrior completely ignored Pax. *Where to go?* Nothing. There was no place to hide. *Jump from the bridge* was all Aren saw as a last chance to live—and a bad one at that.

Aren exhaled in defeat. *I'll not survive the leap.* He stared at the warrior as the exalting manifestation chosen to annihilate him was almost ready to be unleashed. A dark object passing in front of Aren right to left with a whoosh startled him. He jumped as his skin prickled. He felt the vibrations sweeping from his right to his left, in the trail of the dark featherwing as a scintillating crystalline wall of the Powers rose in the featherwing's wake. The wall stood between Aren and the warrior as red and black unleashed his Powers. Aren felt and watched the waves of blues, violets, and reds slamming into the crystalline wall where it exploded into a sheet of lightning so bright Aren had to shield his eyes with his blistered hands. It lasted moments, then was gone . . . all of the Powers. Peeking from behind his pained hands, Aren saw more of the bridge's timbers sizzling, except for those from where the featherwing had placed the wall. Aren exhaled with a sigh of relief.

"Curse you Ebons!" the red and black-armored warrior yelled after the dark featherwing. Returning his gaze on Aren, the warrior drew his heavy bladed sword. "Then we will do this with bloodstains."

Aren watched in horror as the warrior took his first step at him. *What do I do now?* Wide-eyed, he froze in place. All he could do is stare at the Light-Taker closing on him. Suddenly, Rogaan appeared behind the warrior having jumped up on his back slipping his bow string over the red and black helm and using it as a garrote against the large warrior's neck.

"You will not harm him, *Vassal*!" Rogaan declared in a grunt. Aren could see the half Tellen's muscles strain as he spoke through gritted teeth. Rogaan used his body to pull back on his bow, tightening the metal garrote against the warrior's neck. Aren realized, for the first time, how big this warrior stood. Easily a head above Rogaan and with more bulk in that armor.

Vassal? Did Rogaan speak of him as . . . Vassal? Aren swallowed hard. *The warrior in battle with the Shunned on the Khaaron?* In Aren's quick scrutiny, this *Vassal* was more dangerous to him than the *Shunned*. *At least the Shunned had some demented plan for me. This Vassal wishes me lightless and obliterated.*

Aren had little hope Rogaan could stop this *Vassal* from obliterating him. Then, Trundiir and Esizila both drove their bodies into the *Vassal's* armored legs causing the warrior to stumble before regaining his balance. They continued grappling and fighting with fists and appendage-leveraged moves. The *Vassal* fought hard against them to keep his balance, striking them with sword pommel and his powerful gauntleted fist. The four of them grappled, sending themselves slamming up against the tower stonework, knocking loose and off chips of the larger blocks. Appearing in the tower archway, Daluu stood waving at Aren and the others to come and follow him quickly. His feet able to move now that he had a place to go that wasn't to his death, Aren ran, hoping to avoid the other four battling. When Pax and Suhd saw Aren approaching, they grabbed the wobbling Dajil and pulled her through the tower archways following Daluu in his dark Ebon Circle wears. Aren kept looking back at the four grappling like a father with three of his children at play. *Serious play.*

Several simultaneous vibrations alarmed Aren, causing him to stop and look back at his . . . *friends* in battle with a most powerful foe. Arcs of lightning sparked between the *Vassal's* red and black armor and the three. A swift kick to Trundiir, a stiff punch to Esizila, and a backward slamming of Rogaan against the block stone of the tower found all three of them on the timbers scrambling to not be the *Vassal's* first mark for his sword. *The vibrations are intensifying . . . becoming tremors.* Aren leaned left to peek around the *Vassal*, who was now looking at him from less than twenty strides. Behind the *Vassal* stood two figures. Aren recognized them both. Ezerus . . . and Luntanus Alum. He swallowed harder than before as he fought to control his own fear. The *Vassal* took notice of what held Aren's attention and turned to see what could be more important than to look his own death in the eyes.

"Aren!" Daluu's voice was somewhere behind him. "It's too dangerous to remain here."

"Come with us, mystic," Pax encouraged in his defiant way.

"Flee, Aren," Dajil's shaky voice most shocked Aren.

He was about to turn when the tremors shook his mind as a barrage of blue lights and lightning arced from the *Shunned* at the *Vassal*. The first volley struck the *Vassal's* back or an unseen shield of some kind, forcing the *Vassal* to stumble toward Aren. *That* caused Aren's heart to skip several beats. *Too close! Too close!* The *Vassal's* armor seemed to have somehow absorbed or thrown off the *Shunned's* attack, and now he turned to face his foe. He *Vassal* parried the second volley of blue lights and lightning from Luntanus Alum with his own manifestations of Agni Powers. The parried Powers found themselves blasting tower stone all around the *Vassal*, sending flying in all directions chipped and shattered shards of sharp rock. In the midst of the chaos, Rogaan and Trundiir collected up Esizila, and all set off running toward Aren. When they met up with him, they all turned to watch the wonder of light displays . . . dangerous displays of the Powers.

"Even with your renewed abilities, Enshag of the Dingiir . . ." the *Shunned* projected his voice with Agni Powers somehow Aren was certain of it, "you cannot stop me. And I cannot let you take them from me. Behold! Your temple is in flames, and *I* have the Agni keys."

The *Shunned* pointed west to the temple hills of Anza. A top one of the hills near where Aren and Rogaan experienced the Chorus of *Kunsag*, a temple was indeed engulfed in flames.

"You have always been a dragon of chaos . . . child of Tiamat," Enshag, the *Vassal*, declared. "You can never gain the *Ra'Sakti*. In your hands, the world will be all flames as you threaten the cosmos."

"And commanded by you with the *Ra'Sakti* in their hands," the *Shunned* retorted as he motioned a hand at Aren and the others standing behind Enshag, "the world is to be enslaved by you with the return of your kind."

Aren felt vibrations coming from both Enshag and the *Shunned*, no . . . more lengthy tremors in their exaltations, rapidly growing in strength . . . like nothing he felt before. "We need to leave."

"Yes. Quickly," Daluu added from somewhere behind. "We are witness to a new legend of days yet to be. They are joined in mortal battle . . . something we dare not be here to share."

Aren felt both the legends let loose unbridled Powers at each other. A rainbow of colors shaping the lines of Agni Powers colliding in between them, opposing walls of Powers battling to annihilate the other. It sparked and brightened, strengthening quickly as a sphere growing between them.

"Run," was all Aren said in a soft, disbelieving voice . . . with a sense of doom.

They all turned and ran as fast as they could to get as much distance from the battle as possible. As they reached the end of the timbers of the bridge and stepped on a flagstone and dirt area at the bridgehead, Aren turned to look, still unbelieving. The *Shunned* and *Vassal* were relentlessly still at each other. Neither yielding. He felt the Powers stronger than ever . . . immense. *How much of the world will break from it?*

The brown and white featherwing fluttered to a hurried landing just in front of them and spread its wings while facing them and its back to the battle. Aren felt more vibrations . . . a shield of some kind. Like the wall of scintillating crystalline the dark featherwing had manifested earlier.

"This is very grave," the Ebon Circle *Kabiri* announced to everyone. "Aren, set forth your shield and exalt it until you no longer stand. Everyone . . . get close and lie low."

Uncertain if they could survive what was coming, Aren focused on creating his vaporous shield as he felt the *Kabiri* manifesting his own and setting it inside of Aren's just outside the featherwing's manifested wall. He felt the wielded Agni Powers by the *Shunned* and Enshag starting to waver and spear uncontrollably. It was then Aren felt another manifestation, powerful in its own manner. Above. He looked up. Plunging through an opening in the gloomy clouds and toward the battle on the bridge was the dark featherwing. Its black feathers and outstretched talons engulfed in lightning that left a trail of burnt sky. The featherwing plunged in silence. The three Powers met. A brilliant flash forced Aren and the others to shield and advert their eyes as the ground shook violently, and the roar of wind rose in a moment of deafening sound. All went dark.

Chapter 37

Path's Veil

The choking air started to settle around them as some sunlight managed to penetrate the veil. His head and body hurt fiercely as he did his best to cough out the dirt and debris that found its way into his mouth and throat. An eerie silence filled the air all around. Nothing spoke in the wilds. No voices spoke from civilization. Tears filled his eyes trying to clear them of the same debris he coughed, and his face felt soaked in tears that flowed down his cheeks. At least, he hoped the wetness came from tears.

"Is everyone with breath?" Rogaan asked in a dulled manner while lying prone. Daluu and Esizila replied immediately, grunting and groaning, then started coughing. Pax and Suhd followed the same. Dajil groaned, then answered with a coughing fit. Aren remained silent, giving Rogaan concern he was badly injured . . . or worse. Then, in a prolonged groan, the Evendiir answered he was breathing.

"What was all of that?" Rogaan coughed out, expecting either Daluu or Aren to answer. Silence filled the air making him anxious that neither of them understood their shared experiences.

"Powers of the Agni," Daluu finally answered with a groan. "With a nasty adjunct of the master, a *Shunned*, and that Ancient."

"You speak of the gods," Aren commented, then spit out something. "I feared that was what I saw . . . and felt."

The group remained silent for long moments. Then, when they heard a weak caw, they struggled, regaining their feet and began looking for the featherwing. Esizila found it first after removing several large branches and fronds it was trapped under. The once brown and white feather shook off dirt and sticks clinging to its feathers, then jumped up onto a rock protruding above some loose debris. The Ebon Circle guardsman jumped back as if he feared touching it as it cawed more strongly, but with a sadness. It stared into the cloudy gray veil of dust still settling to the ground. It seemed to see something no one else could. The animal then took to cleaning its feathers. Unnerved by the featherwing's behaviors, the group began looking about for anything that would give knowledge of which direction Anza lay. The debris grew less solid as the moments passed, pulling back the veil hiding the wilds close to them. A mess was the wilds with fallen and broken trees, crushed bushes, large stone blocks thrown about, and broken branches and sundered plants filling in between. *Amazing none of us got struck or hurt by a tossed stone.*

As the cloud of debris thinned, Anza . . . or what was left of it, came into view. All stood in awe seeing the sun cast slanting shafts of light through the clouds across the desolation. Nothing remained of the bridge or the walls of the ravine separating Temple District from Coiner's District. The ravine now seemed wider. Even the ground under the bridge was scooped out to look like a bowl. It was now filling with waters from the rivers.

"Father . . ." Rogaan moaned.

"He never made it close to the . . . bridge," Dajil struggled to speak half in her squealing tones and half more huskily as she spoke through gritted teeth. Closest, Rogaan made to help her up from her knees. She weakly tried to wave him off, but Rogaan felt stubborn about getting her up and out of the tangle of broken branches. After several more attempts at waving him off, she eventually accepted his assistance to stand.

Looking at her face and eyes, Rogaan saw instantly she was in great pain. "Daluu, is there something you can do for her?"

"Possibly . . . She appears strong," the Ebon Circle *Kabiri* commented on his observation of her. "Though she bleeds in many places and those lashing stripes under her armor must hurt."

"Can you . . ." Rogaan asked again. He recalled the brutal whipping she received earlier.

"Yes . . . some," the *Kabiri* answered.

As the *Kabiri* mumbled and placed his hands on Dajil to complete his manifestations, Rogaan looked at Pax and Suhd. Suhd threw daggers at him in her stare as Pax stared wide-eyed at his sister.

"What?" Rogaan asked honestly with wide eyes on Suhd. Suhd said nothing. She just crossed her arms as she intensified her glare. Rogaan wanted Suhd to understand he wanted to return a small sense of gratitude to Dajil. "She is hurt . . . and she helped me in the Farratum jail."

Suhd's brows raised, giving Rogaan that "indeed" look. Pax gave Rogaan the big wave-off, signaling him to not ask or explain anything more with both his eyes and waving his hand at his side while trying not to let his sister see him do it. Suhd then made a "humph" and stomped off toward Aren and the still-grounded featherwing.

"Ahhh-gra-ahhhhhh," Dajil groaned.

Rogaan looked back to Dajil and Daluu finding the *Kabiri* holding the *Tusaa'Ner* guardswoman by the head keeping her from falling over. Dajil looked worse than before the *Kabiri* did his healing on her. Waving Daluu off and rejecting any more assistance, she stood on her own.

"I'm better," she said in a tone unlike her high-pitched barking when giving orders. Her continued wincing told of wounds still painful, but evidently bearable to her. "My gratitude, *Kabiri*."

Rogaan thought her tone pleasing and started to stare at her. Dajil saw Rogaan and gave him her own "humph" and walked off as she spoke at Rogaan. "Don't see me like that."

Rogaan watched openmouthed as Dajil took a spot not far off with her back to him, then stared at the mess of Anza. He looked to Daluu, then Pax for help or at least understanding of what he did wrong. Both appeared not to want to get in the middle of things by looking away and at their feet. A heavy slap on his back surprised Rogaan. Looking at who struck him found a grinning Trundiir.

"The world is afire. Anza suffering a destruction of the ages. Legends of old seek powers to subjugate us, and the ancient gods threaten return, fulfilling the prophecies ending us all." Trundiir spoke loudly in his deep voice as he made a sweeping wave of arm at the desolated Anza, then patted Rogaan's shoulder. "And you, my Tellen friend, have woman troubles."

Daluu and Pax grinned, then started snickering. So did Esizila and Aren. Suhd and Dajil just glared at them over their shoulders. Rogaan uttered a grunt of what he wanted to be words, then gave up.

"You will never win where the wind is wrong." Trundiir winked at him as Rogaan realized his mistake. Dajil now stood downwind of him. Rogaan saw her deliberate act moving to keep her sway from influencing him. She knew and took that influence away. Looking at her, she glanced back and nodded, then returned to her staring at Anza. Trundiir then purposely changed subjects. "At least you still have your *Light* . . . as do we all."

"We be free of dem?" Pax asked. "Have der *Lights* been taken?"

"The *Shunned* of legend, a dragon crafted to destroy the gods, and an Ancient . . . a god?" Daluu asked his own question to Pax and the group.

"Who is this Ancient you speak of?" Dajil asked without taking her eyes from Anza.

"Enshag . . . is an Ancient, a serpent Dingiir of the warrior spirit, knowledge, and Protector of the Ancients. He's the creator god of the *Sentii*," Daluu answered, almost reciting from memory. After a long moment of silence, Daluu looked about at everyone and found them staring at him with slack jaws in disbelief. He swallowed, then offered further explanation. "Histories of the Ancients are taught to all *Kabiri* of the Ebon Circle."

"You knew who he was and didn't speak of it to us?" accused Aren.

"No. Only after I heard the *Shunned* speak his name did I come to know who we did battle with," explained Daluu.

"He calls himself the *Vassal*," Rogaan added to the conversation.

"*Vassal* . . ." mumbled Daluu. The *Kabiri* appeared to be trying to remember something but what it eluded him.

"How we be gettin' across da river and back ta Anza?" asked Pax.

"No crossing those swift waters or the snapjaws," Trundiir stated with firm confidence in his knowledge.

"He speaks true," Daluu confirmed. "Some have attempted. None have succeeded. All *lightless*. No getting across the river unless you can *travel*."

"*Travel?*" Pax asked.

"Using the Powers of Agni to move from one place to another without walking," answered the *Kabiri*. "Just as Enshag . . . the *Vassal* appeared on the bridge in front of us."

"The *Vassal* can . . . *travel?*" asked Rogaan. Alarmed at first, Daluu thought the *Vassal* was likely not *lightless*, then revealing him as being the Ancient Enshag, and that Enshag has the power to *travel*. And . . . *Enshag has plans for me*. Rogaan exhaled loudly trying to control his growing fear that this was not over. *Not close to being over.*

"What do we do?" asked Aren before making his thoughts known. "We can't stay here. Even if we found a way back to Anza, they'd be hunting and jailing us."

"Be der another bridge crossin' da river?" Pax asked with a hopeful tone.

"My remembrance of this place is . . . no," Trundiir answered.

"None to my knowledge," added Daluu. He looked to his Ebon Circle guardsman who shook his head as well.

"As I remember, there is a mine some marches into the mountains . . ." Trundiir started to offer a plan to survive the wilds.

"No!" Suhd protested in a hushed scream. "No one can be goin' into dese mountains. It be forbidden."

"We have little choice, young one," Trundiir replied.

"You can no take us der . . ." Tears were freely flowing from Suhd's eyes. "We be losin' our *Lights* ta da mountains . . . or worse."

"Da Ancients," Pax added.

"The mine offers protection from the wilds," Trundiir explained. "These mountains are no place to be out in the open by day and certainly not by—"

"The nights are certain death without a large guard," Dajil joined the discussion. She winched as she moved yet made no complaint. "It's why we were to have so many on our journey to Vaikuntaars."

"Will the Dark Robe come for you?" Rogaan asked of the *Kabiri* with a mix of hope and trepidation. Everyone looked at Rogaan wondering if he were talking to them.

"No," the *Kabiri* soberly answered. "He will come for *you* and your Evendiir friend."

"Why them?" Dajil winched out her words.

"They hold the keys to Vaikuntaars . . . I think," answered the *Kabiri*.

"Some things make sense now," Dajil mumbled, just loud enough for the others to hear. Then, she offered. "Ah . . . Anza's *Tusaa'Ner* put supplies at the mine for our journey."

"When were ya goin' ta tell us of dat?" Pax asked with an accusatory tone.

Dajil gave Pax an unhappy slit-eye stare at his question and tone. She looked to Daluu and Trundiir, then spoke. "I suppose you two are leading us there?"

A caw rang out from the brown and white featherwing, startling everyone. It took off, climbing then circling them twice before heading off into the mountains.

"I think he is leading the way," the *Kabiri* spoke as he followed the featherwing with his gaze. Daluu's eyes suddenly went wide as he stared off into the distance. "Ah! I remember the song . . ."

Ancients sent to heavens high,
Watch their creations live and die,
Never to touch thy earthly ground,
While thy accord remains sound,
A lost son finds his way,
Opens thy forbidden on thy day,
Son of Sons Seven calls the Fathers,
Returning Powers to thy temples,
Where thy Vassal Awaits.

Epilogue

Coils Old and New

V iscous fluids flowing from her mouth and nose alarmed Nikki as she started to feel and hear again. She hoped it was drool but feared she bled from the intense tasering she recalled suffering. Voices vague at first sounded as if in an argument. Opening her eyes, she found a blur of darkness with shadows moving above her . . . *I think*. No longer did she feel pressure on her chest from the armored boot. *Where am I?* she asked herself, feeling disconnected from the voices and her surroundings except for the stone or concrete she lay upon.

"You are lax in respect and becoming a . . . bother!" That familiar voice filled Nikki with dread.

In the voice . . . no, she felt it deeper, *conflict*, within him, as Nikki quickly started regaining her vision. She now made out Agent 19, still standing above in her gray suit and what appeared still to be the patio area with Tyr super soldiers filling the rest of her vision. Agent 19 never took her eyes from something or someone else while addressing the cloaked shadow. She addressed the shadow in a low but forceful tone that was almost delicately done.

"I am fulfilling my duty," Nikki heard Agent 19's voice, filled with defiance as her words trembled. "She is mine . . . as are they . . . to be used for Him."

Several of the Tyr turned their heads at Agent 19's utterance of "Him." The blond agent seemed to feel uncomfortable at their gaze and in what appeared a familiar situation. She then added as if pressured to do so, "Insh'Allah."

"I will consent you them when I am finished," the cloaked figure told the gray-suited agent. "If you are able to . . . succeed. They are more lax in respect than you and frightfully more dangerous."

"I can manage with my Tyr," Agent 19 quietly boasted. The cloaked one simply gave out a dissatisfied grunt.

Something felt strange about Nikki's throat. Reaching up, she felt a metallic collar ring solidly locked around her neck. A flash of panic rippled through her as dread filled Nikki that she was somehow made a prisoner . . . and still in the hands of Agent 19 . . . and Him.

"What is this?" Nikki croaked out with a quivering voice. How much quivering came from fear or her trembling muscles she didn't know.

"I wouldn't play with that," Agent 19 warned Nikki while keeping her eyes on Rogaan and Aren . . . and occasional glancing at her cloaked companion. "Trigger it, and you're dead in a couple of seconds. It's called a Kill Collar."

"Why?" Confusion filled Nikki, her voice still with a tremble. "You're the law enforcement for the U.N., aren't you? The law doesn't do things like this. I'm no danger."

Irritation washed through Nikki. Not her emotions . . . His. She decided to lie quietly for a moment hoping the sensation would pass. As the seconds ticked off in her head, Nikki continued sensing His irritation . . . atop determination and hidden desperation. Agent 19 now seemed to be ignoring her while not about to provide answers to her questions. Instead, her attention was back on Rogaan and Aren, who appeared to be positioning themselves for a fight to come. Nikki felt them too. Aren with guarded confidence and Rogaan with his headstrong determination that meant he would see whatever was to come to the very end.

"Forget of us?" Rogaan sardonically asked. He no longer tended to the still-unconscious Miller. Dunkle now looked after him as Anders stood near. Anders's eyes were fixed on Nikki filled with painful worry.

Nikki felt Aren manifesting and exalting as if expecting a battle of the ages. He did it quietly and without much body movement. She also felt the cloaked one do so as well, also without making much of a show of it externally.

"I have need of the Dari you carry," the cloaked one spoke in Antaalin to Rogaan and Aren.

"You have no such need," Aren rebuffed, also in Antaalin. Now, loaded for ravers and more in Agni manifestations, Aren verbally engaged their longtime nemesis. "You have weaker forms for healing and restitution."

"Another has need of stronger healing," answered the cloaked one.

"Their bodies cannot endure it," Aren rejected.

"We three may be the only . . . mortals able to consume food and drink made of the Dari." Rogaan also rejected the idea of allowing these modern humans to consume the ancient foods of the gods. He then added, "And the Dingir sustenance always gives a chance to see our *Lights* taken from us."

"Who are you allied with, Ezerus?" asked Aren in a tone as serious as Nikki ever heard from him. "Dari-made drink heals the body and mind. Dari-made food prolongs life and may grant use of the Agni if one keeps his *Light*. The gift of the Ancients comes with dangers."

"He too wants the gift . . . again," Ezerus replied.

"Again?" Rogaan asked.

"Provide me the Dari; you can have this one in exchange . . . without the poisonous restraint." Ignoring Rogaan while casually sweeping his hand at Nikki, Ezerus cut to the heart of what he wanted and was willing to give up. Nikki realized she was his leverage and that he was indifferent to her living. She felt that of him. Ezerus continued speaking in Antaalin, obviously to keep everyone but him and the other two from the Bolivian cave from knowing what transpired between them. "The other whore is yours, as well. An irritation I can be without. And her . . . *Super soldiers* should make good play for you. They are with agendas separate from us. You should end them."

"What of your . . . *super soldiers?*" Rogaan asked.

"My *Cmpax Soldats?*" Ezerus sounded almost playful, then turned solemn. "They are what is called Russian. Big, strong, with no happy mood. They fight because that is what they are, not because they follow king or Ancient. Some are too good at following orders."

"More men-machines . . ." Still speaking in Antaalin, Aren carried a strong sense of disdain for the cybernetic warriors. It was so strong that Nikki easily felt it despite her present predicament.

"We have come forward in time to a wondrous new world." Ezerus slowly swept his hand across the expanse of the resort. Rogaan and Aren flinched at his arm motions and looked ready to unleash all they had. Nikki felt both of them alarmed at Ezerus's wave. "A new world with new friends to make and some old friends to be reacquainted."

"Friends . . . *you*, Ezerus?" Rogaan mocked as he spat his words in Antaalin.

"Many merits to you making few my friends," countered Ezerus in a disdainful tone.

"Agnis would destroy those of this world." Aren changed the focus of their talk back to the matter at hand. "Wielding Agni powers cause want and craving to inflict upon those without the gift."

"It will end this world as it ended ours," Rogaan added. "These peoples are not ready for such ability."

"They are already destroying themselves," Ezerus stated in Antaalin as if lecturing on his observations. "Humans of this age are unkind to each other, purposely deceiving in everyday affairs, claiming injustices and slights as a tool to get at what they want, and seeking the destruction of those they find disagreement with. You must see it . . . a few days observing their news tells much."

"Not all behave in the manner of which you speak," Rogaan challenged.

"You have not been consuming enough of their talk and news, ol' friend," Aren observed of Rogaan. "We have been in shelter among good peoples of this age. My visits to their world's . . . *Web* tell of great strife among the city-states, deep mistrust in the peoples, and the Game of Houses played by many in their lofty halls and in their streets."

"I have no wish to see another troubled world end," Rogaan growled.

Nikki felt Aren's distraught before he spoke, more to Rogaan than Ezerus. "Their archives, their . . . history, their . . . news, give vision to a world of people split between their religions and further split by their . . . they call it . . . *politics*."

"I am aware of their . . . *politics*." Rogaan growled in agreement with Aren's words. "I see their . . . *technologies* all around, watching their peoples with what I suspect is great scorn. They are only different in the tools used from what we left burning."

"Their archives reveal their rulers . . . their authorities . . . leaders of *governments*," Aren seemed to feel a need to complete his friend's thoughts and education in current affairs. "The authorities . . . *government* leaders, who believe in their *governments* to solve the people's problems, have largely won out . . . tyrants using the authority of their states enslaving populations by denying them resources and services forcing compliance."

"When were you to speak of this?" Rogaan asked in frustration of Aren.

"My apologies . . ." replied Aren with a sincere tone of regret. "I know how much you value individual freedoms—"

"The people of this world call it *liberty*," Rogaan interrupted as he looked at the metal poles with cameras and other sensors hidden behind black glass. They were all about the resort. He looked west to the sea and found something new. Nikki felt him touch the presence. Concentrating on seeing vague images in Rogaan's mind, Nikki saw the fleet of hovering black drones in the distant dark skies revealed to him by the presence. Flashes from a growing crowd of onlookers, many in their costumes and others in less, and with some at the boundary of the patio. Nikki felt Rogaan's concern for these bystanders.

"Forget of us?" Ezerus mocked Rogaan's earlier mocking of him.

Rogaan returned his attention on Ezerus and his Cmpax Soldats, the Tyr, and Agent 19. Nikki felt Rogaan's resolve building. She wasn't able to figure out to what it was building, but the half Tellen was achieving great strength in it.

"The Dari?" Ezerus ask in a tone matching his shortening patience.

"You say you have reacquainted with old friends?" Rogaan seemed to be making a point of something to Ezerus. "Who?"

"I am not to reveal him . . ." Ezerus replied in a sneer.

"That reduces much of the possibilities," Aren commented to Ezerus's frustrated reply revealing something he had not intended.

"One . . . actually," Rogaan corrected his friend. Nikki felt Rogaan and Aren silently exchanging some understanding, but what she couldn't figure out. "Ezerus, you said this acquaintance wants the Dari for healing and to regain his body's and mind's bond with the Agnis?"

"That's . . . his goal," Ezerus flatly replied.

"I saw into the minds of the Tyr I speared with my gauntlet on the Im'Kas . . ." Nikki felt an unsettled feeling fill Rogaan. "They were devoted volunteers to their cause, their religion. They endured great pains having their Tree of Life changed, severely, and greater pain endured when their bodies were cut, and nonliving parts made whole to them. The mixing . . . their minds now tortured by *technologies* and control from their authorities. They are no longer their own in choice. A crescent moon atop that blue symbol on their armor . . . what does that mean?"

Rogaan stood pointing at the Tyr closest to Nikki. Still lying on the ground with the Kill Collar rubbing her skin, she couldn't turn her head or move to see what he pointed at. Agent 19 seemed uncomfortable. To Nikki's knowledge, she didn't understand Antaalin or what was being spoken, but when Rogaan pointed at the Tyr near her, she visibly looked at it.

"United Nations," is all Ezerus said.

"Makes for better understanding . . ." Aren spoke. "The Crescent Moon controls that government."

"Not all of it . . ." Ezerus clarified with some disdain.

"You're adversary to them?" Aren asked, though sounding more like an accusation. "Is that why your Cmpax Soldats watch the Tyr ready to attack? Why the two closest to you watch you so closely?"

Nikki became alarmed at Aren's revealing that the super soldiers around her were at odds with each other. They had impressive arsenals and were a danger of blowing up everything. In her present predicament, she wished she had paid more attention . . . *any* attention to politics to understand better who was doing what to whom. Nikki then felt Rogaan interacting with the presence again. He whispered something to Aren she couldn't make out, but the feeling she sensed from them was that of steel-clad resolve.

"I see you have spied them." Ezerus made a rhetorical statement to Rogaan and Aren.

"Your flock of . . . what do you call . . . *drones* to our west . . ." Rogaan stared directly at Ezerus as he revealed some of what he saw from the presence. "Or more of your Cmpax Soldats jumping from their high-flying chariot or the fast-flying disk ship approaching far from the east?"

A flash of alarm from Ezerus struck Nikki at Rogaan's reference to the discoid-shaped ship. Ezerus must have visibly shown his alarm as Rogaan and Aren seized on it as a weakness.

"Your master—" Aren started to dig into Ezerus's emotions.

"Not my master . . ." Ezerus denied with a snarling growl. Nikki felt a growing anger in Ezerus, born of frustration at not having complete control of his actions and decisions.

"You have not challenged me for the Wind," Rogaan revealed seeking some acknowledgment from Ezerus. "Not once have I felt you poking at my bond with it. He has your *Ra'Sakti* . . . your sword . . . does he not?"

Nikki felt Ezerus struggle mightily to rein in his emotions and focus on the task he was growing desperate to succeed at.

Ezerus stiffened his back, knowing what he was about to ask would be denied. "The Dari?"

"No," Rogaan answered.

"A fight you will not win," Ezerus warned.

"With us, Ezerus . . . It is *always* a fight," Rogaan nodded to Aren.

A chill sensation struck Nikki as Ezerus started manifesting something powerful. Fearing what he was intending . . . most likely killing everyone, she desperately screamed into Ezerus's mind, "No!"

Ezerus staggered at Nikki's intrusion. Confused a moment and looking around for his attacker, he then realized what had happened. The cloaked shadow turned his fierce glare on defenseless Nikki.

Another chill washed over Nikki as Aren quickly executed a manifestation. She immediately felt pain as a cold-hot sensation snapped into existence about her neck, then painfully pushed her head to one side, twisting her neck. She wanted to scream, but whatever new was around her throat prevented her. Horrified at the sound of the Kill Collar activating, Nikki stared at Rogaan as she waited for the prickling in her neck and for her death to soon follow. Nothing. Realizing Rogaan now held his drawn blue steel bow . . . aimed directly at her, Nikki felt terror explode through her. Rogaan released his arrow. It came directly at her. She was unable to move. Her neck held immobile. The arrow came at her eyes, then fell away slightly passing just to her left and below her jaw. She felt the arrow strike to the side of her neck as a metallic clinging sounded out. The Kill Collar went flying, broken, off to Nikki's right, dripping its deadly venom. Fearing she had been injected with venom, Nikki raised her right hand to her throat to check for blood. A wetness atop a strangely smooth surface surrounding her neck now covered her hand. Fearing it her blood and venom, she looked at her hand . . . to find nothing but a clear film of wetness covering her fingers. Relief pulsed through her as the immobile manifested thing about her neck disappeared in a glow of fire, stingingly singeing her neck.

Chaos exploded all about her. Gunfire erupted from the Tyr trying to kill Rogaan and Aren and some of the Cmpax Soldats. The Soldats returning fire with electromagnetic guns built into their arms quickly downed several of the Tyr. Projectiles whizzed by Nikki as they flew everywhere striking low walls, poles, robotic service units, ALFs, and downed transhumans . . . killing them. Some of the crowd near lay dead on the ground with most of the remaining now running understanding this was not a skit but a real battle with death. Still, some idiots stood in harm's way taking videos and images. Aren protected Dunkle and the rest with his shielding manifestations while Rogaan deflected bullets meant for him by his armor and a blue steel buckler now on his left forearm. He continued raining arrows at Ezerus and the Cmpax Soldats while almost ignoring the Tyr. Rogaan's arrows easily punched through the Soldats, then returned to him to be reabsorbed into his arm guards. The Soldats that lived after an arrow strike concentrated their fire on Rogaan, their EM-propelled projectiles either bouncing off or shattering on Rogaan's blue, red, and black steel armor. Ezerus and two of his Cmpax Soldats battled Rogaan and Aren with more EM weapons and the cloaked one's manifestations of light and lightning. Aren parried most of Ezerus's manifestation, leaving only a few of the light and lightning strikes to hit Rogaan. Nikki felt Rogaan in pain but resolved and determined to win the day. Ezerus too was in pain from Rogaan's arrows and possibly some of the flying bullets. He bled from his arms, his left leg, and a spot to the left of his heart and lungs.

Looking around, Nikki realized she had been forgotten in the battle. A powerful sense of relief filled her. *I must get somewhere protected.* She got to her feet and took no more than four steps before she felt the electrifying grip of Ezerus's scintillating vaporous tendril wrap around her. *Damn . . . I can't move.* Anger, then panic, filled Nikki as she felt a sentient connection between her and Ezerus . . . and something . . . someone else. It frightened her more than she expected or wanted, making it difficult for her to form a logical thought. He drew her to him no matter how hard she fought against it. As he drew Nikki to his left side, he nodded to his Cmpax Soldats who sent a volley of EM-propelled projectiles and several micro-rockets each at the others. Ezerus manifested a swirling man-sized ring of light not far from them in the opposite direction. The resort lit up as a sequence of thundering booms deafened Nikki as much as struck her with powerful shock waves and flying debris. Disoriented, she tried her best to make sense of what was happening. Ezerus still had her wrapped up in his vaporous tendril as he was walking quickly toward the step-gate. *No. If he takes me through that, they'll never find me.*

"*Silence, whore,*" came into Nikki's mind. She realized Ezerus was able to hear her thoughts. Another ripple of panic gripped her. She struggled against the tendril vapors. Nothing. *They aren't affected by anything I do physically.* She caught sight of Ezerus's left forearm. *Bleeding . . . significantly. He's wounded.* A thought came into her mind that she quickly tried to hide from Ezerus by thinking of something else . . . the glowing swirl of the ring ahead. *A last hope.* Timing the swing of his arm, Nikki reached out with her right hand and grabbed Ezerus's forearm, more specifically, his open, bleeding wound. She dug her fingers in. At first and despite the pain she inflicted, Ezerus simply looked at her passively as he continued walking without pulling his arm away. Then, his eyes shot wide open as he yanked his arm away from her grip. He stopped walking, surprising his Soldat escorts.

"Keep moving, wizard," one of the Soldats commanded in his synthetic voice.

Ezerus ignored the command as he looked at his upper forearm. Nikki sensed Ezerus's concern grow more intensely as she felt the sickening sensation fill his body. The step-gate started to flicker as did the scintillation of the vaporous tendrils holding her. Ezerus swayed, then staggered. Nikki felt his thoughts turn unfocused. The step-gate vanished, plunging them all into a gloom with only some of the resort's emergency lights still working. The tendrils restraining Nikki started to give a little, then vanished.

"You whore . . ." Ezerus dropped to a knee, struggling to remain conscious. He spoke in Antaalin. Nikki felt him fiercely fighting the effects of what she put into his veins. Then, to her surprise, she felt another mind but didn't know where it came from. It wasn't Rogaan or Aren. "You poisoned him."

"Damn right I poisoned him," Nikki spoke back at the words. "Wait, what are you talking about, 'him'? Why are you talking in the third—?"

A powerful grip on Nikki's right forearm sent streaks of pain through her body. She saw the electrified left gauntlet of the Cmpax Soldat crushing her arm as she fell to her knees. She looked up into the dark facemask of the unknown soldier as he looked down on her impassively. The shocking electrification kept pulsating through her body. *He's not letting up. He means to kill me.* Nikki felt her heart flutter. *He's killing me.* Lightning streaked around and past her, brightening her surroundings. Ezerus fell to the ground. The other Soldat returned fire at something or someone. The Cmpax Soldat shocking Nikki to death reconfigured his right forearm into another weapon. Then, it fell to the ground, severed from the rest of the Soldat's arm. A blue steel sword blade then viciously slid in front of Nikki's eyes, as if used in a stabbing attack. Its blade edge facing upward. With a sound like a zipper, the blade sliced upward splitting the Soldat from chest to head into two halves that begrudgingly fell away from each other. The gauntlet crushing her arm pulled free of her forearm as it fell to the ground with the rest of the transhuman corpse inside. Standing with blade high in another ready-to-strike stance, Rogaan looked to the remaining Cmpax Soldat standing over Ezerus. The Soldat fired a burst of EM-propelled projectiles that Rogaan, easily blocked and deflected with his buckler and armor. The Soldat then reconfigured both of his forearms into the same weapons the dead Soldat just had as a large, disked-shaped object flew to a stop overhead, appearing without warning or with any sound.

"You do not see that regularly," remarked Rogaan in English, looking up at the classic discoid-shaped UFO. "It is more imposing close then from the eyes of the Wind."

A shaft of white light emitted from the underside of the ship engulfing Ezerus and his Soldat guardian directly below. The two started levitating, then were drawn into the ship.

"No, you don't!" Aren challenged the taking up of their foes. He stood not far away from her and Rogaan. Anders and Dunkle stood next to Aren and on either side of Miller who looked to be disoriented. They started moving in Nikki's direction, helping Miller make his way.

Nikki felt Aren manifest something she was unfamiliar with, then started exalting it. *Oh, he's meaning to do something destructive.* She felt the malevolence in his intent. Rogaan sheathed his sword, then willed his *Ra'Sakti* to form his bow. An arrow formed as he drew the metallic weapon. Its broadhead started glowing blue, then intensely white. He unleashed it at the hovering ship. Nikki thought he would have gone for a kill shot on Ezerus, but instead, the arrow passed through some kind of energy field surrounding the UFO before viciously cutting and embedding into the ship's hull. Nikki felt Rogaan calm himself, blocking out distractions. He touched the presence. The half Tellen was collecting information on the ship, sending it to the presence, above.

Aren unleashed a ball of fire . . . no, plasma, at the hovering ship. It struck the ship's underside just as Ezerus and the Soldat disappeared into the UFO. The ball of fire erupted into a brilliant flash of red-orange before dissipating. The silvery surfaced disk-shaped ship appeared to bear darkened scorch markers on its underside. Yet, it hovered steadily. Suddenly, flashes of light pulsed from the ship. Aren threw up his arms defensively just a moment before the first pulse of light struck his Agni-created shield. The pulses hammered Aren's Agni defense sending residual energies in all directions, ripping apart everything they struck. Several exploded the concrete near Dunkle, Anders, and Miller, sending all three of them flying. One landed next to Nikki and Rogaan, where the half Tellen turned and used his armored body to shield Nikki from the blast. Both went tumbling, coming to a stop a short distance away. The energy pulses stopped.

Dunkle was helping Miller to his feet when the ship fired another volley of energy pulses down at Aren. The Evendiir staggered backward, then to his knees as he angled his Agni defenses, sending the residual energy pulses away from the rest of them and toward more Cmpax Soldats approaching from where they first confronted Ezerus. Nikki felt Rogaan's intense dread in his concern for Aren's survival as he stood up facing the UFO while reaching out to the presence. Nikki felt him connect with it. It felt powerful. With an intense growl, Rogaan made a motion like he was throwing the ship to his right. The UFO shuddered, then rotated in protest in the direction Rogaan motioned, redirecting its energy pulses onto the squad of Cmpax Soldats approaching Aren. Several Soldats blew apart when struck. The others scattered for cover.

Miller staggered up to Nikki, his white skull on black shirt now torn in several places. His costume weapons belt and harness were damaged in several spots. He bled from multiple cuts, some fairly large. Upon reaching Nikki, he stretched out his right arm for help to stay standing. Nikki embraced the bleeding Miller, trying to keep him from falling.

"Dunkle gave me this and said for us to get to the tower over there." Miller spoke lethargically with his Southern drawl heavier than usual. He held out a strange-looking hexagon-shaped data chip made of what looked like blue steel. As Miller flipped it over, Nikki gasped when she saw and realized embedded in the blue steel was a small dark-colored Agni stone. "He's helping Anders back there and will catch up."

A light pulse exploded on concrete not far away, tossing up the man-made stone, striking them with bits and pieces of the resort. Looking to see what happened found Rogaan with his *Ra'Sakti* shaped into a shield, like the first time she saw it back on the Wind Runner. He appeared to have deflected the pulse with his shield.

"We must go," Miller insisted. "I have Dunkle's data files. They're important to get to HQ."

Nikki looked to Rogaan for an answer of what to do. The half Tellen returned a conflicted look. Nikki knew he felt it too. Keeping his eyes on the ship above, Rogaan called out to Aren in a loud voice in the Antaalin tongue, "How are you enduring?"

"I'm not beaten yet," Aren replied loudly in Antaalin, but with uncharacteristic bravado. "Get to the step-gate in the tower. I'll be with Dunkle and Anders. We'll be right after you."

"More drones approach," Rogaan warned his old friend of what he saw from the Wind's eyes.

"Then, give this flying ship another spin and get running," Aren demanded of his ol' friend as he joined up with Dunkle who was now half-carrying Anders. "I'll keep the rest of these Soldats *Tusaa'Ner* from reaching the tower."

Nikki felt torn at leaving Anders behind, wounded as he was. She felt her own feelings mix with Rogaan's at leaving Aren behind to hold back the ship, drones, and Cmpax Soldats. Her bond with the half Tellen told her he reluctantly made a decision affecting them all.

"Aren, Heavenly Hammer." In Antaalin, Rogaan yelled out to Aren after he defended himself from another volley of light pulses. More Soldats suffered injury from Aren deflecting them. Aren then looked at Rogaan, at first not understanding. Then, he nodded his head in agreement realizing what Rogaan meant to do. Nikki didn't understand either of them.

Another growl and sweep of arms by Rogaan sent the UFO awkwardly rolling and rotating about. Rogaan collected Nikki and Miller before making for the closest high, tower like ride at the speed of a fast walk. It was the best Miller could do.

"Is this the path, Miller?" Rogaan asked the wounded crewman, now in English. Miller looked up long enough to see where they were going before nodding yes.

Another straining arm gesture from Rogaan forced the UFO about in the sky, behind them, as they briskly made their way on an overly wide path of concrete-mimicked stone paving slabs. Rogaan kept them moving along the path despite their curiosity to look back at the desperate battle Aren waged. The path soon led them to a tall stone block-mimicked structure with huge waterslides high atop the building snaking off somewhere into the darkness below and away from the tower. Pulses of light streaked past them with a loud sizzle striking the concrete in front of them, exploding. Bits and pieces of the concrete went everywhere striking them and sending Nikki and Miller back into Rogaan where they bounced off the half Tellen, then fell. Another pulse of light struck Rogaan as he turned with his *Ra'Sakti* reshaping into a blue steel shield. He went tumbling down in a bright ball of electrical discharge and smoke.

"Rogaan . . ." Nikki feared for his life, then stopped worrying. She felt him, his anger and determined mind matching the pain from his burnt flesh and wounds.

Rogaan rose from a cloud of debris and smoke with his *Ra'Sakti* reconfigured into his bow, his skin blackened where the energy pulse struck him around his armor. Nikki wanted to scream from the pain she felt through their bond knowing she only experienced a shadow of what he did. Rogaan unleashed another glowing arrow. It flew with great speed striking the disk-shaped ship now hovering several hundred yards away. The topside of the UFO's hull exploded in a blazing bright display along the path of the arrow. When Nikki's eyes adjusted enough to see, she saw a large, red-glowing fissure in the ship's surface. The UFO then protested against another forced rotation to the left, mirroring Rogaan's grunting gesture.

"Get in dwelling!" Rogaan commanded in his broken English. He made a ripping gesture down and away with his left arm. Another light displayed on the underside of the UFO caused the ship to wobble in the air. Rogaan returned his attention on Nikki and Miller. "Travel! And find us the step-gate, young Miller."

"Aren and Anders?" Nikki asked of Rogaan as she passed him. She no longer felt the Evendiir.

"Get inside," was Rogaan's only response as he held up his arms allowing his arrows to return slamming silently into his blue steel arm guards and reabsorbed.

Miller, now moving with a struggle up a flat set of stone-mimicked steps but doing so on his own, passed through the open set of large double doors to the building. Nikki and Rogaan followed. The gloomy inside of the building looked to be something imaged out a science fiction story of the lost civilization of Atlantis. Emergency lights were on that dimly illuminated the place. Miller led them through a large hall, then to an alcove with a door. He entered an access code on a white-green keypad that appeared after he waved his hand over a spot on the wall. The holographic keypad turned red. Nikki heard Miller curse in his Southern drawl. Again, he entered the code. The keypad turned red again.

"Let me at it." Rogaan was short in temperament speaking in Antaalin. He pushed past Nikki giving opportunity for her to smell and feel his burnt skin. She shivered in revulsion and gagged. "None of that. You are needed to get out of this with our *Lights*."

The door opened just as Rogaan made to smash it with his blue steel-covered fists. The eyes and face of a young blond woman dressed in a revealing green elf costume met them.

"It's about time you got here," the beautiful young woman chastised. "We've been waiting for you. What's going on out there?"

"Who are you?" Nikki asked with a hint of jealousy as she looked at almost a double of herself.

"They're your doppelgängers," Miller answered for the young woman. "They're the sleight of hand Dunkle eluded to earlier."

The building shuddered at a series of thunderous explosions. Debris flew across the hall as dust fell from all over the place. Nikki looked all around. She immediately feared for Aren and Anders . . . and Dunkle. *If Ezerus and his gang are attacking us in this building, then they must be dead.*

"Are they still . . ." Nikki looked to Rogaan for answers.

The half Tellen had that distant look. His eyes surrounded by black, burnt, scabbed over skin that looked to be in the advanced state of healing. In Antaalin, he replied. "They still fight a good battle . . . against Soldats and . . . drones. The floating chariot is meaning to destroy this place."

The building shuddered again, and again, at more thunderous explosions from the UFO. Rogaan gestured for everyone to get inside the room when the high ceilings and walls collapsed all around them.

Dust and debris filled the air making it difficult to see more than an arm's length away. Nikki felt Rogaan's strain before seeing him struggle to hold up the wall next to them. It fell as a complete structure, heavy and not as the fake stone blocks would have suggested.

"Get inside . . ." Rogaan grunted at Nikki and Miller. With unsaid protests, they climbed over the debris and into the room. Rogaan grunted as he made his way to the doorway, holding the weight of the wall up as he did.

Nikki stood in horror as she looked around the moderately sized room. Moonlight from an opening in the ceiling far above and one emergency light were the extent of their gloomy illumination. Next to Nikki, her once-beautiful doppelgänger hung bloody and lifeless, impaled on multiple broken rods of rebar embedded in a large chunk of fallen concrete. An Aren look-alike lay on the floor with half his head crushed in from falling debris. A Dunkle look-alike suffered the same fate not far away. Nikki could make out three bodies under another fallen section of wall. They all appeared dead.

"We need to make haste," Rogaan demanded of them. Looking at Miller, he asked a direct question. "Where is this step-gate?"

Miller pointed to the far wall as he stumbled to the bodies crushed under the fallen wall. The step-gate wall appeared to be untouched in the destruction of the room, but Nikki only saw a stone wall.

"Where's the gate?" Nikki asked with growing anxiety.

"It's hidden behind a nanomolecular wall coded to Dunkle's and my biometrics and DNA," Miller answered as he checked for life in the Rogaan, Anders, and Miller look-alikes.

"Leave them and get to the wall," Rogaan commanded.

"This one is still alive—" Miller was kneeling over the Rogaan look-alike.

"Leave him now," Rogaan demanded without looking at his doppelgänger.

"But he's alive," Miller protested.

Rogaan grabbed Miller by his shoulder harness and lifted him into the air, carrying him to the far wall, then placing him back on his feet. Nikki felt Rogaan's sense of urgency. It was real to him, even though she didn't understand what was driving it. "Reveal the step-gate."

Miller reached out to several places along the wall as another series of thunderous explosions shuddered the building again, and again. More debris fell, some on top of the fallen wall with the pinned survivor. The newly fallen debris fell directly on the now-assumed dead survivor. Miller's attention fell firmly on the Rogaan look-alike. A smack on Miller's shoulder from the half Tellen pointing at the wall got him to put his hand on another spot. The outline of his hand glowed red, yellow, then green; then the wall seemed to melt away revealing a gateway that appeared exactly like the one Nikki fell into back in the Bolivian cave—starting all of this. Nikki shivered at the sight of the thing, two eight-foot blue metallic obelisks standing about eight feet apart. Each of their four sides was about a foot wide at the top, flaring out to a greater width at their bases. A blue metal cross brace spanned the space between the obelisks at the bottom where they were largest. There were far fewer symbols and inscriptions on these obelisks than what Nikki remembered of the one she fell into in Bolivia. A shallow hexagon-shaped inset in each obelisk was at identical heights, four feet from the bottom brace. Nikki remembered the insets being triangular in shape on the other step-gate.

Rogaan held out his upturned palm at Miller. It took a moment for Miller to realize what Rogaan was asking for before he placed the blue steel hexagon-shaped object . . . the step-gate key, into Rogaan's hand. Rogaan wasted no time placing the key into a matching indention on the blue steel metallic frame of the gateway. The Agni in the key glowed blue as the step-gate came to life just as the one did in Bolivia that Nikki now thought she experienced a lifetime ago. Its blue steel frame reflecting the shimmering curtain's glow of energy and matter brought back her unsettling memories of being lost and floating in a universe of nothingness.

"Quickly, young Miller," Rogaan demanded. When Miller hesitated, Rogaan grabbed and pushed him through the gateway. He disappeared as if walking through a wall of dark, rippling water. Rogaan held out his hand to Nikki. He sensed her fearing the shimmering curtain of energy. He spoke in Antaalin. "This one has been prepared for us. It is safer than remaining in this room."

Fearing being trapped inside the step-gate, a Möbius loop in modern terms, Nikki took baby steps forward trying to delay entering it. Rogaan gave her a knowing look giving her the courage to take a breath and step forward.

"Do not forget the Heavenly Hammer, my ol' friend." Rogaan spoke to someone in Antaalin as Nikki felt herself stepping into the watery void of liquid energy.

Holding her breath, she felt herself inside a rainbow tunnel made of energies colorful beyond description. She felt nothing . . . no vibrations, no sounds, no movement, not even time. It was as if she were in a set of virtual reality glasses in a soundproof room, floating. The visual complexity of the tunnel was breathtaking, beautiful, and mesmerizing. Without warning, Nikki found herself at a watery wall of energy, its semitransparency allowing her to see what lay beyond . . . an empty room. She felt as if she were being pushed from the tunnel by some unknown force. She stepped through the watery wall.

Nikki emerged from the void of liquid energy on her knees, trying to suck in every breath of air she could. Her heart calming, she opened her eyes, finding herself in a smaller room than what she left. It looked and felt gloomy and much more primitive than the resort-staged décor, with a dirt floor and imitation limestone and dried mud-covered walls. Nikki feared the gateway sent them somewhere distant and isolated. Bathed in the shimmering blue-gray glow of the step-gate, Nikki found simple furnishings of several modern wood crates, one with an almost fresh bouquet of simple flowers in a likewise modern manufactured vase. A small open, frameless window above and to her left revealed wherever she was the waning moments of the day she would experience again. *We must be west of Nassau Island*, she thought as a slight breeze of chill air from the window to the frameless doorway told her she was also likely north of where she just came from. The light cast on the walls from behind her started rippling. Realizing she was right where Rogaan would appear, Nikki rolled to her left before rising to a kneeling position. Rogaan emerged from the step-gate as if walking out of a vertical surface of dark waters. A few moments after he stood in the room with Nikki, the step-gate went silent and cold. The room fell into a deeper gloom. It stood as if it had been undisturbed by time. Rogaan had the hexagon-shaped Agni key in his hand. He put that in the top of his small backpack that his over-the-shoulder sword sheaths were attached to.

Not paying Nikki any heed, Rogaan stood motionless with that distant stare. Nikki felt him deeply connected with the presence of the Wind. They were . . . assessing . . . calculating. What? She didn't know. Nikki worried for Aren, Anders, and Dunkle. The step-gate was "off," and Rogaan held the key. They wouldn't be able to activate the gate, even if they could get to it with the rubble of a destroyed building on top of it.

"Hey, my PDA is picking up a signal . . ." Miller barged into the small room from a hallway wanting to share news he thought important. When he saw Rogaan standing stolidly and not paying any attention to him, he fell silent. He realized Nikki was in the room and motioned for her to come with him. She reluctantly followed. The narrow hallway, more of a gloomy cave, just outside the room looked even more abandoned than the room they just left. Walls with the same imitation limestone and mud like covering over what looked like simple stage material beneath . . . drywall and wood studs.

"Look, my PDA is picking up the US national broadcast . . . we must be in the States," Miller told her excitedly. "The PDAs are locked so they don't transmit any data other than our false identities, but they'll receive what any PDA can normally receive."

Nikki was relieved that Miller's averted near-death experience didn't seem to have slowed him down much. The young seaman appeared to be just about normal with his Southern drawl in full blossom. Miller put his PDA in holographic mode, so he and Nikki could both watch the live news feeds. He had several feeds up in multiple display sheets. The news agencies all had their attentions on New Atlantis, watching from different perspectives the battle still ragging on the island. Several different cameras watched as Aren fought off Cmpax Soldats and Tyr. The audio commentaries of the news anchors were all over the place. A few were just commenting on what they saw without embellishment or grandstanding. Most made commentary with wild speculation of what was unfolding. They all got their speculation completely wrong. Some of the Tyr and their wedged-shaped drones were attacking the Soldats in addition to Aren. Nikki watched as Aren seemed to be doing everything possible to provoke attacks on himself . . . bolts of light, lightning, balls of fire, and things Nikki wasn't certain of but looked nasty when they struck. *What in the hell is he doing?* she thought to herself. Another feed was on the discoid ship having just finished pulverizing to dust the tower ride building they just left. Surprisingly, with all the Soldats and Tyr and their drones raining projectiles and energy blasts at him . . . and *there's Dunkle and Anders just behind him*. They were huddled behind Aren and his failing vaporous shield and a new shield she didn't recognize. *No!* Aren struck the discoid ship again, with what she thought was an exalted blast of lightning. It got the ship's . . . Ezerus's attention as it too rejoined the attack on the Evendiir with those deadly light pulses.

"That is good, ol' friend . . ." In Antaalin, Rogaan spoke in a low voice as if talking to himself.

"He's going to get them all killed," Nikki complained in a fit of growing despair. "What's he doing?"

"Bring them closer . . ." Rogaan talked to himself again.

Nikki glanced at Rogaan finding him still motionless just as she left him. She felt in him both a powerful determination and a deep concern, growing by the second, for Aren. *What are they up to?*

"Now, ol' friend . . ." Rogaan spoke calmly at first, then not so calmly the second time. "Flee, Aren!"

Nikki watched as Aren fought off the Soldat, Tyr, their drones, and the ship with his right hand and formed a personal step-gate with his left. At a nod from Aren, Dunkle helped Anders quickly through the rainbow-colored circle of swirling energy. As soon as they were gone, Aren leaped into the gate. A moment later, the rainbow circle vanished.

"What just happened?" Miller asked no one in particular.

"Watch," Rogaan answered calmly from the other room.

The discoid ship started accelerating away when all the displays filled with brilliant white flashes. The closest feeds went blank. The more distant feeds, from drones or aircraft or ships some miles out and from high-rise hotels, watched multiple brilliant explosions on the resort battlefield, each looking like a miniature nuclear detonation. Nikki counted three or four. One of the news feeds watching the battle from a high vantage point over the harbor on Nassau Island was blinded by another larger detonation where Nikki recalled passing by several U.N. ships anchored when they brought the *Sukkal* into the resort port. A mushroom cloud rose over the western outer zone of the port and more over the northwesternmost part of the resort. Nikki stared on in awe and horror as a growing number of news feeds showed devastation, though most of it localized. The rest of the resort grounds were left largely without damage except for broken windows in the hotels and other buildings and loose umbrella-type features. The port showed damage only around two sunken U.N. frigate-sized ships, one broken in half and partially sunk in the harbor channel. The other near and still sinking with a badly bent hull and rolled over on its side. Both were engulfed in flames.

"What in the hell did you hit them with?" Miller asked Rogaan without taking his eyes from the news feeds.

"Heavenly Hammer," Rogaan answered in English as he walked to them. When he stepped out of the room, the step-gate disappeared behind a solid singular wall that reformed as if water flowed in from all directions. More nanomolecules.

Several more news feeds popped up display sheets on Miller's PDA reporting similar explosions at the U.N. port facilities in Freeport, Bahamas, and Guantanamo, Cuba. The Guantanamo facility report spoke to most of the base along with the port being destroyed. Nikki and Miller looked up at a solemn Rogaan.

"What is a Heavenly Hammer?" Miller asked with his eyes again glued to his PDA's holo-display sheets.

"A hard metal pole in a blue steel container let fall from the Wind," Rogaan answered in English as he looked off distantly again. "This one, into small poles to limit devastation only to what is . . . needed."

"How many?" Miller seemed not to want to stop asking questions.

"Eleven," Rogaan answered as he kept with his distant stare.

"Eleven Rods from God!" Miller sounded awed. "I count only six or seven in the news feeds."

"Four Tyr ships in waters east of the island are now to be lost to the sea," Rogaan answered solemnly, yet a bit absently,

"You and Aren maneuvered all of them in close to keep from harming everything and everyone around them?" Nikki asked her rhetorical question, truly wanting Rogaan to answer.

Rogaan appeared to take a moment to translate Nikki's words before returning his attention to whatever he was doing that made him stare distantly. "Indeed. I destroy the evil ones, not the . . . multitudes."

Nikki smiled at Rogaan's casual honorableness. Yet, she knew his roguish side that allowed him to do what he must for the greater good he knew. Watching the ancient half Tellen at task, all-in, doing what he does, with a sense of noble purpose, gave Nikki a sense of promise for the future and a warming in her heart. And a pang of guilt rippled across her feelings.

"Anders!" Nikki spoke his name aloud without intending to. Wanting to keep the others and Rogaan off the scent of her feelings in turmoil, she thought quickly to ask of the others. "Are you searching for Aren, Dunkle, and . . . Anders?"

Rogaan nodded, then spoke. "First, to make to be safe the Wind. To hide it again. Many of your world . . . seeking for it now that I have revealed it. Their flying ships are able enough to make trouble. Then, I able to find my ol' friend and the others."

Nikki realized she had little for an idea of where they were at, except maybe somewhere west of Nassau. There was something familiar about this place, yet it was long abandoned . . . except for someone who kept fresh flowers in a rather plain stage representation of an ancient, primitive room. Curious, Nikki decided to go outside of the cave in the waning moments of dusk to look around, hoping to get better oriented. Stepping from the cave like hall, she found herself in an open courtyard of dirt and large gravel meant to simulate arid desert conditions, though much of the area was grown over with different types of plants, some that now sat dormant for the winter. What were several life-sized Roman legionnaire statues lay broken and strewn about near the cave entrance. To her right sat broken in halves a large imitation circular stone, as big round as a tall man . . . taller than Rogaan. One of the halves had tendrils of dormant vines wrapping much of it. Familiarity with the place teased Nikki. Not just of physically being here, but of the theme. Turning around, Nikki found a wall of simulated limestone and dolomite. Much of it was covered in dormant vines. Looking higher, she found what she remembered from her early childhood when her parents had taken her on a hushed trip exploring their religion. In the dusky light, above in a patchwork of repairs of modern lumber and ropes, stood the three life-sized wood crosses of the crucifixion of Jesus Christ.

Also by
B. A. VONSIK

Primeval Origins: Paths of Anguish
Book One of the Primeval Origins Epic Saga

Multiple Award-Winning Primeval Origins: Paths of Anguish (2nd Edition) is the first book of the epic origins story of mankind, our heavenly hosts, and the eternal war between good and evil where all is revealed, through characters both past and present, and tellings of humanity's heroic struggles against terrible tyrannies, deadly dinosaurs, and ancient gods as the origins of our End Times is revealed, answering the question, "What if all of our myths and legends are true?"

Myths and Legends...just fables and fantasies for those taught to scoff at them is understood, as I was taught when a graduate student in the sciences; scorn and ridicule the forbidden. Myths are just...myths. Legends are just...legends. Then, I discovered different, in a South American dig where my life went upside down after finding what should not be with what we thought we knew so much about. My consciousness, my Light, plunged through a maelstrom bound to those of our undiscovered history. I witnessed through the eyes of ancient warriors, Rogaan and others, a wondrous human civilization of old, grand beasts and dinosaurs, and celestial gods of myth in what the modern Hopi and Maya branded our First World-Age. An age deep in blood and conflict born of gods and new man covetous of true powers and self-motivations loosing upon their world tyrannies, energy forces...sorceries, and abominations affronting Creation. Sealing the fates of the age, sword-messengers, warrior angels, risen new to bring forth the Harbinger of Creation's Judgments, slayers of civilizations...both of men and gods, the Horsemen. I am bound to them. In the here and now, standing at the precipice at the end of mankind's Fourth World-Age, I fear what is to come from the others...the Horsemen of Prophecy. And yet, I have hope for what follows. As our ancients did in tablets of clay teaching us our undiscovered past, I Nikki, now share these steel bound epics with you before the sounding of the trumpets.

Also by
B. A. VONSIK

Primeval Origins: Light of Honor
Book Two of the Primeval Origins Epic Saga

Multiple-award winning Primeval Origins: Light of Honor is the second book in this epic Fantasy/ SciFi story telling of the origins of mankind, our heavenly hosts, and of the eternal war between the goodness of the Light and the evils of Darkness. Join in the grand adventure revealing humanity's heroic struggles against terrible tyrannies, deadly dinosaurs, beasts of old, and ancient gods answering the question, "What if all of our myths and legends are true?"

Fleeing across the sea from enemies familiar and unknown, the crew of the Wind Runner and I fight for our lives as we struggle to keep safe our strange and ancient cargo, the unconscious Rogaan and Aren. We have need the help of these warriors of old as we battle deadly Tyr super-soldiers of the New World Order, now commanded by the forces of the Crescent Moon, intent on taking our ancient cargo for themselves. I suffer horribly the wrath of the Tyr when protecting the unrisen Horsemen, hurling me to the brink of death and back into the ancient world of mankind's first civilization, reliving the past through the eyes of the then young and aspiring warrior Rogaan and the mystic Aren. As my Light, again, plunges into the maelstrom of our deep past experiencing a culture both simultaneously primitive and advanced, as our ancient ancestors struggle against self-corruptions and unseen powers born of jealous entitlements by their celestial gods and unknown intelligences. In these remembrances, I am witness to terrible injustices and impossible trials levied by the covetous tyrannies against Rogaan, Aren, and many others. In the here and now, I find rising deep questions about humanity's origins and the seemingly eternal battle between the goodness of the Light and the selfish evils of the Darkness. I, Nikki, now standing at the precipice at the end of mankind's Fourth World-Age, bare testimony of our undiscovered history, in these blue steel epics, revealing the origins of the Horsemen of Prophecy… before the sounding of the trumpets.

Learn more at:
www.outskirtspress.com/PrimevalOriginsLightofHonor

CPSIA information can be obtained
at www.ICGtesting.com
Printed in the USA
FFHW010709101119
56017654-61910FF